ANDREW TWEEDDALE

A Remembrance of Death

First published by Tweeddale Consulting Ltd 2024

Copyright © 2024 by Andrew Tweeddale

This is a work of fiction. Characters, corporations, institutions and organizations in this novel are either the product of the author's imagination or, if real, used fictitiously without any intent to describe their actual conduct.

First edition

ISBN: 978-1-7396122-2-1

This book was professionally typeset on Reedsy.
Find out more at reedsy.com

To
Alexander James Tweeddale

'Love like rain cannot choose the grass on which it falls.'

AFRICAN PROVERB

Foreword

A Remembrance of Death is intended to take the reader through some of the darkest moments of our recent history and how, as a society, we still make the same mistakes today. It does not seek to apportion blame but invites the reader to question the lessons that history teaches us. It recognises the British Empire's many mistakes, but sets them in a historical context. It touches on the forced removal of Jews from Europe, their systematic extermination during the Second World War and the villagisation of the Kikuyu during the State of Emergency in Kenya. Like the central protagonist, Basil Drewe, the reader will also see that a lie will spoil a thousand truths.

I was interested in many of the issues the book addresses, as my father lived in London during the Blitz and then in India and Kenya following the war. I also had a professional interest in the way that countries treat other cultures from my studies of jurisprudence and my connection with the International Bar Association's Human Rights Institute. Information about the trial at Nuremberg was obtained from the Avalon Project and the Harvard Nuremberg Trials Project. Information relating to the cross-examination of Goering and life in Nuremberg was taken from David Maxwell Fyfe's letters at the Churchill Archives Centre. Documents relating to the Mau Mau uprising were examined at the Kew Archives as well as the court cases before the English High Court.

Although *A Remembrance of Death* commences where my first novel *Of All Faiths & None* concludes, it is a stand-alone novel that can be read on its own. The novel was short-listed for the Yeovil Literary Prize and received a high commendation, with the judges describing it as, "prose with a classic sensibility ... evoking a clear and present time and place, the characters

i

lifting effortlessly from the page with authentic dialogue and engaging set pieces."

If you would like to find out more about the characters and the background to the novel, visit my website at https://www.ofallfaiths.com/ and sign up to my mailing list at https://www.ofallfaiths.com/contact-8 to get free stories, my blog and newsletter.

I

Part One

Chapter 1

September 1917

Oxford was a city of lost souls and forsaken beliefs as the Great War endured into its fourth year. The spectres of the fallen were everywhere; in the college bars, cycling down the Banbury Road, and punting on the Isis. They blended into the grey stone buildings and their deafening silence rang out. In deference to the dead, the university authorities cancelled the inter-collegiate rowing regatta, the Head of the River, for the first time since it started just over a hundred years ago.

Basil Drewe arrived into this dark milieu for the start of the Michaelmas term. He took a horse-drawn cab from the railway station to Keble College, wondering what he should say on his arrival. He was not precisely certain of the etiquette; it was something he would have discussed with his eldest brother, but Adrian had died near Ypres in July of that year. As the cab made its way through the streets of Oxford, with its ancient colleges, churches, and endless bicycles, Basil wondered whether he should have delayed coming up for a year and stayed with his parents. However, their grief was all-consuming and nothing he could say or do could relieve it.

Keble was built in polychrome brick with only two quads – Liddon and Pusey – and was considered a new college, as it was only fifty years old. Over that half-century, ivy had grown up to hide some of the Victorian gothic brickwork. The college was a stone's throw from the faculty of law, and it had concerned him that he might struggle to walk to tutorials if he were too far away. It was also next to the Ashmolean Museum where he could indulge his love of ancient history. His left leg had been broken in a fall a few years before, and he had metal plates and bolts holding the bones together. The choice of Keble was against the wishes of his father, who favoured Christ Church, with its long tradition of moulding the prime ministers of the United Kingdom. It was the first time he could remember arguing with his father on any matter and he had been surprised when his father conceded the point.

When the cab pulled up at the lodge, Basil got out and paid the driver the precise fare plus a five per cent tip. His valise was placed in front of the porter's lodge and inside he was asked his name.

"Basil Drewe."

The porter looked down his list. "Mr Basil Charles Drewe," came back the confirmation, as if Basil's omission of his middle name was a singular deficiency. "Pusey, second floor," the porter added brusquely, "and your luggage arrived this morning." The porter looked up from his list and saw Basil leaning on a walking stick. "You could be moved?" Basil paused and looked at the grey-whiskered porter with a scar under his left eye and immediately decided that this was a man who would not appreciate the slightest amount of inconvenience.

"No, the second floor will be fine," said Basil and he followed the underporter, who picked up his valise. On entering Pusey, the underporter called out his scout's name, Scoley, and a thin, wiry man with buckled front teeth and short black hair hurried down the stone stairs at the end of the corridor.

"One of your gentlemen," said the underporter. "Mr. Drewe."

"Your luggage is in your room, sir," said Scoley, as he took the valise and climbed back up the stone stairs. "You'll need to be a bit careful in winter, sir. These steps get icy and can be hellish."

"Thank you," said Basil, wondering whether he would regret not taking the offer of ground-floor rooms.

"Here you are, sir, the second door on the left. The bathrooms are at the bottom of the corridor. Meals are taken in the hall and are served from seven in the morning, twelve-thirty, and seven-thirty in the evening. Gowns are to be worn except on formal nights and drinks can be taken half an hour before dinner." Basil saw his surname on a plaque on the door as he entered the small living room. Scoley handed over an envelope. "Most things that you need to know, sir, are in here. If there is anything else just knock on my door."

Basil looked around the room. It was spartan with a desk and chair by the window and on the adjacent wall was a fireplace with a small sofa and two matching wingback chairs placed around it. The fireplace seemed to Basil to be so small that he wondered whether he would even be able to brown toast. An empty bookcase stood near the desk, which was so tiny that it would hold only half of the books that he had shipped from home. Opposite the fireplace was a door to his bedroom, which was even smaller than the living room and equally as bare.

"The linen is changed on Tuesdays and the cleaner comes Mondays, Wednesdays and Fridays," continued Scoley. "Once you have some prints up and fill the bookcase, it will feel more like home, sir." Basil forced a smile, as his idea of home and Scoley's seemed to be different.

From down the corridor, a student was shouting Scoley's name as if his life depended on it.

"That's Mr Templeton, sir, a third year. Most demanding, unfortunately."

Scoley handed over the room keys to Basil. "Just one last thing, sir. Your neighbour arrived this morning from India, a Mr Laxman Choudhury, who is studying for a doctorate in philosophy. I assume you will not have a problem living next to an Indian gentleman?"

"No, not at all," replied Basil and, as Scoley left his room, he wondered why it would be an issue.

Basil looked out of his window towards the college entrance. He could just make out to his left the library and beyond that was Liddon Quad and the chapel. He thought, I'm an Oxford undergraduate, and suppressed a smile. He relished that feeling of accomplishment and success. That morning, when he had left his home at Wadhurst Hall, he had promised his father that he would come back with a first in jurisprudence and, as he watched groups of students scurrying around the quad, he wondered whether that little show of arrogance and bravado would come back to haunt him – but a gentleman's word is his bond.

Chapter 2

While nearly every freshman would depend solely on their scout's experience in the first few weeks of university, that was not the case with Jonathan Bruton. While other freshers had to call for their scout to explain to them roll calls and chapels, Bruton seemed either to instinctively know what was needed or did not care. He knew where he should be and when. Tailors, tobacconists, and wine merchants came and set up accounts with him in the first week. He ignored most of the fresher clubs, only joining the polo club and the Oxford University Officer Training Corps. By the end of his third day at Keble, Bruton knew the names of each of the freshers in Pusey and was on nodding acquaintance with some of the less stuffy third years. As he walked into Pusey, he would shout to Scoley to arrange an innumerable number of matters, which in the first week included having flowers sent to a local girl and the booking of a room in his name at the Randolph Hotel as, he explained, his parents would be visiting from South Africa. Bruton was one of those students that Scoley would soon describe as 'most demanding, unfortunately'.

Basil first met Bruton on the last day of freshers week. As he slowly climbed down the winding stone staircase, he heard Bruton shouting for Scoley to order more wine from Loeb's.

"That wine merchant's an imbecile," Bruton shouted. "When I asked for six Bordeaux, I meant cases, not bottles."

"Good morning," said Basil.

"You must be Drewe," responded Bruton.

"Yes, Basil Drewe." Basil extended his hand.

"Jonathan Bruton," came the reply. "And before you ask, the accent is South African. I think my room is under yours, so I better apologise for the noise."

"Yes, I was going to come and have a quiet word about that," said Basil.

"Sorry, but it might also be a bit rowdy this evening, as I'm having some officers over who are billeted here. We're planning to dine together and then have a few drinks in my room. Join us and make up an eight?"

As it was a Friday and lectures were not starting until the following week, Basil agreed. "How did you know my name?"

"Scoley gave me a rundown of everyone in your corridor. Apart from you and Choudhury, I think I have met everyone, and I rather guessed by your complexion you weren't Choudhury."

"So, I'll see you at seven?"

"Seven is perfect," said Bruton, "and would you mind bringing a bottle or two? Unfortunately, I've been rather let down by Loeb's."

Basil watched as Bruton casually wandered towards the main gate and then put his head in the porter's lodge. A few seconds later he could hear the irascible porter laughing. Basil immediately warmed to the gregarious Bruton. He, on the other hand, had been there for five days and still hardly knew anyone. Basil turned and went and got his bike. He leant down and put his bicycle clips around the bottom of his suit trousers, lifted his leg over the crossbar and rang the metal bell for good measure. He pushed himself forward with his good leg and started pedalling slowly until he heard the porter shouting at him not to cycle in the quad. After dismounting, he pushed the bike slowly towards the gate, feeling that he was being watched by every underporter and scout in Keble. Outside on the street, he again mounted his bicycle. He hadn't ridden a bike for over six years since the accident with his leg but had decided to buy this from a third-year law student who took Basil's money, shook his hand firmly and completed the sale with the words *"Caveat emptor"*.

From the college, Basil turned left and left again, heading for Jericho and then out to Port Meadow, which was the old common that stretched to the village of Wolvercote. The bicycle gave him a newfound sense of freedom that he had not felt for a long time. Someone had suggested that while at Oxford he visit Godstow Abbey and then stop at the Perch Inn for a spot of lunch and an afternoon beer. It was only three miles away and with his bicycle, it seemed possible. But after five minutes of cycling, his left leg began to ache, and he compensated by peddling harder with his right leg and letting his left leg do less.

Godstow Abbey had been built nearly eight hundred years before and was the final resting place of The Fair Rosamund, the mistress of Henry II. When he was much younger Basil had been told a story that the king had abducted Rosamund from Basil's ancestor, Drogo de Teigne. When Rosamund was poisoned, the king blamed Drogo and had him pursued across Dartmoor and chased him down with his hounds. Basil had thought the story nonsense but a distant relative of his, the rector Archibald Drew, insisted it was true. Archibald had also told him about Godstow Abbey.

"I came up to Oxford, borrowed a bicycle," Archibald said, "cycled out there and spent an afternoon searching for the grave of Rosamund. I discovered that in the sixteenth century, a German traveller had found the gravestone and written: 'Here in the tomb lies a rose of the world, not a pure rose; She who used to smell sweet, still smells – but not sweet.'" Archibald had stifled a laugh, almost embarrassed by the story that he was telling a young boy. "So," he continued, "if you decide to go to Oxford, you should take the time to visit the old abbey. It's one of the most tranquil places I know, but you must search for the grave of Rosamund. After all, your family history and hers are tied together."

Basil leant his bike up against the ruined church and sat on a broken-down wall. He rubbed his leg for a good ten minutes before deciding to slowly walk around the graveyard. He wondered whether he would be able to sense the presence of Rosamund, and then smiled to himself, realising the stupidity of that thought. After ten minutes of walking, he sensed nothing except the aching pain in his left leg and sat once again on the old dry-stone wall and looked across the churchyard for an hour or two. In this rich, green field the derelict abbey, with its roof long since fallen in, had become a part of the landscape. Grass grew out of the stone walls where the mortar had fallen out over time. Birds sat quietly on the topmost parts of the church viewing below them the fields, where, on occasion, voles and field mice might be caught. Across the fields and through a copse of trees was the river and Godstow Bridge. The sun, high in the heavens, reflected the colours of autumnal trees onto the river. A single mallard swam under the bridge and as the water parted between its paddling palmate feet, Basil got up, let out a deep sigh, mounted his bicycle and cycled back along the towpath in the direction of Oxford. He did not want silence and tranquillity; he had a life to live. It was why he had decided to come to Oxford and get away from his parents who were in perpetual mourning for his dead brother Adrian.

He would have loved to have come here at another time with Adrian and his other brother Christian. He would have loved to come before the war and the devastation that it wrought on his family and before his injury. He imagined that Adrian would have done something similar at Cambridge when he was a student, rowing up the river with friends and spending an afternoon lying on the banks, drinking champagne.

The Perch Inn was in the village of Binsey, which was on the opposite side of the river from Port Meadow. It was a traditional white plastered building with thatched roof, and once had a row of riverside aspens beside it. They had been cut down nearly forty years earlier, which had appalled the great poet, Gerald Manley Hopkins, so much that it forced him to write:

'My aspens dear, whose airy cages quelled,
Quelled or quenched in leaves the leaping sun,
All felled, felled, are all felled;
Of a fresh and following folded rank
Not spared, not one...'

Basil had been taught the poem when he was at school, but it now seemed more profound with the fallen lights of Oxford's student soldiers. Outside, in the garden of the inn, were benches and tables, where on clement days dons, masters and students alike would walk down the weed-winding bank of the river to lunch. However, the garden was almost empty. Basil placed his bicycle beside one of the empty tables and went in and ordered a glass of wine and poached salmon.

As Basil cycled along the footpath later that afternoon, he could make out, across the river, a polo match taking place. He pulled on his brake as hard as he could to stop and watched the two teams of four charging backwards and forwards between the goals. Basil knew that with the metal plates in his left leg, he would never be able to ride a horse again, and his heart ached. Of all the things that he loved, before his accident, it was horse riding that he missed the most. A battered bicycle with bad brakes was hardly any substitute.

***

"Were you watching our polo practice from across the river?" asked Bruton later that evening as the waiting staff poured coffee.

"Yes," said Basil.

"Do you ride?" asked Bruton.

"Not anymore, not since my accident."

"Tell me to mind my own business," said Bruton, who was tapped on his shoulder by the person sitting on his other side and at once passed the port to his left. "But what happened to your leg?"

Basil looked up at the vaulted roof of the dining room and said, almost inaudibly, "Well that's a story." He brought his eyes downwards. On the walls were portraits of deans of the college, long since dead, who stared back at Basil with paternal concern. In a time when hundreds of students had lost their lives in the war, it seemed to Basil churlish to complain about an accident that had happened years ago.

"I fell from a cliff face," he finally said. "A long time ago now."

A sub-lieutenant in the Officer Training Corps looked over and said, "Lucky you're not a polo pony – they would have put you down."

Basil forced a smile and said, "Yes, I suppose that was lucky."

"Actually," said Bruton, "in South Africa we don't put down nearly as many horses as you do in England. We treat a lot of fractures and breaks, and they heal remarkably well."

The port had made its way around to Basil, and he eagerly filled his glass before passing it on to Bruton. The six officers at the table had spent most of the evening talking about the war and the third battle of Ypres. It was just outside of Ypres that Adrian had been killed, and Basil desperately hoped the conversation would move on as it brought back too many painful memories.

"What are you reading?" Basil asked Bruton.

"Classics," said Bruton. "I have an interest in Roman military history. And you?"

"Jurisprudence," said Basil. "Although classics would have been my second choice."

Bruton was initially surprised by Basil's knowledge of Roman history, although as Basil explained, Latin was a prerequisite for studying law. Basil had a hundred questions for Bruton about the course, and they discussed Marcus Aurelius and Pliny.

"I have a copy," said Bruton, "of Aurelius's *Meditations* somewhere. Do borrow it if you want."

"I will," said Basil, who looked down at his near-empty port glass and tapped the shoulder of the person to his right.

When they got back to Bruton's rooms, Basil and the six officers were four sheets to the wind. More wine was demanded by the officers. Bruton brought out two bottles and opened them. As he came to Basil to pour out a glass, he quietly asked whether Basil had remembered to buy a bottle or two. Basil excused himself for a moment and went up to his room. He reappeared a few minutes later with a case of wine and gave it to Bruton.

"I asked Loeb's to send me two burgundies," said Basil. "And instead of getting two bottles, I got two cases."

"You have an account with them?" asked Bruton, who seemed surprised that Basil managed to do what he could not.

"I charged it to my father's account," said Basil.

"Well, we'll try not to drink the second case this evening," said Bruton, who patted Basil on the back, "for your father's sake."

Chapter 3

Basil did not recall how he managed to get back to his rooms. When he awoke, he still had his trousers on. He had no idea what time it was, though he knew he'd missed breakfast. Fortunately, on a Saturday there were no lectures, and no one would come to clean his rooms. By the side of his bed was a large glass of water and an empty bucket. He could not remember putting either there and wondered whether Bruton had helped him up the stairs and put him to bed. He drank the water. His mouth was clammy and there was a sharp pain behind his eyes. He swivelled his legs over the side of the bed and sat up, at once regretting it, and buried his head in his hands. He went through the process of trying to piece together the evening's events.

Basil recalled that they had played a drinking game. They had gone down to Pusey quad with his bicycle and each of them, one at a time, had cycled around the quad with their hands off the handlebars while drinking a glass of wine. If any of the wine spilt, the cyclist would have to drink another glass as a forfeit. If the cyclist succeeded, everyone else would have to drink a glass of wine. The noise had brought people to their windows and out onto the quad. At eleven o'clock the dean had come out and put a stop to the revelries. However, by this time they were all blind drunk except Jonathan Bruton, who did not spill a single drop of wine.

"Get behind me," Bruton had said, as he walked back towards his room. "And all of you shout '*memento mori*'."

"Why?" Basil had asked.

"Because when a Roman general paraded through Rome after a great victory, he would have someone walking behind him shouting that. It would remind him that death was inevitable," said Bruton.

Once they had returned to Bruton's warm room, Basil had little recollection of what happened afterwards. He assumed that he must have fallen asleep in a chair and later in the evening made his way to his room. He thought he would feel better after a bath, so put on a shirt and went down the hallway towards the bathroom. He returned twenty minutes later to find Scoley by his door.

"Mr Bruton left this for you, sir," said Scoley.

"What is it, Scoley?"

"Mr Bruton didn't say. When he went out this morning, he asked me to put it under your door an hour or two before luncheon." Basil took the envelope.

"I trust we didn't make too much noise last night," he said.

"Enough to wake the dead," said Scoley. "However, everyone enjoyed your little cycling game. Even the dean waited nearly half 'n hour before putting a stop to it."

"Thank you, Scoley."

"Don't thank me," said Scoley. "If there is anyone you should thank it is our Mr Choudhury. It was he who found you slumped against your door at midnight, and it was he who got you in your rooms and put you to bed. A proper gentleman is our Mr Choudhury."

When Basil opened the envelope, it was an invitation to lunch at the Randolph Hotel at one-thirty. Basil looked in his wardrobe for clothes suitable for luncheon at Oxford's most elegant hotel. He asked himself what Adrian would have chosen if he had gone to a similar place in Cambridge, and picked a pair of dove grey flannel trousers, a blue striped shirt, a grey tie, and a blue blazer from Turnbull & Asser.

It was a short walk from the college to the Randolph Hotel, and he arrived precisely on time. He was shown into the restaurant where Bruton sat with a local girl called Enid, who on occasion worked as a barmaid at the Old Bookbinders Ale House and was said to be keen on Bruton.

14

"I'm afraid," said Basil, when lunch had finished and Bruton was suggesting they have a bottle of port, "that I have a tutorial to prepare for on Wednesday." However, if truth be told, Basil was getting the distinct impression that if he did not leave soon, he would start feeling like a maiden aunt chaperoning Bruton and the girl he had invited.

Basil excused himself, walked out of the hotel to the feel of a coolish autumnal wind and then crossed the road and went into the Ashmolean Museum. He wondered how Bruton could be so carefree, nothing seemed to bother him. Basil knew that he couldn't be like that. He felt that unless he applied himself, he would never succeed in becoming a great lawyer. His brother Adrian had excelled in everything he had done, and he thought that if his parents could be equally proud of him it might somehow lessen their grief. He decided to walk through the museum but after a few minutes of looking at the exhibits, Basil felt a familiar twinge in his leg. He knew that if he walked any further the pain would increase, and he sat down beside a statue of the Buddha. As he thought about his brother, he found himself welling up, overwhelmed by feelings of loss. He still could not believe that Adrian had been killed. If there was anyone who should have survived the war unscathed it was Adrian, who embodied everything that a gentleman should be – strong, honourable and dutiful. Everyone seemed to love him – especially his parents. Perhaps, thought Basil, he should have remained with Bruton and spent the afternoon drinking. Bruton would have made him laugh and he remembered that the previous evening, when one of the officers had ridden his bike into a wall buckling the wheel, Bruton had refilled his glass, smiled, and said, as he looked at the broken bicycle, "Fortunately, a small injustice to one's feelings can be cured by wine."

Chapter 4

Basil walked into the Junior Common Room, which was almost pitch black except for the faintly glowing embers in the fireplace. However, as his eyes became accustomed to the darkness, he saw a figure sitting in a chair by the window cradling a cup. Basil wandered over and sat down opposite him.

"Scoley said I might find you here," said Basil. "I seem to keep on missing you. You're usually gone by the time I surface, and I haven't seen you dining once."

"They don't cater for vegetarians," said Laxman Choudhury. "With breakfast, I can always have porridge or an omelette but for the evening meal there is usually nothing for me to eat."

"Well," continued Basil shyly, "I just wanted to thank you for helping me into my room during my first week."

"Actually," said Laxman, who took a sip of his tea, "I have helped you into your room on three occasions in the last month. You seem to be able to perfectly negotiate the stairs but then you give up when you need to put your key in the lock and fall asleep in the corridor."

"Ah," said Basil, who felt himself blushing. "Three times did you say?" Laxman nodded. "Well in that case," continued Basil, "just a thank you seems a little bit churlish. Can we dine out one evening? I will arrange dinner and make sure there is something suitable for you."

"It would be a pleasure, Drewe," said Laxman. "However, just so you know, it is not just animal meats that I don't eat. My religion also forbids

16

the eating of animal fats."

"But eggs are fine?" said Basil, remembering that Laxman had said he sometimes ate an omelette for breakfast.

"And cheese," added Laxman.

"And cheese," Basil repeated and wondered where on earth they could go.

**

During the next few days, Basil contacted every restaurant, hotel and pub in Oxford to ascertain the extent of their vegetarian options. The responses ranged from the imbecilic to incredulity. One hotel manager suggested bacon as an option as he considered it was not a proper meat. The Randolph Hotel would do a vegetarian alternative; however, the grandest hotel in Oxford hardly seemed a suitable venue for a quiet, informal dinner. In the end and out of despair, Basil sent a cable to his mother who replied the next day saying that she had been able to speak with her distant cousin Emily Lutyens, who was a vegetarian, and that a guesthouse on the Botley Road had a nice dining room and did good vegetarian food. Basil contacted the guesthouse and although it usually only catered for paying guests, it was prepared on this occasion to make an exception.

The landlady of the guesthouse had previously lived in India until her husband died in a railway accident when two trains collided at Barara station in 1908. When she heard that Basil wanted to bring an Indian student from Oxford for dinner, she agreed and spent the next day roasting and grinding dry spices.

"Choudhury," the landlady said, after Laxman and Basil had introduced themselves, "isn't that a Bangladeshi name?"

"It is," said Laxman, "although my family lives in Assam, to the northeast of Bangladesh."

"My late husband and I," said the landlady, "lived in the north of India for many years. He worked as a manager for the railway company until he passed away." She sat Basil and Laxman down at a table that could easily have fitted four people. "I hope you don't mind but when Mr Drewe told me he was dining with the first Indian PhD student at Oxford, I took the liberty of preparing some of my favourite Indian food."

"I could smell the spices when we walked in," said Laxman. "It reminded me of home."

The dining room of the guesthouse was homely, with flock wallpaper and a small chandelier. There were six tables, where guests would have breakfast and those who wished for an evening meal could eat. The floors were covered with almost threadbare rugs. When the landlady returned from the kitchen, she brought two plates.

"It's aloo ki tikki," she said as she placed the plates before Basil and Laxman. Basil looked at her perplexed. "Potatoes with peas and spices," she explained. "Just cut each potato cake and dip it in the mango chutney."

"It smells wonderful," said Laxman. "I didn't think I would ever be eating Indian food in Oxford."

A biryani, with okra, carrots and beans, was served, accompanied by dahl cooked in coconut milk with a temper of cumin, mustard seeds, and chilli. There was a masala bell pepper curry and a tomato soup with paneer, yoghurt and coriander. A dessert of gulab jamun came afterwards with its small, sweet doughnuts swimming in a sticky syrup.

Basil was initially unsure what to make of the food. The spiciness of the masala bell pepper curry made him hiccup, and he remained uncertain about the texture of the dahl. However, the gulab jamun made up for any reservations that he had, as did the sweet lassi, which he slurped down with the meal.

"We would have a meal like this every weekend when I was growing up," said Laxman wistfully. "My aunts would come to our house and all the children would be thrown out so that they could be in the kitchen without being disturbed. Most of the boys went to the playing fields to play cricket or we would go to Padham Pukhuri, which is a small island in the middle of a lake in our town. I was the eldest child and have four younger brothers and a sister."

"I had two elder brothers," said Basil, "and no sisters."

"Sisters can be tricky," said Laxman, who stuck his fork into the last gulab jamun and swirled it around the sweet syrup before swallowing it in one go.

"My sister is called Majda. She was supposed to play with the other girls but whenever we played cricket, she would demand to join us and then embarrass most of the boys by her ability to hit a ball out of the ground."

"She sounds incredibly strong," said Basil.

"She's as skinny as a rake," said Laxman, "but she has this wonderful eye and could hit a ball as sweetly as a nut."

"I used to play cricket," said Basil, "but that stopped when I had my accident as I couldn't run anymore."

"But you can still bowl and bat," said Laxman.

"Not really," said Basil. "I was a medium-paced bowler and because I cannot run, I can't bowl with any speed."

"Have you thought about learning to be something different?" asked Laxman. "The best spin bowler in our village is a cousin of mine who had polio as a child. He can hardly walk, let alone run, but he can spin a cricket ball that most people can only swing blindly at."

"I don't know," said Basil. "What would be the point? I would never be very good at it."

"That you will never know," said Laxman, "until you try."

Basil paid the bill, which was a paltry sum and much less than it would have cost him if he had gone to eat at a restaurant. Laxman charmed the landlady and asked whether she would be prepared to cook for him and a small group of Indian students he knew. She agreed.

"They are a terrible group of people," said Laxman apologetically to the landlady. "All of them to a man have been spoilt by their mothers and normally I would not impose them on anyone, but none of them like the bland English food we have in halls."

***

Basil limped as he and Laxman made their way back to college along Botley Road. He pushed his bicycle with its new front wheel, holding onto the handlebars to give him some support.

"Why don't you cycle?" said Laxman. "You would be back at halls in less than five minutes."

"Then we would not be able to talk," said Basil.

19

"But this is causing you discomfort," answered Laxman.

"You get used to it," replied Basil, who hoped that one day it might prove to be true.

"I'm sorry," said Laxman, "however, it is pleasant for me to walk with you. We Indians tend to wrap ourselves up from the cold and hurry with our heads down from one place to the next. When I walk with you, I see things from a different perspective."

"What do you mean?" asked Basil.

"I have time to look up, to appreciate the beauty of this city and the clear night sky. I can also see that every journey you take requires a certain amount of determination. I simply go from one place to the next but for you it takes effort. I respect that."

Basil thought about what his thoughtful companion had said and realised that it was probably true, but he would give anything not to have the pain that went with every journey.

"I'll tell you a secret," continued Laxman. "All my Indian friends would have left me where we had dinner and cycled back to their halls. However, if an Englishman says he will walk beside you, then he will do exactly that, irrespective of how arduous the journey is. We Indians laugh at that, telling each other it is naivety, but really in our hearts, we admire that determination. It is perhaps why your country rules half the world and why my country is still ruled."

"Does that upset you?" asked Basil.

"Yes," said Laxman. "More than anything, however, independence is coming to India. People are saying that there will soon be a new Act of Parliament where more powers will be given to Indians to rule themselves. However, for many Indians, the real question is not whether independence will be given to us, it is when it will be given."

Basil looked at his watch. On a Friday evening, he knew that Bruton and his officer friends would be drinking at the Old Bookbinders Ale House next to the canal. He was about to suggest that they go, Laxman could always have a lemonade; however, as quickly as the idea came into his head it disappeared. Bruton's chums were almost sure to rag him for being

Indian, and then there could be an awful scene if Laxman didn't take the ragging well.

"Can I ask you something," said Laxman, "and I don't mean to pry."

"Of course," said Basil.

"Who is Adrian? The other night when I woke you up in the corridor, you mentioned his name. I think you said, 'I can manage, Adrian.'" Basil had no recollection of having said it and, for a moment, he felt that it was impertinent of Laxman to have mentioned it. However, he had wanted to talk about Adrian to someone for a long time, to share his loss with a friend. Laxman was thoughtful and empathic, unlike Bruton or any of his other friends.

"Adrian was my eldest brother. It was just a few months ago that he was killed near Ypres, saving someone else. I think about him a lot."

"I could not imagine losing one of my brothers in the war," said Laxman. "There would be nothing so sad as not saying goodbye to him."

"It hit my parents the hardest, especially after what had happened to Christian." Laxman looked over at Basil but said nothing. "Christian was wounded on the Somme in 1916," continued Basil. "He led a company of men across no man's land and was blinded in the attack. He never regained his vision and lives alone, rarely going out. That was the first thing that hurt my parents and when Adrian died, I think it was just too much for them to bear. My father had a heart attack when they delivered the news, and my mother has been overcome with grief. I sometimes think that when they look at me, they wish Adrian had lived and I had died. He was always their favourite. He was everyone's favourite."

Laxman stopped and turned to Basil. "I can tell you, even though I have never met your parents, that that is not true."

"Perhaps," replied Basil. "But sometimes I feel it."

"It is strange," said Laxman, "that in my religion we do not dwell on guilt. If a person does a wrongful act, they might feel regret or remorse, but they should then deal with the consequences of the act. A very wise person once said to me after I argued with my father that 'I need to forgive myself'. I was so angry with him because he would not let me come to England to

21

study, as he thought it too expensive and unnecessary for the son of a civil servant. I was told that if I did not forgive myself, I would build a wall around me which would prevent me from being able to communicate and I needed to communicate if I was to change his mind. I calmed myself down and a day or two later I set out every reason why I should study at Oxford and after he listened to me, he relented and agreed that I could study here."

"Who was the wise person?" asked Basil.

"My younger sister, Majda."

***

Despite the cricket season having finished a few weeks earlier at the end of September, Laxman was able to round up a few Indian undergraduates who were prepared to spend an afternoon at the cricket nets with the assurance that he would feed them with the best Indian food in Oxford. When they saw Basil cycle towards them, they looked at Laxman and asked why he had invited him.

"Two reasons," said Laxman. "First, he found the place where I am going to take you to dine, which was no mean feat, and second, I like him."

"Why do you like him? You are always complaining about the students in your halls and their drunken parties, behaving like animals and vomiting everywhere. Why is he different?"

"Because he is the politest drunk I have ever met. If I tried to help one of his friends I would be sworn at and told to get my black hands off, but Drewe will just say 'Thank you and I'm so sorry to have inconvenienced you'. I sometimes think that there is a lot of truth in that saying *in vino veritas*."

Despite their initial misgivings, the group of Indian undergraduates got on with Basil, and when Basil suggested that two of them, who were also studying law, join his study group, the walls between them fell.

However, the focus of the afternoon, and subsequent ones, was on bowling and teaching Basil how to spin a ball. He practised finger spin, but it was wrist spin that he seemed to excel at and by the end of term he felt he would soon be good enough to play for the college team. He could field on the boundary and bat with a runner. In turn, the Indians invited him to their now-weekly dinner at the guesthouse on Botley Road, and by the time the Christmas break arrived, he would nonchalantly pile spoonfuls of vegetable jalfrezi onto his plate.

Chapter 5

It had been months since Basil had been home to Wadhurst Hall and he was picked up at the station by the chauffeur Poley. It was a chilly December afternoon and there was still frost on the ground. Despite the cold, he wore no coat but a thick Arran jumper and a wool jacket. Laxman, on the other hand, was wrapped from head to toe with the addition of a scarf and gloves to ward off the cold.

"And this is Mr Laxman Choudhury," said Basil, as he passed the bags to Poley. "Laxman is doing a doctorate in philosophy and has been helping me with my off spin."

"You've been playing cricket?" asked Poley.

"A little," said Basil.

"Is he any good, Mr Choudhury?" said Poley. "And please don't spare his blushes."

"With a little more practice," said Laxman, "he will be good enough to play for one of the college teams. He has a cricketer's brain."

"A cricketer's brain," replied Poley, laughing at the phrase. "Whatever do you mean by that, sir?"

"He might bowl three balls the same line and length and then he will bowl something just a little different and that's when he can get into a batsman's head. Unless they are watching attentively, they won't know whether the ball will turn just a little, or a lot, or go straight on. It's when you can put that kind of doubt in someone's mind that you know that they will be walking back to the pavilion shortly afterwards."

"Master Basil gets that from his father," said Poley as he loaded the last bag into the boot of the car.

"And how are my parents, Poley?" asked Basil.

"Unchanged, I'm sorry to say."

***

Wadhurst Hall was more than Laxman had hoped. He knew that Basil's family were rich, having grown up in Assam where tea plantations are two a penny and where the name of the Home and Colonial Stores was still said with some reverence. For decades they had been the biggest buyer of tea in India. Even now their name carried great weight, although many new general stores were starting up that were, little by little, eating into the market share.

Laxman was given a room near Basil's in the main part of the house and was amazed that there were two panes of glass to stop the cold from getting in. Fires were lit every morning and replenished in the afternoons and evenings and there were times over the next four weeks when Laxman was able to walk around the inside of Wadhurst Hall in his shirt sleeves and a jumper.

Basil noticed the differences; the little ones and those of larger import. Christmas decorations were not put up, except in the main living room, and the New Year's Eve ball was cancelled – the first time in Basil's memory. He did not see much of his parents. His father locked himself away in his study for most of the day and his mother stayed in her rooms, often in bed. When she got up each day, she still wore black as she had done since Adrian's death. Only at mealtimes would they appear, and these were now almost silent affairs. His other brother Christian had come up from Drewsteignton where he lived, but he also hid away in his rooms. Basil decided that he should take Laxman out each day to show him the estate, a little at a time. On each short walk, he would stop and introduce Laxman to the estate workers. Basil would lean on his walking stick and catch up with the gossip. Afterwards, they would go to the library and study and when they were bored try and complete *The Times* crossword. Basil also organised trips out to house parties in the evening or to the theatre in

Brighton, where Laxman saw his first pantomime.

Although she said little, Laxman liked Basil's mother, Lady Frances, and noticed the similarities between her and Basil. She knew everyone's first name, irrespective of how long they had worked on the estate, and did not possess airs and graces. However, Laxman could see the sadness that she carried with her, as if some part of her had been cut away. Sir Julius spent his days in his office working until the early hours. He was brusque with everyone and made it clear he did not want to be disturbed. He acted as if he was just carrying on with things, but Laxman could see the pretence. Their grief gave them no time for either Basil or Christian and Laxman understood why Basil had wanted to leave them and go to Oxford.

It was, however, Christian for whom Laxman felt the greatest pity. When Basil had said that Christian had been blinded in the war, he had not said that he had also been horrifically burnt. Laxman noticed how Christian silently moved around the house like Banquo's ghost, unbidden and scarred. Laxman saw how Christian would hide himself away for most of the day and at mealtimes remain silent to avoid becoming the centre of attention. He seemed to be ignored by his parents and it was therefore with some surprise that one morning, after breakfast, Christian came into the library, tapping his way with his cane, and sat down opposite Laxman.

"You must think we are all terribly rude," said Christian, "especially me. You've been here for nearly two weeks, and I've hardly said more than three words to you."

"Not at all," said Laxman, putting down his book. "I can understand how difficult it must be for you."

"I'm not sure you can," replied Christian.

"You're right. I have no idea about the life you lead."

"I thought coming up here might help my parents, but I think that seeing me just emphasises what they have lost. That's why I've been hiding away. Nothing has changed since the day they heard that Adrian had died. In the last few days, I've been thinking of going back home but I wanted to speak to you first to see how Basil is."

"He's coping," said Laxman. "He drinks, I think too much on occasion

26

but then I don't drink at all. You know that academically he excels? My Indian friends who study jurisprudence say that he is certain to finish top of the year, which is no small achievement."

"I'm pleased," responded Christian. "He always had a streak of determination."

"But why go home?" asked Laxman. "What will you do there?"

"Nothing," said Christian. "Absolutely nothing. That's the problem. I live in the smallest village in the quietest county in England. No one knows what to do with me and what can a blind man do?"

"Almost everything," said Laxman. "There's music."

"I'm an artist... was an artist."

"There is a Chinese saying that 'even a blind man can appreciate the beauty of pottery'."

"I'm not sure I understand," Christian responded.

"The beauty of a pot is not just what it looks like but how it feels. In India, some blind men earn a living making ceramics and the most skilled can make beautiful sculptures."

Christian sat quietly for a moment. He had been so angry following his injury on the Somme that he had not even contemplated that he could make a new life. He didn't have to work, and so he had sat doing nothing and slowly the self-pity had taken hold. He suddenly thought back to Celia Lutyens, who had cared for him after his injury and who had left for America six months ago. He wondered how she was. The last thing she had said to him was 'You need to move on with your life'. He realised he hadn't, and he realised that that had to change.

"And what about you, Laxman? What are you going to do when you leave Oxford?"

Laxman thought about his answer. He looked at the fireplace for a moment and then his gaze went to the windows, and he stared out onto the moorlands that were so different to his home in Assam.

"Is it such a difficult question?" asked Christian.

"I want to go into politics and work for the independence of my country."

***

When news circulated that Mr Basil Drewe wanted a potter's wheel and enough clay to make a terracotta army, there was a look of bemusement on the faces of the estate workers, but Poley's son, George, took the Rolls-Royce and headed to the lanes of Brighton, returning that evening with everything that was required. A makeshift studio was created in the stable room where once a model of Castle Drogo had taken centre stage. The following day a woman from the Wedgwood factory turned up to give her first lesson to three young men about how to cast a bowl and, as she sat behind Christian, holding his fingers at the bottom of the clay and then slowly bringing them up, as the inertia of the wheel pulled the form outwards, Christian realised that this was something he could do.

Three bowls, which had been fired and painted, were exchanged on Christmas Day. Christian's bowl, which had been painted by their tutor Daisy Makeig-Jones, was given to Laxman. Basil's bowl was given to Christian and Laxman's bowl to Basil. Both Laxman and Basil acknowledged that their attempts at pottery were no better than a child's; however, the bowl that Christian had produced was almost perfectly shaped and smooth and the painting by Daisy was an exquisite scene of fairies and knights in armour going to war.

Laxman watched on as Christian spent hour after hour practising. Long after Daisy had gone home each day, he would continue to work on lumps of clay in the cold stable until his fingers became too cold. His hands would instinctively caress the outside of the clay raising the sides of the pots. Sometimes they would collapse, and he would throw up his arms in frustration. On other occasions, he would throw the greenware pot on the floor, when he felt the imperfections in its casting. At other times he would smile to himself as he ran his fingers down the lip and curve of a vase.

"It's a beginning," said Daisy two weeks later, as she examined one of Christian's vases. "However, there is so much more that you can do, such as carving the clay exterior or cutting it to produce geometric shapes. We've just taken a small first step."

Two weeks into the new year Basil and Laxman packed up their belongings for their return to Oxford. Christian decided that he would go home the following day with the potter's wheel, clay and kiln following. He wished his brother well and shook Laxman's hand firmly as they stood outside Wadhurst Hall and then he heard his mother and father.

"I'm sorry to see you go," said Sir Julius to Laxman. "However, you are more than welcome to return whenever you like and please do not hesitate to contact me if there is anything that I can do for you."

"That is very kind of you, sir," replied Laxman.

"I am serious, Mr Choudhury." Sir Julius looked at his two sons. "Your stay has been most welcome."

Lady Frances kissed Basil on the cheek, as Poley put the final pieces of luggage into the Rolls-Royce and wished him a safe journey, then, for no reason that Laxman could explain, she kissed him on the cheek as well.

Chapter 6

29 May 1918

Basil felt that he had not seen the sunlight for an eternity. His first-year examinations had finished, and, as he returned to his rooms, he was quietly confident that he had done well. He opened his door to find a note from Bruton inviting him to a polo match at the weekend; however, he thought, tonight he would kick up his heels. No doubt Laxman would disapprove if he was found sleeping in the corridor again, but it was now an exceptional occurrence.

He put on his gown and went down the stairs and towards the dining hall. He heard a noise coming from the hall as he strolled in, walking stick in hand. Students were huddled around copies of the evening papers, talking about the Battle of Cantigny – America's first major battle in the war. It was a victory, although, as one student remarked, a large amount of help had to be given by the French.

"Drewe, join me," Bruton shouted from across the room and Basil made his way over. "Where have you been hiding?"

"Exams," said Basil.

"You should have heeded my advice when we first met," continued Bruton. "Studying can always wait."

"You do know that they can send you down if you don't do anything at all?" replied Basil.

"It doesn't matter now," replied Bruton. "Some chums from the Officer Training Corps have decided to enlist with me at the end of term. Now

America has joined in it's all likely to be over in a few months and we've decided we want to do our part."

"I would come with you if I could," added Basil.

"We're meeting later for a few beers at the Old Bookbinders Ale House. Will you join us?"

Basil readily agreed and he thought it was just what he needed. The dinner gong was sounded, the doors of the hall were closed and bolted, and a tasteless meal of celery soup, boiled fish with mashed potato and dead man's leg was laboriously consumed.

"Promise me something, Bruton," said Basil as they got up from the table. "Don't get yourself shot. Seriously, it was hard enough to lose my brother. I would hate to lose a friend as well."

"I'll do my best, but I can't promise you anything," said Bruton, as they walked towards the door. "However, I'll ask you to make me a promise." He stopped as they got to the door of the dining room and looked keenly at Basil.

"If I can," said Basil uncertainly.

"If I don't come back, don't spend one moment feeling sorry for me or yourself. Raise a glass of wine and drink to all the good times we've had."

"I'm not sure I can make that promise," said Basil.

"I would appreciate it if you could," said Bruton. "I know if you make a promise, then neither hell nor high water will make you break your word, and I would be happier knowing that you would be celebrating my life rather than mourning it."

"You have my word then," said Basil and they turned, walked out of the door, down the stone steps and into the quad.

"Do you know," continued Bruton, "that I had a similar conversation with a girl that my parents are keen for me to marry." The bells tolled from the clock tower.

"You've not mentioned her before," said Basil.

"Her name's Margaret, Margaret Ellis. I asked her not to cry for me if I didn't come back from the war. Do you know what she said?"

"I've no idea," answered Basil.

31

"She said, 'Don't worry, Poppet, I'm not the crying type.'"

"She sounds absolutely heartless!" said Basil.

"Actually," said Bruton, "it was at that moment that I thought I might be in love with her."

"And she called you Poppet?" Basil chuckled to himself as he said it.

"If you mention that to anyone, Drewe, I promise you will be limping on both legs from now on. Now come on and the first bottle of claret is on you."

***

The Old Bookbinders Ale House got its name from the rich publishing history within the Jericho area of Oxford. But the strangest thing about the pub was the model railway inside, which had been stuck to the ceiling. It always made Basil smile when he saw it, and he thought he would have liked a train set as a child, but toys were something his father had disapproved of.

As Basil and Bruton approached, they could hear cheering. Initially, Basil thought it was something to do with the Americans' victory at Cantigny, however, as they got closer it was mixed with laughter.

"It looks like they started drinking early," said Bruton.

Suddenly, the two wooden doors of the pub were flung open, and eight cadet officers came tumbling out, carrying above their heads a student. The rest of the pub followed laughing and everywhere there were shouts of "throw him in".

"What's going on?" shouted Bruton to one of the officers he knew.

"A wog came in with a local girl," shouted the officer back at him. "We thought we'd teach him a lesson in manners."

Bruton laughed in response.

Sometimes there is an event where the reality of the situation is too sudden to fully take in. Basil felt disassociated as he watched what happened with everything slowing to a dreamlike pace. He stared at what was happening, noticing everything to the minutest detail, frame by frame – and the noise of the crowd also slowed, so that nothing was comprehensible. Basil stood with an open mouth as he realised that they were carrying

32

Laxman above their heads.

The crowd crossed the road and followed the officers as they headed towards the canal. Basil followed as quickly as he could and arrived to see Laxman being tossed into the middle of the filthy stream. There was a splash as he went under, and a few moments later he surfaced. The officers, who now had had their fun, returned to the pub, except for one, perhaps the most drunk of all of them, who shouted, "Leave him, Drewe! He's just a wog."

"Piss off," said Basil.

"We can throw you in as well," replied the officer, who looked around for his friends.

"Yeah, I suppose if they come back there'll be enough of you to take on a cripple as well."

The officer decided there was no point arguing and, anyway, everyone else had gone. He turned and staggered back towards the pub. Basil looked at Laxman who had managed to get himself to the side of the canal and then at the officer. He thought he saw Bruton at the end of the road but, if he were there, he had gone in an instant.

***

Two weeks passed more quickly than Basil could imagine. There were no lectures or tutorials as they moved towards the long summer vacation. Laxman had been irritable since the evening at the Bookbinders. He was rarely seen in halls and mixed only with his Indian friends. On the times that Basil did see him, he was polite but curt. It was therefore no surprise to Basil that Laxman decided to go up to London for a few weeks before returning to Assam. Keble College was feeling quieter than Basil had ever known it. If Bruton was out, Basil would eat solitary meals in the dining hall. However, the weather was generally warm and balmy, and Basil spent his days touring the Oxfordshire countryside on a new five-geared bicycle that he had received from his parents as a birthday present.

"Hills are the only problem," he said to Bruton one morning over breakfast, "as I must stand up to peddle and that puts too much pressure on my leg. However, on the flat, I have no problem. I went out as far as

Blenheim Palace a few days ago."

"Don't you find the countryside a bit of a bore?" said Bruton. "It's green and very pretty but after you've cycled through it once, every journey's the same." Basil looked at him and decided to let the comment pass. "Talking about your leg," Bruton continued, "I have something for you."

"What is it?" asked Basil.

"A liniment. It smells a bit, but I'm told by one of the stable boys who looks after the polo ponies that it does miracles for muscle pain. He said you rub it into your leg in the area where it hurts." Bruton held out a small flask. "They use something similar on the polo ponies if they have hurt their legs."

Basil removed the cork stopper from the glass vial. There was an overpowering smell of camphor, which reminded him of mothballs and vapour rub. Underneath there was an acrid smell, which he thought was like burnt rubber. Basil did not even want to guess what was in it and quickly replaced the stopper, thinking about pouring it away at the first opportunity.

"If I were you," said Bruton, who could tell from the look on Basil's face that there was only a remote possibility it would be applied, "I would use it. Scoley might complain to high heaven about the smell, but the stable boys promised it would help. He also gave me a list of ingredients just in case you wanted to make some more. Some of the ingredients might be tricky to get but I would have thought with your father's contacts you should not have a problem."

"So, what are your plans this weekend?" asked Basil.

"I'm going up to town," said Bruton, "to meet someone my father introduced to me – Philip Kerr. He's Lloyd George's private secretary and something of a rising star. Why don't you join me?"

Basil shrugged and thought why not – he had nothing better to do.

**

Basil had bought a bottle of wine and was staring at an envelope that he placed in the middle of the table. He felt a profound sense of disappointment, having only been awarded third place in the Martin

Wronker Award for Jurisprudence. Other law students, who had also come to the pub, were congratulating him on his success.

"Great achievement," someone said and patted him on the back.

"Thank you," Basil replied, as he forced a smile. A prize for third place was about the worst thing he could have been awarded. What would he say to his father – he had come third and won a £5 book voucher? It would have been better not to have won anything. He worried that his father would be disappointed and despite every effort to the contrary, he felt sorry for himself and gulped down a glass of wine and then poured himself another.

An hour later, Bruton arrived and sat opposite Basil.

"Did you win an award?" asked Bruton.

"Third prize in jurisprudence," said Basil. "I wrote an essay on inchoate offences, about where you wilfully close your eyes to a likely event."

"I'm not sure I follow you, Drewe," said Bruton.

"Say one of your fellow officer cadets tells you he wants to borrow your pistol for target practice. You lend it to him, and he robs a bank. Are you guilty of aiding and abetting him?"

"No," said Bruton emphatically.

"But if he said he would rob a bank, then what?" asked Basil.

"Obviously, I would be guilty," answered Bruton.

"The grey area is when you suspect he might do something but do not know. For example, he has robbed a bank before."

"I wouldn't be so damned stupid as to lend him my gun," answered Bruton.

"But if you did," said Basil, "and, for example, you knew he had money problems. My essay was about when a person does not know what is going to happen but closes his eyes to an obvious risk – when a person is wilfully blind to what he should see."

Chapter 7

December 1918

The ground was covered in frost and a clear blue sky lit up the day. Sir Julius stood in front of the granite stone walls of Castle Drogo with his two sons. From where he stood, he could see miles into the distance where oak, ash and beech trees seemed bleached in the cold morning. In the Teign Valley below them, that stretched from Dunsford to Chudleigh, the meandering Teign River continued its course as it had done since time immemorial.

"I cannot remember the last time I was here with both of you," said Sir Julius.

"It was before the war," said Basil. "It must have been seven years ago, the stone-laying ceremony to mark your fifty-second birthday."

"That long ago?" replied Sir Julius.

"Actually," replied Christian, "we've never all been here together." He paused. "It was that day when Basil fell coming up the escarpment. He never reached this point. Adrian and I have been here with you, but never with Basil."

They stood silently for a few moments as the icy wind blew up the Teign gorge. Basil looked down the sharp sloping escarpment and his stomach knotted. Sir Julius pulled up the astrakhan collar of his coat and then turned his face away from the wind.

"I wanted to speak to you about the future," said Sir Julius. "I wanted to know what your plans were. I need to make some decisions about my companies and wondered whether either of you had any interest in joining them."

Basil looked at his brother. As the eldest surviving son, it seemed that it was a question for Christian; but as he looked at his brother, he knew what the answer would be.

"No, sir," said Christian. "Even if I wasn't blind, I don't think I would want to manage a company, and being blind creates an impediment I don't believe I can overcome."

Sir Julius said nothing but turned his head towards Basil.

"If I am being honest," said Basil, thinking about what he would say next, "it is not something I have ever considered. I had always assumed that Adrian... but you know."

"I do know," said Sir Julius, "which is why we are having this conversation. If my boy had not been killed in battle, we would not be here... but he was, and we are. Your mother and I have grieved for him for over a year; however, I must draw a line as it's been eating away at our lives all that time, and so I have started thinking about selling most of my interests in the Home and Colonial Stores and then spending some time travelling with your mother."

"Yes, sir," said Basil.

"I would remain the chairman of the company, but my involvement would be less. However, if you were interested in joining the company I would delay my retirement until you were ready to step into my shoes."

"But that would be years away, sir. I have another eighteen months at Oxford and then I thought about spending a year or two abroad in India working as a clerk to a judge. I don't want to disappoint you, sir..."

"It would only disappointment me, Basil," said Sir Julius interrupting, "if you did something to which you were not committed."

"Yes, sir."

"Would you like some time to think about it?" asked Sir Julius. Basil nodded his head. "So shall we say that you will give me an answer at Easter?" Again, Basil nodded.

"That's settled then," said Sir Julius. "Now let's find Lutyens as I am freezing out here. He should be around here somewhere, and I need to talk to him about the design of this castle."

They started slowly walking around the stone walls. Christian put his left arm on Basil's shoulder and tapped ahead as they walked.

"Tell me what the castle is looking like," said Christian.

"The walls are being constructed and at some places, they are more than twenty feet high. There are granite blocks everywhere but I am guessing that this is only about a quarter of the castle."

"Is it just the walls that are being built?"

"Yes," replied Basil. "However, every granite block is a different size. Some are small and others must weigh more than a tonne." Basil stopped and directed Christian's hand to the wall. "Can you feel the different sizes and textures of the granite blocks?"

"Yes," said Christian. "And what colour are they?"

"Primarily grey, but there are areas of white and orange and even black in some places. Behind the granite walls, there are bricks, which I suppose are the internal walls."

Edwin Lutyens stood talking to the site foreman, wrapped up warmly in a thick wool trench coat. He held the bowl of his pipe in his left hand, as he explained where the foundations for the next section of the walls should go. When he saw Sir Julius walking briskly in his direction, he patted the foreman on the shoulder and held out his hand to Sir Julius.

Basil had not seen Lutyens for seven years and he seemed much older than he remembered. Lutyens's hair had thinned and was all but white, as was his moustache. Despite being barely fifty, Basil thought he looked as old as his father who was nine years his senior. His round-rimmed glasses gave him the air of an elderly Latin teacher who would attempt to befriend their students with terrible Latin jokes. Basil smiled as he was greeted by Lutyens. He had forgotten how genuinely warm and welcoming Lutyens was, and he could not help himself saying how well Lutyens was looking.

The cold was biting into Sir Julius's bones, and he quickly wanted to finish the meeting and get back to the Rolls-Royce, and so he interrupted the introductions and asked for an update on the works.

"They are progressing well," said Lutyens, "but as the weather has now turned, work on the walls will stop as we can't mix cement in these conditions. It's the water in the cement," explained Lutyens. "If the water expands then the cement will be useless. What we can do is continue to dig more foundations unless the ground freezes and we'll continue to lay aggregates for the driveway."

"And when will the work on the walls start again?" asked Sir Julius brusquely.

"March probably. February, if we're lucky."

"I will then make my final decision on whether you should omit the other wing at Easter. Thank you," he added, shook Lutyens's hand and then turned and walked towards his car. Lutyens followed beside Christian and Basil.

"I'm pleased to see both of you," said Lutyens, "and I was so sorry to hear about your brother, Adrian. My deepest condolences. When we read about his death both Celia and I were heartbroken."

"Thank you," said Christian. "I saw her just before she left for America."

"I can't recall the last time I saw her," said Basil, "but I do remember she used to love the stories that you used to tell."

"I still tell a tale or two on occasion," replied Lutyens. "My wife and children came back from America only last week. I don't know if you recall, but my youngest daughter Mary is only twelve and, although she pretends that she is far too grown up to hear stories, she still demands that I tell one before she goes to bed. Fortunately, I was recently given a book of fables when I was in India, so I have a stock of new tales to tell."

"Can you remember any of them?" asked Christian.

"A few," said Lutyens, who took his pipe out of his mouth. "There was a fable I heard about a blind man and a cripple, but I am not sure that you would want to hear it."

"I think I would," said Christian, as he walked slowly towards the car, with his hand on his brother's shoulder.

"Once upon a time," began Lutyens, "in a small village there lived two brothers who fought like cat and dog. One of the brothers was blind and the other had been crippled in an accident and could not walk a single step. Whenever they spoke to each other they would argue ferociously.

What one did would upset the other, and vice versa. For years this enmity raged until one day they swore never to speak to one another again. As fate would have it, a fire broke out one hot and dry summer day and began quickly consuming everything in its path. Everyone from their village ran away in fear for their lives as there was no way to stop this raging inferno. In the villagers' panic, the blind man and his brother were forgotten. The two brothers now had a problem. The blind man could not tell which way to go to escape the fire, and the crippled brother, who could see the path to safety, could not take that path. So, both were stuck, but the desire to live was greater than their hatred for each other, so they decided to work together to save their lives. The blind man put his brother on his shoulders, who then directed him on which way to go to escape, and working together they became not only brothers but true friends."

Lutyens shook their hands and said his goodbyes as they reached the vehicle and, as he turned, Christian asked whether he would pass on his best wishes to his daughter Celia.

"Celia," said Lutyens, "is still in America."

"She didn't come back with your wife?" responded Christian.

"I am sorry to say," said Lutyens quietly, "that we have lost touch with her."

"Nothing has happened to her, has it, sir?" asked Christian.

"No, nothing like that. It was an affair of the heart," answered Lutyens and put his pipe in his mouth.

"Get in the car and shut the door," shouted Sir Julius to Christian, "or I'll catch my death of cold."

II

Part Two

Chapter 8

October 1922

Set in a valley near the Topatopa mountains, Ojai is a small city in California with orchards of apricot and orange trees. From a distance, the summit of the mountain range looks bereft of any trees or shrubs. The clouds often fall below the tops of the mountains and in wintertime, the highest peaks are white with ice and frost. The surrounding fields are lush and verdant, with excellent farmlands. It has a climate that is neither too hot nor too cold. For more than a millennium, the Chumash Indians lived and roamed here before they were systematically exterminated or sent to live on the Santa Ynez Reservation. These first people had a rich culture, which can now only be seen in their cave art and in the stories that have been passed down. When settlers came to this area, they named the town that they founded Nordhoff. Following the Great War, the name of the town was changed to Ojai as Nordhoff was considered too German. In the Chumash language, Ojai means 'the Nest'.

In the spring of 1922, Krishnamurti and his younger brother Nitya came to live in Ojai. Nitya had just been diagnosed with tuberculosis and needed a warm dry climate. Krishnamurti was given a parcel of land a few miles outside of the city as a sanctuary. There are dry-stone walls on each side of an unmade driveway as you enter the property. The driveway itself is flagged with trees of ash and white fir. The main house is built of pinewood, which had been painted white, and there are several bungalows dotted around the estate, which have been converted from old bunkhouses when it had been a working ranch. Krishnamurti once said, "If I had nowhere to go in the world, I would come to Ojai. I would sit under an orange tree; it would shade me from the sun, and I could live on the fruit."

At the age of twenty-seven, many theosophists still believed that Krishnamurti would one day transform into the new World Teacher, an enlightened spiritual leader such as Buddha, Krishna or Jesus. However, as each year passed, doubts began to take hold. Then, on the 17th of August 1922, Krishnamurti began what he thought was a spiritual awakening. He felt a sharp pain in the base of his neck and writhed in agony for almost three days, unable to eat and in a state of constant delirium. He was unchanged after the event. Two weeks later he started to have attacks almost nightly, which Krishnamurti and those who looked after him referred to as *the process*. He was exhausted after each of these attacks and would spend the day resting or outside in the shade meditating.

The theosophist movement waited, expecting that soon he would appear as the World Teacher.

***

After having lived for almost five years in a suburb of New York, Celia Lutyens came to Ojai and in the quietness, surrounded by the trees and fields, she burst into tears. She was tired, as it had taken her more than six days to travel to Ojai. She held the hand of her four-year-old son, who tried to hide the fact that he was equally as tired as his mother. However, once Celia began to cry, Robert could not prevent the tears from flooding down his cheeks.

Before starting the short walk along the driveway, Celia straightened her woollen plaid skirt and tidied her son's hair, which was sticking up after a night with his head against his satchel that held his prized crayons and colouring book. She carried in her large handbag a letter from Krishnamurti with the address. It was not a long letter and was written in Krishnamurti's solid, masculine handwriting. The nub of it was that he had news from London and asked if she was able to come and visit him in California for a holiday.

On the journey, Celia had told Robert about Krishnamurti, about how she first met him when she was fourteen, and how he came to live with her at their house in Bloomsbury in London. As the train made its way first to Chicago, she told Robert about Krishnamurti's life in India and explained that Krishnamurti's father had obtained a job as a secretary at the Theosophist Society and how he brought his youngest sons, Krishnamurti and Nityananda with him.

"It was there," said Celia to Robert, "that they were identified by one of the leaders of the Theosophist Society who said that Krishnamurti's aura was almost perfect and that Nitya's aura was nearly as strong."

"What's an aura?" asked Robert.

"It's a light that comes from the body that can only be seen by certain special people with spiritual powers," replied Celia.

Robert Lutyens continued to listen to his mother. When he became bored of the stories of the mystical Indian who they were going to see, he would stare out of the window, where in the night, when the sun had sunk below the horizon, the vast stretches of water seemed silent, airless and dead. The moonlight flooded through the window of the train and reflected off the Great Lakes, which seemed ghostly white. He was excited as it was the first time he had been away from New York. However, there was also a feeling of trepidation as he journeyed into the unknown. His mother had made Krishnamurti and his brother Nitya sound strange and supernatural, and he felt for the first time a sense of unease.

The following day the train proceeded to Iowa and then Nebraska, with its tall-grass prairies and savannas. The sun beat down relentlessly and the passengers opened the windows of the train for air. They travelled along an iron track which had been laid by fifteen thousand Chinamen, who had been treated little better than slaves, fifty years before.

As the journey progressed, Celia started telling Robert about her parents and their interest in theosophy and how her mother looked after Krishnamurti and Nitya when they came to England.

"Your grandmother would read to them," said Celia. "She would read anything so long as it was educational and there were times you could see Krishnamurti sitting in front of her, daydreaming as he lost interest. If I had done the same, I would have been scolded but Krishnamurti couldn't do anything wrong and as soon as he was out of the house he would go into the garage and tinker with his bicycle and then, when he was old enough, he bought himself a motorbike."

"What are my grandparents like?" asked Robert. "You never talk to me about them, or my father."

"I told you he was killed in the war," said Celia. Celia looked away from her son. She was tired and it was a conversation she did not want. She had promised herself that she would never talk about Robert's father, Adrian. She had loved him more than anyone else and he had betrayed her. She sighed and hoped that Robert would go back to his colouring books.

"What was he like?" demanded Robert.

"He was very handsome, just like you," replied Celia. "Now get on with your colouring."

"Tell me more," whined Robert.

Celia sighed again and relented. "Your grandfather's name is Ned. He is charming and smiles a lot, and he loves stories and smoking his pipe. He has white hair, and the top of his head is bald. When you meet him, he will start talking to you as if you were his closest friend and as if he had only seen you yesterday; however, that's how he treats everyone. Your grandmother's name is Emily. She is very different to your grandfather and can be quite stern. She belongs to lots of organisations and always has a hundred things to do but when she's at home she likes to read in quiet and doesn't like to be disturbed."

His appetite partially sated, Robert got out his crayons from his satchel and opened his colouring book. He decided to try and draw his grandparents based on his mother's description of them. Neither figure that he drew, when he closed his colouring book, was particularly fetching.

The Southern Pacific Railroad took Celia and Robert from San Francisco towards Los Angeles. The train went along the coast with its long stretches of sandy beaches and softly lapping waves. They got off the train at Ventura and took a bus twenty-three miles to Ojai. It was a mountainous route and, as they started getting closer to Ojai and into the valley, Robert noticed that palm trees grew everywhere. Ojai was a small city that had expanded significantly in the last decade. The town had been transformed five years earlier from a dusty, ramshackle collection of old West shops made of wooden planks nailed to wooden frames into a unified design of public architecture and parks. It had a population of around five hundred families, with two hotels, a post office, an arcade, a pergola, a tennis club and a golf club. The town had both an elementary and a high school and had plans to build a second high school and was in desperate need of teachers. Rows of arches went down the main street and an old-style Spanish church had been constructed. If Lutyens had been with his daughter and his grandson, he would have described the town as being built in the Mission Revival style of architecture, which harked back to the old Spanish colonial days. Many of the houses had also been renovated and had enclosed courtyards with large adobe walls and low-pitched roofs of clay tiles. Often the walls were stuccoed and painted white, like the Andalusian houses in the mountain villages of Spain. Ojai was prosperous, however, there was an underlying tension between those who had modern values and money and those who had been left behind when the town had been developed.

***

Krishnamurti sat in a cane chair, wearing a white silk shirt and a blue blazer despite the heat. It was as if he were receiving a special guest on whom he wished to make a good impression. He had not seen Celia for over six years and wondered if she had changed. It had saddened him when the split in the Lutyens family occurred because he thought of Emily as a surrogate mother and Celia as a headstrong sister. Emily had told him that Celia had eloped with a soldier on her journey over to America and that they had had a child. Krishnamurti doubted the story, as he remembered Celia as impetuous, but not foolhardy. Equally, Emily was awful at lying and, as she had told the story, she had blushed furiously.

When Celia and Robert entered the room, Krishnamurti stood up, came forward, and without the slightest hesitation kissed Celia on both cheeks, as he would do a sister. He patted the boy on the head, whereupon Robert's hair, which Celia had tried to flatten, sprang up again.

"How are you?" he asked.

"Tired," said Celia. "It was a long journey."

"Let's get you settled; we can talk later. How long are you staying for?"

"It rather depends," replied Celia.

The bungalow that was given to Celia and Robert was bigger than their apartment in New York. The living room had a small veranda that looked out onto a field of orange trees. There was an assortment of cacti in the little front garden. The two tiny bedrooms were white and spartan and, except for a few pieces of artwork that had been painted by previous occupants, the walls were unadorned.

Despite it still being the morning, Robert was happy to go to bed and left a trail of clothes as he walked from the bathroom to his bedroom. Celia eyed the bathtub with a desire that she had not felt for a long time. When Robert was asleep, she put a copper on the stove and then filled the bathtub, lay in the hot water and closed her eyes. She thought about what she wanted from her life. She could not imagine going back to New York and continuing to work in a hospital. Each day that she awoke she was still tired and each night she was a little more fatigued. She did not know how long she could continue working in a busy city hospital and being a mother. Things had to change but she knew that would involve compromises and she wasn't good at compromising.

***

When Celia came to New York in November 1917, she was met by a chauffeur on the quayside and was driven to her mother's apartment in Manhattan, an expensive and fashionable area of the city. If her mother was missing London, she did not indicate it and would only say that she would not return to that damp and dreary place until the war was truly over and when it was safe for her two youngest children, Mary and Elisabeth. Emily kept a stony silence when Celia arrived. She allowed Mary and Elisabeth to make a fuss of their elder sister, however, after a few hours, the excitement waned and the two young girls left, both having arranged afternoons out with friends.

"At least it doesn't show too much," said Emily when they were alone. She looked at her eldest daughter. Celia noticed her mother's pinched lips.

"Who have you told about it?" continued Emily, glancing down at Celia's stomach.

"Except for you, father and Aunt Gertrude, no one else knows I'm pregnant. I told everyone I was coming here to look after you and the girls because you had flu."

"Thank goodness, at least we'll have no problem getting that thing adopted and avoiding a scandal," said Emily.

Celia took in a deep breath. She had realised that sooner or later she was going to have this conversation with her mother and had prepared for it on the journey across the Atlantic.

"I'm not having my baby adopted," said Celia. "I'm going to keep it even if there is a scandal."

Emily looked at her daughter; her cheeks flushed. "Have you lost all your senses?" she said, doing her best not to shout. "It'll be the ruin of us. You know your father will never get another commission! Celia, for goodness' sake, don't disgrace me or your family."

Celia stood her ground and looked around at the sumptuous apartment that her mother had rented. "Why can't you say that I met a soldier and eloped? Say that you have disowned me. I'll get a job…"

"You, get a job?" said Emily incredulously. "What on earth do you think you can do?"

"I can be a nurse," said Celia testily, "or a teacher."

"You can't live on a teacher's salary," Emily said, now losing her self-restraint. "You can't bring up a child on a nurse's pay."

"I can if Father arranges an apartment for me. You seem to be living in the lap of luxury here."

"You selfish, spoilt girl!" Emily hissed. "You expect your father and me to make do, just because you couldn't keep your legs closed."

"You have no idea what you're talking about," shouted Celia. "You've no idea what love is, and you probably never will. You treat people with cold indifference, especially Father. I wouldn't expect anything like this," said Celia, waving her hand at the opulent apartment. "Just something where I can live and be far enough away so that I won't run into you or Mary and

Elisabeth."

Emily, who had never walked away from an argument in her life, responded in equal measure but when tempers cooled, Emily realised that she had no option but to agree to Celia's plan. She telegraphed her husband, who pulled some strings with the American consulate and a visa for Celia was granted. Emily rented a cheap flat in Yonkers and Celia had little trouble obtaining a position in a local hospital, given her experience as a nurse in the war.

When things had settled down, Lutyens wrote to Emily asking how long it would be before Celia could return to England. Emily wrote back saying that she could never return because they would face a scandal and that Celia had made her bed. With a deep sense of sorrow, Lutyens agreed and spoke about his eldest daughter only when asked.

When Emily returned to England in the first week of December 1918, she hardly if ever mentioned her eldest daughter. However, while Lutyens thought about his daughter every day, Emily rarely ever did until one day in September 1922 she received a letter from Krishnamurti.

"My dear Mother (I hope you don't mind me calling you this, Emily, but you have been more of a mother to me than anyone in my life),

"I have told you about the 'process' that has been happening to me which is still ongoing. I have been suffering severe pains & sickness although the experiences I have encountered have also been marvellous and beautiful. During the days I meditate. On one occasion, I saw above me a Star, bright and clear, and felt the vibrations of the Lord Buddha and I beheld Lord Maitreya. I was so happy, calm and at peace. I have drunk of the clear and pure waters at the source of the fountain of life and my thirst was appeased. Never more could I be thirsty, never more could I be in utter darkness. I have seen the Light. The fountain of Truth has been revealed to me and the darkness has been dispersed. I am God-intoxicated.

"During my meditations, I have thought about forgiveness and what it means, and my mind has often come back to your separation with Celia. I know that you feel that you have been hurt. Time will either heal that hurt or you will deliberately set about cultivating forgiveness. Forgiveness must I think be something different

to compassion because love and compassion know no hurt. Love exists when the 'me' element or the 'I' element of our thinking is not dominant. You know that a person who thinks about themselves more than others cannot truly love or have compassion.

"To obtain a state of love or compassion one must therefore give up hurt. You must decide whether you want to continue to feel hurt and then, hopefully, one day, you will forgive her, or you must give up hurt and feel love and compassion. If you choose the former path, you are simply strengthening the 'me' and the 'I' elements and this is not true love or compassion. So, it is very important, my dear Emily, to remember why you feel hurt. Is the hurt to do with your feelings of pride or self-respect or some other 'me' or 'I' feeling? When you come to realise that Celia has caused you no real hurt, you will be able to comprehend love and compassion. I have always believed that you are capable of real love and compassion, and it would make me so happy if I learnt that your daughter was back with her family.

"Always with you in my heart
K"

Chapter 9

Ojai was at its most beautiful in late autumn. When the sun came up from behind the Topatopa mountains, there would often be a hint of dew on the ground, as the coldish nights gave way to morning. There had not yet been a frost that year, which the farmers said was uncommon for October, and fruit could still be found on some of the trees.

The estate where Krishnamurti lived was called the Pepper Tree Retreat and it lay on the east side of the Ojai valley. An old, large pink pepper tree grew near the main building, which produced fragrant-smelling pink peppercorns. Six people were staying at the retreat when Celia arrived. Krishnamurti and his bother Nitya lived in the main house. Rosalind Williams, a companion and nurse to Nitya, had a small bungalow. Two theosophists from Australia, who were rarely seen except at mealtimes, had another bungalow and the estate manager, who lived there permanently, had rooms in one of the bunkhouses. The chores around the retreat were shared, with everyone taking turns to clean, shop, and cook.

Celia was woken by Robert in the early afternoon, who complained he was hungry. She dressed and they walked over to the main house and found Krishnamurti on the veranda, reading a book. Nitya and Rosalind had decided to take a walk after lunch and the two Australian theosophists were in their bungalow meditating.

"The introductions can wait until this evening," said Krishnamurti, "when we have dinner. However, let me prepare you something to eat." Krishnamurti looked at Robert and asked what he liked.

The young boy immediately answered, "Hot dogs."

"We are vegetarian here," replied Krishnamurti.

Robert thought for a moment before asking, "What exactly is a vegetarian?"

"Someone who doesn't eat meat," answered Krishnamurti, as he led them through the house to the kitchen.

"No meat, ever!" said Robert. "Not even hamburgers?"

"We can fry some mushrooms and put them in bread and make a mushroom burger," suggested Krishnamurti.

Robert looked at him as if he were quite mad. Everyone knew that a burger was made of a beef patty in a bun and had a liberal amount of ketchup and mustard on it. You could even add fried onions or a slice of cheese or bacon. Putting mushrooms in bread did not a burger make.

"What else do you have?" asked Celia.

"Cheese," said Krishnamurti, "or something from Mr Heinz." Krishnamurti opened a cupboard to show an array of tins of soups and baked beans. "If I were to be completely honest, cooking is not my forte."

"How about a cheese sandwich?" suggested Celia.

Robert casually nodded his head, indifferent to the suggestion.

Krishnamurti took out the ingredients from the pantry and Celia started cutting and then buttering the bread. Once Robert had started eating the sandwich, Krishnamurti and Celia sat down at the other end of the kitchen table.

"I wanted to speak to you," said Celia quietly. "I understand from your letter that you have news from my mother."

Krishnamurti frowned for a moment as he collected his thoughts. "I asked Emily to think about why she was hurt by what you did."

"She made it quite plain to me five years ago that she didn't want a scandal."

"But will there be a scandal?" Krishnamurti asked quietly. "Emily has told everyone that you fell in love with an American soldier on the crossing to America, that you married him and became pregnant but that he died a few months later in the war."

Krishnamurti got up and went to the tap and poured three glasses of water. He placed one in front of Robert, gave one to Celia and took a sip from his glass. Robert had got out his colouring book and pencils from his satchel.

"What are you drawing?" asked Krishnamurti.

"An aeroplane," said Robert.

"He loves aeroplanes," said Celia to Krishnamurti.

"Have you ever seen one?" asked Krishnamurti.

"Lots," answered Robert, "and when I grow up, I'm going to be a pilot."

Krishnamurti smiled and left the boy drawing another plane high in the sky. He sat next to Celia and again lowered his voice.

"Once Emily realised that it was only a hurt to her pride, she found that she could forget the hurt or, at least, forgive it."

They talked for another hour after Robert had gone out to play in the garden. Krishnamurti told Celia that he intended to leave Ojai in May and go to the Theosophical Society convention in Chicago in June, before returning to England.

"And would it be possible for Robert and me to stay here until May and then go back to New York or England with you?"

Krishnamurti thought for a moment. "There is nothing here for a child to do," he said.

"I can enrol him at the school in Ojai for six months until we leave, and he won't be any bother. I can also help look after Nitya."

"You'll find things very provincial here," said Krishnamurti.

***

The next morning, Robert picked the last of the Valencia oranges from a tree in the fields and ran back to his bungalow with the fruit in his arms so that his mother could squeeze them. With a glass of orange juice, he ate a breakfast of French toast, which he smothered in Heinz's ketchup to Celia's horror. Celia had told him that tomorrow he would be enrolled in the kindergarten in town.

Robert again felt a sense of unease. When they had left for California, he had understood that it would be a short holiday, he had not expected them to stay. All his things were in New York in their apartment – his clothes, his toys, his memories. He had not even said goodbye to his friends, and now he did not know when he would be returning home.

***

The sky was the colour of an anvil when Celia hitched the horse to the buckboard. Storm clouds gathered in the distance as black as coal and faraway thunder rumbled like a score of hammer blows on a darkened forge. She was about to change her mind about taking the buckboard into town when Robert appeared, wearing a sou'wester, oilskin poncho and carrying his satchel.

"Where did you get those?" asked Celia.

"Señor Manuel gave them to me," answered Robert. "He said I could wear them, and he left a set for you."

Manuel, or, to give him his full name, Manuel Hernández Garcia, was the estate manager. He was short and stocky and as strong as a mule with a full, black moustache and deep brown eyes that would almost close whenever he laughed. He had left a wife and four children in his hometown of San Felipe when he had come across the Mexican border looking for work and was fastidious in sending back three-quarters of his wages to his family every month.

Once Celia had hitched the horse to the buckboard she went back towards her bungalow and saw Manuel tending the vegetable garden.

"Will it rain?" Celia called out, looking up at the dark clouds in the distance.

"*Si*," answered Manuel, "*creo que lloverá a cántaros.*" Celia looked at him momentarily, unsure of what he had said. "It's going to rain cats and dogs," he translated. "If you're going into town, I'd take the truck."

"I can't drive," said Celia.

"Then you're going to need to wear those oilskins," said Manuel, glancing up at the sky.

***

The Ojai kindergarten was held each morning in the Boyd room at the Women's Club – a small, slate-roofed wooden building that had been painted green for as long as anyone could remember. The women of Ojai

55

only ever used the clubhouse on the weekends and in the late afternoons, when they would meet after playing tennis.

In September 1922, twenty-three children attended the Ojai kindergarten. Miss Clara Newman, who ran it, was young and from a good but not well-to-do family. When Celia introduced herself to Clara and enquired about a place for Robert, she was met with a score of questions about her background and education.

"And your husband," asked Clara, "is he here or still in New York?"

"Robert's father died in the war," responded Celia.

Clara Newman gave the customary words of condolence that had become so common after the war. She then asked Celia what she had done before the war.

"I was at Cambridge," said Celia. "I read English."

"And what are your plans while you're here in Ojai?" asked Clara.

"I've no plans," said Celia. "I suppose I should find myself employment."

The next morning when Celia and Robert arrived at the Ojai kindergarten, they were met not only by Clara Newman but the principal and a teacher from the Bristol Secondary School. While Celia had slept soundly in her bed, the telephone wires of the town buzzed and the possibilities of employing her were discussed at length. Cambridge may have been 5,400 miles away but its name, even in Ojai, was almost as well-known as Stanford. To have a teacher at the school who had studied at Cambridge, even if she had not finished her degree, would give Ojai a great deal of prestige – and the women of Ojai thrived on that.

Celia was somewhat at a loss as to what to say when an offer of employment was immediately made, subject to proof of references. She would have to teach most subjects including reading and writing as well as basic mathematics. Her class would consist of a range of ages, as many children never got further than eighth grade, and would consistently repeat years. She asked how she could pick up Robert if she was teaching at the school. The principal said that they would arrange her working day around Robert's timetable and that on the few days when she was still teaching, Robert could be escorted to the school and wait in the library.

A week later, when telegrams arrived confirming her good standing, Celia began teaching at the Bristol Secondary School. Given the enthusiasm of the principal and teachers in employing her, it had not occurred to her that some others in town might resent her presence. It started with the Hamilton children – three boys aged seven, thirteen and fifteen who had a troubled history at the school. The eldest boy had left after punching a teacher. The middle and younger Hamilton boys were often in detention for fights.

After a knife fight which involved Ethan, the middle boy, Mr Hamilton was told to come to the school to discuss the children's behaviour. He took the view that children getting into knife fights was as common as anything in his time and that Celia "was making a mountain outta nothin'." He said he would give his son, 'a whoppin' and, as he left, chewing on a piece of tobacco, remarked that Celia had no right to preach when an unmarried woman was livin' with injuns.

Chapter 10

February 1923

The sun had set some hours before, and the world had gone from red to an intense blue and then to black. In the distance, the katydids sang, and the crickets chirped. Nitya sat writing in his journal, something he did daily. Celia and Robert took the dinner plates to the kitchen and washed them. Manuel was outside, cooking tacos from a recipe his mother had given him, and where he hoped the scent of the cooking meat would not be smelt.

"Where did you get that recipe from, Rosalind?" asked Krishnamurti.

"My eldest sister gave it to me. When you're the youngest of four children, all girls," said Rosalind, "you pick up things."

"I was the eighth child born to my parents," said Krishnamurti, "but I never learnt to pick up anything in the kitchen."

"It was delicious," said Nitya, "and, as we all know, my cooking is even worse than K's."

After Celia returned from washing the dishes, she said that she needed to get Robert back to their bungalow and put him to bed. As usual, Robert complained. It was Nitya who suggested that they move to Celia's bungalow, and they lit lanterns and walked the sixty metres along an unlit winding path to where Celia and Robert were staying. In the darkness of the evening, they looked like a procession from a pre-Raphaelite painting – the women in long white cotton dresses and the men in white shirts and flannel trousers and all of them carrying lanterns.

Once Celia had tucked Robert in bed and told him a story that her father had once told her, she went to the living room to join the others. Rosalind had brought with her some fruit and was slowly eating grapes, one by one. She had short dark hair, blue eyes and an angular face, with a chin that protruded slightly. She had turned twenty in June and when she decided to move to Ojai her parents had not objected, as they were both theosophists and considered looking after Krishnamurti's younger brother an honour. She brought with her an enthusiasm about everything she did, even when making dinner, and it was this that made her liked by everyone.

Nitya, like his brother, was handsome and parted his hair in the middle. His features were not as pronounced as those of Krishnamurti, who had an owlish look, with a slightly pointed nose, large eyes and a wide mouth. Nitya was, in contrast, more classically attractive with a more relaxed manner than his elder brother. If Krishnamurti was at times passionate, Nitya was objective. However, both brothers could talk all evening, although it was Nitya who was able to put everyone at ease. They talked about Krishnamurti's upcoming talk in Chicago and then his trip to England from New York.

"Nitya and Rosalind have decided to come with me," Krishnamurti said.

Celia thought about her options and saw that going back to New York with Krishnamurti was logical – she could then decide whether to stay there or return to England. Staying in Ojai was not an option. While she was enjoying being at the Pepper Tree Retreat there was an undercurrent of hostility that she sometimes felt when she was in town. She put it down to being an outsider. Most of the people she spoke to had never left the town and many she thought disapproved of her living on a farm with two unmarried Indian men.

"I suppose," said Celia, "it makes perfect sense for me to go with you, although I am still in two minds as to whether I should go back to England."

"What would you do if you went back?" asked Rosalind.

"I've no idea," said Celia. "I've been avoiding thinking about it for the last few months."

"If you would like some advice," said Nitya, who nestled a cup of mint tea in his hands, "I would contact your friends and tell them you are coming home. They will be delighted to hear of your return and will want to support you."

"Yes," said Celia. "However, there are also some bitter memories I will need to face, and everyone I know will ask me about Robert and his father." Celia paused. "I had this overwhelming love for him, which unless you have been truly in love you cannot understand. You can't understand it from reading a book or someone telling you what love is – you must feel it. Robert is so much like his father in looks and mannerisms. In America, no one knows me. In England, I will always have to be on my guard and will have to avoid talking about Robert and Adrian."

Suddenly Celia realised what she had said. She had mentioned that name which she had not told to anyone – not to her mother, nor her best friend, Jenny Stanton, nor Christian Drewe. She felt that she had inadvertently opened the box with all the dark secrets in the world and she could not replace the lid.

"Please," she said. "Please forget what I just said."

Krishnamurti, Nitya and Rosalind agreed never to mention the name again. However, in the next room, peering through a crack in the door, Robert sat listening intently to the conversation and now began to wonder who Adrian was.

Chapter 11

Robert said he felt unwell, which was not so much a lie as a half-truth. He had slept restlessly the night before, thinking about the father who had died before he was born. He rubbed his eyes and yawned, taking little notice of what the kindergarten teacher was saying until she repeated, quite tersely, that they had to go to the senior school so that he could wait for his mother who was still teaching. The senior school was a maze to Robert and as they made their way to the library, he saw a boy standing in the corridor facing the wall wearing a dunce's cap. Robert was unable to stifle a giggle and the boy turned and scowled at him. It was the first time Robert encountered one of the Hamilton boys.

After Celia had finished teaching, she collected Robert and walked with him across town towards the stables where the horse and buckboard had been left. They walked along Ojai Avenue and Robert, as he often did, asked his mother whether they could stop at the ice cream parlour before going home. Celia, who had just been paid, did not need much convincing and they went in, ordered, and sat at a corner booth.

It was three weeks until Robert's fifth birthday in March and Celia had still not found a suitable venue for his party. But, as they sat sipping soda and melted vanilla ice cream through a straw, Robert saw an opening – and asked whether he could have his party at the ice cream parlour. Celia thought about it for a moment and then went to find the manager.

Joshua Hamilton was the youngest of the Hamilton children and two and a half years older than Robert. Joshua's mother had died two years after he was born. His father worked at the saloon in town and while he mostly stayed sober when he worked, he spent what he earned on whiskey after the bar closed. As Robert sat sipping his ice cream soda the three Hamilton boys came in. Deke, the eldest, never attended school after he had hit a teacher. He looked around the ice cream parlour without any expression on his face. When Celia saw him, she was reminded of the soldiers who had suffered shell shock, as he had the same cold, blank unfeeling eyes. Above his thin mouth, he had a cut, which his father had given him during a belting. His nose had been broken and Deke did not recall whether that had been received in just another fight or was one of the many presents from his father.

When Joshua saw Celia, he pulled Deke's arm and pointed towards her. Celia saw him out of the corner of her eye but decided to ignore him. However, when she felt Deke staring at her, the hairs on the back of her neck went up. For a moment she thought about staring back but she heard a warning voice telling her not to do it. The boys came up to the serving counter, where Celia stood with the manager discussing whether she could book the ice cream parlour for twenty children.

"Three sundaes," said Deke, as he leant on the counter.

"I'll be with you in a minute, young man," said the manager.

Deke stood to his full height. He was nearly two inches taller than Celia and taller than the manager.

"Three sundaes, now," Deke demanded. He then looked at Celia. "You're that teacher what lives up at the Pepper Tree place, ain't ya?"

"Yes," said Celia.

"And you've been punishin' Josh 'cause he ain't no good with learnin'."

"No," said Celia, turning to Deke. "I punished Joshua because he was being insolent."

"Well, he says different, and Josh is many things but he ain't no liar."

"I told you my reasons," said Celia, who then turned back to the manager. "Why don't you serve them and then we can finish the booking."

"You havin' a party, are ya?" asked Deke. "I'm lookin' forward ta gettin' my invitation in the post." The other two Hamilton boys laughed.

"Boys, take a seat," said the manager. "I'll bring your order over in a second. That's three nickels."

Deke slammed the coins on the counter and the manager picked them up and opened the till.

"You wouldn't be interested in coming," said Celia tersely to Deke. "It's for little children."

"While they're playin'," said Deke, "you and me could play as well. Pa said you already had one little bastard, so you might not mind another."

Deke grabbed hold of Celia's arm as she raised it. No one had ever called her son a bastard and she stood staring at Deke, her face flushed. She hated herself for not having the strength to slap him.

"Leave her, son," said the manager. "You don't want another run-in with the sheriff."

Deke let go of Celia's arm and the boys turned and went over to an empty booth. Celia took a deep breath and tried to calm herself. Her face still felt flushed, and she didn't want Robert to see her like that.

"They're all bark," said the manager. "You and your boy finish your sodas, and I'll see you on the third of March."

Celia went back to Robert, who had been watching. She felt the Hamilton boys looking at her.

"Are you all right, Mummy?" asked Robert. "What did they want?"

"Nothing," said Celia. "Just finish up, it's time to go."

"But I'm only halfway through," Robert whined in response.

"Just hurry up," replied Celia. "I have a pile of books to mark this evening and your laundry doesn't do itself."

As they left the ice cream parlour, Celia again felt that she was being stared at. She started talking to Robert about nothing of importance and thought about why she had punished Joshua Hamilton that afternoon. She had asked him to read a page from *The Pilgrim's Progress* and he had stumbled over nearly every word. The other children had laughed. When she had asked him what the problem was, he said that when he tried to read the words the letters jumbled themselves up and that it wasn't his fault. The children had again laughed, and Celia concluded that as she was still relatively new, he was probably making fun of her.

***

Something about Deke Hamilton disturbed Celia. She had looked into his eyes and seen nothing but hate – it was a blackness where nothing shone out. She wondered what had caused it and, for a second, felt sorry for him until she remembered that feeling of panic. Robert had noticed that something was wrong. He did not know what it was, but Celia knew he had sensed her fear – it was as clear to her as a rainbow when one sees sunlight scattered by raindrops.

Celia's feelings of disquiet were gone the next morning, like a passing cloud over the Topatopa mountains. She and Robert were both up early and she suggested that he find Manuel and get some eggs for breakfast. At the coop, Manuel was throwing feed out for the birds and said to Robert to go collect the eggs himself. A few moments later Robert came out rubbing his fingers with no eggs.

"They bit me," said Robert.

"They'll do that," said Manuel, who continued to put feed out for the birds.

"How can I get the eggs?" whined Robert. Manuel looked over at him.

"You get used to their pecks. You show them who is in charge and take them." Robert thought about Manuel's answer and looked doubtful. "You can always put the front of a spade between you and the chicken and while they peck at that, you reach under and take the egg." Robert still looked doubtful. "Come with me," said Manuel, putting down the bag of feed, "I'll show you."

Robert came out of the chicken coop with four warm eggs in his hands.

"*Es facil*," said Manuel.

"*Si*," said Robert. "Does it work on bullies?"

"*Si*," said Manuel. "You must show them you're the boss – never let yourself be bullied or it won't stop."

"But Krishnamurti says you must avoid violence?"

"Señor Krishnamurti doesn't have to get the eggs in the morning," answered Manuel.

Chapter 12

Robert's birthday party was a success, although, by the last hour, the young children had become unmanageable. Twenty children, each with a slice of cake wrapped in a napkin, left the ice cream parlour and, as the last one went, the manager sighed with exhaustion. He knew he had a good hour of cleaning before he could reopen the parlour for the Saturday evening crowds that came before the performance at the cinema.

"Do you need a hand?" asked Celia, who was pretending not to notice the carnage that twenty children had caused.

"You run along, Miss Lutyens," replied the manager. "It's starting to get dark, and you have a long journey home."

Celia and Robert both wore coats wrapped tightly around them and she had a blanket which she put over their legs. The sun had just set and, above her, the moon gleamed brightly. There was a dampness in the air. The buckboard rattled as it went along the cobbled street of Ojai Avenue. As they left the city limits, the sound changed as the horse trotted along a cinder track. There were farms on both sides of the road and, as Celia's eyes got used to the dark, she could see creatures moving. The moon-feeders were waking and coming out. Away across a field, she spotted some deer, who had come down from the mountains in search of food. She pointed them out to Robert as the buckboard rolled slowly forward. The deer looked around, their ears pricked up in case a farmer was out protecting his crops. The deer moved slowly into the crop fields and then lowered their heads to eat. A stag stood guard, looking, and listening as his herd ate.

The buckboard turned off the main road and started going uphill towards the Pepper Tree Retreat. It was Robert who first saw the shapes of three people coming down the road and pointed them out to Celia.

"Who do you think they are?"

"I can't tell," said Celia. "They're probably going into town."

A coyote howled in the night and Celia shivered.

**

On a Saturday evening, Manuel would drive into town in his truck, have a meal, drink a few beers, and then see a movie. About four hundred metres from the entrance of the Pepper Tree Retreat, he saw the buckboard. It was on the side of the road and as he got closer, he saw a struggle taking place. Joshua Hamilton let go of Robert and ran, as soon as the truck pulled up and Manuel got out of the vehicle. Ethan Hamilton received a kick in the ribs that sent him sprawling and clutching the side of his chest. Deke rolled over when he saw Manuel's foot swinging towards him, stood up and pulled out a knife.

Robert ran to his mother and buried himself in her arms when Manuel and Deke started circling each other. Manuel watched his opponent closely and realised that Deke knew how to use a knife. He did not lead with the knife and kept it close to him, thrusting out quickly whenever he got close to Manuel. Deke used his free hand to punch at Manuel, trying to find an opening in his defence. Manuel crouched with his arms in front of him. He kept moving to the side, always watching the knife. When he had positioned himself between Deke and his truck he shouted:

"Celia, can you get to my truck?"

Celia said nothing but got up and, with Robert still clinging to her, moved towards the vehicle.

"There's a rifle in the back," said Manuel.

It was then that Deke stopped watching Manuel and looked at Celia. Manuel moved in, quickly hitting Deke on the left side of the face. He stepped back immediately as the knife was thrust forward. Manuel was surprised that the boy had not gone down. He had hit him hard and then he saw blood glistening above his eye. Deke wiped the blood away. Manuel heard the unoiled hinges of the truck door squeal and knew that Celia had got to the truck.

"It's time to walk away," said Manuel. He knew that the next thing that Deke would do would be to try to rush him, get in close and stab him as many times as he could. He had not expected to hear a rifle shot.

The force of the shot knocked Deke backwards and he went down with the knife dropping from his hand. He didn't say anything for the few seconds he lived afterwards. He just looked up at the blackness of the night with the stars shining in the heavens.

Manuel turned and looked at Celia, who had lowered the rifle. "You didn't have to do that," he said.

"If you had arrived a few minutes later, they would have raped me."

Robert got out of the vehicle and ran to his mother.

"I hate it here. I want to go home," said Robert.

"I want to go home as well," said Celia quietly to him, although they were both thinking about very different places.

***

"Another bad dream?" asked Rosalind. Celia nodded her head and sat down on the bench on the porch. She cupped a glass of milk in her hands. There was a slight mist in the air, which lay upon her arms and caused the hairs to stand up. She felt uncomfortable and wanted to rub her skin. She had felt something similar two weeks earlier when she had fired the rifle.

"The dreams will go," continued Rosalind, "but it will take time."

"It's good of you to stay with me," said Celia. "I don't think I could have stood to be alone right now."

"Was it the same dream?" asked Rosalind.

"Yes," said Celia. "I feel that I can't move and there is a weight on me that is dragging me under the ground and, as I sink, I'm choking, and I try to break free. It is then that I hear voices in the blackness – judging me – telling me that I must fight harder. I know the voices, but they're voices from a dream that I can't remember and there is one voice, more solemn than the rest, urging me to fight and I can smell something sweet like honeydew melon." Celia took a sip of milk. "And then the empty blackness seems to pull back and I am looking at his eyes – the boy's eyes – the one I shot – and I see my reflection in them, and I'm paralysed with no strength."

"It will get better," said Rosalind. "Time is a great healer."

Celia said nothing in response. They had all said the same sort of thing to her – Krishnamurti, Nitya, the doctor, and the sheriff.

Robert said little and clung to Celia. It was as if he was feeling the same pain but had no way to articulate it, except to hold onto his mother and hug her. Manuel said almost nothing to her, except when she asked him a direct question. His silence felt like a rebuke as if he did not understand her reasons for firing the gun.

"Have you decided what you'll do?" asked Rosalind.

"Go back to New York," said Celia. "As soon as the sheriff says I can leave the county, I'll go back to my apartment in New York and from there... well I don't know. I want to go home – back to England. I always felt safe there and that's what I want more than anything now."

***

The dreams did not go away and were as vivid two weeks later. Rosalind spent much of her time sitting with Celia, and during this period Krishnamurti and Nitya survived on a diet of Heinz's finest cuisine. Both men would alternate between heating spaghetti in tomato sauce or macaroni with cheese and mushroom sauce. Nitya later remarked that their lives had been saved solely by the invention of the can-opener. Manuel would get everything they needed from town and would take Robert with him if Celia was asleep. Except for his mother, Robert only felt safe with Manuel as if he sensed that the short, burly Mexican would never let anything bad happen to him.

Rosalind tried to encourage Celia to talk. Not about the shooting or how she felt about it but about her life before the shooting, before Ojai, and before America. At first, Celia was reticent but soon realised that as her mind began to fill up with the memories of her youth, the more recent memories diminished. And so, Rosalind and Celia spent most afternoons sitting on the veranda wrapped under warm furs talking about Celia's past.

"And boyfriends," said Rosalind, "you must have had dozens of them in New York. Don't tell me there wasn't a doctor or two who turned your eye."

"I was too busy trying to make ends meet," said Celia. "Besides, any man who did look at me ran a mile when they found out I had a small boy," said Celia.

"Men are like that," said Rosalind. "When you find one who's not frightened to love you and everything that comes with you then you have to hold onto him."

Celia didn't answer and they continued to sit on the bench with the fur skins wrapped around them watching as the sun made its way westwards. After a few minutes, Celia shivered and pulled the furs around her a little closer.

"Penny for them," said Rosalind.

"I was thinking about Robert's father," said Celia.

"Do you want to tell me?" asked Rosalind. "Manuel and Robert are in town so there is no one to overhear us."

"When he died," began Celia, "I felt like someone had torn out my heart and stamped on it. I loved him and hated him all at the same time. It was complicated, he told me he loved me but then married someone else. I would suddenly burst out crying for no reason at all. Even six years later, I can't look at anyone else without comparing them to him and they always come up short. When I was with Robert's father, I just felt happy, so happy as if my heart would burst."

"You must have known him very well to feel like that."

"No not really, which is the thing that confuses me. However, the last time we saw each other I felt that we could finish each other's sentences and if we said nothing it was because we both knew what the other was thinking."

"I sometimes feel that with Nitya," said Rosalind, who at once laughed with embarrassment.

"Nitya?" said Celia. "I thought it was K who you liked?"

"K is unobtainable," replied Rosalind, "and he has sworn himself to celibacy."

"I suppose that rather puts a damper on choosing him," said Celia and

Rosalind laughed, and then for the first time in what felt like years, Celia laughed as well.

***

By the end of March, the sheriff had finished his investigation. Although the two Hamilton boys were too young to face court proceedings, they were not so young as to escape being flogged at the jailhouse until they could not stand. Their father carried out the whipping in front of the local judge and the sheriff, and the two boys bore the scars on their backs for the rest of their lives. As to the shooting of Deke, the sheriff found that it was a case of self-defence. The Hamilton boy had a knife and showed an intent to cause grievous bodily injury. Many of the townspeople felt aggrieved, though there were only a few who openly criticised the sheriff's decision.

Celia and Krishnamurti talked about her leaving, and though he tried to persuade her to stay, she would not be moved.

"All I want at the moment," said Celia, "is to feel safe. Is that too much to ask for me and my son?"

"Of course not," said Krishnamurti, "and know that when you leave here, you will still have all my love." He leant forward and kissed her on both cheeks as he had done six months earlier when she had arrived at Ojai. He then picked up Robert and hugged him.

"Let us say *au revoir*," said Krishnamurti to Robert, "and not goodbye. *Au revoir* means 'until we see each other again'."

Nitya and Rosalind also said their goodbyes and Celia got into the truck, which Manuel was driving, to take them to the bus station.

It was the first time Celia had been out of the Pepper Tree Retreat in nearly a month, and they drove along the road where she had been assaulted. When they got to the spot where the attack had taken place, she closed her eyes and counted to fifty before opening them. She hoped that she could put the past behind her, but as soon as they got into town, people gawped at them like they were a circus attraction.

Manuel said nothing. At the bus station, he unloaded the bags and gave them to a porter.

"I'm sorry," said Celia.

"I'm sorry as well," said Manuel. "However, this last month has made me think about what is important. It's time for me to go back home to my family." He then reached into the vehicle and got out a colouring book. "There are lots of aeroplanes in it," he said as he gave the book to Robert, "and remember to look after your mother."

Manuel waited outside the bus. Robert pulled down the window where he sat and looked at Manuel and smiled. As the bus began its journey to Ventura, he waved.

Celia sat back in the seat. She felt as disillusioned as the day she had arrived; her dreams lying in an overgrown graveyard of half-remembered faces. The bus would take her first to Ventura and then she would take a few trains to New York. Her job as a nurse was no longer available and she knew she would struggle to make ends meet, put food on the table, and buy clothes. She realised that sooner or later she would have to go home to England, but first, she needed to give Robert some continuity. She owed him that.

***

Celia held three letters in her hand as she went inside the post office. It had been two years since she returned to New York. She had done almost nothing in that time except try to give her son stability and had walked him to school each morning and picked him up in the afternoons. She had managed to get some part-time work teaching the piano. It paid little and, even with the money she received from her father, it was barely enough to live on.

She had struggled with the letter to her father, and the drafts that had been torn up and binned were testimony to this. The letter that she finally sent was short and just said that she intended to return to England in the first week of December that year after the lease on her apartment had expired. This would give her time to arrange a school for Robert. She asked whether she might stay at the family home until more permanent accommodation could be arranged. The second letter to Cristian Drewe was equally as short and said that she would be returning to England at the end of the year with her son Robert and she hoped he was well and getting on with his life. The third letter to her oldest friend, Jenny Stanton, was longer and more personal. She wrote about everything that had happened to her and the insecurity she felt. In all candour, she asked Jenny if she could assist in finding her a suitable husband.

She walked back from the post office towards her apartment and stopped at the butcher's. She would make Robert's favourite meal – hamburgers. As she queued, she thought about the last two years. Robert still clung to her and had not made friends at school. He still seemed unsettled and often cried at night and, she thought, he needed someone who could encourage him to stand on his own two feet and bring him out of his shell.

"What can I get you, ma'am?"

"Half a pound of mince," said Celia, and looked in her purse, hoping that she would have enough money. Scrimping and saving, it was hardly a life at all, and she wanted so much more for her son. If things had been different, she might have remained in New York, but both she and Robert were treading water. She had almost no friends and no prospects. When she got home, she looked around the tiny apartment that she had lived in for over seven years and knew that she was doing the right thing in leaving a country that had never been her home.

III

Part Three

Chapter 13

March 1922

The fountain outside Middle Temple Hall trickled water as it had done in Lord Mansfield's day. The Benchers of Middle Temple had ignored the leaking pipe for so long that its deficiency was now considered with something like affection. On a greyish March morning, when the sun had yet to burn away the mist, Basil and his friend, David Maxwell Fyfe, wandered past the old fountain on their way to their chambers at Hare Court. Basil kept his hands in his pockets as he hurried past the old red stone buildings without noticing them, his mind too busy thinking about the Abraham case to properly appreciate their reverential beauty. As he turned into Middle Temple Lane, he felt a twinge in his left leg and realised that he hadn't rubbed on any liniment that morning.

"And why are we coming in this early?" asked Maxwell Fyfe, with his light Scottish accent. "No one will be in chambers."

"Because Rowledge's junior left the Abraham brief there last night and I want to read it. There's a rumour that Rowledge wants to get the measure of all the pupils which is why we're all going with him to court." The bells of St Clements chimed seven times above the grey slate roofs of the oldest Inn of Court and then there was silence as if a thousand years of learning sucked every sound out of the air. They entered the door of 2 Hare Court.

"I'll go and get the brief," said Basil.

In the early afternoon at court 3 of the Old Bailey, Horace Rowledge KC brilliantly summarised the evidence and the law in the case of *R v Abraham*. He explained to the jury that his client not only had to threaten to kill the victim but that the prosecution had to prove that he intended that the victim would believe that the threat would be carried out. He leaned forward towards the jury, with one hand placed firmly on the table in front of him.

"The prosecution would have you believe that my client intended to cause the victim to fear that he would be killed." Rowledge stopped, stood fully upright, turned, looked directly at the defendant and then pointed his outstretched arm towards him. The jury looked at the defendant. "Members of the jury, the prosecution's case is that my client, all five foot and one inch of him, would put in fear of his life a man who was over six feet tall. A burly man who had served in the war and had been awarded a medal for bravery. Members of the jury – use your common sense. Picture the scene, the landlord is bearing down on my client who is standing at the dartboard, armed only with a dart. My client accepts he shouted, 'Get back or I'll kill you' and then threw the dart, but this was bluster as he feared that the publican would injure him. As my client said, when the police arrived, he only intended to part the landlord's hair."

A member of the jury laughed. The judge took off his reading glasses and looked down at the juror, who fell silent.

"Continue, Mr Rowledge," said the judge, and Horace Rowledge did so, setting out the case for the defence, point by point. When he sat down Basil was equally convinced of Stephen Abraham's innocence as were the twelve good men and true. An hour later a verdict of not guilty was reached and they left the Old Bailey and walked back along the Strand towards chambers. Horace Rowledge stopped at the Old Cock Tavern and took out his pocket watch. It was three o'clock on a Friday and there was no need to hurry and after all, he thought, a win in the Old Bailey didn't happen every day. He pushed the wooden doors open. The inside of the building had changed very little since the mid-eighteenth century when it had become a favourite for both journalists and barristers. The room was dark, and the gas lights fluttered as the door opened. Horace Rowledge headed for a small area at the back of the tavern where there were several booths. He called to the landlord, requested a bottle of his usual claret and looked at

Basil, Maxwell Fyfe and the two other pupils.

"You don't have anything pressing do you?" he asked as the claret and five glasses arrived.

Chapter 14

July 1922

Basil, Maxwell Fyfe and the two other pupils sat in the conference room of 2 Hare Court. The rays of a rich July sun flooded through the window. Basil stared out and could see, above the rooftops, the rounded end of the Inner Temple church that had been constructed at the end of the twelfth century. It had been designed, like so many churches that the Templars built, to mirror the Church of the Holy Sepulchre where Jesus had been buried. The Templars had gone to war with the Muslims when they refused to hand over the Holy Lands. In a world so big and beautiful and full of different people, Basil wondered why anyone would think that God could be parochial and favour one religion over another.

"Were you listening to me?" said the senior clerk to Basil.

Basil turned his head and looked at the grey-whiskered clerk in his striped trousers.

"Of course," replied Basil, "the West London Magistrates' Court on Monday morning."

"No, Mr Drewe, not the West London Magistrates' Court, I said the Wimbledon Magistrates' Court. You really will have to do better." The senior clerk moved on to Maxwell Fyfe. "It's just a noting brief, Mr Maxwell Fyfe." His hands were empty when he came to the two other pupils. "I'm sorry, gentlemen; however, I'll speak to the other members of chamber and see if I can rustle up some work for you next week."

"There's nothing?" questioned one of the pupils.

"It seems that the criminals of Wimbledon like Mr Drewe." The clerk turned away and, remembering something he had forgotten, turned back to Basil and added, "You will see from your instructions that your client is one of three co-accused. Mr Rowledge is representing one of the others and the third has also instructed King's Counsel, so they will be expecting some assistance."

Basil said nothing. He had no idea why King's Counsel would need help from him, or even why he would be instructed on the same case and decided to ask Maxwell Fyfe what he thought the senior clerk meant. The brief, tied in its pink ribbon, was thicker than anything he had been given before.

In the last three months, he had done his fair share of bail applications, pleas in mitigation and a few trials, although these were mainly for drunk and disorderly or solicitation. It had been one of these trials that had first got Basil recognised by a small London firm of solicitors when he had a pickpocket acquitted on the basis that the police evidence might have been unreliable. From then on work seemed to come in quite regularly. It was not nearly as glamorous as Basil had thought it would be, but he knew he was just taking his first steps. However, those moments when his clients were acquitted made up for it. He would stand in the courtroom feeling euphoric when a jury said, 'not guilty' and if one innocent person was acquitted then he was making a difference, even if it was only a small one. He remembered Horace Rowledge once saying to him over a glass of claret, that the rule of law applies to everyone, whether they are the poorest beggar on the streets of London or the King of England.

***

It was getting dark as Basil and Maxwell Fyfe walked back to chambers after having dined. The gas lamps that lined the stone pathways within the Inner Temple flickered, bringing to life shadows in every doorway and alcove. They ignored their ghostly army of watchers and continued talking as they took the same steps that ten thousand barristers had taken before them. Basil was in a reflective mood, and it had been noticed by Maxwell Fyfe.

"What was that noting brief about?" asked Basil.

"I just have to sit in on a meeting about international treaties and record

79

what's been agreed."

"It sounds dull," said Basil.

"It's fascinating," said Maxwell Fyfe. "And what's your case about?"

They stopped for a moment at the stairwell of 2 Hare Court. The number of the building was carved into the white stone above the doorway. Basil took out his keys and fitted one into the heavy lock.

"It's about coining money," said Basil. "Rowledge and the other King's Counsel are representing the men who coined the money, and my client is the one who laundered it. They could get a life sentence and my client could get two years with hard labour." Basil pulled on the iron handle of the heavy wooden door. "I still don't understand why the clerk said that Rowledge will be expecting some assistance from me."

Maxwell Fyfe stubbed out his cigarette before entering the damp stairwell and said, "I asked about that. You'll be expected to take the magistrates through the facts of the case as Rowledge and the other King's Counsel won't have been inside of a magistrates' court for decades."

"I was rather hoping that I wouldn't have much to do as I have a hectic weekend. Apart from having to prep for this appearance at the West London Magistrates'…"

"*Wimbledon* Magistrates'," Maxwell Fyfe corrected him.

"I'm meeting my mother and brother tomorrow," said Basil, ignoring the correction, "and on Sunday I'm having lunch with my sister-in-law."

"I didn't know you had a sister-in-law?" said Maxwell Fyfe.

"She married my eldest brother, Adrian, who was killed in the war, and each year she invites us for a luncheon on the anniversary of his death. Usually, I get out of it but this year my father asked if I could make the effort as he's not well." Basil closed the door behind him and started going up the stairs. "It's been five years since he was killed."

"I don't think you've ever talked about him to me," said Maxwell Fyfe.

"I don't talk about him much to anyone now and just try and remember the good times I had with him. A friend once told me he would want me to get on with my life and I suppose I do, though sometimes it feels like work is all I have."

"What about that female medical student that you see once in a while?" asked Maxwell Fyfe.

"She's a friend's sister and I promised him I would look after her while she's studying here. There's nothing more to our relationship than that."

"Well, it looks like you're stuck with the law but then, as we both know, she's a jealous mistress."

***

"You're sounding just like a barrister," said Christian, "and you've not even taken off your coat."

"My coat is off," said Basil. "However, you say you're moving to Austria in two weeks, and you don't expect me to have a thousand questions."

Basil walked to the other end of the room, picked up the phone and asked room service to bring up two gin and tonics.

Christian listened as Basil paced around the hotel suite. It was the first time he had been with his brother since Christmas. Christian could hardly remember the last time Basil had gone to Drewsteignton to visit him – perhaps fifteen months ago – and from what their mother said, it was nearly as rare for Basil to go back home. It seemed to him that Basil's work had almost become an obsession.

"Mother has been complaining that you've become a stranger," said Christian.

"Whenever I go there, they ask me if I've met a nice girl and when they can expect grandchildren. I'm twenty-four, for God's sake, and you know what they're like. Mother is always saying how Adrian used to visit every other weekend and that he would have given them grandchildren by now. Father still looks at me with disappointment ever since I told him I did not want to take over his company. He doesn't say anything, but you can tell from the silences." Christian sighed. He knew exactly how Basil felt. "Where's Mother?" asked Basil.

"She said she was tired and has gone to lie down in her room."

Basil slouched in an armchair. "How was the journey coming up?"

"Tedious," said Christian. "Four hours on two different trains with Mother is enough to try the patience of a saint."

"So," said Basil, "tell me why you are moving back to Austria?"

"A friend of mine, Tomas Skeres, got in touch with me a few months ago and then came over from Austria. I used to study with him at Klimt's studio before the war. When he was over, he suggested I should go back to Austria and stay with him and set up a studio and sell the vases and pots I make."

"What does his wife think about that?" asked Basil.

"Tomas isn't married. You could say Tomas is a confirmed bachelor." Basil looked at his brother and was about to ask Christian what he meant when Christian added, "And yes, I mean exactly what you are thinking."

"Doesn't it bother you?" asked Basil.

"Not particularly," answered Christian. "Tomas is discreet. He is effusively charming. When he met Mother, he walked up and kissed her on both cheeks. She adored him. Father, on the other hand, loathed him. Anyway, I intend to stay with Tomas for a month and if I like living there, I will sell the house in Drewsteignton and buy an apartment in Vienna, if Father loans me a little money."

There was a knock on the door and a waiter came in with the gin and tonics.

"What about you?" said Christian. "How is your life of law?"

"Law is like a jealous mistress," said Basil, quoting his friend Maxwell Fyfe, "and I'm afraid I have little time for anything else."

Chapter 15

One entered the Faceys' estate at Havering-atte-Bower from Orange Tree Hill. On a clear day, you could see the East End of London, as the sprawl continued to eat into rural Essex. The Bower House had been designed by Henry Flitcroft; however, it was ignored by architectural and country life magazines. It was a square block of red brick, and the previous owners had tried to give it some character by adding two side extensions. The estate had been bought by the Faceys nearly thirty years earlier, but now it was mainly empty, except when Jane wanted to hold one of her weekend parties.

Jane continued to use her maiden name, Facey. Her marriage to Adrian Drewe had been so short that she saw no purpose in adopting a married name that no one knew her by. She greeted her guests as they came in with a forced smile. Her hair had been cut short into a Dutch boy bob, her cheeks were rouged, and she wore a burgundy cloche hat, which the milliner had described as *à la mode*. In her bare feet, she looked diminutive when standing next to her fiancé, the Right Honourable Peter Grayson, and had therefore got into the habit of wearing high heels. She spent most of the afternoon with her arm tucked through her fiancé's as if they had been conjoined at birth and started nearly every conversation with the words, "When Peter is in the House of Commons" and ended them with, "Don't you think he would make a wonderful prime minister?"

"I'm so very pleased you were able to come," she said to Basil. "I was just thinking the other day that we only ever met once or twice – at your mother's New Year's Eve ball and, of course, when I married Adrian."

Basil decided not to correct her that he had not been at the wedding, as he had been taking school examinations at the time. Peter Grayson, who was ten years older than Jane, looked indifferent when she mentioned her previous husband. He handed Basil a gin and tonic.

"You know everyone here, I assume?" said Jane.

Twenty people made up the small dinner party, all friends of Jane and Peter. Basil looked at the group and had no idea who any of them were and doubted whether any had been friends of his brother. He, however, liked the look of a tall woman with short black hair and dark eyes and decided that this was someone he should get to know.

"I don't think I've met everyone," replied Basil, looking over to the woman with short black hair.

Jane introduced him to Margaret Ellis. He listened as she spoke about a comment that George Bernard Shaw had made that week.

"Shaw," she began, "said that if you want to know why our aristocracy consists of a large proportion of intellectual idiots, then you need to look no further than to the fact of the well-to-do Englishman's habit of getting rid of his children at an early age under the ruse of having them educated." Margaret paused, slowly raised her hand to indicate she had not finished speaking and added, "I do not think so – but it may explain why Shaw hates schools. He is not nearly as intelligent as likes to think he is, and I understand that he was beaten particularly severely at school for being so arrogant."

Basil smiled at the remark. Here was someone who would stand her ground. He continued to listen as Margaret made one sardonic remark after another, and when they sat down at the dining table, he made sure he was next to her.

Jane was known to throw lavish lunches – however, this occasion appeared to be the exception that proved the rule. Basil wondered whether she had decided to play down the occasion for the benefit of her new fiancé. Basil looked across the table to where Christian and his mother sat. Both looked miserable. Basil dipped his spoon into the Brown Windsor soup, tasted it and winced. It reminded him of dining at halls in Oxford. He turned to Margaret, who was adding a good dose of salt and pepper to the soup.

"Have we met before? Your name sounds familiar," said Basil.

"I can't recall, but it's a possibility," replied Margaret Ellis. "We do have a mutual acquaintance – Jonathan Bruton."

"You know Bruton?" said Basil.

"A family friend," said Margaret. "He's been posted to the Transjordan so I have not seen him for a few months, although, he will be back in August."

"I haven't seen him for years," said Basil. "The last time we saw each other was at the end of his first year at Oxford when he enlisted."

"He told me that you two had lost touch." She took a pencil from her purse, scribbled down Bruton's address on a scrap of paper and handed it to Basil. "Just in case you want to renew your acquaintance." Basil looked at the piece of paper and thought how good it would be to see him, although a reunion with Bruton better not happen on a weekday. He remembered all too well the nights that he was found drunk and asleep outside his rooms in Keble.

Margaret turned to the man on the other side of her and began talking. Basil listened as she spoke. She flitted from subject to subject and like a beautiful butterfly, stopping only long enough to leave an initial impression. Depending on the subject she could be razor-sharp or her words could be as meaningless as the wind in dry grass. The man that Margaret was speaking to was ensnared in the giddiness of the conversation.

Basil wondered, as he listened, whether there was more substance beneath the surface; whether if she were alone, she would be able to talk more deeply about each of the subjects she had glided over. But then it was not just Margaret, he thought; everything seemed superficial since the war ended. Maxwell Fyfe had said the same thing to him and said it was a consequence of the fear of death that everyone had lived with during those years; that if they did not say everything they had to in ten minutes, they might not say it at all. The need to do everything at a frenetic pace had become a fashion. Everyone drove fast, drank fast and spoke so fast that there was not enough time to take anything in.

Suddenly Margaret stopped talking and turned to Basil.

"Are you finding this interminable?" she whispered in his ear.

"Yes," answered Basil.

Margaret shifted in her seat and leant over towards Basil. He could see the top of her ivory chemise under her cocktail dress.

"It might get more interesting this evening," she said almost inaudibly. "You never know."

"I hadn't planned on staying over," replied Basil.

"You should. There's plenty of room and sometimes it can be quite fun." She drank down her glass of wine and looked at the waiter to refill it at once.

Basil felt she was toying with him, like a cat with a mouse. He did not know whether she was half serious with her suggestion; however, she immediately turned back to the man on her right and once again began to talk to him about something inconsequential. The course that followed was equally as bland as the soup, consisting of a fillet of plaice swimming in butter. The meal ended with an Eton mess.

Jane got up from the table and opened the patio doors of the dining room which had views down across Havering County Park. In the distance, there was a tall thin water tower. Most of the guests came out and were milling around on the terrace. A butler with a tray of drinks stood at the patio and Basil took two glasses of champagne as he and Margaret walked out.

"Pretty, isn't it?" said Margaret to Basil as she looked out over the countryside. Basil nodded and passed her one of the glasses. Across the terrace, he noticed that Peter Grayson was talking to his mother and Christian. Peter had lit a cigar and the smoke billowed up into the air and then Peter's face broke into a smile.

"So, you know Gertrude Jekyll," said Peter.

"She prepared some designs for the gardens at the castle we're building in Devon," said Christian. "Before the war, she asked me to do a few paintings of the gardens at her home. I liked her, but she is a formidable woman with a mind of her own."

"I came across her," said Peter, "during the war. I was having lunch with

86

the First Lord of the Admiralty, and he told me that she had camped out at his office until he gave her an interview. She said to him that she wanted to do something for the war effort, but Winston was having one of his brusque days. She said that if he thought the Germans were troublesome, it was nothing to the havoc that a spinster from Thursley could cause."

"And what did Mr Churchill do?" asked Lady Frances.

"He gave in. Miss Jekyll and Dr Haden-Guest were at that time trying to get an old hotel converted into a hospital and Winston arranged for all the materials to be supplied. It was somewhere near Euston."

"The Endsleigh hospital?" said Christian. "I was sent there during the war."

"It is quite unbelievable what a few people can achieve with a little bit of determination and focus," said Peter. "Lutyens also worked on the design for free, which was a first for him."

"And his daughter worked there as a nurse," added Christian.

"The one who went to America," said Jane, looking at Peter.

"Ah, her," said Peter. "I hear that trouble follows her."

"Why do you say that?" asked Christian.

"It's nothing," said Peter. "And certainly not a conversation for a memorial luncheon for your brother."

Jane hugged his arm and smiled in a self-satisfied manner. "Don't you think he would make a wonderful prime minister?" she added, looking up at her fiancé.

Basil wondered what they were talking about, and then noticed that Margaret was again chatting to another man.

"How can you dismiss modern art with just a wave of your hand?" she asked the person to whom she was speaking.

"I'm not..." answered the man.

"But you are," she said, "in the same way as you say Mozart is better than Mahler and Thomas Hardy is better than Ford Madox Ford."

"But that's not exactly what..."

"Dismissing everything modern is quite provincial. Those sublime paintings by Wyndham Lewis can't be classed as nonsense."

She had already finished her glass of champagne and Basil waved for the waiter to come over. He suddenly felt a tap on his shoulder.

"We're thinking of going," said his mother. "Christian is feeling tired, and I have one of my heads."

"Pardon the intrusion," said Basil to Margaret, "but unfortunately it looks like I will have to leave early. However, before I go let me introduce you to my mother, Lady Frances, and my brother Christian."

Margaret smiled broadly and said it was a pleasure to have met them. As she smiled, Basil noticed a little smudge of red lipstick on one of her teeth. She was about to turn back and continue her conversation; however, Christian interrupted.

"We've met before," he said. "I will never forget that voice."

**

That evening Basil stood in a smoke-filled bar at the bottom of the King's Road, slightly drunk. He had no idea that it had been Margaret Ellis who had given him a white feather nearly eight years earlier, but then it had happened so quickly. He hadn't thought about that day for years and, if he was being honest, wouldn't have been able to identify her a week after it had happened. It must have been bitterly cold that day, as they were wearing coats, scarves and hats. One of them held a white feather, the symbol of a coward, between her index finger and thumb and shoved it towards him. It all happened so quickly that he could not remember much about it. He tried to relive the moment, but it was so long ago. Celia had then arrived and said something to him, it might have been 'sorry'. And then what? However, something made him think about that moment again. Why had she said sorry? She hadn't done anything. He recalled that she had then shouted at the two women to leave him alone, and Christian came back and stood next to Celia and there was one almighty argument until Margaret threw the white feather at Christian. He couldn't believe that Christian still remembered the sound of her voice.

**

"I need to get my brief and go to the West London Magistrates," said Basil to Maxwell Fyfe the next morning as he arrived in chambers.

"The *Wimbledon* Magistrates' Court," said Maxwell Fyfe, shaking his head.

"I was pulling your leg," replied Basil. "I know precisely where I need to be."

He picked up the bundle of papers and went outside where a waiting taxi would take him to Wimbledon. As the taxi took him across the river and out to the suburbs, Basil rehearsed what he would say to the magistrates. The case would then be referred to the Crown Court for trial, given the severity of the charges. His client had previously had bail refused. Basil considered whether he should make a further application, and decided he would as there was nothing to lose.

Later in the afternoon, Horace Rowledge stood beside his senior clerk and told him that chambers would offer a tenancy to Basil and that he would convince Basil to accept it.

"You won't get the measure of him unless you see him on his feet," said Rowledge to the clerk. "His understanding of the facts of the case was first class. No one expected his bail application to succeed, but he had spotted an inconsistency in the police papers, and he simply kept bringing the magistrate back to it."

"But is criminal law something that we want chambers to be known for?" said the clerk.

"Having a proper trial advocate in chambers after I have gone is not something to be sniffed at," said Rowledge. The clerk nodded his head. He may disagree, but the decision was not his to make.

"And who else are we taking on?" asked the clerk. "I assume Mr Maxwell Fyfe."

"There is a view that there simply is not enough work in chambers now to take on a second tenant. Drewe has his work, but Maxwell Fyfe is dependent on cases being given to him that other members of chambers would normally do. Also, although no one doubted his calibre, he is a little dour."

"Will you tell him?" asked the clerk.

"Of course," said Rowledge, "and I have spoken to a friend of mine, George Lynskey, who's head of chambers in Liverpool, and suggested that Maxwell

Fyfe should contact him. It's a good set of chambers."

Chapter 16

18 December 1925

"I am so pleased that you could come," said Mrs Rowledge to David and Sylvia Maxwell Fyfe, and then she looked enquiringly at Basil who had arrived alone to the Inner Temple Christmas Ball.

"Basil is putting us up," said Sylvia. "So, David and I have decided to make a weekend of it."

Basil smiled. He had not seen Maxwell Fyfe since August when he had been best man at his wedding. Maxwell Fyfe's wife, Sylvia Harrison, was charming, as she steered the conversation away from Basil's lack of a plus one and towards the gown that Mrs Rowledge was wearing. She had the same charm as her brother, Rex, who was just beginning a career on the stage.

"I nearly had to bail out," said Maxwell Fyfe to Basil. "However, Sylvia insisted and who am I to say no? She's been complaining that since we got married all I seem to do is work."

"It's because, my dear," said Sylvia, kissing Maxwell Fyfe on the cheek, "that's all you ever do and then you complain that you are working too much."

"The last weeks have been hectic," continued Maxwell Fyfe. "We're pushing to get the Locarno Treaties signed."

Basil took a sip from his glass of champagne. Similarly, he had been working non-stop and was now regularly appearing in the higher courts, but nothing as glamorous as the work that Maxwell Fyfe was doing.

"I've been following the news," said Basil.

"One thing we must do," Mrs Rowledge said to Sylvia, as she gazed across the room of people in black tie and evening dresses, "is find someone for Basil."

Basil looked down at his patent leather shoes and thought that Mrs Rowledge was becoming just as bad as his mother.

"He brought someone to our wedding," said Sylvia, and then turned to Basil: "What happened to her?"

"She was just a friend's sister," answered Basil.

"She seemed quite a ripe tomato," added Maxwell Fyfe.

Sylvia pinched her husband's arm and whispered, "You shouldn't be noticing that kind of thing on your wedding day."

"Her life was in India and mine was here," said Basil, thinking that the evening was now going in a direction that he couldn't stomach.

"Oh, East is East and West is West, and never the twain shall meet," said Mrs Rowledge and sighed. She continued to look around the Great Hall of Inner Temple. If truth be told, she admitted to herself, she had not seen anyone who would be a suitable match for Basil. He needed someone with spirit and personality. Mrs Rowledge looked at an array of women who were talking or dancing in elegant long evening gowns. A few of the women were attractive, in an English sort of a way, but seemed more interested in their appearances and were standing in groups giggling. Some of the young ladies looked very bookish and, as she continued to survey the women of the room, she noted that a disproportionate number of the younger ladies at the ball wore spectacles and were not blessed by Aphrodite. Many, she thought, were probably not blessed by Athena either. She sighed again and then she saw a young woman standing with her father.

"Do you know Jenny Stanton?" asked Mrs Rowledge. "She's Patrick Stanton's daughter."

Basil said he hadn't made her acquaintance, and Mrs Rowledge guided him over and made the introduction. Basil asked her to dance, but it was a rumba and so by the end, his leg was in excruciating pain. He escorted Jenny back to her father and returned to his friends.

"She seemed nice," said Maxwell Fyfe as Basil approached.

"I'm not sure she wanted to dance," said Basil. "She said she was waiting for a friend to arrive, and hardly said anything else."

The Great Hall of the Inner Temple was magnificent. Above the richly carved double wooden doors that led one into the hall, was a minstrel's gallery where a small orchestra played. Above the musicians were stained-glass windows and then wooden panelling with paintings of Lord Chancellors. During the day, coloured light flooded in through the windows, each bearing a different coat of arms, while in the evening, the rich patina of the dark wood shone in the candlelight.

When Celia arrived, she was hugged by Jenny Stanton and the two women found a corner to talk. Celia talked about her life in New York and Jenny gave her all the news about everyone and anyone she might know in London.

"And did you hear that Margaret got married?"

"Margaret, really?" responded Celia. She hadn't thought about Margaret Ellis for years and wondered whether time had made her softer.

"To an officer in the British army. I think his name is Jonathan. They had a big wedding out at Cliveden. His family is from South Africa and seems to know everyone in that circle."

"Did you go?" asked Celia.

"She has a new circle of friends," said Jenny diplomatically. "To be honest I haven't seen her for years and the last I heard she had moved to Transjordan where her husband had been posted."

"And what about you?" asked Celia. "Is there anyone you're making whoopee with?"

Jenny burst out laughing.

"You can't ask me that," said Jenny. "It sounds so American, and the answer is no. However, I love what you're wearing." Celia raised a questioning eyebrow. "You're more glamorous than anyone here."

Celia hadn't thought that the way she spoke or looked had changed. When she arrived in America everyone spoke differently, and everyone wanted to be glamorous. She had tried to embrace the American ideal and now realised that in England both her dialect and manner of dress marked her out. She felt a sense of innate satisfaction that her friend, at a ball at the Inner Temple, thought of her as glamorous. She was still quite young; not yet twenty-nine. She thought that if she acted quickly, and did not let life slip away, everything was still possible.

"Is there anyone here I might know?" Celia asked.

Jenny pointed to Basil. Celia took a deep breath and stared towards him across the Hall. He didn't look like either of his brothers – although he had dark hair, green eyes, and a strong jawline. Basil was not as tall as Adrian and, in Celia's opinion, not nearly as handsome. While Adrian had been toned and muscular, Basil was thin and wiry. However, he had confidence, which could be seen in the way he held himself and talked. It was not arrogance, which his father had, or insouciance, which Christian had when he was younger. Basil had a casual assuredness, like his mother.

"I might go and ask him to dance," said Celia.

Jenny looked at her friend. "Isn't that a bit forward?"

"Not at all," said Celia. "Anyway, we are related, although distantly."

Basil was again listening to Maxwell Fyfe explaining why the Locarno Treaties were so important when he felt a tap on his shoulder. He turned to see a woman with auburn hair, which had been tied up and was held in place by a silver headband encrusted with faux diamonds and feathers. Her dress was ivory and came down just above the ankle. Stitched into the gown at the neckline and the waist were hundreds of tassels that shimmered when she moved. She wore white silk gloves that came to her elbow. A long chain of pearls hung from her neck and were matched with pearl earrings. However, he hardly noticed any of this but just stared into her bright, sparkling green eyes and then her mouth which was shaped like Cupid's bow.

Basil had never seen her before at any of the Inner Temple functions. She was more beautiful than any of the women there and for a moment he was unsure what to say and started blushing.

"Basil Drewe," she said, smiling at his embarrassment. "I was hoping you were going to ask me to dance."

Basil looked at her and smiled back, hoping he had not gone as red as he felt. Maxwell Fyfe stopped talking and then just said one word to Basil, "Tomato," and Basil hoped that he was not referring to the colour of his face.

"Would you care to dance?" asked Basil and placed his walking stick beside a chair. As they crossed the dance floor, Basil asked, "How did you know my name?"

"Guess," said Celia.

"I don't know any Americans," said Basil.

"I'm not American."

"But your accent?"

"So, you don't remember me?" said Celia.

"Perhaps a hint?" asked Basil.

"I bandaged your leg when you fell off a cliff in Drewsteignton."

"Celia!" said Basil and smiled broadly.

"That took some time," replied Celia, who tried to keep a straight face. "Most men don't usually forget me." She had almost forgotten what it was like to flirt and was enjoying the feeling. She smiled to herself as she remembered that he had the same look on his face as a boy when he had stood staring at her in Gertrude Jekyll's kitchen a decade earlier.

"In my defence," said Basil, "I was only thirteen when we first met, and you hardly spoke to me at all."

"But we did meet at my Aunt Gertrude's house years later." She remembered that Christian was there with Basil. Basil would have been sixteen, she thought, and she would have been a few years older. She remembered that she had teased him as he stared at her in the kitchen when she made lemonade.

"But that was only for a few hours," Basil said.

The music started playing and, to Basil's relief, it was a slow-paced promenade and not something modern like a Charleston or a tango.

"I am so pleased that they are playing something slow," said Celia. "It will give us a chance to talk as we dance. I want to know everything that has been happening to you, Christian, your parents and Castle Drogo."

Basil told her about Christian's move to Austria, how the castle was now only half the size of the original design, and the grief that his parents had suffered following the death of Adrian. It seemed to Celia that he was much more measured than either of his brothers and more conservative. However, there were moments when he said something or, just for a second, when the light caught him, that Celia was reminded of Adrian and then suddenly that feeling was gone and, in those moments, Celia felt a surge of happiness followed by an acute sense of loss.

Celia wanted to know everything about Christian. She asked a score of questions about how his injuries had healed, his life in Austria, and whether he had more operations to restore his sight. Basil told her that Christian had carried on living at Drewsteignton until three years ago when he moved to Austria.

"The doctors told him there was a chance that his sight might be partially restored," said Basil, "and they had operated on him almost four years ago. However, it wasn't a success and he sank into a depression, and it was then that Tomas Skeres contacted him."

"Tomas Skeres;" said Celia, "wasn't he someone whom Christian knew in Austria?"

"They were both artists at Klimt's studio," said Basil.

"What's he like?" said Celia. "I remember that Christian always had a story about going to the clubs with Tomas."

"First, he called Christian 'Kit' as we did before the war, and he wasn't embarrassed about Christian's disability. When they went into Brighton, for example, he would describe the journey, where they were and what he was seeing. Christian said that when they walked along the promenade at Brighton, Tomas would point towards people and might say that they were wearing the most awful knitted blue bathing suit, or he would describe the buildings. I suppose I didn't ever think to tell Christian what a room looked like because it was so ordinary, but a blind person has no idea."

"It sounds like Tomas was a tonic."

"More than that," said Basil. "Tomas just has a wonderful ability to paint a picture as he talked."

"Were your parents against Christian going back to Austria?"

"No. I think Mother knew in her heart that Christian would be happier there and Father arranged an apartment for him in Vienna."

"And Castle Drogo?" asked Celia. "How is that coming along?"

"It won't be complete for a few more years; however, Father and Mother will soon be moving into what has been completed. Once Adrian died, I thought that Father might sell it. If the truth be told, it has rather become an albatross around his neck. Mother doesn't want to go there but then who in their right mind wants to live in a castle on a moor in Devon?"

"I would... if I had the money," said Celia.

For most of the evening, Jenny Stanton had stood on her own. She danced occasionally and spoke only to her parents. She had not seen her oldest friend for eight years and within half an hour of arriving Celia had left her alone. She had not changed one iota, thought Jenny. She could be so thoughtful but also so self-absorbed. She remembered that before the war Celia, Margaret and she were inseparable. They did everything together and no boy could come between them. That was before that day at Liberty's when they agreed to hand out white feathers to men who had failed to enlist. Margaret had never forgiven Celia for standing against her. Even now, when Celia's name was mentioned, Margaret seethed with rage. She looked at Celia as she sat deep in conversation with Basil. Jenny remembered that when her brother had been injured in the war, Celia had visited him nearly every day in the hospital until he got better and because of this, Jenny's parents adored Celia. Jenny knew that whatever Celia did she would be able to forgive her. However, as she looked at Basil, she could not help but wonder if she would break his heart.

***

The next morning Basil rose early and made a pot of tea. He sat in the kitchen thinking about the night before.

"How's David?" he asked, as Sylvia came in looking to make a fresh pot. She saw the kettle was on the stove, refilled it and put the gas on.

"Hungover," said Sylvia. "He's buried his head under the blankets and refuses to say a word until I've brought him a cup of tea."

"He did seem a little the worse for wear when we left last night."

97

"I've also been tasked to find out how things went with you and that attractive woman."

"I don't kiss and tell," said Basil and sipped the barely warm tea he had made earlier. "She's a distant cousin of mine, and I last saw her about eight years ago. She was a nurse and looked after my brother Christian during the war, and then went out to America to look after her mother. I suppose I was a little infatuated with her then."

"And now?" asked Sylvia.

"You do like to get directly to the point," said Basil.

"When you're married to a barrister, you have to," answered Sylvia with a smile.

"If anything," said Basil slowly, "she's perhaps more beautiful now than when I first saw her. Anyway, on the ship to America, she met a soldier and married him." Sylvia stopped washing out the teapot and sat down, listening as Basil continued. "He was killed in the war, and she has a son Robert who is now nearly eight. She decided to come back to England this year and wants to send her son to school here. She told me that she had tried to give America a go, but it was too difficult on her own with a child."

"And will you be seeing her again?" asked Sylvia.

"I think so," said Basil, "but there's something that concerns me." The kettle began whistling on the stove and Basil got up and turned off the gas. "We talked a lot about my brother Christian and what I had been doing; however, when I asked her anything about her husband or what had happened to her over the last eight years, she just changed the subject."

"You can't be surprised about that," said Sylvia. "If I was in her shoes, I would want to keep my secrets until I got to know someone. She must have been terrified telling you about her son. Most men would run a mile if a woman they had just met said she had a child."

"It's not that either," said Basil. "No, it was something else."

"Perhaps," said Sylvia, "she finds it uncomfortable being out socially with men. There are a lot of women who still feel that they are betraying their dead husbands when they are with another man."

"It may be that," said Basil, shaking his head as if he was unconvinced.

"And you mustn't be angry if she doesn't want to tell you about her husband," continued Sylvia. "Can you imagine that for her this is a betrayal? It's not like they had been divorced or separated. She had the person she loved most taken from her in a war. If David died tomorrow, I don't think I would ever want to talk about it to anyone – not now, not in a score of years."

"Don't worry," said Maxwell Fyfe, as he stood at the door. "David won't die tomorrow. He'll die right here and now if he doesn't get that cup of tea."

Sylvia got up and swirled hot water around the teapot, emptied it and then put in a spoonful of tea for each cup, and one for the pot. She looked at Basil in his green paisley dressing gown as he sipped slowly at his cup of tepid tea. She would need to have a word with him about the apartment. It was fine for a man, but so much of it was already dated. She decided that that conversation could wait until another day and, as an afterthought, said, "She may not be ready to commit to you, she may never be ready. If you go ahead and see her again, you must understand that."

Chapter 17

April 1926

Basil looked at himself in the mirror as he stepped out of the bath, regarding his rake-thin physique. He glanced at his deformed left leg which was horrendously scarred and thin. He over-compensated with his other leg, which was strong and muscular so that one leg now seemed to mock the other.

In lieu of much else in his life, he devoted himself to his work and knew that there were only a handful of barristers in London who were better advocates. It was how he measured his success – by winning those cases that everyone said were impossible to win.

He took from his wardrobe an elegant cream suit, a blue Egyptian cotton shirt, and a silk tie with yellow diamonds. He dressed and then again looked at himself in the mirror as he rested on his cane. He smiled. A well-cut suit from Savile Row could hide a myriad of sins. He sat down, put on a pair of brown brogue shoes and, as he left his apartment, picked up a fedora hat. He had not put liniment on his leg, even though he was likely to have to do more walking than was usual. He knew that the liniment had an awful smell, and he did not want to leave the wrong impression. He was used to hiding his pain behind a smile.

The taxi took him to the British Museum. It would be the first time that he would meet Robert, who was with Celia for the Easter vacation. The British Museum was perfect for the introduction as it was not far from where Celia was living and there were thousands of things for a young boy to do. Basil had not been to the British Museum for years, but as someone keenly interested in ancient Greek and Roman history, he was happy to play at being the guide. He had thought about showing Robert the Egyptian artefacts, including the golden death mask of Tutankhamun that Howard Carter had discovered a few years earlier in Egypt, but in the end he decided on the Elgin marbles.

***

"Most of the sculptures," said Basil, as he pointed out the various friezes to Robert, "were taken from the Parthenon in Greece by Lord Elgin."

"Do they belong to the Greeks?" asked Robert.

"No," replied Basil. "Lord Elgin rescued them when Greece was under the control of the Ottoman Empire. He feared that they would be damaged, so he paid for them and arranged for the marbles to be brought to England for safekeeping."

Robert looked at the beautiful friezes and statues.

"Do you like them?" asked Basil. Robert shrugged. "The story on the marbles depicts the Greek myth of Centauromachy."

"What's that?" asked Robert.

"It's the story of the battle between the Greeks and the centaurs, who were mythical creatures – half-man and half-horse. The centaurs lived in the forests of Thessaly and when the Greek king Ixion died the centaurs tried to seize power. If it wasn't for the Greek hero Theseus, who slayed many of the centaurs, the Greeks would have lost the battle."

"I've heard of Theseus," said Robert, "at school."

"There are some drawings of him in another room," said Basil. "We could go and see them if you're interested.

"Could we see the Egyptian mummies?" asked Robert.

"Yes, of course," answered Basil. "But I do need to sit down for a minute. I'm afraid my leg is rather hurting."

"Mummy said you hurt your leg in a fall," replied Robert.

"Yes, your mother was there and put my leg in a splint. I was just a few years older than you."

Basil looked at Celia, who was casually occupied with a statue of a Greek warrior. He watched her and realised she had no interest in the British

Museum or its treasures and then, feeling as if she was being watched, she turned and looked for her son. Basil and Robert walked over to where she was standing.

"I'm afraid," said Basil, "that I will need to sit down for a while. Robert said he wanted to see the Egyptian mummies. Why don't you take him, and I can catch up with you in twenty minutes or so."

"We can all wait together," suggested Celia.

"Let's not spoil Robert's day," answered Basil. "I'll catch up with you shortly." He smiled and then added, "It's quite all right."

Basil found a bench and sat down. He pulled out a bottle of liniment from his jacket pocket and thought about rubbing some on his leg. However, he was conscious of the smell of the tincture and decided to leave it until later. He rubbed his leg vigorously for a few minutes. He had forgotten how young boys liked to be constantly moving and thought that Robert was like he was at that age.

Robert and Celia found the room with the Egyptian artefacts, and she walked beside him as they went from one sarcophagus to another.

"The coffins," said Celia, reading from a card, "are actually in these sarcophagi."

Robert shrugged.

"What do you think of Mr Drewe?" asked Celia. Robert stopped and looked at his mother.

"He's very nice and he knows lots and lots of stuff," said Robert. "He was telling me all about the war between the Greeks and the centaurs. Do you like him?"

Celia thought about her answer.

"Yes," she said. "I like him a lot and we've become good friends. It's nice being with someone you feel comfortable with."

***

Living at her parents' house was an ideal choice for Celia. Her sister Mary and her mother were travelling with Krishnamurti in India and would not be back in Europe until the summer. Her father was in Delhi, carrying out the final designs on the new capital. He only came back to England every other month or so and would then usually be away dealing with projects that he had neglected. Her youngest sister Elisabeth was studying music in Paris at the École Normale de Musique, although she was suffering from depression following the death of Nitya from tuberculosis. Her brother Robert had married Eva Lubrynska, the talented fashion designer, and was socialising almost every evening. The house in Marylebone, which her father had recently bought, was therefore empty, except for a handful of staff. Both Celia and Robert therefore had more space than they had ever known in their lives.

Celia, however, knew that when her mother returned home in late July, it would be time to find herself a permanent place to live. It would be the unforgiving looks and bitter tongue which would hurt. While on the surface it appeared that Celia and her mother had reconciled, Celia knew that when she was there, she would have to tread on eggshells. She and Robert would be endured but after a time, Celia thought, living with someone so disapproving would become intolerable.

She therefore contacted Jenny, and together they started looking for somewhere for Celia to live. However, with the allowance that her father gave her, Celia could only afford a small apartment in a run-down part of the East End of London. Then, one evening, as she had dinner at the Savoy with Basil, he suggested that she consider somewhere like Marlow, which was on the river and with an excellent grammar school. Basil drove them out there the following weekend, and, although the town was attractive, Celia felt she would be too far away from everyone she knew.

"The problem," Celia said to Basil, "is that I want to support myself, but I also want to be there for Robert and until I finish my degree there aren't many jobs for me to do except work as a nurse or a schoolteacher."

"So, finish your degree," said Basil, as they ate a light lunch at a little pub by the river.

"I can't afford it," said Celia. "I need a job and I can't afford to send Robert to a public school – even if I wanted to." Celia looked at her son who was kicking a ball in a small park opposite the pub. "And even if I could afford to rent anything in Marlow, which I can't, there is nothing but a little cottage hospital here and a boys' school, so there's no chance of me getting a job."

"So back to London," said Basil.

"Back to London," said Celia, sighing. "But thank you anyway, you've been an absolute dear driving Robert and me out here for the day, and for everything else you've done recently."

"I like being with you," said Basil. "You know that. I always have done."

"And I like being with you," said Celia, and as she got up from the table, she kissed him. She had only meant to kiss him on the cheek, but he had turned to look at her and the kiss fell upon his lips. She looked at him for a moment and he stared back at her, blushing slightly.

"I do have one other place to suggest," said Basil, who got up from the table, "but let's get back to London. Isn't your father arriving home from India this evening?"

"Yes," said Celia.

The drive back to London took them past Maidenhead, Slough, and Hammersmith. New towns were being built everywhere and train lines, the underground and roads followed. The countryside around London was changing rapidly, and Basil wondered how everyone would be able to live when each was living cheek-by-jowl with their neighbours. Basil drove into Belgravia and pulled up in front of his apartment in Cadogan Square.

"What are we doing here?" asked Celia.

"It's where I live," said Basil. "I wanted you to see it." Basil got out of the car and opened the door for Celia. "I have an apartment on the top floor but fortunately there's a lift."

Celia looked at the white stuccoed building and went inside. The elevator took them to the fifth floor and Basil opened his door.

"I wanted you to see the view from here," Basil said, as he led Celia and Robert to the living room. Below the building, they could see the beautiful, terraced gardens which spread over seven acres with tennis courts. "It's a special place. It's like living in the countryside but you're in the centre of London, and some of the best schools are around the corner."

"Why are you telling me this, Basil?"

"Because you know how I feel about you and there's something I've been wanting to ask you and I've no idea what your answer will be."

Chapter 18

The April sun was overhead; however, despite it being a cloudless sky, Celia needed a blanket around her legs. She nodded at a few people that Basil had introduced to her as they also sat down to watch the polo match. Basil had taken Robert to the stables, to see the polo ponies. Behind her was Ham House, where the cantankerous Earl of Dysart lived. It was said that his wife had run off at the start of the century and that he had lived alone with no heir in the house for the last twenty-five years. Rarely was the Earl of Dysart ever seen in public, but he continued the tradition of polo matches being played on the estate.

Basil and Robert walked back from the stables and sat down beside Celia.

"I said that Robert could learn to ride after we're married," said Basil.

"You still have to ask my father," said Celia.

"I'm meeting him later this afternoon."

"Mister Drewe," said Robert, "may I ask you a question?"

Basil turned to Robert. "Ask away."

"Could you teach me how to play cricket?"

"Of course I can," Basil said. "But don't you know how to play already?"

"They didn't play cricket in America," said Robert. "And at school, nobody ever picks me to join their team because I'm not very good."

"We can't have that," said Basil, and ruffled the boy's hair. "We'll soon have you hitting the ball out of the ground."

He turned to Celia and asked how long Robert had left of the Easter holidays. Celia said another week and Basil suggested that they go down to Castle Drogo the following weekend.

"I haven't been there for years," said Celia.

"I happen to know your father will be there next week," said Basil. "And I know that my mother will want to meet with you. I can also arrange a game of cricket on Sunday morning, weather permitting."

***

"You don't mind if I call you Basil?" said Lutyens as he chewed at the stem of his unlit pipe.

"Not at all, sir," said Basil.

"Well, Basil, I understand that you have something that you would like to ask me about my daughter."

"Yes, sir," replied Basil. He took a deep breath. In the days and hours before, he knew exactly what he would say to Lutyens but now, sitting in front of him, his mouth had gone dry. He hadn't felt this nervous since his first appearance in front of a magistrates' court as a pupil barrister. "I wanted this opportunity to talk to you privately because, sir, with your permission…" Basil took another breath and looked at Lutyens who appeared not to be flustered by the event at all. "I would like to take Celia's hand in marriage."

"And what does Celia say about this?" asked Lutyens.

"Celia?" said Basil. He had anticipated that Lutyens would simply say he was delighted, shake his hand and order a bottle of champagne in the traditional way. He had not thought there might be a question-and-answer session on the matter.

"Yes, Celia. She does know that you will be asking her."

"Yes, sir. We've discussed it of course and – subject to your blessing – I believe she will consent."

"Is there any doubt?" said Lutyens, who was enjoying watching a rising barrister stumbling to find his words. However, he liked Basil and could not think of a more decent person to marry Celia. He liked his straightforward honesty and that when he spoke, he looked you in the eye. He did, however, have a nagging doubt that Basil may not be the perfect match for Celia, who as a child had been so wilful and headstrong and dreamed of heroes.

"It's what both of us want," said Basil emphatically. He took another deep breath. "Would you like to see the ring?"

"Is it a large diamond?" asked Lutyens.

"Yes, it is," said Basil enthusiastically.

"Then there is no need to show it to me," said Lutyens. "I am sure Celia will be perfectly pleased with it and when she shows it to Emily and me, I can then make the appropriate noises at the appropriate time."

The smile left Basil's lips.

"Well, that's all I wanted to talk to you about," said Basil. "Except to confirm that you will be going to Castle Drogo next weekend as it would be pleasant for you, Celia and Robert to spend some time with my family and myself. I understand from Celia that Lady Emily is currently abroad in India."

Lutyens looked over to a waiter who stood discreetly in a corner and nodded at him.

"Attending another conference on theosophy," said Lutyens. "One always wonders how they have so much to talk about. Do you know anything about it?"

Basil shook his head. "Not a thing I'm afraid."

"You would be very sensible to keep it that way," said Lutyens. "However, as my wife is quite high up in the Order, I would caution you to read up on the basics before you meet her."

"I'll ask Celia about it," suggested Basil.

"And to answer your earlier question," continued Lutyens, "yes, I had planned to go to the castle next week and can stay on for the weekend."

A waiter arrived with an ice bucket, champagne and two glasses and placed them on the walnut table between their two chairs.

"Celia is suggesting a wedding in late August. Would you and Lady Emily be amendable to that?" Lutyens thought for a moment and nodded. "And how is the castle coming along? It has been a while since I was there."

"There's not much more work to do on it, except for the North Wing, and your parents don't use that."

"So will it be completed by next year?" asked Basil.

"A few years more, I'm afraid," said Lutyens. "There is still a lot of work to do to terrace off the formal gardens and build the laundry rooms and other outbuildings."

"It seems to have taken as long to build your castle as it did to build the Taj Mahal," stated Basil.

Lutyens shrugged; however, when he considered the time that it had taken the analogy seemed accurate. The main difference, however, was that Sir Julius still wanted to save every penny he could and therefore only a few stonemasons were working. Ustad Lahori, the architect of the Taj Mahal, had hundreds of people working on the build. The design of Castle Drogo had been completed years ago. That was what had interested Lutyens. He now only went there to keep his client happy and because his final payment for the works was linked to the completion of the project.

Chapter 19

When one approaches Castle Drogo from the driveway, there is a square tower that borders it and looks as if it is the tallest part of the castle, but this is deceptive as the other side of the castle is built on an escarpment. Only from the opposite side can the castle be truly appreciated as it rises out of the rock. The entrance to the castle is at the end of the driveway, where above the wooden doors and arched stone doorframe is the heraldic lion of the Drewes and the family motto, *Drogo Nomen Et Virtus Arma Dedit*. Lutyens explained to his grandson that this meant 'Drogo is the name and valour gave it arms' and that Sir Julius had decided to omit more than half of his original design, which meant that the door had to be located on the side rather than facing the driveway.

"If you can imagine," said Lutyens as he pointed to the area in front of the door, "here was to be a mirror image of the castle that you now see, and the main door would have been at the start of the drive. It was an exceptional design."

Lutyens remembered the many drawings that he had done back in 1910 and 1911, where the shape of the castle was more of a 'v' rather than a straight line and the great halls and dining room had been situated to look out over the expanse of the moor.

"Why did he change it?" asked Robert.

"There may have been many reasons," said Lutyens, "but only God and Sir Julius know the true one. It may have been the cost, but I have always thought that after his eldest son died, Sir Julius no longer saw the purpose of having such a big castle."

"Did he die in the war like my father?" asked Robert.

"Yes, just like him," said Lutyens.

"I can understand why he might be sad," said Robert. "I can't picture my father at all but thinking about him makes me sad."

"Let's go and find your mother and Basil," said Lutyens, "and remember what I told you. When you meet Sir Julius and his wife, you address them as Sir Julius and Lady Frances."

"What's Sir Julius like, Grandfather?"

"When I first met him, he was very impressive. He had stores in nearly every city and shipped in tea and foods from around the world. He dressed impeccably and politicians would come running when he snapped his fingers. However, after the death of his son, he became more withdrawn."

"Is there anything to do here?" asked Robert, looking around at the vast endless moor that spread out in each direction as far as one could see.

"Lots, if you like fishing, swimming, riding and walking."

They entered the hallway, which was dark and foreboding. In an alcove stood a tall grandfather clock made of dark wood. A pendulum swung slowly and made a clicking sound as it fell back from its highest arch. A portrait of Adrian Drewe was on the wall next to the clock, showing him in a dark suit and wearing an old Etonian tie. A gold chain crossed his waistcoat, where he would have kept his pocket watch. In his left hand, he held a red book with his finger at a certain page, as if the artist had caught him by surprise reading.

"That was Adrian," said Lutyens to Robert. "He was the son that died in the war."

"Adrian?" said Robert. "Sir Julius's son was called Adrian; did Mummy know him?"

Lutyens nodded and Robert looked at the painting for a few moments longer until Lutyens said that they should go.

"Were they close friends? Mummy doesn't speak much about growing up in England," Robert said, as they continued walking down the hallway until they came to a tapestry of Don Quixote by the drawing room.

"I don't really know," said Lutyens. "Come along," he added a little impatiently, "there is so much more to show you."

"But can't you tell me more about him?"

"I didn't really know him that well," said Lutyens, "but I shall tell you a story later on."

Robert looked at his grandfather. "I would like that," he added, and thought he would need to bide his time and ask about Adrian later.

***

The dining room of Castle Drogo was built on the escarpment with its dramatic views across Dartmoor. The ceiling was ornately corniced, and the large dining table could comfortably seat twelve people and sixteen at a push. The floor was made of oak planks, two inches thick and around the door frames was the same oak, with beautiful and intricate carvings. The oak had been felled and cut locally. On one wall was a tapestry of a battle in front of Vienna, which, according to Sir Julius, he had bought some years earlier, but he did not, at the time, have a wall big enough to put it on.

Sir Julius sat at the head of the table with a recent portrait, which he had commissioned, hanging on the wall behind him. The artist had captured him in a grey suit and buff waistcoat, with a silver tie and tie pin. His wife had specifically asked the artist to give him a genial look and to make him look at least ten years younger. Sir Julius was more than content with the result, which he considered a mirror image of himself. On the opposite end of the table sat Lady Frances. She had recently turned fifty-five and was eleven years younger than her husband. She had never wanted to move from her beloved Wadhurst Hall, where she had lived for over thirty years. However, being of a character onto which no moss would gather, she soon found that there were plenty of things that needed her attention and that Exeter, although an hour away, was a pleasant place to develop a circle of friends.

Celia sat on one side of the table with Basil beside her and Robert sat on the other side, next to Lutyens. Lutyens looked around the room with some pleasure. Proportionally and aesthetically the room, he thought, was perfect, as was much of the castle and although the design had to be radically reduced per Sir Julius's wishes, Lutyens was pleased with his creation.

The meal that was served was a delight to Lutyens – with both a fish and a meat course. The wines were impeccable, as he expected, and the dessert managed to have a creamy richness as well as a tartness from a deep mango sauce. If good manners had not prohibited it, he would certainly have asked for seconds.

"Grandfather," said Robert as the dessert plates were swept away, "are you going to tell us a story?"

"You must," said Lady Frances. "I haven't heard one of your stories for years and I so miss them."

Lutyens moved his chair back from the table and looked at Robert and then at Basil.

"This," he said, "is an incredibly old story and like very old stories it contains at its end a lesson for us all. I wasn't sure whether I should tell it because at times we all fall short, and necessity's sharp pinch sometimes makes us tell half-truths rather than the whole truth. However, it is a story which we can all learn something from."

With the introduction completed, Lutyens began his story.

"Once upon a time, there lived a wise man called Mamad, who never lied. All the Masai tribesmen knew who he was and admired him. One day the king called Mamad to his court and asked him whether it was true that he had never lied. 'It's true,' said Mamad. The king then asked him whether he would ever lie in his lifetime and Mamad said 'I'm sure I will not.' Several days later, the king who believed he was wiser than Mamad, called him back to his court and said that he had arranged to go hunting and held his horse by the mane with his left foot already in the stirrup, as if he were about to mount. He told Mamad to go to the summer palace and tell the queen that he was going hunting and would be arriving there for lunch the following day with his whole entourage and that she should prepare a big feast. Mamad bowed to the king and went to the queen. Then the king laughed and said, 'We won't go hunting and now Mamad will lie to the queen. Tomorrow we will laugh on his behalf.'"

Lutyens stopped and looked at his grandson.

"So, what did Mamad say to the queen?" asked Robert.

113

"Well," continued Lutyens, "the wise Mamad went to the palace and said to the queen that it was for her to decide whether to prepare a feast or not as he was not sure if the king would come. 'Tell me, will he come, or won't he?' asked the queen. However, Mamad said 'I do not know whether he mounted the horse and put his right foot in the stirrup, or he put his left foot back on the ground after I left.' When the king came to see the queen on the next day, he said, 'The wise Mamad, who never lies, lied to you yesterday.' However, the queen repeated what Mamad had said to her, and the king realised that the wise man never lies but says only that which he has seen with his own eyes."

***

Basil had corralled Arthur Poley and his son George for the game of cricket, and they had put up some nets in the hope that not too many balls would be lost over the escarpment. Lutyens also agreed to umpire and even Celia, who had never understood or seen the sense of the game, agreed to join in.

From inside his study within the castle, Sir Julius heard the noise of a family at play and put down his pen. He looked at the instructions he had prepared to his solicitors Stern, White & Elston. The instructions had been prepared weeks ago, but he had not signed and sent them. They requested his solicitors to prepare a notification to the Board of Directors that he, Sir Julius, would be retiring as chairman of the Home and Colonial Stores with immediate effect and that an extraordinary general meeting needed to be called to nominate his replacement. He realised he had to step down as his health was deteriorating, and doctors had been called on several occasions over the last few months when he had pains in his heart. He stood up and went to the window. A knock on the door surprised him, and his wife came in with a cup of tea for him.

Lady Frances stood next to her husband peering out of the window at five people trying to teach a young boy to play cricket.

"Do you think they will be happy together?" she said, looking at her son.

"I don't know," said Sir Julius. "What do you think?"

"It certainly won't be the easiest of marriages. He adores her, you can see it in the way he looks at her. However, I'm certain she doesn't feel the same for him. She likes him, don't misunderstand me, but when all is said and done, he's always going to be second best."

"He may already know that," said Sir Julius. "Have you spoken to him about it?"

"What can I say?" said Lady Frances. "He would hate me if I interfered."

"I think they will be fine," said Sir Julius, who then looked at Celia. "Basil has a habit of working at things until he's successful."

"I hope you're right," replied Lady Frances, "but I do worry that she will break his heart." She looked at Celia's son who was swinging the cricket bat aimlessly at anything that was bowled to him. "Her little boy is a delight," she continued. "Do you know who he reminded me of when I first saw him?"

"Yes, I saw that too," said Sir Julius.

"Why don't you go out and join them?"

"I don't know," said Sir Julius. "Not at my age."

"Your age!" replied Lady Frances. "You can still run rings around a man half your age." She continued to stare out the window. "You know, you'll regret it if you don't go out there." She looked down at the table at the unsigned instructions. "Sign that document before you go out," she said, "and I'll make sure it's posted."

Five minutes later, Basil and the two Poleys looked on in astonishment as Sir Julius walked determinedly towards them.

"I thought a little exercise wouldn't do me any harm," said Sir Julius as he went past Basil.

"I didn't think you liked cricket, sir?" responded Basil.

"I never had time. I'll be the wicketkeeper." And with that Sir Julius Drewe took up his position behind Robert.

"Bowl some slow straight ones, Basil," shouted Sir Julius, "so I can see what this young man can do." Robert missed the next three balls and clipped the fourth.

"We need to get your stance right," said Sir Julius, who came around the wicket and showed Robert how to stand.

"Feet sideways on, knees slightly bent," said Sir Julius, "and keep the bat straight."

"It feels awkward," said Robert.

"Now for the next four balls," said Sir Julius. "I don't want you swinging that thing, I just want you to stop the ball by your feet."

Robert restrained himself from asking what the point of that was and decided to do as he was told.

"Watch the ball," shouted Sir Julius as it flew in. To Robert's amazement, the ball hit the centre of the bat and fell to the ground. He picked it up and threw it back to Basil.

"The secret to cricket," said Sir Julius, "is to watch the ball and let it come on to you. It's like life, never go looking for trouble but just see what needs to be done and deal with it."

Robert could hear behind him Sir Julius telling him to "watch the ball" as the next ball was bowled. He concentrated on keeping his bat straight and the ball again hit the centre and fell harmlessly in front of him. The next two balls bowled suffered the same result and Robert beamed.

"Now," said Sir Julius, "I want you to play the next ball that Basil bowls. Take a step towards the ball when it hits the ground and keep your bat straight. Knock it back up the pitch to Basil." Sir Julius took the bat and showed Robert the movement he expected to see. When Basil bowled the ball, Robert took a step forward and cleanly hit the ball back towards Basil.

"He's got a good eye," said Lutyens to Celia.

"Now bowl an off break," shouted Sir Julius to Basil.

"What's an off break?" asked Celia to her father.

"It's when you spin the ball," said Lutyens. "Robert should think that the ball will be missing the wicket, but when the ball hits the ground, the spin pulls the ball back towards the stumps."

Celia looked on as Robert stood in front of his wicket watching the ball as it travelled along a path which looked like it would go wide of the wicket by a good foot, but it then turned when it bounced. Despite Robert trying to prod the ball away it clattered into the wicket knocking the bails clean off.

Robert looked deflated and stared at Sir Julius.

"Lesson two," said Sir Julius. "You must always play the man."

"That doesn't make sense," said Robert.

"It makes perfect sense," said Sir Julius, standing to his full height. He walked up to Robert and said quietly, "Whenever you play a game, whether it's cards, football or cricket, you have an opponent to beat. Understand what your opponent is thinking, and you are halfway to winning. When Basil is bowling the most important thing is to watch him right up until the ball is in the air. Watch how he holds the ball, watch his run up and most importantly, watch what the ball is doing when it leaves his hand."

"So, if I see the ball spinning," said Robert, "what do I do?"

"You reposition yourself, knowing that the ball will be coming in from a different angle, or you can move forward to where the ball pitches and you play it from there." Two more off breaks came in from Basil. Robert missed the first but the second caused George Poley to dash across the grass to stop the ball going over the escarpment.

Robert took turns as a bowler, fielder and wicketkeeper. He tried to put spin on the ball without success. "Master the basics," said Sir Julius when Robert seemed dejected. "Line and length. Get that right and you will not go far wrong."

Two hours later as they wandered back to the castle, Sir Julius put his hand on Robert's shoulder.

"You'll learn nearly all your life lessons playing games," said Sir Julius.

"What do you mean, sir?" asked Robert.

"The games we play teach us things. With team games, we learn that a well-drilled and disciplined team can beat any other team, even if it has better players. That's why people say that the leaders of our country are made on the playing fields of Eton."

Celia smiled, listening to this conversation, as she walked back towards the castle with her father.

"I don't think I've seen Robert enjoy himself so much for a long time," she said.

"Can I ask you something, Celia?"

"Of course."

"Do you remember when we came here years ago on the train? Just you and me and I was working for the War Graves Commission?"

"Yes, I remember," said Celia.

"I had come back from France a few weeks earlier and had seen rows and rows of little crosses across the battlefields where those brave soldiers had fallen. And do you remember you asked me something on the train?"

Celia looked at her father as they walked. "Not really," she said.

"You asked me, 'Do you still love Mother?' Well, now I have a question for you. Do you love Basil?"

"Of course I do," she responded.

Lutyens stopped, bent down, picked up something from the ground and put it in his pocket.

"What was that?" asked Celia.

"Something you may have dropped," said Lutyens. "A little piece of the truth."

Chapter 20

31 August 1926

"Once upon a time," said Edwin Lutyens and then paused. He looked around the Old Hall of Lincoln's Inn. At one end was a wooden screen designed by Inigo Jones, and, on the opposite wall, was Hogarth's painting of Paul before Felix, which he looked at for a moment and then picked up a glass of water, took a sip and began again.

"Once upon a time in China, there lived a girl named Chen Lien who was very self-conscious about a large scar on one of her eyebrows, caused by a childhood accident. She refused to look at herself in a mirror and, if she did see the scar, she thought it hideous. As she grew into a young woman, she spent more time alone in her garden. One day a rich young man named Wu-Tang was visiting Chen Lien's neighbours and saw Chen Lien in the garden, stitching embroidery and humming to herself. He was immediately entranced by the young woman, who moved as gracefully as a willow branch and whose sweet voice stole his heart. It so happened that Chen Lien sat with her good side facing toward him, and Wu-Tang thought her the perfect vision of a soul mate.

"'I have found my bride!' Wu-Tang declared to his parents when he arrived home. And so, his mother went to Chen Lien's parents. After the usual discussion of gifts, the mother returned and asked to speak with her son. 'Wu-Tang,' said his mother. 'As you know, the young woman is from a good family and carries herself with the grace of a princess. But there is something you may not know about her. You should know about a flaw to her beauty.'

119

"'I have seen her with my own eyes!' exclaimed Wu-Tang. 'I will not hear you speak of any flaw!'

"The wedding therefore went ahead. However, as Chen Lien stood in her wedding dress, she felt uneasy and wondered what Wu-Tang would think when he saw her. As Chen Lien watched her husband-to-be laughing and talking with guests, she worried, 'If he had been told, why wouldn't he try to glance at me to try to see the scar through my veil? How can he be unaware of it?'

"After the wedding ceremony, the two of them were alone. The new husband lifted his bride's veil and was startled when he saw her eyebrow. Chen Lien saw the surprise on her husband's face and said, 'Wu-Tang, did not your mother tell you of my bad eyebrow?' The young man was silent. Chen Lien continued: 'When I was a little girl, my family was travelling far away to visit friends. I was playing in their garden when a little boy threw a heavy stone. I'm sure that he did not wish to hurt me, but it hit me on the forehead, and cut this gash where you now see a scar. I am sorry that I cannot come to you, my husband, perfect in every way.'

"'Oh, my bride,' said Wu-Tang at last, 'what was the name of that little boy who threw the stone?'

"'I do not know,' said Chen Lien, 'he was a visitor there like myself.'

"'Was the garden in which you were playing that of the Li family in the city of Peking?' whispered Wu-Tang. Chen Lien looked at him in surprise. 'My parents told me,' Wu-Tang continued, 'how I once threw a stone and cut the forehead of a little girl in the gardens of the Li family. It must be destiny itself that we are now tied with the silken cord of marriage so that I might finally make amends to you for the injury I caused. And now I know exactly what I must do.' Wu-Tang therefore called for the finest black ink and his thinnest writing brush, and with the brush and ink, he drew a new eyebrow right through the scar. It was thin and curved, like a willow leaf, and it was so much like Chen Lien's other perfect eyebrow that no one could tell them apart. For the rest of their lives, the two lovers lived together. Every morning Wu-Tang painted a new willow-leaf eyebrow over the scar that he had made and the two of them lived their lives in perfect contentment."

For a society wedding, there were not many people, but Celia had said that she wanted something small. Lutyens knew most of the guests. There was his wife and his three other children – Robert, Mary and Elisabeth and their partners – as well as Gertrude Jekyll who had made the trip to London despite her deteriorating health. There was Basil's brother, Christian Drewe, who had journeyed from Austria with a friend he had known before the war. There was Basil's mother – however, Sir Julius was too unwell to make the journey – and then there were their friends and some cousins.

"I first met Basil on the night before his accident when he broke his leg," continued Lutyens. "I must say that he was an exceptional young man even then. He went about things with a sense of determination and was not overcome by the circumstances that affected him. I recall Celia's godmother later saying that when faced with adversity Basil got on with things with a quiet modesty."

Lutyens stopped for a second and took another sip of water. "I was aware that Celia and Basil had met each other a few times after Celia had returned from America. However, a few months ago Celia said to me, as we were having breakfast, that she thought she was going to receive a proposal of marriage and that Basil might be calling to see me in the next few days. Rarely, if ever, am I stumped for words, but I had not seen that coming." There was some mild laughter around the hall. Lutyens waited a moment and then continued. "Basil duly asked whether he could see me and a few days later we arranged to have dinner at my club in London."

Lutyens again looked down at his notes and removed the top sheet of paper. He smiled slightly, his full, white moustache curved upwards and then he continued.

"Most fathers of the bride have a meeting with the groom for one purpose only." Lutyens waited a moment to give effect to what he would say next. "They are there to ensure that the groom is suitable and can provide adequately. However, when one is sitting opposite a barrister who happens to be the son of the man who has commissioned you to build a castle, that conversation will inevitably be somewhat short." Lutyens let the laughter die away. "After a few minutes of speaking with Basil, I was left in no doubt of his sincerity and that he was prepared to adopt Celia's son Robert and give him his name. There was nothing more to ask him, and I happily gave my consent for their marriage."

Lutyens looked directly towards Celia and Basil sitting beside him at the table. He then turned back to the guests and said, "I believe that all things should be built on good foundations. I hope that the love that these two young people have for each other will endure over time and their marriage will last to the end of their days." Lutyens raised his glass and the words: "The bride and groom" were repeated by the guests.

When he had sat down, Celia leaned over and whispered to him, "What made you choose that story? I don't have a scar like Chen Lien."

"Not all scars can be seen," said Lutyens. "Anyway, why do you think that you are Chen Lien in my parable?"

"Because I am the bride," responded Celia.

"The purpose of a parable," replied Lutyens, "is to teach us something and if I had simply repeated one of my old stories you would not have learnt anything at all."

"And what should I learn from that story?" asked Celia.

"That if you hurt someone you must always make amends and seek their forgiveness."

***

"I hadn't realised that Father was so unwell," said Christian. Basil looked at his elder brother. The burns on the side of his face had healed over the years, however, there was still nothing that could be done to restore his sight, and he wore a pair of opaque, round, brass-rimmed glasses.

"He's been deteriorating for some time," replied Basil. "Before you go back to Austria, we should have a chat about matters. You also need to speak to him."

"That sounds rather ominous," replied Christian.

"It's not meant to be," responded Basil.

Drinks were being served in the crypt of the Old Hall and Christian's friend, Tomas Skeres, wandered over with a glass of champagne in his hand.

"Are you enjoying yourself?" asked Basil.

"It's all been divine," said Tomas, in a slightly high-pitched tone. "The food was perfect, and the wine and champagne are exquisitely delicious." Tomas took a sip from his fluted glass and smiled as if to prove his point. "But I am afraid to say that the music is a cacophony."

Basil glanced over at the three-piece ensemble, tucked away in a corner.

"It's a composition by Celia's younger sister Elisabeth," said Basil. "For our wedding."

"Aah," said Tomas. "And you like it?"

Basil paused. "Let's just say that Celia wanted it played and, as we all know, it's all about the bride on a wedding day."

"It sounds like there's a story to tell," said Christian.

"Not really," said Basil. "Do you remember that boy, Krishnamurti? I think you met him before the war?"

"Yes, I heard him speak in London."

"He had a brother, Nitya. It seems that Celia's two sisters were taken with him. Anyway, to cut a long story short, he died at the end of last year of tuberculosis. Both sisters were distraught, and Elisabeth suffered from depression. Celia thought it might cheer her up if we played her composition."

"She'll be the only one," said Tomas, more to himself than anyone else.

Basil decided it was time to speak with his other guests. "It was nice to meet you finally," he said to Tomas. "Has Christian introduced you to Celia?" he added, as he was about to go.

"Not yet," said Tomas. "And I missed her when she came to Vienna a few months ago."

Basil looked over at his brother. "I didn't know that Celia had gone to see you a few months ago," he said. "She didn't say."

Christian turned towards Tomas and slowly said, "I think Tomas is mistaken."

"Possibly," said Tomas, who moved his gaze from Basil. They carried on speaking for another five minutes or so about inconsequential things and then, after Basil had left, Tomas lit a cigarette and offered one to Christian.

"Why did you lie?" he asked.

"Let's go outside," said Christian. "This is not a conversation I can have here."

They walked slowly across the lawns of New Square. Georgian buildings of greyish-brown brick surrounded them on three sides. Dark olive-green wooden shutters had been installed on the first-floor windows of the buildings on the eastern side of the square. It was a reminder that not even one of the fortresses of the bar was immune from the occasional attempt at breaking and entering. Tomas described all this to Christian as he held his arm and walked slowly around the lawned quad. At the southernmost end of the quad was a bookshop underneath an arch. Tomas looked at the books in the window.

"Do you have any idea," he said, "what Arbitration and Securities is about?"

"Why?" said Christian.

"Because that's the title of a book I'm looking at."

"Ask Basil," said Christian. "It's something to do with treaties between countries. He talked about it once, but I stopped listening after a few minutes."

"And talking about Basil, what were you going to tell me?" As he finished his question, the church bells of St Clement Danes began to toll.

"What have I told you about Celia?" asked Christian.

"All you have ever said is that she looked after you when you were injured in the war."

"During the war, she became infatuated with my brother."

"Basil?" said Tomas.

"No, my older brother Adrian, who died at Ypres." The bells stopped ringing and a silence settled over Lincoln's Inn. "But then everybody loved Adrian. He was a born leader and quite brilliant at everything he did. Everybody fell under his spell."

"Ahh," said Tomas.

"When I left the convalescence home, Celia looked after me at Adrian's house in Drewsteignton. It was Celia, more than anyone, that helped me to get back on my feet and for that, I owe her more than I can ever repay. After a few months, when I could look after myself, she would each month come down from London for a few days, examine my wounds to see that they were healing properly and make sure I was improving. In June 1917 she came down with her father. Adrian was there. It was an uncomfortable couple of days."

"Why?" asked Tomas. They started slowly moving back towards the Old Hall. Once again Tomas held Christian's arm as they walked. In his other hand, Christian held a white cane and tapped the area in front of him.

"They went out riding one morning and they were late getting back. They concocted a story that Adrian's horse had thrown a shoe. Adrian was in a strange mood. He was terse with me, and Celia was crying when he left. I didn't see her again until the start of November when she went to America, and I hugged her goodbye."

"And your point?"

"I believe she was pregnant. I could feel it, or at least sense it."

"Aah," said Tomas again.

"And her child, I am told, has more than a passing resemblance to my dead brother."

"And what do you know for certain?" asked Tomas.

"Absolutely nothing, which is why I've said nothing to Basil."

"So why did you lie about her visit to Austria?"

"She came to ask me what, if anything, I had said to Basil about her and Adrian. As I just told you, I had said nothing. Adrian had married someone else, and no one needed to know what had happened before."

"And that was that?" said Tomas.

"I asked her whether she was in love with Basil. She said that in time she believed she could love him, and I accepted that. She said that she had told Basil she was going away for the weekend to see friends, and could I forget she had visited? I agreed to say nothing about her visit and so when you told Basil she had visited, I had to either break my word to Celia or tell a white lie."

Chapter 21

Jonathan Bruton and Maxwell Fyfe stood in silence, in black evening dress, smoking cigars under the vaulted undercroft of the chapel, beside the Old Hall. A hundred years earlier, distraught and destitute women would have left their newborn babies there when they couldn't care for them. The Inn of Court adopted these orphans, and each was given the surname of Lincoln. The undercroft was ornately decorated with stone carvings of flowers imprinted onto the arches of the roof.

"Have you spoken with Basil?" Maxwell Fyfe finally asked.

"We caught up earlier today," said Bruton. "He was telling anyone who'd listen about the cricket match at Lord's and how Jack Hobbs' score was the highest ever recorded at that ground. If he carries on, he'll be divorced by the end of the evening."

"I know, I had to pry him away from the wireless this morning," said Maxwell Fyfe. "I was worried that if he didn't get a move on, he'd miss his own wedding." Bruton grinned, put the cigar to his lips and then slowly exhaled the smoke. He watched it as it swirled around the vaulted roof. "Weren't you at Oxford with him?" continued Maxwell Fyfe, who threw his cigar onto the floor and stepped on it.

"We were in the same halls in our first year," said Bruton.

"Has he changed much?" asked Maxwell Fyfe.

Bruton thought about it for a second. When he had spoken to Basil earlier in the day, he had noticed a difference in him. He was more measured in his responses and not as carefree. He seemed guarded, more reserved, a pillar of society. He could not imagine Basil now falling asleep in the corridor by his room or riding his bike around the quad with no hands on the handlebars. Bruton wondered whether they still had anything in common and doubted it. The only thing that they now shared was a memory of Oxford.

"He's changed a little," Bruton finally said, not knowing how he could explain what he felt to someone he had just met.

"You will excuse me won't you," said Maxwell Fyfe, "but I should go back to my wife. I think the music has started and she'll want to dance." Maxwell Fyfe held out his hand and Bruton shook it.

The three-piece trio had moved upstairs from the crypt into the main hall and, given some freedom to play, they had chosen a waltz from *Sleeping Beauty*. Maxwell Fyfe wandered over to his wife, Sylvia, with a glass of champagne for her. She was talking to Celia's parents and the conversation had focused on the General Strike which had happened a few months earlier. Maxwell Fyfe listened to the exchange until he was asked for his opinion.

"I rather hope that this sort of nonsense won't happen again," said Maxwell Fyfe, "and certainly the government is going to legislate on the issue."

"It may be nonsense to you," said Emily Lutyens, "but if your salary was cut overnight and your hours of work increased, you might have a different opinion."

Maxwell Fyfe tried to smile but was not in the mood for an argument about politics. As a lawyer who was standing as a Conservative member of Parliament, he held opinions that not everyone would agree with. His party's position was that it was better to have a poorly paid job than no job at all. However, all he managed to say was, "You're probably right." He leant across to his wife and suggested they dance, and she readily agreed. Emily looked at her husband as they stood alone.

"I suppose we should be grateful," she said.

"Grateful," answered Lutyens, "for what?"

"That Celia has finally married so well." She looked over at the head table where Celia was sitting next to Basil. "Without my unconditional forgiveness, this marriage would never have occurred. I had a talk with her the other day."

"About what?" asked Lutyens.

"About being a wife," answered Emily. "She has a role to play, and I wanted to make it clear to her that everyone expects her to fulfil that role." Emily continued to stare at Celia as she carried on speaking. "We all know that Basil was not her first love, but, as I said to her, he must be her last. Society is always so unforgiving of a woman who does not play her role to perfection."

"And what did Celia say to that?" asked Lutyens.

"You know how she can be. She was straight on her high horse telling me to mind my own business, but I told her it was my business and that our fortunes were still very much linked to that castle. I think she realised that, but I do worry that she is marrying him for the wrong reasons."

"Yes," said Lutyens, almost apologetically.

"She's not in love with him," continued Emily. "She's marrying him for security. Also, I think that what happened in Ojai knocked some of the stuffing out of her."

"Do you think it's that?" responded Lutyens, who also looked at Celia and Basil. "At least they both have good hearts. Wasn't it your grandfather who said that a good heart is better than all the heads in the world?"

"The problem with you, is that you're a romantic," said Emily and leaned across and kissed her husband on the cheek.

Basil felt as if he were being minutely examined as he sat on the top table next to his wife, and so turned and whispered in Celia's ear, "You do look wonderful."

"Thank you," said Celia, who then tried to stifle a yawn. "I hadn't thought it would be such a long day."

"You're not regretting it?" said Basil.

"Of course not," said Celia. "I saw you were speaking to Christian earlier."

"Yes, he's in good form. When was the last time you saw him?"

Celia put her hand under the table and rubbed her foot once more as Basil had managed to step on it when they danced.

"I don't know," she said. "It was just before I went away to America; so probably nearly nine years ago."

"So, you won't have met his friend Tomas Skeres?"

"No," replied Celia. "I know of him but what's he like?" she asked, as nonchalantly as she could.

"More Oscar Wilde than Douglas Fairbanks I would say. I asked him what he was reading on the train from Vienna, and he said, '*Chéri* by Colette' and then added, 'Everything by Colette is simply quite delicious and mischievous.' When I asked him about politics, he looked at me as if I had offended him."

"Why?"

"He said, 'In Austria, we seem to have some very naughty boys who like dressing up in uniform and throwing stones.' Christian said that there had been one or two incidents with fascists attacking Jews and artistic types in the streets of Vienna. When I asked what was being done about it, Tomas said 'Nothing is being done. Unfortunately, the grown-ups have buried their heads in the sand and are all reading Winnie the Pooh stories.'" Basil grinned. "I wanted to correct him that one couldn't read a Winnie the Pooh story if you had buried your head in the sand, but something told me that he might not find it funny. He did say," and Basil turned his head and looked directly at Celia, "that he thought you had recently been to Vienna to see Christian."

"He was obviously mistaken," said Celia. "I've never been to Vienna." She looked away from Basil and saw Jenny Stanton, standing on her own. "You will excuse me, darling," she said hurriedly and stood up, "but I do need to speak to Jenny and introduce her to some people."

***

Later that evening, when Celia had gone to get ready for bed, Basil decided to make sure everything was ready for their honeymoon to Italy. He had arranged to stay in a palace in Frascati, where Celia had stayed with her parents when she was a girl. The suitcases were packed and ready to be taken to the train station. He decided to get the passports, train tickets and Italian lira from the safe and leave them out so there was no chance of forgetting them. He placed the money and the documents on the table, got himself a glass of water and sat thinking about his wedding day.

Robert had been packed off to his grandparents. The little eight-year-old had been the perfect page boy at the wedding, holding an ivory pillow with Celia's wedding ring on it. He was quite angelic and smiled at everyone. Basil's mother adored him as he stood perfectly still in a small sailor's suit that was just a little too big for him. His green eyes lit up as he held up the cushion with the ring on it and he smiled as if he knew a secret that no one else at the wedding could guess.

Basil picked up Celia's passport. On the inside page of the blue passport, there was a photograph of Celia from almost ten years ago, looking straight ahead and unsmiling. The passport had on the first page a stamp from her trip to America and nothing else. Basil turned the page and then he saw a stamp of an eagle with its claws holding a hammer and sickle and the name of a city underneath it: 'Wien'.

Celia called from the bedroom and asked whether he was coming to bed.

"Coming!" he shouted back, closed the passport, and placed it on top of his own. He tapped his finger slowly on the table. He was not sure he wanted to know why both his brother and his wife had lied to him in the last few hours.

Celia was up early the next morning. She had bathed and dressed and found herself in the kitchen when she heard the bedroom door open, and Basil go into the living room. He put the radio on and found a station that was playing some modern American songs.

"Can you change that," Celia called out, "to something classical?" Basil turned the dial and settled on something he thought sounded like Beethoven.

"I think everyone enjoyed themselves yesterday," he said, "with the possible exception of Maxwell Fyfe."

Celia stood in the kitchen for a moment, watching the kettle boil. She hadn't enjoyed herself. Basil and she had hardly danced, and she objected to him cross-examining her about things that had occurred before they were married. She hadn't told him about Vienna because it was none of his concern and, she thought, a gentleman would know better than to pry.

"What happened to Maxwell Fyfe?" asked Celia.

"He got a broadside from your mother for his views on the General Strike and also got caught in a conversation with Bruton about British foreign policy."

"I didn't have time to speak to your friend Bruton. He seemed to be enjoying himself. He's in the army, isn't he?"

"He's stationed in the Transjordan but was recalled to England to help with the General Strike," said Basil. "His wife is still there. I liked him a lot when we were at university, but army life seems to have hardened him."

Chapter 22

July 1929

Celia Drewe clutched hold of her degree as if she feared that the university may ask for it back. At the age of thirty-three, she had finally received a Bachelor of Arts in English. She walked slowly across the black and gold-chequered floor towards the main doors, stifling an urge to run. She hoped she could maintain an academic reserve, but as she walked, she smiled broadly, looking left and right as everyone politely clapped. When she saw her husband, she could not help but wave. Dressed in a gown and mortarboard, she looked every bit a graduate of King's College London. She had curled and combed her hair into a poodle bob so that the mortarboard would sit on her head. As she left the chapel on the Strand she saw Jenny Stanton, who waved at her.

"Congratulations," shouted Jenny. Celia rushed to her and kissed her on the cheek.

"Thank you for coming."

"I wouldn't have missed it, and my parents send their love." Jenny looked around. "Where's Basil?" she asked.

"He's still inside," said Celia. "He suggested that we wander down to the Savoy, as he's booked a table for tea and said he would meet us there when the ceremony has finished."

"I'm so delighted for you," said Jenny, as they walked. "I don't know how you managed to do it and look after Robert, although I did think that if you had more children then that would put a spanner in the works."

"Basil and I agreed not to," said Celia, "until I got my degree." She waved at another female graduate who was standing with a group of students whom she knew.

"Do you want to stop and join them?" asked Jenny.

Celia hesitated for a second. "No, I want to catch up with you. We haven't seen each other in an age, and I'm meeting them tomorrow for dinner." Jenny took hold of Celia's hand and squeezed it lightly. "Now, tell me," continued Celia, "how's married life?"

"It's nifty," said Jenny. "We've been living it up for the last few months. He's still so goofy about me and I've got some wonderful news. I was going to tell you later, but I can't wait." Celia looked at Jenny, who was more animated than she had ever seen her. "I'm pregnant."

"Oh, that's the bee's knees," said Celia.

"It is, isn't it!" squealed Jenny. "Except for Jonny and my parents, you're the first person I've told. I don't think I've ever been this happy. And what about you, Celia? Now you've finished studying are you planning to have more children?"

"Basil would like a family," said Celia, as they arrived at the Savoy. "But I'm not sure that I want to start one straight away. But I'm so happy for you."

Celia was shown to a table in the Thames Foyer, with its glass-domed atrium, where a pianist played in the middle of the room. A waiter arrived at the table.

"Two glasses of Laurent-Perrier," said Celia.

"I'm not sure I should be drinking," said Jenny.

"One glass won't hurt," said Celia, "and we are celebrating." The waiter asked whether there would be anything else and Celia replied that they were waiting for her husband who would be arriving shortly.

"Have you spoken to Basil about it?" asked Jenny.

"Well, that's the rub," said Celia. "He's always wanted to start a family of his own and when we got married, I persuaded him to hang on for a bit."

"Ahhh," said Jenny.

"And he's been so awfully good about it. He hasn't once tried to change my mind and he's looked after Robert when I've been studying at the weekends."

"It sounds as if you're in a bit of a pickle. What do you want to do?"

"I don't know," said Celia, "that's the frustrating part. I don't want to be a barrister like Basil or an architect like my father. All I know is that I don't want to be a stay-at-home mother with a brood of children." Celia looked at Jenny. "Sorry, that may have sounded insensitive."

"It's what I've always wanted," said Jenny. "To have my own house and family. Knowing that every day I could do what I wanted. It'd be just perfect."

"But," replied Celia, "don't you want to do something with your life?"

"I think bringing up a family," said Jenny, acerbically, "is doing something with your life."

"Of course it is," responded Celia. "Of course, you're right. I didn't mean it like that. But women have just been given the vote this week and don't you want to go out and shake this country up?"

"Why would I want to do that?" replied Jenny. "This country has given me everything I could ask for."

Celia waved over the waiter and asked for a second glass of champagne.

"I suppose," said Celia, "I have been thinking a lot about my aunt Constance this week, my mother's sister who died a few years ago."

"Yes, I remember," said Jenny. "She was one of the suffragettes."

Celia thought about what she would say next. "Did you know that when she was imprisoned in Holloway, my aunt Constance used a hairpin to cut the letter 'V' into her breast, just over her heart? It was the first letter of 'Votes for Women.'"

"Really?" said Jenny. "She did that!"

"She was going to cut each letter into herself, right up to her face. However, the prison guards took away the hairpin."

"I should think so," said Jenny. "That's horrible."

"I think that she was incredible," said Celia. "She had so much determination."

"But we now have the vote."

"But isn't that just the start?" said Celia. "It's what we do with it. If we all just vote in the same way our husbands and fathers vote, then what's the point of having the vote? If we don't make a difference, then everything my aunt went through was meaningless."

When Basil arrived, he kissed Celia on the cheek as he came around the table and fondly greeted Jenny.

"Have you ordered?" he asked.

"We thought we would wait," said Celia.

"I don't think I have been as proud of anyone in my life," said Basil, who waved his hand towards the waiter and ordered afternoon tea for three.

"Are you going to join us with a glass of champagne?" asked Celia.

"I'm afraid not," said Basil. "I must be back at chambers later this afternoon. I still have work to do."

"And no more for me," said Jenny.

"Jenny has some news," said Celia and then proceeded to tell Basil what it was. "We were also talking about the Equal Franchise Act and what my aunt Constance did in jail."

"Is that really a topic for the lunch table?" said Basil. "I'm sure Jenny, in her condition, really doesn't want to hear about what she did to herself."

"You're right of course," Celia said, through clenched teeth. "It's just that I was excited."

Basil turned to Jenny as the plates of sandwiches arrived, with tea. "I think it's the best news I've heard in a long time. Please send my congratulations to Jonny and I hope I'll see him at the club soon. Did Celia tell you we're now planning to start a family?" Basil took one of the salmon sandwiches and took a bite. "It will be perfect if our children grow up together like you and Celia did." Basil turned to Celia. "You should have one of these, they are delicious."

IV

Part Four

Chapter 23

September 1930

The fog rolled in upon the moor and Basil slowed the car to almost a walking pace and then stopped. He peered through the windscreen as veils of fog continued to fall, and, in its folds, the sounds of the world disappeared. Celia and Robert looked at Basil, as the twins slept blissfully unaware in their carrycots. Their journey had come to an abrupt halt.

"How far away are we?" whispered Celia.

"Just a few miles," replied Basil. "But I daren't go on as I can't see more than a yard or two in front of me."

"How long will it last?" asked Robert, who rolled down the window in the back of the vehicle and put his hand out to feel its wetness.

"Roll the window up," said Celia quietly but firmly to Robert.

"These fogs usually blow over quite quickly," said Basil, "and it may be clear thirty yards ahead, but you just can't tell."

They waited in silence for ten minutes, not wishing to wake the twins. Basil then decided to walk up the road and try to see how far ahead the fog stretched. Robert asked whether he could go with him and when the two had left the vehicle, Celia looked back at her two sleeping babies. They were three months old and still only slept intermittently and rarely at the same time. If Howard was awake, Catherine usually slept and if Catherine was awake, the devil would not be able to stir Howard. It was only the rocking motion of the car that had made both sleep at the same time and Celia was on tenterhooks that one or both would wake up. She wanted a cigarette, although she had told Basil she had given up. She swallowed as she looked at the two sleeping faces and felt like crying.

It was the first time they had been away for months, but their vacation had not begun well. The twins had both started crying at around three in the morning and bleary-eyed, Basil and Celia had got up to deal with them. After they had rocked the two children back to sleep, Basil suggested that as he was awake, and they were packed, they might as well make an early start down to Devon. They carried the twins to the car and Basil went back for Robert, who he helped down to the car still wrapped in an eiderdown. Celia made some sandwiches and a thermos flask of coffee for the journey, and they started their drive when not even the sparrows were awake.

After staring into the fog, Basil looked behind him. He could just make out the lights of the car and decided it was not safe to walk a step further.

"You know," he said to Robert, "my brother Christian once got lost on the moor and it took over a day to find him." Robert looked at Basil. "How far can you see ahead?"

"Not far," said Robert.

"Me neither," said Basil. "Let's go back to the car."

"Is Mummy all right?" asked Robert.

Basil stopped and looked down at his stepson. "Yes, Mummy's fine, she's just very tired. Hopefully, after our holiday she'll feel better."

"It's just," said Robert, who was unsure whether he should break a confidence, "Mummy sometimes cries for no reason."

"I know," said Basil, who had in the last few months often been on the sharp end of Celia's tongue. "But Mummy will feel much better after a holiday." They slowly walked back to the car. Despite the assurance he had given to Robert, Basil felt that things were not right, and he did not know what to do, except give Celia time.

When they arrived at Castle Drogo, the twins were crying uncontrollably, and Celia had buried her head in her hands. Robert did his best to comfort everyone and Basil, who had managed to blank out the noise, felt he was close to screaming. Lady Frances stared into the vehicle and immediately acted – Celia's nanny, who had arrived the day before, was called and whisked away the twins. Robert and Celia were summarily sent to bed.

Basil was told to find his father and have breakfast with a few strong cups of coffee.

"If anyone knows what to do in these situations, it's your mother," said Sir Julius to his son, as he drank a third cup of coffee, despite the orders of his doctor.

"I don't think I have ever felt this tired, sir," said Basil, who, if truth be told, wanted to go to bed himself.

"It will get easier," said Sir Julius. "It just takes time."

"It's been months. I walk around in a daze for most of the day and during the nights I only get a few hours' sleep between the incessant crying." Lady Frances walked in as Basil was talking and sat down next to him. "And the hardest part of it," continued Basil, who felt he was rambling on uncontrollably, "is Celia seems like a different person to the one I married. She sleeps most of the time and when she is awake, she doesn't want anything to do with the twins or me."

"She needs a proper break," said Lady Frances to her son. "Won't her father be in India at the beginning of the next year for the inauguration of New Delhi? Why don't you send Celia there for a family holiday with Robert and leave the twins with us?"

"Do you want them?" asked Basil. "They cry constantly, and we haven't worked out how to stop them, except for picking them up and carrying them around all night."

"Haven't you yet worked out that the baby that cries the loudest gets fed," said Sir Julius. "You just have to leave them; they'll stop in time."

"But how do you ignore the incessant noise, sir?" asked Basil. "It tears my nerves to shreds."

"Fortunately," said Sir Julius, "I live in a castle, and I am certain that Lutyens will have included a dungeon somewhere. It's the kind of joke he thinks is funny!"

Chapter 24

13 February 1931

"It's breathtaking," said Celia, as the open carriage took them slowly through the All-India War Memorial Arch. "Is it all you hoped it would be?"

Lutyens said nothing but smiled and continued to smoke his pipe as they proceeded along the Kingsway. The inauguration of New Delhi was to last a week and on the first day, four dominion columns were to be unveiled by the Viceroy of India to a fanfare of trumpets. A procession of carriages took the dignitaries along the Kingsway to the Secretariat buildings. Lutyens sat in an open-top carriage with his wife and two of his daughters, Celia and Mary. As one of the leading architects of New Delhi, he was given a position of honour in the procession and, as the carriage moved slowly forward, he explained that the All-India War Memorial Arch was in recognition of the Indian men who had died in the Great War and the third Afghan war.

"From here," said Lutyens, "you travel about a mile to the Secretariat buildings and then the Viceroy's House is in front of you. The four dominion columns are gifts of friendship and unity from the four other great British dominions: Canada, South Africa, New Zealand and Australia."

As the carriage came towards the end of the Kingsway, Lutyens pointed to the two Secretariat buildings, which were behind the dominion columns, and told Celia that Herbert Baker, another architect, had designed these. The buildings were made of soft cream and red sandstone from Rajasthan.

"They are in the Indo-Saracenic Revival style. My idea was for the Viceroy's House to be a classical building to stand above them, but Baker insisted they be placed on the same level," continued Lutyens. "He knew full well that the rise in the road would obscure the Viceroy's House from a distance, except for the dome. If you do have to speak to him, do maintain an attitude of indifference to his buildings."

As the dominion columns were unveiled, Celia saw that atop each one was a brass ship, to represent the trade between the dominion countries and the emblem of each dominion country was marked at the bottom.

"The columns have a political purpose," Lutyens continued, "along with being gifts, they are intended to indicate that soon India will become a part of the British dominions. It's a suggestion that India's independence is coming."

***

New Delhi lies just to the south of Delhi, which is as old as the Mahabharata and surrounded by stone walls. The Red Fort was constructed just south of the walled city for the Mughal emperors and was completed in 1648.

"It is called Lal Qila," said the guide to Robert, "or the Red Fort, as the English call it. It is a palace and was once as great and as grand as any in the world with its towers, domes and minarets. The river that runs beside it is the Yamuna, which starts its journey in the Himalayas. In Hindu mythology," continued the guide, "the goddess Yamuna used to bathe and drink the water of the Yamuna and it was said it would absolve a person of sin."

"Can I drink it?" said Robert, who thought it smelt vile. The guide laughed and his young face broke into a smile.

"No," he replied. "When the city of Delhi developed, and the British made it their capital, the waters became undrinkable as sewage was pumped into the river."

Celia hardly heard a word as the guide continued talking to Robert. Robert was enjoying his day out, although he also seemed to love the pomp and circumstance of the inauguration. Celia was pleased to be away from the crowds and her parents. At moments she still wanted to cry. She felt tired most of the time and could hardly concentrate. When she left for

India, she had hoped that it might be the tonic she needed, but she still felt in the doldrums. She worried about what she would do when she got back and how she would be with the twins. Incessantly crying babies was not how she pictured her married life. While marriage had given her the security that she had wanted, she hated not having her own money and independence. It was the little things that made her grind her teeth together, such as when Basil asked about an expense on their joint account.

"What happened to the Red Fort?" asked Robert.

"When the city was invaded in 1739 by Nader Shah of Persia, it was sacked, and all the precious materials were taken…" The guide sighed. "All the gems and gold and silver of the Peacock Throne were stolen." He held his arms wide as he looked at the walls. "When the Mughal emperors declined in power the fort was taken by the Persians and then was left to rack and ruin. When the British came to India, they used it as a fort."

"What was the Peacock Throne?" asked Robert.

"It was the most splendid of all thrones ever made," said the guide. "Three hundred years ago the greatest of all the Mughal emperors, Shah Jahan, was ruler of Delhi and held court at the Red Fort. Shah Jahan wanted to be as great as King Solomon and had a magnificent jewel-encrusted throne built. It took years to make and cost more than the construction of the Taj Mahal. He chose two enormous gemstones to adorn the throne. These were the famous Timur Ruby and the Koh-i-Noor diamond. The storytellers say that when the Persians sacked the city it took seven hundred elephants, four thousand camels and twelve thousand horses to carry away all the gold and jewels."

"And the Koh-i-Noor diamond is now in the crown of Queen Mary," said Celia.

Celia heard a clackety-clack noise, the sound of metal on metal. For a moment it reminded her of the war, the sound of a bolt of a gun repeatedly hitting metal. She thought about Adrian and then remembered the face of Deke Hamilton as he lay on the ground staring up into the night. She shivered in the warm air and suddenly felt like crying. A tear welled up and she turned around to watch as a train went over a bridge nearby. Its metal wheels clanked repetitively on the joints of the track. People sat on top of the train carriages as they made their way back to the countryside from the city.

"They are Untouchables," said the guide. Robert walked over to his mother and took her hand.

"Why are they called Untouchables?" asked Celia, trying to pretend that there was nothing wrong.

"Because they do not fall within one of the recognised castes," said the guide, "and therefore have no place in our society, except to do those jobs that other people will not do. Some people think that this is India's greatest shame." The guide turned and looked again at the Red Fort. "Let us go inside," he said. "I will show you some of the great rooms in the fort where the carving of the sandstone is exquisite." He walked slowly to one of the great gates and spoke to the soldiers at the door who let him in. "Let's not dawdle," he shouted back to them. "There is so much to see and tell you, and so little time before we need to get back."

Celia took a small lace handkerchief from her bag and wiped the tear away.

Robert watched his mother and because he did not know what to say or do, he wished that Basil was there.

***

The gala ball at the Viceroy's House was opulent and was held in the centre of the palace beneath the dome, in a room called the Durbar Hall. The room, like the dome, was round and supported by jasper pillars that sat on white blocks. Above the pillars were semi-circular recesses where the stone was carved in beautiful symmetric patterns. Behind the pillars were corridors where one could travel the circumference of the room without ever having to cross the main floor. There were no chairs within the room except for the two thrones that sat at one end. In the early evening, the room was lit up by the sunlight that shone through the dome. The white marble and porphyry on the floor had been so highly polished that the jasper columns could be seen in its reflection.

"The word 'durbar' means a court in Persian."

Celia turned around and looked at a tall Indian man dressed in a sherwani, the long-sleeved outer coat that was fashionable with the Nawabs, the old rulers of Benghal. It was fitted at the waist and fell below the knee. The coat was adorned with intricate stitching of exotic birds, made up of gold and silver thread. Underneath the coat, he wore white cotton pyjamas and soft tan loafers.

"Good evening," said Celia. For a moment she wasn't sure whether to introduce herself or ask for a glass of champagne.

"You don't recognise me, do you?"

"I'm sorry," said Celia, who stared vacantly at him.

"Less than half a day has gone and already you've forgotten me."

Celia continued staring at the face of the young man. Again, she thought of Adrian and then realised that he had been their guide at the Red Fort that morning.

"I'm so sorry," she said. "I wasn't expecting to see you and, well, not dressed like that. Are you working here as well?"

The young man laughed, a full rich and warm laugh that made people look and smile. When he stopped, he said to Celia, "Not exactly. Your mother and Miss Besant asked me to find you. They have gone outside into the gardens and charged me with escorting you to them."

As Celia walked into the gardens, a glass of champagne in her hand, there was a heady scent of jasmine. Under the full moon with its chilly light, she could make out the hedge mazes, flowerbeds, and bridged waters at various levels, all framed in the red sandstone that Herbert Baker had used to build the Secretariat buildings. There were fountains like heaps of pennies and gazebos in red and cream stone. There were terraced battlements of flowers that went up like bastions and stone pergolas. It was ornate, unnatural, and intricate; something her godmother, Gertrude Jekyll, would have hated.

"I see that Devjeet has found you," said Annie Besant as Celia arrived. Celia had not seen Annie Besant, the head of the Theosophist Society, in many years and Celia thought that she must now be in her eighties.

"Devjeet?" questioned Celia.

"Maharaja Devjeet Patel," replied Annie Besant.

Celia looked at her guide. "You didn't tell me," she said apologetically, and then turned to her mother and Annie Bessant and, in a more accusing tone, asked, "Why didn't either of you tell me?"

"You said you wanted a guide," said Emily, "and Annie simply arranged one. I had no idea until this evening that you were being escorted around the Red Fort by one of India's most eligible men."

"I said that I needed a guide, and he offered his services," said Annie Besant. "And who am I to say no to a maharaja of the northern territories?"

Celia turned again to Devjeet and could not help smiling.

"Why on earth would anyone," she said, "let alone a maharaja, offer to escort a drab, middle-aged woman around Delhi?"

Devjeet looked at her, smiled and replied, "Actually I had no idea what you would look like when I offered my services as a guide; although, I should say, my description of you to my sister was neither middle-aged nor drab."

Celia did not know what to say but continued gazing at his beautiful face and deep brown eyes. Devjeet took a step closer to Celia and whispered, so only she could hear, "Why do you look so curiously into people's faces; do you expect to find your lost dead there?"

Chapter 25

28 February 1931

They spoke in whispers, as they had done for the last hour. A sudden knock on the door made them stop and hold their breaths.

"Celia, are you in there?" It was the sharp tone of her mother. "You'll make us late," she said firmly, and then they heard her footsteps as she walked back down the wooden hallway.

Celia suddenly felt unsure of herself and covered herself with a silk sheet, trembling.

"I should go," he said.

"You should never have come," she replied, looking at him as he sat up on the side of the bed. He had broad shoulders and the muscles on his chest were pronounced from hours of playing polo. She could not see a spot or blemish on his olive skin. She smelt the cedar and citrus of his cologne and wanted to put her hand through his beautiful black, oiled hair. He was everything that Basil wasn't. She watched him as he looked for his clothes and then he turned towards her. She caught her breath, wrapped the sheet around her and sat up, placing her hand on his arm. The shutters on the veranda door were down but she was certain that there would be people working in the garden.

"How will you leave?"

"I thought I would wait until you left and then go ten minutes later."

Celia thought she heard someone on the veranda and for a moment was frightened that her mother may have returned. A minute passed but there was no other sound. She started to get up.

"Don't look," she said. As she went into the bathroom, he noticed that she was still shaking slightly. She closed the door; he took out his cigarettes and lit one as he waited. When she came out, wearing a white slip, he saw that she had been crying.

"No one will find out," he said in a reassuring voice, and for a moment she smiled. "Even if one of the servants did see us, they would not say anything. They know their place. When you see your mother just say that you had a headache and were sleeping."

She put on her clothes and afterwards sat down in front of her dressing table to do her make-up. He walked over, put his hand gently on her shoulder and kissed her neck. She didn't want him to stop and hated herself for feeling like that. She adored him but she pushed him away, telling him that she had to go. When she was dressed and her make-up faultless, she slid back the bolt on the door, opened it slightly and looked down the hallway. She turned, intending to tell him that there was no one there, but then saw Robert running down the hallway towards her room.

"I'll see you later," she said, as she closed the door behind her.

***

"Another one of your heads," said Emily. "You poor thing, every Tuesday and Saturday afternoon like clockwork for the last two weeks."

Celia ignored the barbed remark.

"You also suffer from migraines, Emily" said Lutyens.

"The difference, Ned," said Emily, "is that I have no idea when one of my migraines would come on."

"Perhaps," said Celia, "it's caused by always having the house fumigated?"

"Speaking of foul smells," continued Emily, "have you started smoking?"

"No, why would you ask that?" replied Celia.

"I noticed the other week that your room smelt of smoke." Emily turned to her husband. "If we are going to get to this concert this evening then we really must get a move on."

"I'll make sure Robert is ready," said Celia, who took hold of her son's hand and started walking towards his room. She felt uncomfortable. She was certain that her mother knew something as she made one pointed remark after another.

When she had gone Lutyens looked at his wife. "Should I arrange for a doctor to see Celia?" he asked. "It's always difficult to know what the cause of these things is."

"Sometimes, Ned, you can be so dense," Emily retorted.

***

The Lotus Pond Garden was lit up with torches in the early evening and the players arranged themselves around a mimosa tree. The beautiful dusky pink powder puff flowers shimmered in the light evening breeze, giving off a honey scent. There were three of them; a middle-aged man with short jet-black hair and a waistline that showed an appreciation for gulab jamun, a younger, thinner man with a nose of similar shape to that of Lord Wellington, and the beautiful Begum Akhtar, the celebrated singer of ghazals and dadras. The middle-aged man played the tabla, the Indian drums that are played with the timpanist's fingers. The younger man played the sitar. Begum Akhtar sang songs of longing and promise, which, if Celia could have understood, would have broken her heart.

Cushions and rugs had been strewn on the floor for the guests. Many of the young men smoked hookahs and blew the fragrant smoke into the air. They lay trance-like listening to the music and occasionally talking when a piece finished. Away behind them, the servants were preparing a selection of snacks and pastries. In deference to his English guests, Devjeet had set out a table and chairs for the Lutyens family to sit around and placed it a few paces away from where the Indian guests were lying on the ground.

In the hot evening, Emily constantly waved a fan as she sat listening to the music.

"Are you enjoying it, Emily?" asked Lutyens.

"It's very spiritual," said Emily, "as if it's rooted in nature."

"And you?" said Lutyens to Celia.

Celia hesitated for a moment. She had found the first few ghazals intriguing but the longer it went on the more difficult she found it. However, she did not want to appear discourteous as Devjeet had arranged this for her and her family, and very few people could claim that they had been invited to an evening listening to the famous Begum Akhtar.

"I'm enjoying the evening," she said. However, she was not surprised that Robert had gone off exploring the gardens. Lately, he had been acting differently and had at times been curt with Celia.

"And what about you, Father?" asked Mary. "Do you like it?"

"It's not my type of music," said Lutyens. "I find it all too unstructured, like Indian architecture. There were moments when I thought it was beautiful but, to my ear, there is nothing that holds it all together."

The music stopped and after the applause subsided Devjeet wandered over with Begum Akhtar. He asked how they were enjoying the recital and, like the English family they were, they began enthusing about the performance.

"A ghazal," said Begum Akhtar, "is a form of poetry. A literal translation of the word *ghazal* is a conversation with women."

"Would you mind translating one for us?" asked Celia.

"The last song I sang," said Begum Akhtar, "which Dev asked me to sing, was by the great Mirza Ghalib. When the words are translated you lose the balance of the poem, but the meaning is:

"Life becomes even more complicated
when a man can't think like a man...
What irrationality makes me so dependent on her
that I rush off an hour early, then get annoyed when she's 'late'?
My lover is so striking! She demands to be seen.
The mirror reflects only her image, yet still dazzles and confounds my eyes.
Love's arrows have left me the deep scar of happiness
while she hovers above me, illuminated.
She promised not to torment me, but only after I was mortally wounded.
How easily she 'repents', my lovely slayer!"

"It's both beautiful and sad," said Celia.

"Like much of what Ghalib writes," said Begum Akhtar. "He can see into the heart of a person and say what is there in just a few perfect words."

"Ghalib is my favourite of all the Mughal poets," added Devjeet, who took out his cigarettes and lit one. "He wrote:

'*I was unable to relate the state of my heart to her,*
while she failed to appreciate the nuances of my silences.'"

He smiled slightly, and gazed at Celia, looking into her eyes for just a second more than a mere acquaintance would have done.

"Your cigarettes have a distinctive smell," said Emily, who looked intently at him.

Celia sat silently, hoping that he would ignore the comment. She also prayed that her mother would change the subject. She couldn't say anything herself. If she rose to the bait, her mother would know she was hiding something.

"They're Russian," said Devjeet. "I have them made especially for me in London in Jermyn Street and shipped here. Would you like one?"

"I don't smoke," said Emily, "but Celia may have started."

"You didn't tell me," said Devjeet, who offered her a cigarette.

Chapter 26

The first Round Table Conference to discuss the future constitution of India concluded on the 19th of January 1931. It had been a partial success, although the Indian National Congress, or as they were colloquially referred to, the Congress Party, had not attended. They were still advocating a campaign of civil disobedience and many of their leaders, including Gandhi and Nehru, were imprisoned. The Conference had reached some form of agreement. It concluded that on achieving independence India should be run as a federal state and have dominion status.

On the 26th of January 1931, Gandhi was released from prison and met the British viceroy, where it was settled that, in exchange for stopping the civil disobedience, or as Gandhi called it, the Satyagraha, the Congress Party would have an equal negotiating role at the next conference on India's future. The leaders of the Congress Party were slowly released from prison. Laxman Choudhury, who had been imprisoned for civil disobedience under Bombay Regulation XXXV of 1827 and interned at the Yerawada Prison with the Congress Party leaders, was freed on the last day of February 1931. There had been no trial and no sentence. When he left the stone-built prison, with its heavy wooden doors, he was distinctly thinner.

Laxman Choudhury's father was a civil servant, as was his father before him. For five generations, the ancestors of Laxman had held posts in government. Even before the British invaded in 1826, when Assam was still an independent state and under the rule of the Ahom people, the Choudhury family had held advisory positions in court. They were not a family of warriors or poets. They were not rash or imprudent but lived cautious lives, avoiding danger. They appeared to have a sixth sense, they knew when they should be seen and when not to put their heads above the parapet. They counted numbers and advised on fiscal matters. They kept meticulous records detailing every transaction that the government made and their ledgers, without fail, always balanced. It was in this way that they survived from one dynasty to the next. Even the British, with their sense of order and perfect administration, saw the value of the Choudhurys.

Laxman's father looked like a civil servant. He was bald and had a small black moustache which was flecked with grey. He was overweight, but not to such a degree that one would have thought him obese. His eyes were chestnut brown and quite small. His nose was well proportioned, and he had a wide mouth with thickish lips. Laxman bore many of these features, except that when he walked out of Yerawada Prison he was thin and still had a full head of black hair. Laxman's father would later remark that his son was the first Choudhury in his family to be imprisoned but never said whether he was proud of this fact or horrified by it.

Laxman worked alongside Gandhi, although in public he went unnoticed. Laxman was not a natural orator and avoided the limelight, as countless generations of Choudhurys had done before him. However, he had a deep knowledge of Indian politics and generally believed in Gandhi's philosophy. He wanted an independent India now – not when the British thought it was in their interests to leave. He wanted a single state ruled by a majority, for the benefit of everyone. He did not believe in the caste system and wanted equality, which was often mistaken by the British as being sympathetic to communism. He would often be asked his opinion by the leaders of the Congress Party and, when he spoke, people listened – not because he spoke well but because his arguments were always considered.

Laxman found Gandhi's philosophy of life both simple and compelling. He believed that love was the most powerful force in existence and reasoned that if hate had been superior to love, humankind would have already destroyed itself. In this way, Gandhi taught that change could be affected through non-violence and that the actions of an aggressor against a non-violent adversary would ultimately fail.

From prison, Laxman went home to see his family in Tezpur. He decided against going immediately to Delhi and craved the comfort of the place in which he had grown up and where he could always have a homecooked meal and a clean bed. When he paid for his train tickets he groaned as he realised that the British had chosen to imprison him on the opposite side of India. He arrived tired at Tezpur train station after four days of travel and haggled with a tonga-wallah to take him to his parents' house near the Mahabhairab Temple.

As he climbed into the tonga, newspaper vendors were shouting, "Newspapers, one anna only! Gandhi and Jinnah at odds – read for one anna only!" He leant out of the tonga, gave the vendor an anna, and took a paper.

As the horse clip-clopped along the main streets, the driver exchanged salaams with his fellow tonga-wallahs. Laxman noticed that there were lines of policemen out on the streets. The tonga turned into the road in which Laxman had played as a child and he saw the plastered stone walls of his home with the large wooden gates that were bolted shut. He climbed down from the tonga, paid the driver an anna and a half and rang the bell. He heard the man say something to his horse and then the crack of the whip. The horse turned and went back the way it had come. A servant hurried to the gates, looked out through the spyhole and asked who it was. When Laxman said his name, the four metal bolts that barred the door were pulled back.

"Why are the gates bolted at this time?" asked Laxman as they walked toward the main house.

"There was rioting again last week," said the servant.

"Against the British?" asked Laxman, who had not read a newspaper for nearly a year.

"Between Hindu and Muslim," came the reply from the servant. "But we are safe here. Neither Musselman nor Hindu would dare threaten your family."

Laxman's great-grandfather had been a man of considerable means and had built a house near the temple. He had survived the passing of Assam to the British and was able to retain some of the hidden wealth of the Ahoms, which he later invested into a property. He constructed a main house with an internal courtyard and, besides the walls which surrounded the property, he built smaller houses for the servants. Outside the house, as one went away from town, the road became unpaved and shanty housing had been constructed around a municipal tap. Sanitation in this area was poor and mosquitoes and flies swarmed in the unclean conditions. Those who lived and worked in the house and grounds were paid and treated well, and, over time, the Choudhurys improved the conditions of the local area where many Muslims lived. The family was therefore respected by the whole community and, when the violence began, they seemed to be spared from its effects.

***

Majda Choudhury looked at her older brother as he sat in the kitchen wiping the last vestiges of red lentil dahl from a terracotta bowl with a roti. As he ate, he turned the pages of his newspaper.

"Maa is buying fresh spices from the market," said Majda. "She'll never say it, but you're her favourite."

"Oh, I know," said Laxman, as he slowly chewed the last piece of roti and savoured the buttery taste of the dahl. "And she does tell me."

"You asked Maa who her favourite child was, and she told you it was you?"

"Only when we're alone. She would of course deny it if you asked her."

"I'd never think of asking her," said Majda emphatically.

"And you're Pita's favourite."

"I am not," said Majda, although she knew, as she said the words, that that was a lie.

A servant came over and took the bowl.

"So, tell me the news," said Laxman. "I heard as I came in that there had been riots."

Majda waited until the servant had left the room before saying anything.

"The Muslims are worried about the Congress Party's proposals," said Majda. "They are saying that they risk changing one imposed ruler for another."

"That's nonsense," said Laxman. "The Congress Party simply want a unified India controlled by a majority government. The Muslims will form part of that government."

"But a minority part of it. The majority will always be Hindu," said Majda. "The Muslims want a federal system where they can have control over their affairs. I assume that you heard in prison that at the first Round Table Conference, there was an agreement that the future constitution of India should be federal rather than unitary."

"I did," replied Laxman, "but that kind of agreement will never happen. It is not what most people want and not what the Congress Party wants. The British can't ignore us. They have tried that, and you've seen what's happened."

"And Jinnah is now saying no constitution will be acceptable to the Muslims of India unless there are safeguards as to their rights and interests," continued Majda. "That's what's causing the rioting. The Hindus in Assam are worried that we might become a Muslim state and the Muslims are worried that they will have no say in how they are governed."

"Which is why we need a unitary solution so that we can have represen-tation from everyone and there is one law for everyone." Laxman looked at his younger sister. "But what about you and Maa and Pita? How have you all been?"

"Nothing changes here," said Majda. "The world is as it was when we were children. Pita still goes to work every day and Maa still buys enough food to feed an army. I asked her why she bought so much, and she said she never knew when all her children would come home to visit."

"And what about you?" asked Laxman.

"I still have my clinic in Nagaon, and I spend half my time trying to find funding for it." Majda paused for a second, smiled slightly, and asked, "Is there any way I could get a grant from the Congress Party?"

Laxman laughed. "We don't have any money. If you want a grant, you will need to get it from the British government, they're the only ones with money. But what about you? Anyone in your life?"

"No one," said Majda.

"Is Maa still looking for a suitable man?"

"Fortunately, she has given up on that," said Majda.

"So, are you still getting over that broken heart?"

"It mended a long time ago," replied Majda. "However, that does remind me, you received a letter by airmail last week from Basil Drewe."

Laxman reread the letter and placed it on the table. He had not heard from Basil in nearly five years, not since he received an invitation to his wedding in London. He had not been able to go and so sent a card and what he thought was a fitting present. He received a note from Celia, nearly two months later, thanking him for his unique gift and saying that if he was ever in London, he would be more than welcome. He had never gone back to England.

In the letter Basil asked how Laxman was, wrote that he fondly remembered their time in Oxford, updated him about having had twins and having adopted a stepson, said that his wife was currently in Delhi and that he had heard from Celia's mother, Lady Emily Lutyens, that Celia was currently unwell and having intense migraines. Basil concluded the letter by asking Laxman for two favours. First, to visit Celia when he was next in Delhi and tell him how Celia's health was. Basil wrote that he was in two minds about whether to come out to India, as his father had recently had another heart attack and, as the prognosis was not good, he was reluctant to do so unless necessary. Second, he asked Laxman to see Mrs Clarke at the tea plantation near Devi Singh Gat and ascertain whether the house on the lake could be used by the Lutyens family if they wanted to get out of the heat of the city.

"I'm at a loss," said Laxman to Majda, who had been trying to read the letter on the table in front of her, but it was upside down. "Why on earth would he ask me to drop in on his wife? I'm a doctor of philosophy, not medicine. It would have been better if he had asked you. And why didn't Basil write to Celia's mother who is with her and ask her the question?"

"There may be a hundred reasons," said Majda. "If Lady Emily Lutyens heard that Basil's father was seriously unwell, she might not want to unduly worry Basil."

"And how did he know about the house at Devi Singh Gat?"

"I told him about that place," said Majda, who stopped trying to read the letter and stared out into the courtyard. "It was a long time ago when I thought my life would take a different course."

Chapter 27

Emily was up early and was issuing orders to every servant to ensure that their bungalow was spotless, each hedge trimmed, and every blade of grass reduced to the requisite height. Robert was also up, and for once he and Emily were alone in the dining room eating breakfast and talking about a common interest – the arrival of Krishnamurti.

"I was five when I went to Ojai and stayed with K," said Robert. "I didn't like it there."

"Why ever not?" asked Emily.

"Because the people were mean."

"K and Nitya weren't mean to you, were they?" asked Emily, in a tone of voice which Robert always found slightly intimidating.

"Oh no, not them," said Robert, who looked at Emily. "They were always nice to me. But the folks in town didn't like us much. Some of the boys at the school called Mummy a squaw."

"But K is not that type of Indian," replied Emily.

"That's what Mummy told me to say but they shouted 'an injun's an injun' and that if I didn't lock my door at night I would be scalped."

"You should ignore those kinds of children," said Emily. "They're just uneducated."

Emily had not seen Krishnamurti for eighteen months since he had dissolved the Order of the Star in the East and turned his back on theosophy. He said that the Truth will not be discovered through a religion or sect – these are things which are a barrier to the Truth – but that each person must find their way to it.

160

"Individuals should," said Krishnamurti, "be free from all fears – from the fear of religion, from the fear of salvation, from the fear of spirituality, from the fear of love, from the fear of death, from the fear of life itself."

And so it was, with a few words, Krishnamurti drove a wedge between himself and the theosophists that had followed him as the next World Teacher for nearly twenty years. For Emily, the dissolution of the Order of the Star in the East touched something more primordial in her. When he was a young boy, she had looked after Krishnamurti as a mother and waited for him to say, "Follow me". If those words had been uttered, she would have given up everything: her home, her husband, and her children. She now felt bereft, having been told that her beliefs were misplaced.

In the year after Krishnamurti dissolved the Order, she refused to believe that it was over. She understood that Krishnamurti had been able to transcend personal love, but she could not. She thought that what he was saying was too abstract for most people who live in the real world with family responsibilities. She thought he was running away from real life, and she wrote to him telling him so. He wrote back saying that it was she who had to change her emphasis. She tore up his letter and decided to join her husband and family in India for the inauguration of New Delhi. It gave her the chance to take stock and when she heard that Krishnamurti was coming to New Delhi and wanted to see her, she assumed that he was going to say that he had made a mistake.

Krishnamurti was still handsome. He parted his dark hair in the middle which he swept back over his ears. There were, however, streaks of grey that ran through it, which gave him a sense of gravitas. His eyebrows were black and full, and he had a tendency, which some people thought was affected, to lower his head and look up with his deep brown eyes, often clasping his hands in front of him, as if he were about to pray. He smiled more often than he frowned and when he laughed it was an honest, deep, resonant laugh. With age came an assuredness that he had not had when he was younger.

"Look at you," said Krishnamurti, as he entered the Lutyenses' bungalow in New Delhi, "you've grown so tall." He stood for a moment looking at

Robert before opening his arms wide and hugging him. Mary, who had also not seen Krishnamurti for a few years, hoped that she would also get a hug. Emily could not stop her lips from pinching, as Krishnamurti all but ignored her. Krishnamurti kissed Mary on both cheeks, then Celia and turned to Emily.

"I've become old," he said, "but you do not look any different to me from the last time we met. Have you forgiven me, Mother?"

Emily hesitated a moment before she lied to him.

***

"I suppose you can say I'm free now," said Krishnamurti to Emily later that morning.

"You were always free," said Emily.

"No, I mean spiritually," responded Krishnamurti.

"So, do you think you have become the World Teacher?" asked Emily.

"Yes, in the pure sense but not in the traditional, accepted sense of the word. I won't be performing miracles, as that would be a betrayal of the Truth; but, if you listen carefully, you will hear the Truth in what I say."

"And what will you do now?" asked Emily. "Your philosophy that the Truth cannot be found in a religion or along any path is impossible for most people to understand. Most people need to be guided; you must see that."

"But there is no path, Emily. Everyone must achieve enlightenment by taking their own path because everyone is different. Anyone who tells you that you can achieve enlightenment by simply praying before an idol or reading a prayer book is a charlatan."

"Then don't be upset," said Emily, sternly, "if people don't understand you. How can a disciple follow you when you say there is no path? To be honest, I don't understand it myself."

"All I can do, all anyone can do, is give you the tools to find your way," said Krishnamurti. "I can talk to you about love and duty and the need to help your fellow man, but these are just tools like a compass that points you in a general direction."

"Let's not dwell on it," said Emily. "I don't want to be cross with you. I want to be happy because you are here, and I want this evening's party to be a success."

Out of the corner of his eye, Krishnamurti saw Robert by the door.

"Will you excuse me, Mother?" said Krishnamurti. "I think your grandson wants me." As he walked towards the young boy he could not help smiling. Robert had been five when last he had seen him in Ojai and now, he was almost thirteen.

"You'll be shaving soon," said Krishnamurti.

"I was so sorry to hear about Nitya," said Robert. "When Mummy heard she cried all day."

"Nitya would not have approved of anyone crying, although I have cried many tears for him and miss him every day," said Krishnamurti.

"It's nice to see you again," said Robert. "How long are you staying for?"

"Just a day or two," said Krishnamurti. "Where's your mother?"

"She's with Devjeet in the garden," said Robert. "She's always with him nowadays. She thinks he's the bees knees and is all hotsy-totsy around him."

"I'm not sure what that means," said Krishnamurti.

Chapter 28

Emily had decided that she needed a banqueting hall for her party, and her husband was duly tasked to arrange one. However, while Emily had visions of the Viceroy's House, which had been designed by her husband, this was neither possible nor realistic. The Imperial Hotel was newly opened for the inauguration of New Delhi. The restaurants were excellent, the service was impeccable, the gardens were spacious and with Italian marble floors and Burmese teak and rosewood furniture, it was considered superb. To obtain the largest reception room at the hotel, at short notice, Lutyens had to call in a multitude of favours and the cost of the evening was exorbitant. With pinched lips, Emily accepted the venue, noting to her husband that it fell far short of her expectations and was nothing more than second-best.

The guest list was a mixture of British and Indian dignitaries, as it was a party in honour of Krishnamurti's return to India. Despite his recent statements, Emily invited the leaders of the Theosophist Society in India, including Annie Besant, with the hope that they might change his mind. She also invited Herbert Baker and the leading public figures of New Delhi. There were then one or two people who knew Emily's father, Robert Bulwer-Lytton, when he had been viceroy in India. Finally, there were people whom she knew such as Devjeet Patel, who Emily could not ignore without offending. At the bottom of the list, she had written in hand the name of Laxman Choudhury. She had received a telegram from him saying he was coming to New Delhi after receiving a letter from Basil and wanted the opportunity to meet her and Celia. In total, there were just over one hundred and forty people who had been invited.

***

After two hours of handshaking, namaste and philosophical argument, Krishnamurti was exhausted and found a table in a corner of the garden where he could quietly sit for as long as he could. It took him a few moments before he realised that someone was already seated in the furthest corner hidden by the bushes. Krishnamurti looked at the young Indian man whom he did not know.

"I'm hiding," whispered Krishnamurti conspiratorially, "please don't tell anyone."

"But aren't you the guest of honour?"

"Yes," said Krishnamurti, "but even the guest of honour sometimes wants a minute's peace. I don't think we've met."

"I am Laxman Choudhury," said Laxman who raised his hands and put them together.

"A pleasure to meet you," said Krishnamurti, returning the gesture.

"I am a friend of Celia Drewe's husband, Basil, in case you were wondering."

"I have not yet had the fortune of meeting him."

Laxman picked up a cup of tea that he had placed on the table before him and sipped at it. "Would you mind if I asked you something?" he said. "Although this may, I'm afraid, sound a bit odd."

Krishnamurti peered at Laxman through the darkness. "Go on," he replied.

"How do you find Celia? I ask because her husband received news that she has been persistently unwell."

Krishnamurti thought for a second. "I only recently arrived in Delhi, but she seemed to me to be in excellent health."

"Yes," said Laxman, "I have only seen Mrs Drewe here, but I didn't get the impression of a woman who is enfeebled."

Robert came running up.

"Everyone's looking for you, K," he said, slightly breathlessly. "I was told I had to go and find you."

"Well, now you've found me," replied Krishnamurti, "you can sit down, and I will introduce you to Mr Laxman Choudhury. He knows your stepfather." Krishnamurti then formally introduced Laxman to Robert.

"How do you know Basil?" asked Robert.

Laxman smiled. "We were at university together."

"You went to Oxford?" said Robert, sceptically.

"Don't sound so surprised," replied Laxman. "There are quite a few Indians at Oxford. We were in the same halls."

"What was Basil like?" asked Robert.

"He was a good friend, who would stick beside you through thick and thin," said Laxman, who then turned to Krishnamurti. "May I ask you something about Indian independence? As a member of the Congress Party, I am interested in your views." Krishnamurti nodded. "Why have you never spoken about it?"

"My answer," said Krishnamurti, "is probably not something you will want to hear. However, if you aim to stop violence and live harmoniously with your neighbour, whatever race or religion, you must give up the absurd toys of nationalism, of organized religion, of following somebody politically or religiously. That is our problem in India. Everyone is a Hindu, Muslim, Christian or a Sikh. However, if you are earnest about unity then you must free yourself from infantile acts, from calling yourself by a particular label, whether national, political, or religious; and only then shall India have peace."

"You believe that?" answered Laxman. "If India simply gave up demanding its freedom, we would be under the British yoke for a thousand years."

"Your battle is to change their minds," said Krishnamurti, "and then, most importantly, not to replace one form of control with another. When you look at the world and what is happening you see we are on the brink of a precipice. Civilization, which man believes in, may be destroyed; the things which we have produced, tenderly cultivated – everything is now at stake. For man to save itself from the precipice, there must be a revolution of self-knowledge, not a bloody revolution."

"I hope you don't mind me saying this," said Laxman, "but that sounds like a dream world. In some ways, I envy you for that, but the British have ¹ ruled India for nearly one hundred years, and you might be surprised to know that India is now more illiterate today than it was fifty or a hundred years ago. There can never be a revolution of self-knowledge until we raise the quality of education of all Indians so that they can understand the concept of self-knowledge."

"There you are mistaken," answered Krishnamurti. "It will always be easier for the very poorest to make this journey because they have less to give up. The tricky thing is to convince those who are the wealthiest in society to give up their possessions and for them to understand that those things are meaningless."

Robert sat half-listening to the two men talk. Politics and philosophy bored him, but he did not want to go back to the party either. His mother was with Devjeet, and she was laughing at almost anything he said. He wanted to go back to England where he now had friends at school. He wanted to go back and be with Basil and go to Castle Drogo in the holidays with Sir Julius and Lady Frances. He understood that they had left England because Celia needed a restful holiday, but she seemed perfectly well now.

It made Robert jump when he heard his mother's voice behind him.

"I've found you," Celia said. However, as Robert turned, he realised that she was not talking to him but to Krishnamurti. He could just see Devjeet walking back to the party in all his finery, and he smiled to himself that at least his mother would not make an idiot of herself in front of K.

"I was not hiding," replied Krishnamurti, "or at least I was not hiding very well as I seem to have been found by everyone." He winked towards Robert. "And I also could not ignore one of our most important guests."

Celia looked at the man in the corner with his short black hair and plain blue sherwani. She did not recognise him from any of the events she had been to in the last few weeks. He stood up and extended his hand towards her and introduced himself.

"Laxman," she repeated. "Sorry, I know the name but I'm afraid I can't place you."

"He's a friend of Basil's," said Robert, "from Oxford."

"I received a letter from your husband," said Laxman, "telling me you were in India, and I took the liberty of contacting your mother to introduce myself and she kindly sent me an invitation for this evening."

"Yes, of course," said Celia, who looked over her shoulder. Devjeet was not there, and she felt relieved. "I remember that you sent an interesting vase as a wedding present."

"It was made by a blind potter in our village," said Laxman. "I hoped Basil and you would like it, and that you might tell Christian."

"Christian?" said Celia. "Sorry, I don't understand?"

"Of course, you wouldn't," said Laxman, blushing slightly. "When I was at university, your husband kindly invited me to Wadhurst Hall one Christmas where I met Christian. I suggested that Christian try pottery and told him about a blind potter from my village. Basil thought it was such a clever idea that he arranged for a potter's wheel and clay, and we spent a week or two that winter in a freezing room making pots. To be honest we were awful at it except Christian who seemed to have a natural ability. And how are you enjoying India?"

"It's just about perfect," said Celia and placed her hands on Robert's shoulders. "We are having the most wonderful time."

Robert looked up at her and thought for a moment about contradicting her, but then thought better of it.

"I am pleased," said Laxman, "as it is the most captivating country, although Krishnamurti and I would likely argue all night about what the most beautiful area is."

"It is where our hearts are," said Krishnamurti, "and my heart will always be in southern India."

"And mine in the north," said Laxman, laughing.

"And mine is here," said Celia.

"Not in England?" asked Krishnamurti.

Celia did not respond and then blushed because she could not think of what to say.

"I suppose I should get back to the party," said Krishnamurti, who started standing up. "Unfortunately, I am not able to spend longer here as I must go on to Adyar soon."

"And I must meet with the Congress Party tomorrow," said Laxman.

Chapter 29

The Yogmaya Temple had been rebuilt in the early nineteenth century, but a temple had stood in the same spot long before Christ was born. The beautiful hard white stucco front of the temple had the images of numerous gods and goddesses carved into it. In the sanctum of the temple was a statue of Yogmaya, made of black stone and placed in a marble well.

By the time Celia arrived at the sanctum, she simply did not care who Yogmaya was or her relationship to Shiva or any of the thousands of other deities that Hinduism seemed to possess. Robert was out of sorts, but then he had been irritable for the last few weeks. However, Emily was fascinated and wanted to find out about each god or when a part of the temple had been destroyed and rebuilt. Celia wished everyone but Devjeet would disappear so that she could be alone with him. She felt ecstatic when she was with him and, when he was not there, sadder than she could ever recall.

As Devjeet led them through another sacred corridor, Celia looked at her watch. Only an hour or two more and they would make their way back to their villa for lunch and then, she thought, this banality could turn into joy. Robert would have lessons and her mother would go to her room to meditate. Mary and her father would go exploring the city and she would claim to have another migraine.

"You seem to be in another world," said Mary.

"I am just finding it so humid in here," said Celia. "I feel that one of my headaches is coming on."

"Don't let on," said Mary, "because it's supposed to be a surprise, but

Mother is arranging for us to go to Assam for a few months as the weather here gets warmer."

Celia stopped and gasped and then bent over double trying to catch her breath.

"Mother," shouted Mary, "Celia's unwell."

Her mother, father, sister, and Robert surrounded Celia, all trying to give her advice. However, all Celia could do was look around for him. Her head was swimming, but she could not see him anywhere and then he came into focus, coming back through the entrance door of the temple.

"The carriages are being brought around," Devjeet said. "We should get her home as soon as possible."

Celia could hardly tell how she got back to her room. Her sister helped her into bed, closed the blinds to the veranda and told her she must sleep. Mary sat reading until Emily came in later that afternoon and told her that she would take over. Once her sister had left, Celia sat up in bed.

"There's no need for you to stay, I'm quite all right."

"You nearly fainted."

"It was so hot," said Celia.

"Before I go, I need to ask you something," said Emily.

"What?"

"Are you pregnant?"

"No," said Celia as forcefully as she could. "What on earth would make you think that?"

"You look at him in the same way as you used to look at Robert's father."

"I've never told you who Robert's father is."

Emily took a deep breath. "You act as if I'm stupid. I've always known who Robert's father was. The way that you used to moon about after him. My only regret was going to America and letting you slip from under my wing."

"It could have been anyone," said Celia. However, she knew her mother would not believe that, and she did not either. However, she wasn't prepared to admit that Robert's father was Adrian. If she did, then she feared the comfortable and secure life that she had built for Robert and herself would start crumbling away. She didn't know what Basil would do if he found out and that uncertainty worried her. If the boot were on the other foot, she would not be able to forgive him.

"It was never going to be anyone," said Emily. "You were never a girl who would sleep with just anyone. It had to be the one. That's why I had reservations about your marriage to Basil."

"What do you mean by that?"

"You look at your husband," said Emily, "and hope he will turn into his brother and then you're resentful when he doesn't. I told you that you must play the perfect wife and you're here acting like a fool."

"At least I'm happy here," rasped Celia. "Basil's thousands of miles away and he'll never know. It was he who suggested I come to India, and it was you who introduced Devjeet to me. None of this was my idea, so, just let me stay here."

"That, I won't do. We're going to Assam and that's an end to the matter," said Emily. "And you can wipe those tears from your eyes."

***

Celia only ever saw Devjeet again on two occasions in those final days in Delhi, when circumstances could not prevent them from meeting. It may have been that Devjeet's father had received news about the affair and ensured that the devil would no longer find work for idle hands. Perhaps Devjeet himself realised that the affair had run its course and that a clean break was the only prudent course. Celia never found out why he did not contact her again and when she boarded the train to leave Delhi, he was not there to say goodbye.

"What are we going to do in Assam?" asked Robert as they settled themselves in the carriage.

"I don't know," said Celia, and glared at her mother. "Ask your grand-mother. She's arranged this trip."

However, Robert chose to avoid asking his grandmother, who, lately, was often irascible. He was pleased that they were leaving Delhi but wanted to go home. He had had enough of India. He had no one to play with – no friends, no one to talk to. He decided to ask his grandfather for a story.

172

"A story?" said Lutyens. "That's rather putting me on the spot." However, Lutyens sat back in the seat of the train and looked up at the luggage rack thinking about what story to tell and then smiled.

"Once upon a time, there was a herd of deer that used to live near a village. The deer knew that they had to be careful when they came to the village, especially at harvest time when the crops were tall because the farmers would kill them, fearing that they would eat their crops. At these times the herd of deer would only come to the village at night. One of these deer was a beautiful young doe. She had soft reddish fur, a fluffy white tail and big wide bright eyes.

"One year a young mountain buck strayed into the forest near the village and saw the beautiful young doe. Immediately the buck became infatuated with her. He knew nothing about her or her life but imagined himself deeply in love with her because of her reddish fur and her fluffy white tail and big wide bright eyes. The young buck therefore decided to introduce himself and stood before her entranced by her appearance. He wooed her with beautiful love poetry. The doe smiled, flattered by the attention. From then on, the young buck followed the doe wherever she went. He kept telling her how beautiful she was and how much he loved her.

"When night came the herd decided to go to the village. They did not know that a hunter waited for them, hiding behind a bush. Carefully, the doe walked along the path watching for any hidden danger. The mountain buck, who was still singing her praises, went along beside her. She stopped and said to him, 'My dear buck, you are not experienced, and you do not know how dangerous human beings are, you should not come with me but remain in the safety of the forest.' The young buck paid no attention to the doe's warning. He just said, 'Your eyes look so lovely in the moonlight! Your smile dazzles and confounds my eyes,' and continued to walk beside her. She said, 'If you won't listen to me, at least be quiet!' He was, however, so infatuated with her, that he did not listen. After a while, they approached the place where the hunter was hiding behind a bush. The doe could sense danger and, fearing a trap, she let the buck walk ahead. When the hunter saw the buck, he shot his arrow and killed him instantly. Seeing this, the terrified doe turned tail and ran back to the forest as fast as she could. The hunter claimed his kill and took the deer home to feed his family. When the doe recounted her story, an old wise deer with long antlers said 'It was the excitement of infatuation that killed this buck. Such blind desire brings false happiness at first but ends in pain and suffering.'"

"I hope you have some better stories," said Celia to her father. "It's a long journey to Assam and I didn't care for that one at all."

"We'll be taking it in stages," said Emily. "We'll spend a week in Agra and then a few days in Lucknow before going on to Patna. I haven't decided yet whether we should go to Kathmandu."

"Why on earth would we want to go to Kathmandu?" said Celia.

"To see the temples, and also we could go to the Himalayas."

"Haven't you seen enough temples to last you a lifetime?" said Celia. "I'm tempted to carry on with the train to Calcutta and take the boat home."

However, despite what she said, she had no intention of taking the boat home. Devjeet would be aware that they were going to Assam, and she felt he would follow them there.

Chapter 30

April 1931

Assam felt like another country – green, verdant, and quiet with clean waters. They arrived at the city of Tezpur and were exhausted. Celia's mood had darkened and Lutyens could not revive the spirits of Robert with a story.

"Where are we staying?" said Celia as she got off the train and then helped Robert.

"At a tea plantation a few miles away from here," said Emily.

"What on earth made you choose a tea plantation?"

"Basil arranged it," responded Emily, "after I wired him."

"You wired Basil!" said Celia. "What possessed you to do that?"

"I did it weeks ago when you first started having your headaches. I thought one of us should tell him what was happening, and he suggested that the clearer air at Assam might be a perfect antidote. He sent me a letter by airmail with details of the plantation that he had arranged."

"And how do we get there?" asked Celia.

The four tongas clip-clopped along the street in a procession that made people turn their heads. Two of the tongas were filled with their luggage. When they left the outskirts of the town, and the horses' hooves no longer made a sound on the dirt track, the tonga-wallahs started singing: 'A hundred skies and both the worlds… I've come to you leaving them behind.' By the time the tonga-wallahs came to the third chorus, Robert started humming along. He stopped as he saw a temple ahead and sighed loudly thinking that his grandmother would again drag them around another shrine. However, the tongas rolled past and took them towards the river and to an area that the tonga-wallahs called Devi Singh Ghat.

The estate at Devi Singh Ghat extended down to the Brahmaputra River and in the evening a red setting sun would reflect off the clear blue waters, setting the world alight in a beautiful flamingo pink. Fishermen in long, thin boats would take to the river in the early mornings to fish for carp. They would cast their nets out into the water and pull them slowly back hoping that a few fish had come up to feed in the morning light. By late morning the fishermen would bring their boats to the shore and, around a campfire, eat some of their spoils. They would tell stories or sing folk songs from faraway places, as many races had been brought to the area by the British over time to pick tea.

***

Two weeks after they arrived at Assam, Lutyens returned to Delhi and Emily and Mary decided to leave for Calcutta and take a boat back home to England. Celia was asked whether she wanted to stay in Assam or return with her mother and Mary. She said she wanted to stay. She thought that once they had gone, she could write to Devjeet and could then return to Delhi, or he could come to Assam. Robert settled into his new surroundings and was busy with a tutor preparing for his examinations for public school. After lessons and at weekends, he would cycle into town and play cricket or football with children from the town or tea plantations. When there weren't enough children to make up a team, they would play tag or statues. When he was on his own, he would go to the lake and skim stones or swim in the cool, clear waters.

"Do you like it here?" Celia asked Robert one evening, as they sat down to a feast prepared by their cook. Robert nodded, more interested in putting a spoonful of rich, spicy dahl into his mouth than talking to his mother.

"And are you missing home?"

Robert shrugged and then stretched out his fingers to take an onion bhaji.

"And what about your friends?" said Celia. "You have whined ceaselessly about how you missed them."

Robert swallowed the mouthful of food. He realised that he was not going to get away with simply nodding or shaking his head and that he would have to be a fraction more articulate.

"Yes, I miss them but I'm also making friends here."

"Here?" said Celia. "Who do you know here?"

"The boys that play cricket at the cricket pitch in town and then sometimes we go to Padham Pukhuri." Celia looked blankly at her son. "It's the island park," continued Robert, "and you get to it from the wooden footbridge in town. In English, they call it the lotus pond."

"Oh yes," said Celia. "I did hear someone mention it, but I've not been there."

"What do you do all day?" said Robert; and with those words he thought the conversation concluded and stretched out his fingers for another bhaji.

***

Celia's letter to Devjeet was returned unopened, with a note from Devjeet's father which was short and courteous. It advised her that Devjeet had to go abroad on matters that pertained to the family business and that he was not expected to return for some months, if not longer. The letter also said that his son would thereafter be entering into a marriage, which had been arranged since his birth, with the daughter of another family of similar standing.

Celia lit a match, set fire to the letter and tossed it into the grate in the living room. She then burst into tears and shouted at everyone, including Robert, to leave her alone. That afternoon she sat in the living room in her slip and dressing gown not caring about anything in the world. She was angry with Devjeet for not standing up to his family and angry with herself for being such a fool. More than anyone, she was angry with her mother who had proven again to be correct. She looked out of the window where the sun was setting and could see a lone fisherman standing in his narrowboat on the river, casting out his nets in the hope of making a catch. In the gathering gloom, she decided at once that she would stay on in Assam for just a little longer and think about nothing at all, and certainly nothing about men.

***

On the first weekend in June, Celia, for the first time, walked across the wooden bridge to Padham Pukhuri. The bridge was charming if somewhat dilapidated. The island itself was not large and was covered by a multitude of trees; some a vivid green and some of a burnt red that reminded her of Chinese maples. There were areas scattered around the island that had been lawned to provide picnic spots for families. An estate worker brought picnic blankets, cushions and a hamper of food, which could have almost fed the town.

"No chairs?" asked Celia.

"No chairs," said Robert, "we're going to picnic like my friends do."

There was no shortage of children on the island and as Robert kept playing, she found she could relax with a book. When the exhausted children had finished their games, they threw themselves onto the rugs and cushions and Robert offered them their food, which was quickly devoured. At some point in the afternoon, one mother brought over a tiffin box of carrot halwa and offered a piece to Celia. More women came with different desserts and by the late afternoon, Celia had tried rasgulla, kaju katli and kalakand. As the sun started dropping towards the line of the horizon and the earth took on the hue of the darkest azure, they started packing up their things. Celia looked out across the lake where lotus flowers sat on the water, showing off their perfectly pink flowers, and it reminded her of a painting by Monet or some other impressionist who captured the beauty of the world in dabs of perfect colour.

***

The tea plantation, owned by the Clarke family, was less than three miles from Devi Singh Ghat. Celia decided to borrow Robert's bicycle and cycle the few miles. As she entered the tea plantation she could see on different levelled plateaus the tea plants. Celia stopped and looked down, watching as the Tea Tribes picked the delicate leaves. She cycled past the factory that dried and shredded the tea until she arrived at the plantation house. Twice a week, as regular as clockwork, the English, American and European women who lived on the tea estates would meet at one house or another to ensure that everything in their world was proceeding without hiccup or incumbrance.

"Was that you on the bicycle, Mrs Drewe?" asked Mrs Clarke, knowing full well the answer. "If you ever have a problem, my dear, please tell us and we can send a car."

"I thought it would be enjoyable to cycle," said Celia. A few of the women at the table smiled as Celia said this; however, Mrs Clarke and another lady with equally white hair looked on; neither showing approval or disapproval.

"One must be so careful in this climate, my dear. You have such delicate skin, and it is so easy in this sun to begin to look like a native within a week or two." Mrs Clarke called over one of the servants and sent him off hurriedly to find Celia a parasol.

The afternoon was run with all the efficiency of a Rotary Club meeting. Mrs Clarke and the other white-haired lady considered themselves the appointed leaders of the group, based on age and length of residence in Assam. They were resented by many of the middle-aged women who were wealthier. When tea and sandwiches were brought at three-thirty p.m. and the discussions regarding bridge, whist and solo evenings had been completed, the group of ladies began their usual complaints. This might involve some pointed remarks about India's desire for self-government, or that the utility companies were on strike, or that there was so little food of any decent quality in the shops. The women, including Mrs Clarke, treated Celia with deference, as the daughter-in-law of Sir Julius Drewe, and were keenly aware that their lives of luxury were due, in no small part, to the fact that the Home and Colonial Stores in England sold their tea. Therefore, when Celia said that she had been enjoying picnics on the weekends at Padham Pukhuri, Mrs Clarke did not immediately criticise her.

"You will no doubt soon be receiving invitations from the more well-to-do Indians of the area," said Mrs Clarke to Celia. "One has always to be careful about this." Celia asked why and Mrs Clarke replied, "They do try to impress, and they end up spending a fortune on a folly that they simply cannot afford and then you feel obliged to reciprocate." Celia smiled and said she would take note. She then turned and started talking to an American woman, who had an estate twenty miles from Tezpur. She had once lived in New York, and they shared common ground from Celia's time there.

"I don't always agree with Mrs Clarke," whispered the American, "but on this matter she is talking sense. However, if you are in Tezpur and bump into Dr Choudhury, it is worth taking the time to say hello."

"Dr Choudhury, I don't know him," said Celia.

"Dr Choudhury is female, and, in India, she's the exception that proves the rule."

Chapter 31

June 1931

Dr Majda Choudhury was in her early thirties with long, thick dark black hair, which she mostly tied in a bun above her head. Except for a little lipstick that she would wear on social occasions, she wore no make-up. She favoured traditional Indian clothes and wore a sari with a headscarf. Her face was thin, and she was lean and toned. From long years of reading, she was now forced to wear spectacles and chose a pair of thick, black-rimmed glasses. She did not have a classically attractive face, but there was something in her character that made people look at her twice, and it was her determination to get things done that made most people who met her, respect her.

She had been educated at the London School of Medicine for Women in 1922, as, a few years before, the India Office had opened a hostel for Indian women who wanted to be medical students. She stayed in London for the next three years completing her studies. When she returned to India, she started a small school and clinic near her home in Tezpur and devoted the next years to helping the underprivileged and ill-nourished children of the area. It was not a lucrative calling for Majda Choudhury, and to the despair of both her mother and her father, she remained unmarried. However, she woke each morning with eagerness and purpose.

Celia and Majda met by accident. It was a rainy day in June and Robert was standing under a tamarind tree, trying to shelter from a torrential downpour with two other boys, including Amin Choudhury, Majda's nephew. They had been standing there for the best part of an hour, with their bikes lying on the grass. Robert had missed lunch, which was unusual for him, and so Celia asked that the tonga be readied. Similarly, when Amin failed to arrive home, Majda was asked by her youngest brother to drive to the playing fields in her car to get him. Celia arrived to find Amin being scolded by his aunt, who stood with her feet planted wide apart under a large umbrella. Celia got down from her tonga, put up her umbrella and walked over.

"I'll deal with you later," she said to Robert. "Put your bicycle on the back of the tonga and let's get home."

"I assume you're Mrs Drewe," said Majda, who turned and held out her hand as she introduced herself. "You're staying at Devi Singh Ghat." She said it as a statement of fact and not a question. "And you used to be a nurse."

Celia complimented Majda on her English, and Majda explained she had done some of her medical training in London, and they briefly spoke about the places they had both visited.

"Do drop around," said Celia, after she said goodbye. "You know where I am."

***

At eight-thirty the next morning Majda was standing at Celia's front door at Devi Singh Ghat. When Celia came to the door, she was still in her dressing gown.

"Ah, Dr Choudhury, I didn't expect you."

"I thought you might like a day out in the country," said Majda. "Well, actually, it's less like a day out and more like the beginning of an adventure."

Celia looked at Majda somewhat perplexed. No one came around unannounced or suggested 'an adventure', however Celia was intrigued.

"Fine," she said, after a pause. "It will take me a few moments to get dressed if you don't mind waiting in the living room?"

"Do you drive?" asked Majda, as she walked through the door.

"Not really. My husband tried to teach me, but I just didn't have the knack."

"He was probably a bad teacher," said Majda. "Men usually are. You can practise on the way."

The living room contained numerous chairs and sofas, set around a large coffee table so that one could look out across the grounds and down to the river. A dark wooden cabinet stood in one corner, unadorned by either a photograph or a memento. A drinks cabinet, in the same dark wood, was nearby as well as a bookcase and a sideboard. Majda looked at the books and noted an edition of poems by Federico García Lorca and took it off the shelf. The Spanish poems had been translated and she made a note to ask to borrow them. She looked at Celia when she entered the room. The morning sun flooded through the window and set off the colour of Celia's auburn hair, which hung loosely on her shoulders. Celia smiled, sensing she was being watched and she looked back at Majda.

"Where are we going?" asked Celia.

"To my school and clinic in the country," said Majda.

Celia noted an immobility in her expression, which slightly worried her.

"And why do you want me to come?" asked Celia.

Majda looked at her a little more keenly, as if considering whether she had made a mistake in coming. However, having decided that she had done the right thing she answered, "To meet the children. Shall we go?" She added no more clarification as to who these children were; and, on the journey to the highlands, the mystery fascinated Celia.

***

The Nagaon clinic, with its corrugated tin roof, small leaded window-panes, and big blue shutters stood near the Morikalong River. When it rained there was a constant thud, thud, thud on the roof which would irritate the nerves in no time whatsoever. Celia was told there was little to do or see in Nagaon, except for a few weeks each year when the orchids bloomed. However, away from the town there were lakes, caves, and valleys and not too far away, in the state of Meghalaya, there were beautiful waterfalls and bridges made from the living roots of the trees.

"And one hundred thousand butterflies," continued Majda, "each beating their wings and creating chaos. I think that Meghalaya is the most perfect place in the world. A place to visit and fall in love."

As they drove into the courtyard of the clinic, Celia looked at the run-down building with the main door, hanging from its hinges, and wondered why on earth she was there. The children, some half-baked in dirt but smiling and laughing and running and playing, filled the playground. Celia tried to count them but, as they continued playing their games, she lost track of the numbers and guessed that there were more than forty. Majda explained that the children were split into classes by sex and age. There was also a dining room and an infirmary for sick children.

"While we call it a clinic," Majda said proudly, "it is more of a place where we can feed the children and give them some basic schooling. Most of the problems that we see here are caused by malnutrition."

"Aren't the children fed on the tea estates?" asked Celia.

"These children," said Majda, "don't live on the estates. Most of their parents work in the paddy fields and object that their children aren't working with them."

"Why?" asked Celia.

"Because they need the money to feed their families. They are, however, required by law to go to school, even if there is not enough money to buy them schoolbooks."

As they walked into the school building, Majda greeted each of the children by name and introduced some of them to Celia. Celia looked at them and half attempted a smile.

"The reason I asked you to come is that I must go to Delhi and apply for funding from the British government, otherwise we might have to close. I need someone to look after the clinic while I'm away."

"I can't do that," said Celia, "I've not been trained."

"Of course you can," replied Majda. "You've worked as a nurse in England and the United States. You have more than enough common sense to manage the day-to-day affairs here. I'll be gone for no more than a week, and I wouldn't ask if it wasn't important. If I close the clinic the children will end up working again in the fields and I'll never get them back."

"And how do I get here, each day?" asked Celia.

"You can borrow my car," answered Majda. "I'm not going for another two weeks so we can practise driving here each day."

"And how did you know that I once worked as a nurse in England and the United States?" said Celia, as they entered Majda's office.

"Your husband told me."

"What do you mean, my husband told you?"

"I knew him when I was in England," said Majda. "When I went there to study to be a doctor. I telephoned him when I heard you were coming here. You do know I am Laxman's sister. Didn't he tell you when he saw you in Delhi?"

"We barely said three words to each other," responded Celia. "He said that he had been Basil's friend at university, that he was sorry that he could not come to the wedding and that he wanted to meet me and pay his respects."

"Men!" said Majda.

"Indeed," responded Celia.

"I first met Basil in September 1922," began Majda, "while studying medicine in London. Laxman asked Basil if he wouldn't mind keeping an eye on me while I was there. You know how older brothers are?" Majda looked at Celia, and Celia nodded. "Basil was working as a barrister at Inner Temple and my hospital was just across Waterloo Bridge. We were only a few minutes away from each other."

"How very cosy," said Celia, "although, he's never mentioned you."

"Why would he?" answered Majda. "I returned to Assam in the autumn of 1925, as we both wanted very different things from life." Majda again looked at Celia. "How is he?"

"Basil?"

"Yes, Basil," said Majda, more tersely than she had intended.

"Unchanged," replied Celia. She decided she didn't want to talk about her husband to someone she considered a stranger, and, sitting in Majda's office, she felt at a disadvantage.

"Is he still obsessed with cricket?" asked Majda.

"That's a slight understatement," replied Celia.

"He took me to a Test match at Lord's," continued Majda. "I was excited but all I remember was how cold and damp it was."

"I've never seen the attraction of cricket," said Celia. "Nothing happens for hours on end. It's the epitome of boredom."

"Then you've never hit a ball for six," said Majda. "And how about his leg? Is it any better?"

"No," said Celia, again feeling that the questions were becoming too personal.

"And does he still use that foul-smelling liniment?"

"He does," said Celia.

"Have you tried massaging his leg?"

"Why?"

"In India, we use massage as part of our healing techniques in Ayurvedic medicine. We might place a bag of herb-infused rice onto the skin to relieve sore muscles. I can tell you it smells a lot better than that liniment he got from that horse doctor."

"He tries not to use the liniment when I'm there," said Celia. "He knows I don't like the smell."

Once again Majda studied Celia. "You do know how much pain he's in when he doesn't use it? It's like the worst cramp you've ever had, and he walks around with that pain until he sits down and rests his leg."

"It's not nearly that bad," said Celia. "We have a car, and he drives to wherever he wants to go. Our lives are very different from when you knew him, Majda. We're very happy," she said; however, as she spoke she knew none of it was true.

***

The sun was lowering in the sky when they arrived back at Tezpur. Although Celia had done little, she felt she had a purpose – something she had not felt since she had finished her degree. She was unsure whether she wanted to return the next day but agreed and asked Majda if she could work with the younger children.

"Before you go," said Majda, as the car pulled into the estate of Devi Singh Ghat, "can I ask you something?"

"Yes," said Celia.

"You knew Basil's two brothers, Adrian and Christian. What were they

186

like?"

"Why do you ask?" Once again, Celia felt that her questions were far too personal.

"I'm just interested. Basil always idolised them. I don't mean to pry and if you prefer not to say anything I would quite understand." Celia smiled and paused. She was about to say she would prefer not to discuss them, but then she remembered Adrian in his uniform on the last occasion she saw him. She hadn't thought about him for months.

"Christian was an artist," said Celia, and she smiled as she recalled those beautiful sketches he had drawn of the gardens of Munstead Wood where Gertrude Jekyll lived. "Many people thought he was exceptionally talented, as he was one of the youngest students at the Slade in London and then went to Gustav Klimt's studio in Vienna. Everyone loved Adrian. It was impossible not to love him. He made you feel special. He just had this joy for life. When Basil broke his leg, it was Adrian who slid down the escarpment to get to Basil first and then carried him a mile and put him in a car to take him to hospital. When a barn was on fire and a horse was trapped inside, he ran into the building and dragged an unconscious man from the blaze. In the war, his men adored him and would follow him anywhere and he died giving his life to save another person."

"And Basil?" asked Majda.

"He's stoic, reserved and probably the most honest person I've ever known." Celia looked over at Majda. "Most of the time you have no idea what he's thinking, and I sometimes think he loves his job more than Robert, the twins or me."

"He was the same when I knew him. I believe he wanted to make his father proud of him," began Majda. "However, I know this; if you were in trouble, he is the one person in the world you would want standing next to you."

"And can I ask you a question?" said Celia in return.

"If I can answer it, I will," replied Majda.

"Have you ever been in love?"

"Once," said Majda, looking at the lake behind the house. "Unfortunately, he didn't love me back, and so there was no point going on."

"Can I ask you who…"

However, Majda cut her short. "I need to get home," she said quickly. "I'll see you tomorrow at the same time." Celia smiled to herself. She could guess who it was, and it was good to have at least one stone in your back pocket that could kill two birds.

Celia got out of the car and Majda slid over to the driving seat. She watched as Celia went inside and let out a long, deep breath. She then put the car in gear, turned it around and drove out of the driveway.

Celia could hear Robert in the kitchen talking to the cook as she walked in. He was probably asking again for his favourite dessert of doughnuts swimming in syrup. She stood at the kitchen door listening to them. Robert seemed to have fallen in love with Assam. He had changed so much since they left Delhi, where he had often been sullen and petulant. She suddenly thought about her twins in England and her stomach knotted. It would soon be time to go home, and she did not know what she felt about it. And then there was Basil, and she wondered how she could make their lives work.

Celia and Majda drove each morning for the next two weeks to Nagaon and when Majda went to Delhi, Celia went on her own. Except for a few minor ailments, such as coughs and colds and a grazed knee, there was no need for Celia to apply her knowledge as a nurse. She arranged for an old piano to be brought to the clinic and would play hymns for the children to learn – the favourite being 'All Things Bright and Beautiful'. As she got to know the children, she might pick one up who had fallen over and hug them, especially the little girls with their beautiful deep brown eyes and long lustrous black hair.

When the monsoons came, Celia started planning her return to England. Any thought of returning to Delhi had long since evaporated. Having passed his exams, Robert had been enrolled to start his first term at Eton, and she decided to leave for Calcutta towards the end of August and then have a three-week sail home. She contacted Basil to see if he wanted to meet them somewhere on their journey. She received a telegram in response saying that Sir Julius was again unwell, and he suggested that she might want to return sooner rather than later.

***

Celia's final day at the clinic started with an assembly where 'All Things Bright and Beautiful' was played on the piano and the whole school sang the words, or a variation of them. Celia knew that she would miss being there and when the children, in an orderly line, filed out at the end of the day – each one saying, "Thank you and goodbye Miss Drewe" – she allowed herself a smile. Majda was in the infirmary dealing with a small girl who had scraped her knee and Celia went to find her. She entered to see a five-year-old girl trying not to cry as Majda applied iodine to a graze.

"How brave you are," said Celia to the girl who smiled in response.

"Can I ask you something?" said Majda, as she put the stopper on the iodine bottle and put it back in a cabinet.

"Would it matter if I said 'no'?" replied Celia, keenly aware that Majda's questions tended often to be personal in nature.

"Probably not. Indians can be terribly familiar sometimes," continued Majda, "almost to the point of rudeness. It's a bit like the way you English understate everything." Majda threw away the iodine-soaked ball of cotton wool and washed her hands. "Run along," she said to the child who jumped up and ran out. "What I wanted to ask you is, why are you here? Why did you leave your babies and your husband and come to India?"

"It's none of your business," Celia said matter-of-factly.

"I know," said Majda, "but you've been coming here for the last six weeks. You love working with the children, but you're also scared of them or at least scared of something. I don't understand what could have happened, what could make you leave your children at home? If it would help, speak to me as if I am your doctor rather than your friend."

"Are we friends?" asked Celia.

"I would like to think we have become friends."

Celia took a deep breath. "I suppose," she began, "that it started when the twins were born. I couldn't feed them, so we hired a wet nurse to look after them and they just seemed happier with her than me. I felt that they

189

didn't love me, and it began to frighten me that one day they could hate me and look at me with dark, hollow eyes that have no feeling."

"What do you mean?" said Majda.

"I'm just being silly," said Celia. "It was something that happened years ago."

Majda sat down and looked at her.

"You're not being silly at all," said Majda. "Just tell me about it in your own time."

"There was a boy called Deke Hamilton." Celia stopped and looked at Majda. "Do you know, I've not talked about this for years? I just wanted to forget about it."

"What about the boy?" asked Majda.

"I killed him," said Celia. "I shot him."

Celia stood still. She did not know what to say next or what to look at. She swallowed and choked back her tears and then with the back of her hand rubbed the bottom of her nose. Slowly and in an unsteady voice she told Majda about Robert's party and how they took the wagon back towards the Pepper Tree Retreat; how Deke and his brother had pulled her down from the wagon and how Manuel had arrived in his truck and how she had shot the boy.

"When the twins were born, I could not stop thinking about him, that boy Deke, and when I failed to bond with my children, I thought that God was teaching me a lesson. I know it sounds ridiculous, but I saw so much pain in that boy's eyes and I thought that God would want to punish me if I were so happy."

"Why did you think that?" said Majda.

"Because I had two beautiful, perfect babies and it seemed so unfair that I should have that when I had killed someone else's child. It wasn't right that I should be happy, and I know it's all nonsense, the rational part of my brain told me it was nonsense, but that was how I felt."

"So, it's guilt that you're feeling?"

Again, Celia did not answer immediately and stood staring at the white plastered wall that was crumbling.

"Not just guilt – not just that. I also feel frightened. Frighted that if I love my children too much then something bad will happen to them. I was brought up to believe that there is a balance to everything, that the tallest building has the deepest foundations and I thought that if I loved my babies too much then something bad would happen to them." Celia sat down on the side of the desk. She looked out of the dusty window to the empty playground.

"I once asked Manuel... he was the one who rescued me... to find out about the Hamilton boys. He knew their housekeeper – a Mexican woman called Juana. She used to look after the children until their father got home from the saloon but often, he would turn up drunk and try and... well you know. He used to come home and say 'Who wanna have some fun?' He thought it was amusing – a play on words with her name – and then one night he took things further and young Deke came out and tried to stop him and his father just leathered him with his belt. Juana used to say that the only reason that the other two children weren't beaten black and blue was because Deke used to stand up for them against his father. Juana told Manuel that she guessed that Deke got a leathering most days for the best part of five years since their mother died and that's what made him mean and bitter."

"And how did that make you feel?"

"Wretched," said Celia. "I felt that it wasn't his fault, but I know that if I were in the same position tomorrow, I'd do the same thing again." Celia paused. She continued looking at the empty playground which had been filled with children thirty minutes earlier.

"And what did Basil say when you told him about this?"

"Basil?" said Celia. "I haven't told him. When we got engaged, he promised he would never pry into my past unless I wanted to talk about it, and I have never wanted to. He gave me and Robert everything we wanted for our futures – comfort, security and a home."

"Is that honestly everything you wanted?" asked Majda.

"At the time, yes," said Celia, who turned to look at Majda. She heard in her voice a disapproving tone. "Basil worships me. He always has."

191

"It's the problem with men," said Majda. "They have a habit of putting you on a pedestal, but so few of them have the strength to put you back up there when you fall off."

They sat quietly for a few moments, Celia not knowing what else to say and Majda digesting what she had heard.

Chapter 32

September 1931

Sir Julius Drewe's name still carried enough weight to open doors, and, for Robert, the door that opened was to Eton. Sir Julius had first considered Eton as a possible school for Robert after Basil's engagement to Celia. Basil and Celia were unsure, but an Eton education was not something to be turned down, especially when Sir Julius agreed that he would take care of the fees. Celia and Basil agreed that Robert should try it and, if he did not like it, they would remove him and have him schooled at a day school near their apartment in Cadogan Square.

As Basil walked over the bridge that separated Windsor from Eton, he read out loud little titbits of information about the town, which was of no interest to either Robert or Celia. Behind them, the nanny brought the twins, who were more interested in the swans than their parents.

"Eton was founded by King Henry VI," said Basil, "who wanted to give free education to seventy poor boys. The other boys paid for their education, and they were called the Oppidans, which comes from the Latin meaning town."

Celia and Robert looked over the side of the bridge at the swans as they paddled downriver.

Basil turned the page and continued, "Henry VI also gave a right to swans on the Thames."

Robert looked at Basil and asked, "What is a right to swans?"

"I've no idea," said Basil. "I suppose it means you can eat them."

Robert screwed up his face. "Do you think they'll make gulab jamun for dinner here?"

Basil laughed. "I'm afraid not, but I do know a lady in Oxford who can make it."

"I didn't know you liked Indian food?" said Celia.

"I used to go," said Basil, "to a guesthouse on Botley Road with my friend Laxman and some other Indians and we would eat Indian food. That was during my first year at Oxford."

"You've never told me that," said Celia. "You mentioned Laxman a few times and I met him briefly in Delhi."

They had walked the hundred yards or so to the college entrance. Basil looked at his stepson in his tailcoat, striped trousers and top hat and thought that he looked at home in Eton. He knew, however, that as soon as they left, Robert would be reduced to wearing a bumfreezer jacket and Eton collar until his peer status within the school allowed him to graduate to a tailcoat. Basil gave small words of advice. "Remember, never complain to a schoolmaster if you are being bullied, you go to your fag-master," "Listen to the beaks, but don't cosy up too much," and "Excel at sport – and remember they call cricket players dry-bobs."

Robert nodded as Basil spoke. He knew he had to act indifferently to his mother when he went. It would be seen as a sign of weakness if he even acknowledged her and being thought of as weak at Eton meant your days were numbered. "Finally," said Basil, "if you want to command, then you must first learn to obey."

Celia stood a few feet away from her son. She did not say anything but forced a smile. Robert half smiled back.

"Go and join them," Basil said, looking at a group of boys playing in front of the chapel. "Show them what a Drewe can do."

***

They walked down to the fields by the river, with views of Windsor Castle. They looked like the perfect English family – a young, rich couple with twins and a nanny. A breeze blew and rippled the water. Pleasure boats meandered along the river and siblings of other children, who had been enrolled at Eton, laughed, played and shrieked in the meadows hitting dandelion clocks, knocking thousands of seeds into the air, which floated on the breeze. The plants would multiply and grow the following year, with their bright yellow flowers that looked like lions' teeth, and jagged, bitter leaves. The nanny looked down at twins who sat on a blanket, too young to run and play, and told them that in the language of flowers, the dandelion represents faithfulness and happiness.

"Will he be fine?" asked Celia.

"I think so," said Basil. "You can never tell, but, if I had to wager on it, I would say that Robert will find his feet and once he does, he might enjoy himself. But what about you?"

"What about me?" said Celia.

"You've hardly said two words about your eight months away. How are you feeling?"

Celia looked over at the twins.

"I'm fine," she said. "I needed to get some distance to understand things and my time working in Majda's clinic made me appreciate my life here."

"I hoped you would meet Majda."

"Why?" asked Celia.

"She's like a force of nature. When she sets her mind to something, nothing gets in her way. Even when she was a medical student in England she worked harder and longer hours than anyone else. She started her clinic with nothing – she begged and borrowed the money to buy that building and every week she buys food and medicines, and then pays everyone even though she runs the clinic for free."

"Was she more than a friend, Basil?"

"No... no. She was Laxman's sister and I had promised him I would look after her. Do you know, she reminded me of you."

"Of me?" said Celia. "We're like chalk and cheese."

"When you were younger," said Basil. "You had this desire to do something. You gave up your studies in Cambridge to become a nurse and help the injured – especially Christian. She was the same – she wanted to have a clinic in Assam and help the villagers. You were both selfless and determined, and I always thought that was something incredibly special about you."

Celia leant over and kissed him on the cheek, as they watched the twins.

"Majda also gave me something," said Celia. "It's a mixture of herbs that you blend with warm rice and put in a cheesecloth bag – like a poultice. She says that if you place it on your leg for half an hour and then massage your leg afterwards it will help with the muscle pain."

"My liniment does that," said Basil.

"Yes," said Celia, "but this doesn't smell nearly half as bad as that foul concoction that Jonathan Bruton gave you."

"You get used to it," said Basil.

"No, you don't," answered Celia emphatically.

"So why did working in the clinic help you appreciate your life here?" asked Basil.

Celia continued to look at the twins.

"Everyone was so poor," she said. "They had next to nothing, but the people seemed happier than we were. It seemed to me that we, with all our wealth and privileges, had forgotten the most important things in life. Things like community and respect and love."

Celia then walked over to where they sat and opened her arms and squatted down. The twins looked at her and then Howard opened his arms. Celia picked him up, hugged and kissed him. Basil looked on at his daughter, who looked on stern faced.

"At least we now know who will be the difficult one," he said, more to himself than anyone else.

***

You can't have a rainbow without a little rain, and, like a rainbow, it is impossible to predict when love will appear. On her return to England, Celia found that she again settled into a comfortable existence with Basil. She would not describe it as love – which she had felt for Adrian, and perhaps even Devjeet. However, it was an existence in which she felt content – where the world revolved, and time passed. Basil had not changed – he still focused on his work. When time permitted, he would take Celia out to one of the new fashionable restaurants in London. She, in turn, would make up a poultice of the herbs that Majda had recommended and massage Basil's leg twice a week. She also made a point of finding a job within the first few weeks of returning to England and started working for Dr Barnardo's Homes.

Fostering orphaned children was not a popular idea in England and Celia had to find foster homes in England and abroad. The charity took the view that raising a child in a loving and caring family environment was better than having them live in a home with hundreds of other children. Celia therefore took on the role of liaising with Barnardo's in Australia and Canada and sending children there, where they would be fostered in farms and homesteads. The charity required that there be continuing supervision over these children; first by systematic visitation; second, by regular correspondence. In her first few weeks on the job, Celia noted that this did not always happen and therefore implemented a policy whereby each Barnardo's supervisor in each country had to report back to her immediately and then on a three-monthly basis identifying each child and its welfare.

"Of course," said Celia to Basil, as she put down her first report, "we must take a lot of things of trust. However, the process seems to be working. We give each child two stamped postcards so that they can write to us if they are unhappy or being mistreated." Basil looked up from the history book he was reading.

"That assumes," said Basil, "that they are allowed to keep the postcards and have a way of sending them."

"I suppose it does," said Celia. "But we also send someone to check on the children every quarter."

"Again, you assume that the children will talk to these people."

"I hope you don't mind me saying this, Basil, but having a negative attitude about everything is not your most endearing quality."

"Sorry," replied Basil. "But after a decade of being a criminal barrister, I seem to have lost my ability to see the world through rose-coloured spectacles." He folded the top corner of the page, closed his book and looked at Celia. "Do you want a G and T? I need one."

Chapter 33

25 November 1931

Ecclesiastical Law requires that 'In every church and chapel there shall be provided at least one bell to ring the people to divine service.' In the Holy Trinity Church in Drewsteignton, there are six bells; however, at a funeral, it is usual for only a single bell to be tolled with long pauses between each strike. The church bells at Drewsteignton were rung out on three unprecedented occasions in the last weeks of November 1931. First, there was the 'passing bell' that warned of Sir Julius's imminent death. There was then the 'death knell', which was sounded immediately after his passing. Finally, there was the 'corpse bell' that was rung on the day of his funeral, as the procession approached. In this case, the clapper was half muffled, so that after each loud strike of the bell there was a deadened strike.

The body of Sir Julius lay in the chapel of Castle Drogo for four days until his funeral. The coffin was then carried by his two sons, George Poley and three nephews of Sir Julius who had travelled down from Yorkshire with their families to pay their final respects. George Poley walked behind Christian and whispered to him as they approached the few stairs which they needed to climb before they placed the coffin on the horse-drawn carriage for the mile-and-a-half journey to Drewsteignton. The horses, with their black plumes and livery, snorted as they were held in the cold November morning. Lady Frances sat in a Rolls-Royce with Celia and her grandchildren. Lutyens and Emily were also in a Rolls-Royce, which followed behind Lady Frances and then there were five more cars with Sir

Julius's two brothers and their sons and daughters and children. Basil and George Poley agreed to walk behind the horse-drawn coffin to the church. They had convinced Christian to go with his mother, as the road was in parts nothing more than a cinder track.

At quarter to eleven, when the procession was seen from the tower of the Holy Trinity church, the corpse bell was rung and sounded for the next fifteen minutes as the entourage approached Drewsteignton. Christian again joined his brother and George Poley and when they arrived at the Drewe Arms the procession stopped and the six men, who were the coffin bearers, again lifted the coffin.

No one had expected so many people to attend the small church in Drewsteignton. Despite the cold, the doors of the church were left open so that villagers who came to pay their respects, but who were not able to get inside the church, could hear the service. At the front of the church sat Lady Frances, Christian, Basil, Celia and Robert. In the second and third rows sat Sir Julius's two brothers, their three sons and four daughters, as well as a dozen children. There were more distant relatives in the rows behind. Politicians and businessmen sat on the other side of the church as well as friends. In the front row were two Members of Parliament and Sir Walford Selby, who had for many years been a friend of Sir Julius. The servants who worked on the estate sat at the back or stood lining the walls. The only notable absentee was Jane Facey, who had married Sir Julius's son Adrian for just the shortest period before his death, fourteen years earlier.

Following the service, when they lowered the coffin into the ground, there were tears from Lady Frances. Basil and Christian stood stoically together, both knowing that the last thing their father would have wanted was for them to wear their hearts on their sleeves. Celia stood on the other side of Basil and to her surprise, Robert cried inconsolably. Familiar words were spoken by the vicar as the body was laid to rest with a handful of dust. Lutyens had already prepared a design for Sir Julius's memorial, which would consist of a low granite-framed square with neatly trimmed yew hedges on the northern and southern sides and then another hedge in the middle in the form of a cross.

"He would have approved of the eulogy," said Basil, as he looked around the muddy cemetery on that cold and black day. It had fortunately stopped raining that morning otherwise everyone would have been chilled to the bone. "It was a long journey for you to come."

"Tomas was busy and so a friend brought me from Vienna to Exeter," said Christian.

"I heard," said Basil, "that she's a dancer. I'm not sure that Mother approved."

"She's an acquaintance," said Christian. "She's meeting some family in London and then returning to Austria. That's why I needed someone to accompany me home. I could have paid for a companion, but I was pleased when you agreed."

"I would have gone with you and Basil as well," said Celia. "But I don't think the twins would forgive me if I upped sticks and left, having only just come back from India."

"I'm looking forward to it," said Basil, "I've been wanting to have some time with you."

***

In the dining room of Castle Drogo, with its paintings of Sir Julius, his parents, grandparents and great-grandparents, sat a solicitor from the firm of Stern, White & Elston. Mr Stern was a thin man with straight, grey hair that was parted on the left-hand side. He spoke with the accent of a person who had attended a public school. His briefcase was open and left on the chair next to him and he placed before him a document marked 'last will and testament'. Basil thanked him for coming to the castle rather than making them go to London for the reading.

"The will," said Mr Stern, "is not nearly as complex as it might have been." He looked at Lady Frances. "Your late husband was fastidious when it came to keeping his affairs in order." They listened as Mr Stern read the will, slowly and laboriously, word for word, and when he had finished, he summed up how Sir Julius had disposed of his assets. "Mr Christian Drewe is therefore bequeathed the apartment in Vienna, free of any encumbrances, as well as a gift of two hundred thousand pounds and an annual allowance of twenty thousand pounds. Mr Basil Drewe is bequeathed the apartment in Cadogan Square, London, free of any encumbrances, as well as an annual allowance of twenty thousand pounds. Lady Frances is given a tenancy for life of Castle Drogo and an annual allowance of twenty thousand pounds. She is also given all other real and private property of her late husband. On the event of her death," continued Mr Stern, "the castle will pass to Mr Basil Drewe and will be held on trust in the interim." Mr Stern folded the will and then sipped from a cup of tea that was before him. "Please, if you have any questions, ask."

"The residue of his estate," said Lady Frances. "How will that be managed?"

Mr Stern put on his glasses and reopened the will.

"A Board of Trustees," he said, "which shall include his two sons, myself and two representatives from the accountancy firm that managed your late husband's affairs, will oversee the management of the residue which is currently valued at two point seven five million pounds. The yearly allowances will be paid from this as well as the maintenance of the castle and the other ancillary properties."

"And in the event of a shortfall?" asked Christian.

Mr Stern took off his glasses and wiped his eyes.

"Then the allowances will be paid at a discretionary percentage, but I would not worry about that, Mr Drewe. That is unlikely to happen, save if there is a catastrophe, such as another world war."

Basil looked at Mr Stern. He decided not to ask anything and could go through a copy of the will later. He stared across the table. On the wall behind the solicitor was a large painting depicting a battle scene. It had been bought by his father years earlier, but he did not have a wall big enough for the painting until the castle had been completed. It was a work from 1683 in which the Polish army, led by John Sobieski III, had routed the Turks of the Ottoman Empire outside the walls of Vienna. The battle marked the beginning of the end of the Turkish occupation of Europe and Basil wondered whether the Austrians still acknowledged the debt they owed to their Polish neighbours.

Later that evening when their mother had gone to bed, Basil, Celia and Christian sat in a small living room with a coal fire burning and each with a glass of malt whisky.

"I always thought that as the eldest surviving son, you would have inherited the castle," said Basil.

"I didn't want it," said Christian. "I spoke with Father last year about the will and we agreed that it should be given to you. I'm unlikely to marry and you were always more interested in the castle than I was. At least it can be passed on to your children if you don't sell it."

"And what will you do with your inheritance?" asked Celia.

"I," said Christian, "intend to buy a villa by a lake in Austria and go swimming and fishing in the summer and forget about the world. I might even employ a secretary and write my memoirs, or perhaps a novel."

"And what type of novel would you write?" Celia asked.

"A romance," said Christian. "A doomed and forlorn love between two people who meet at a train station."

"I'm sure you would fill it with more than the usual amount of revolting sentimentality and it would be a fabulous success," said Basil. He finished his glass and placed it on the table. "I never knew you and Father kept in touch."

"It was more frequent over the last few years. He would call me on the telephone just to have a chat. He mellowed in his last years."

"Did he?" said Celia, and she heard the grandfather clock in the hall chime the hour. "Anyway, it's time I went to bed."

***

The train rattled as it made its way towards the south coast where they would catch the boat to Calais. From there they would take a train towards Brussels, stopping near Ypres for a single afternoon, and then on towards Germany and finally Vienna. The compartment on the train was comfortable, although it smelt of stale smoke. Basil had a copy of *The Times*, and they were completing the last few crossword clues.

"H, I, J, K, L, M, N, O," said Basil. "Five letters and the fourth letter's an E."

"I have no idea," said Christian. Basil looked down at the crossword. He had already written in the word 'Water' and had worked out the remaining answers to complete the crossword. "Go on," said Christian, "tell me the answer."

"Water," Basil mumbled.

"And I take it you've done all the other answers," said Christian. Basil again mumbled something and put down the paper.

"So, let's talk about you," said Christian.

"There's not much to say," replied Basil.

"Then," responded Christian, "this journey will be dull. However, if we are being honest, a lot's going on in your life."

"Not really," answered Basil. "Life's sort of back on an even keel."

"Basil!" said Christian, exasperated by his brother's refusal to talk about his feelings. "Your wife goes to India for eight months and you are left holding the babies. She's back now and you are both trying to play happy families."

"It's complicated," said Basil.

"It usually is," said Christian.

"I love Celia. I always have. Even as a schoolboy, I was infatuated with her and then she went away, and I grew up and my relationships with other women didn't work out as well as they could have. When she came back to England, we were closer in age, and I was doing well as a barrister, and she wanted security. However, she never tells me about the important things in her life. The things that frighten her at night, the bad dreams that wake her up, or the things that make her smile and I promised her I would never ask. I told her that when she was ready to talk, I would be here, but she has never wanted to speak to me about her past. I thought, in time, we would grow closer. She would realise how much I adore her and that would be enough for her. But that hasn't happened and when the twins were born," Basil shrugged, as he thought back over the last few years, "things went downhill. I had two screaming babies and an irascible wife all living under my roof. It just got to breaking point."

"That's when you decided that a separation would be a good idea."

"It wasn't a separation, it was a holiday for her," said Basil.

"Call it what you will," said Christian. "And now she's back home and you're as cool as cucumbers with each other."

"I don't know what the problem is. The twins are sleeping, and Robert is at school, but I still feel a distance from Celia, and I don't know why. Don't get me wrong, we are not unhappy. We go out and we enjoy each other's company. It's just that I sense that she doesn't feel about me the same way I feel about her."

"So, what are you going to do?"

"Carry on loving her," said Basil. "It's the only thing I know how to do."

Chapter 34

They left flowers by the grave, just Christmas roses with pure white petals and leathery, dark green leaves. They had taken a cab the one and a half miles from Ypres train station to Vlamertinghe New Military Cemetery. The cemetery was kept in immaculate condition with black, wrought-iron gates between two pillars of brick and Portland stone. In front of the gates was the Great Cross with its iron inlay designed as a sword. On a commemorative marker near the gate, written into the grey-white stone, were words that stated that the land had been given as a perpetual resting place for the fallen from 1914 to 1918. They first went to find the Book of Remembrance.

"The inscription that Father gave was: 'Blessed are the pure in heart for they shall see God'," said Basil.

Over eighteen hundred men had been buried there from every corner of the Commonwealth. After they had found Adrian's gravestone and laid the flowers they walked towards the Stone of Remembrance.

"I'm pleased you convinced me to come," said Christian. "It's over fourteen years since we lost him. How old were you then?"

"Nineteen. I was going up to Oxford that year. I missed him terribly in that year and even now I sometimes hear his voice in my head telling me to do this or that. There was one occasion where I came third in an essay competition and I was thinking how disappointed Father was going to be, and then I heard Adrian in my head saying: 'You won't come third again, will you'."

"I recall," said Christian, "that he was so proud of you. He had hoped to have a long talk about the dos and don'ts just before you went up, but you seem to have muddled through."

They stopped before the Stone of Remembrance – the Great Alter stone as Lutyens had called it.

"Do you know why these are here?" asked Christian.

"As a remembrance to the fallen," said Basil.

"But why an altar stone?" asked Christian.

"I've no idea," said Basil.

"Before the war ended, Lutyens visited Wadhurst Hall to talk about the design of the castle. I happened to be there and Lutyens stayed for dinner. We discussed his work for the War Graves Commission. He talked about his design for a cenotaph in London and then he told us about his idea for a Stone of Remembrance, to be placed in every war cemetery in Belgium and France where a thousand or more soldiers were buried." Christian paused for a moment and placed his hands on top of the altar stone. "The words he used to describe what he saw on the battlefield were a ribbon of isolated graves like a Milky Way across miles of countryside where men were tucked in where they fell. Ribbons of little cross each touching each. He talked about the ideas he had, but there was one constant theme – that it had to be non-denominational because the fallen men were of all faiths and none. He described a beautiful stone altar – plain with no ornate or elaborate carvings – and that it should contain one clear thought."

"Their name liveth for evermore," said Basil.

"Yes, although Lutyens never chose those words. Most importantly for Lutyens, was that the Stone of Remembrance would be facing the West and facing the men who lie looking ever eastwards towards the enemy."

They stood quietly for ten minutes until Basil looked at his brother.

"Are you cold?" asked Basil. "You're shaking."

"Do you mind if we leave? There's just too much pain here."

***

"Let me ask you a question," said Basil, as the train left Ypres railway station on its way to Brussels, Munich and finally to Vienna.

"Go ahead," said Christian, who put down his braille book.

"How can you live with the people who killed our brother?"

"I suppose," said Christian, "that I look at things differently. The Austrians that I knew didn't want a war. If you want to be angry with anyone, be angry with the politicians; people like Cecil Facey who guided the country to the brink of war and then made his fortune on the back of it."

"But why go and live there?"

"I lived in Drewsteignton for years after I was wounded. I was told by my neighbours to stay indoors, so as not to frighten their wives and daughters and if I did go out, I was ostracised and treated like a pariah even though I had been injured fighting for my country. Austria's not perfect but the people there treat me better than my countrymen, even though I fought against them."

"But…" interrupted Basil.

"Let me finish," said Christian. "Is my life perfect? No. I still have nightmares almost every night and wake most mornings wishing I had died on that battlefield. However, I have a life in Vienna. I have friends and acquaintances and we go to concerts, clubs and dinner. I have a small studio where I sculpt and sometimes make pots and vases. Tomas sells some of them at his gallery. I have even started playing the piano. So, is my life better in Vienna or Drewsteignton? It's a thousand times better in Vienna and the Viennese are not nearly as priggish and as stuffy as most Englishmen I know."

"I see…"

"I don't think you do. I don't think you realise how cold and arrogant our countrymen are."

"We may be cold at times," said Basil, "but at least an Englishman can be relied upon to do the right thing."

"Do you believe that?" said Christian. "That myth of the white man's burden that we use to justify our domination of other countries. Think about it again when you stand in a foreign country looking at how poor the people are."

***

The dining car in the train had plush burgundy seats of velvet; there were flowers on each of the tables in small clear crystal vases and menus were handed to them as they sat down. Basil read the menu aloud and Christian chose a smoked mackerel pâté, followed by an asparagus risotto, and then fillet steak with a sauce Diane as his *plat principal*. He decided to wait before ordering dessert but knew that if he was still hungry, he would be finishing with the crêpe Suzette.

"We fight a lot," said Basil. "Why is that?"

The porter came over with a bottle of Montrachet and poured two glasses.

"We do," said Christian, "but more importantly we protect each other and we're not afraid to tell each other the truth. Both you and Adrian looked after me when I was injured, and I know if something happened to me you would be the first person to drop everything and come to my aid." The starters came and they both took mouthfuls. "Why did you choose a career in law? I never understood how you made that decision."

"It was Father," said Basil. "When I was recovering after I broke my leg, he asked me what I planned to do with my life. I hadn't thought about it and told him that. He stood looking down at me for a moment and then said, 'If you want to change the world, be a politician; if you want to affect people's lives, be a lawyer; and, if you want to confuse the masses, be a priest.' I asked him why he went into business, and he said that he wanted to be rich."

"And have you affected people's lives?" asked Christian.

"I think so," said Basil. "Sometimes in small ways but small changes can have large consequences. It's why I believe the law is so important and why I spend so much of my time working."

"I admire your tenacity," said Christian. "However, don't let the law become your mistress. I think that's what you called the law once – a jealous mistress. You're having troubles at home but throwing yourself into your work to the exclusion of your family is the worst thing you can do. There must be a balance to life."

"That's a rather nice speech," said Basil.

"Yes," said Christian. "If I was lucky enough to have your family, I would wrap my arms around them every moment of the day. I would make sure I told them I love them every night and they would be the most important thing in my life."

V

Part Five

Chapter 35

May 1939

The history books would call it the *Anschluss*, meaning the joining. After the Great War the allies had thrown the Austrian Empire to the four winds and therefore it was inevitable that Germany would want to join with it to become a strong, single territory, which they did in March 1938. It filled Christian with a sense of trepidation. Germany had by this time passed the Nuremberg Race Laws, which had taken away all political rights of Jews. When the two countries joined, those laws were soon applied to Austria. Vienna's population consisted of 1.9 million people, of which ten per cent were of Jewish or mixed Jewish extraction. These included many of the city's doctors and lawyers, businessmen and bankers, artists and journalists – some of whom were Christian's friends.

In the coffee shops, everyone talked about the mass emigration of Jews from Vienna. Only a few people were standing up against the Nazis and they were systematically being arrested and imprisoned. Christian heard that many Jews were trying to get to Palestine, England, Cuba or the United States. Out on the streets of Vienna, queues of Jewish people had formed outside the municipal police offices to obtain the required documentation to leave. There had been no let-up, and night and day the lines seemed to get longer. The Jewish emigrants were being forced to pay an exit fee and to register all their immovable and most of their movable property. The Austrian authorities confiscated everything when the Jews were permitted to leave. Things then got worse.

Christian had sat in the living room of his apartment at Tuchlauben in

Vienna in November 1938. He had heard the violence taking place out on the streets, as the first pogrom in Vienna was happening. The papers later called it *Kristallnacht* because shattered glass from Jewish store windows and synagogues littered the streets. All but one of the city's synagogues and small prayer houses had been torched, and any Jewish business was ransacked. The fire brigade looked on, instructed by the Nazis not to intervene unless the blaze got out of control. In the following days and weeks, it was the subject of subdued discussion and people spoke of how it had happened across the whole of Germany and Austria and not just in Vienna. Systematically, the Jews were forcibly moved to the Jewish quarter of Vienna and their cars, houses and possessions were confiscated.

After the violence quietened in the middle of November 1938, the German police officials began arresting some six thousand Austrian Jews and deported them to the Dachau and Buchenwald concentration camps. If the Jews could prove that they had the money to pay the exit fee and would emigrate, they were released. Those Jews who did not have enough money to move to a new country remained incarcerated and were used as slave labour. Rumours about the concentration camps ran rife and what Christian heard scared him.

Dachau was ten miles northwest of Munich. It had been set up as a camp for political prisoners in 1933. Over time the Germans started transporting other groups to it, including communists, Roma, Jehovah's Witnesses, homosexuals and other 'asocials', as the Nazi party called them. It was after 1935, and the passing of the Nuremberg Race Laws, that Jews were sent to Dachau. On the metal gates, as one entered the camp, were three words wrought in iron – '*Arbeit macht frei*' – work sets you free.

***

At the height of her career, Rachel Kraus danced the 'Vision of Salome' at the Vienna Opera House. The newspapers called it 'mesmerising' and with a photograph of her, she was for weeks afterwards a *cause célèbre*. With long dark hair, large brown eyes, full lips and a small cleft on her chin, the description of her as a Levantine beauty was unquestionably warranted. Her photograph, when she danced as Salome, showed her covered with

214

nothing more than a few modest sequins. Numerous German boys cut out her photograph from their parents' newspapers and numerous fathers suddenly found an interest in modern dance, and the cafés where the dancers would frequent. That had been in 1933. She had been popular for a few years after that but when the *Anschluss* took place, and the Nazis took power her star fell as quickly as it had risen.

In May 1939, Rachel was twenty-eight, eighteen years younger than Christian. She had started her career as a dancer at the Vienna State Academy of Music and Dramatic Art in 1928. Her last performance in Vienna was given in March 1938 when she was told that the Academy could no longer employ her because of her faith. Her father, who had owned a bakery, had refused to leave Vienna until *Kristallnacht* when every Jewish person began to fear for their lives. After *Kristallnacht* his business and all his provisions were confiscated, and he was fined by the Nazis. Rachel and her family were forcibly moved to the Leopoldstadt District, the only place where Jews were allowed to live. Rachel's father had no way to pay the fine and could not leave Austria until it was paid. Rachel lived with her parents, however, without the ability to work as a dancer, she could not save any money.

It was at the Yohan café and restaurant in the Stadtpark that Christian had first met Rachel on a summer night in 1931. There had been a dance performance at the Academy that evening, and the troupe had come to the café for a drink. Tomas, who knew a few of the dancers, ordered champagne and they joined their table. Christian was introduced to Rachel, who had spent a few years as a child in London with relatives. Her English was impeccable.

"You've rather drawn the short straw," said Christian.

"Do you think so?"

"I'm hardly Ronald Colman."

"But you have an interesting face," said Rachel. "Most of the men here are anything but interesting and none of them look like Ronald Colman."

They spoke for a while and Rachel was interested in what Christian did in his spare time. They talked about music, and he told her that he played the piano and had a small studio where he sculpted vases. They also talked about books, and he explained that books were sent to him from England in braille.

"And what's your favourite book?" she asked.

"*The Mystery of Dr Fu-Manchu*," he answered without hesitation. "The greatest vile genius that the powers of evil have put on the earth."

"Was he?" said Rachel.

Chapter 36

May 1939

The telephone rang and rang and just as Christian was about to hang up it was answered.

"Good morning," said Christian.

"How can I help you," was the response.

"May I speak to Rachel Kraus?"

"I'm afraid I don't know anyone called Rachel Kraus." However, the person answering did not hang up.

"I was given your telephone number by Herr Engel at the Jewish emigration office," continued Christian.

There was a pause. "Go on."

"I will be leaving Vienna soon and going to my home near Salzburg. My name is Drewe, Christian Drewe. It might be possible for Rachel…"

Christian was interrupted, "As I said, I don't know any Rachel Kraus."

"If you find out where she is, please tell her that I will be in the café where we first met at three p.m. tomorrow."

There was no goodbye or acknowledgement, just a click and then the sound of buzzing.

***

The Yohan café and restaurant was popular with locals and tourists alike. Outside was a large patio with a score of tables, and four large, pink, wooden flamingos standing incongruously at various locations around it. A small oom-pah band played on Friday and Saturday evenings when the weather was pleasant. Christian decided to sit at a table away from other people. If

217

Rachel turned up, he did not want anyone to overhear them.

It was not until a quarter past three that Rachel arrived. She wore a rust-coloured skirt, cream shirt, dark jacket and a beret. It was a nondescript outfit as if she had made a conscious decision not to stand out in the crowd. She sat down immediately before saying a word.

"I wasn't sure whether to come," she said. "You know I could be arrested for being here."

"I'm sorry," Christian responded, "But I didn't know where else to suggest."

A waitress hurried over to the table.

"Tea," whispered Rachel to Christian.

"Tea," said Christian to the waitress, "and also another cup of coffee for me."

Rachel looked at the table until the waitress had gone.

"The reason I wanted to see you," said Christian, "is that I have a summer house near Salzburg. I will be going there shortly and from there you can go to Marseille."

"I don't understand," said Rachel.

"I heard that your family is having trouble leaving Vienna and I would like to help."

Rachel looked at Christian. She could read nothing in his face, which had been so badly burnt in the war. He sat facing her wearing a pair of round dark sunglasses with copper frames.

Finally, she said, "Why?"

"Because you have always helped me when I needed it and because I think of you as a friend," said Christian. "I intend to go in a week or so. Does that give you enough time to organise the paperwork you will need?"

"For what?"

"For going on to Palestine," said Christian. "You'll need to get a tourist visa. They still issue them and once you get to Palestine you can disappear into the crowd."

"How do you know that?" asked Rachel.

"Someone told me how it's done. There are groups who can help you and I'll give you their details."

If Christian had any vision at all, he would have seen the tears brimming in Rachel's eyes. They began to fall unwanted and stopped immediately when she saw the waitress coming towards their table with their drinks. She quickly pulled a handkerchief from her purse and wiped her eyes. She continued looking down at the table as the waitress placed the cups, the teapot and a small plate of sliced lemon on the table.

"Thank you," said Christian to the waitress as she left.

"There is one thing," said Rachel, as she started pouring herself a cup of tea. "I need a thousand Reichsmarks."

"What for?" asked Christian.

"It's for the fine that my family needs to pay to leave Austria."

Chapter 37

Christian had just finished a cup of coffee when the taxi arrived. His cases were loaded, and he locked the door of his apartment for the final time. As he sat in the taxi, as it headed towards the train station, he wondered whether he would ever return to Vienna. He would stay with Tomas for a week or two at his villa at St Gilgen, then to England and finally on to America. He knew that it was time to make a new start, even at the age of forty-six. Old dogs, he thought, could still learn new tricks and he found himself humming a tune, as he mused about the future.

Rachel wore the same clothes that she had worn to the Yohan café. She had left her small suitcase with her parents in third class and had come to find Christian to ensure he was safe on board and did not need anything. She found him in a first-class compartment on his own, dressed as if he were going to meet royalty. Everyone in the Jewish district was struggling to feed themselves and hardly any of them had more than one change of clothes. Christian was, by contrast, dressed immaculately in a double-breasted suit, a silk tie and shoes that had been polished to a point of reflection. He wore a Fedora hat and pulled down the brim so that only those who stared at him could see his face. His luggage had had been stowed away by the guard twenty minutes earlier.

"Almost twenty-five years ago," he said, "I left Vienna on very much the same train." He put his hand to his chest and could feel the St Christopher hanging there on a silver chain, given to him by a nurse who he once loved. "I am fine here on my own," he continued. "Don't worry about me, you ought to be going back."

A knock on the compartment door disturbed their conversation and a guard entered, asking to see their tickets and papers. Rachel handed over her a certificate from the Reich Ministry of Finance, one from the local police authorising her to leave Austria, her passport stamped with a J, and her ticket. Christian took out his train ticket and passport from the inside pocket of his jacket and held them out for the guard to take. The guard went through the papers meticulously, mumbling to himself.

"Is everything in order?" Christian asked after a few minutes.

"We do not allow Jewesses in first class," shouted the guard. "She must get back to where she belongs."

Rachel turned to go.

"She was just returning to third class," said Christian, "she only came to find out how I was." He took off his hat and then his glasses and turned towards the guard. The crater of the socket where his eye once was, was burnt black. His other eye looked up and towards the bridge of his nose, the pupil was grey and milky, but the iris was still a beautiful green.

"She can't be here, ever," shouted the guard. "You know that!" The guard thought for a moment and weighed up his options. The train was just moving out of the station, and there was nothing he could do until it got to Linz.

As she started to leave the compartment, the guard looked at her and hissed, "Dirty Jew."

Chapter 38

The doorbell rang and Basil put down his copy of the *Sunday Times*, leaving the crossword puzzle unfinished. It had been a relaxing morning and Basil had opened the windows of his apartment and could hear children playing in the gardens below. His two children would be tired out when they came back for lunch if the noise was anything to go by. The twins had dozens of friends around Cadogan Place, and he was now surplus to requirements, except for pocket money and to take them out for treats.

"I'll get it," he shouted to Celia, who was in the kitchen talking to their cook. Basil had not expected to be handed a telegram and his first thought, after receiving it, was that his mother might be ill. He opened it and read it quickly.

"Who was it?" shouted Celia from the kitchen.

Basil walked down the hallway and into the kitchen.

"It's a telegram," he said and waved the piece of paper at Celia. "A telegram, from Tomas Skeres."

"What does it say?" asked Celia.

"It says that Christian is missing. That he left Vienna on a train to Salzburg but never arrived."

"That doesn't make sense," said Celia, who held out her hand to take the telegram. She read it. "What are we going to do?" she asked.

Basil took a deep breath and tried to collect his thoughts.

"I'll telephone Tomas and find out what this is all about."

He went into the living room, picked up the receiver, called the operator and told her he wanted to make a long-distance call to Vienna. A few minutes later the operator rang back saying that the number he had given her had not been answered.

"I'll try again later," said Basil, and put down the phone. Celia came in.

"What do you think has happened?" she asked.

"I don't know," replied Basil. "I don't know why he decided to get off the train or even why he was going to Salzburg."

"Or who was with him," added Celia.

Basil sat back down in his armchair. He tapped his fingers on the arm of the chair as he thought about what he should do. The last time he had seen his elder brother was just after the funeral of their father when he went with him to Vienna. He remembered Christian had said something as they went there. He had said that if he were ever in trouble Basil would be the first person to drop everything and come to his aid. Suddenly Basil got up, picked up the telephone and called his clerk, Claude Palfrey.

"I won't be in chambers for the rest of the week," he said, "it's a personal matter." Basil then explained what had happened and they discussed the cases he was dealing with. He asked to see if he could get him travel documents, book him on an aeroplane to Berlin that evening and arrange a hotel near the British Embassy in Berlin.

"I'll call you if there's a problem and good luck, sir," said Palfrey, as he hung up the telephone.

"What have you decided?" asked Celia.

"That I'm going to Berlin and then Austria to find him," said Basil. "I need to make another call, to Maxwell Fyfe."

"Why do you need to call David?" asked Celia.

"Because he was recently posted to the Judge Advocate General's department. He may be able to direct me to the people I need to speak to at the embassy and pull some strings."

After Basil had finished his call, he began gathering his things together.

"Telephone the children every evening if you can, so that they know you're safe," said Celia, "and don't worry about anything here – we'll all be fine."

"I know you'll look after things," said Basil, "you always do."

"Just find Christian," said Celia, "and bring him home safely and most importantly keep yourself safe."

***

As the cab took Basil out towards Croydon airport, he scribbled the things he needed to do in his notebook. In his telephone conversation with Maxwell Fyfe, he had been warned that resources at the embassy in Berlin were stretched and that he would need to do most of the legwork himself.

The Tempelhof Airport in Berlin was far more impressive than Croydon; with a yellow stone façade and white stone rectangular windows, the airport terminal was both modern and utilitarian. A myriad of shops sold everything from pastries to papers. Basil got his suitcase and headed for the exit. All around him, he saw men wearing brown shirts and ties, as well as red armbands with the Nazi insignia. There were groups of them standing next to the customs officials, at the exits and by the cab ranks as if everyone needed to be checked.

Basil would best describe his German as basic; his school had stopped teaching it when he was fourteen just before the Great War. His passport was meticulously examined as he went through the control and was asked a score of questions about the purpose of his visit. He took a taxi to his hotel near the British embassy. The hotel was opulent, and a group of bellboys approached the taxi, taking Basil's bag and directing him to the reservations desk. Again, as Basil went into the reception area, he noticed the brown shirts everywhere. The reception hall was grand, with rich, thick rugs on the floor and ornate cornices on the ceiling. Large mirrors reflected light everywhere.

"How long will you be staying?" asked the receptionist.

"Two nights," replied Basil.

"We will need to keep your passport," said the receptionist.

"Is that necessary?" asked Basil. One of the brown shirts started moving towards Basil. The receptionist looked over and raised his hand to indicate that he was not needed.

"It's just normal practice, Herr Drewe," he said. "We will also give you papers to show that you are permitted to be in the centre of the city."

"A permit?" said Basil.

"There are certain elements of our society," said the receptionist, "that are not permitted into the centre of the city. Jews and the like, you understand."

"Of course," said Basil.

However, as soon as he had uttered the two words, he hated himself. It was not all right, and he did not understand. Two more brown shirts walked into the reception hall and Basil decided to say nothing further. The receptionist handed Basil his room keys, explained where he could have dinner and breakfast and reminded him again that he would need to pick up his papers when he went out tomorrow.

***

Clive Horridge met Basil at the embassy door. He was tall and thin and seemed always to be in a hurry.

"I spoke to Mr Maxwell Fyfe on the telephone yesterday, so I'm aware why you've come to me, Mr Drewe."

Basil looked around. He had expected to see queues of people lining the block but there seemed hardly anyone there.

"Good," Basil said, "I was told you were busy."

"We are," responded Clive. "The Germans prohibited all Jews from coming into the city centre and we had to relocate most of our resources to the Passport Control Office just outside the centre to deal with their applications to leave Germany. We just have a skeleton staff here to deal with every other emergency. If I hadn't received that telephone call yesterday, I would have been there."

"What exactly do you know?" asked Basil, as he was taken into an office.

"That your brother is missing." Clive called to a secretary for tea. "Also, that he was filed as a missing person in Salzburg, four days ago."

"Who did that?" asked Basil. Clive opened his briefcase and pulled out a thin file. He took out the front sheet and looked down.

"A businessman called Tomas Skeres," said Clive, reading from the form. "He has given an address in St Gilgen in the area of Salzkammergut."

"He's a friend of my brother's," added Basil. "I know Mr Skeres. However, the address belongs to my brother Christian."

225

"The report says that ten days ago your brother took a train to Salzburg, but he appears not to have got off the train at Salzburg."

"So, my brother could be anywhere between Vienna and Salzburg?"

"Exactly," said Clive.

"And how many stops are there?" asked Basil.

Clive again looked at the file. "Eight stops between Vienna and Salzburg." He got up and hurriedly left the room, returning a few moments later with a map that he placed on the table. "Let's see where the train stopped," he mumbled, more to himself than to Basil. He traced his finger along the map where the train would have travelled. "Obviously," he added, "we start our search in Salzburg and if that proves fruitless you should look in Linz, as it's the only other major town on the route." He looked up from the map and added, "I know some people in both Salzburg and Linz, I will call them. Also, I'll check to find out whether the train was delayed anywhere. Could you come back tomorrow?"

"And what should I do?" asked Basil.

"Nothing."

"I could try and telephone Tomas Skeres," said Basil "Do you have a number for him?"

"He's in St Gilgen," said Clive, looking again at his file. "I doubt whether they will put in telephone lines there for another hundred years. However, you could send him a telegram." Clive started putting his papers away. "Also," he said, "could you come to the Passport Control Office tomorrow morning?" He scribbled the address on a piece of paper and handed it to Basil.

Basil looked up at the ceiling, as he lay on his back in his hotel room. He closed his eyes and thought about the day's events. A set of heavy velvet drapes had been pulled across the double-hung sash windows, which stifled the sounds of the city outside. He could on occasion still hear crowds of young men leaving the beer hall across the road, and wondered whether he should go down and have a drink before going to sleep. Deciding against it, his mind turned to his telephone conversation with Maxwell Fyfe. He hadn't seen Maxwell Fyfe in years as they were both so busy with their respective careers. Basil had said, jokingly, that he rarely saw Celia now, as she was also so busy with work.

He did not know when he had started to lose contact with Maxwell Fyfe. They were both married, both with families and living at opposite ends of the country. However, when they were younger, they made time to visit – Maxwell Fyfe and Sylvia coming down to London for weekends, and he and Celia going up to Liverpool. However, since becoming a member of Parliament and King's Counsel, Maxwell Fyfe did not seem to have the time for anything. There was also perhaps a little jealousy. Basil had expected to become a King's Counsel two years ago, but someone in the Lord Chancellor's offices did not appear to think that he was cut from the right cloth. Maxwell Fyfe's star was rising quicker than his and he wondered why that was the case.

One reason he could think was that Maxwell Fyfe seemed to be able to juggle countless balls without dropping any, and, Basil suspected, it was due to his wife, Sylvia, who worked tirelessly for him. Celia seemed almost to have no time to help with his career, she was too busy to attend the bar dinners or for social evenings in chambers. As sleep evaded him, Basil wondered what had happened to all his other friends. Over the years he had lost touch with all of them, including Bruton and Laxman. Whenever he went out now it was to functions that Celia arranged or to dinner parties with her friends – Jenny Stanton and her husband and the women she worked with.

Celia's star was also on the rise. After six years working for Barnardo's, finding homes for thousands of children in England and abroad, her work was rewarded with an MBE. It was Celia who was recognised and acknowledged when they went out, while he still had to wear the sobriquet of a junior barrister. Celia then gave up her position in Barnardo's and started working for the *Kindertransport* programme. Basil had thought it was a mistake. However, everyone applauded her for her fierce determination to ensure that as many Jewish refugee children came safely to British shores. She worked tirelessly in this role, and Basil spent more time with the twins. He spoilt them – he knew he did – despite Celia saying that he should be firm but fair. They gave him unconditional love and because of that, they knew precisely how to manipulate him.

He picked up the telephone again and asked the operator to make a long-distance call to England – Kensington and Chelsea 5638. He put down the receiver and waited until the operator rang back saying that a connection had been made.

"Is that you, Celia?" said Basil. "I'm sorry, the connection is quite poor."

"I can hardly hear you, dear," said Celia. "Have you any news?"

"Nothing at all, except that Tomas filed the missing person's report and that he's at Christian's villa in St Gilgen. I've got an address, and I'll send him a telegram tomorrow to say that I'm coming."

"And anything about Christian?"

"Nothing. I spoke with someone at the embassy who wants to help, but no news now. How are things there?"

"All fine. The twins have done their homework, and I had a call from Robert earlier this evening from university. There's a girl he wants me to meet – I don't think it's serious."

"I was thinking that when I get back, we should spend more time together."

"We're always together, dear, and as you know, things are so hectic here that I really can't spend any time away. You understand that?"

"I was thinking about a holiday," said Basil.

"That would be lovely, dear; but not right now. Perhaps at Christmas, we can go away, or perhaps you could take the children to see your mother one weekend."

"I was hoping that we could do something, just us two."

"I do as well, but I can't stop what I'm doing now. You do understand that?"

"We don't need the money, Celia. We could both stop working tomorrow."

"I don't do this for the money, it's important to me. I told you that I need to make sure that every refugee child who is trying to escape Germany is safe. Now, I've got to go, dear. I have a call with a boarding school who might be able to take two dozen children."

Basil listened to the buzzing of the telephone, long after Celia hung up.

Chapter 39

Basil arrived at the passport control office at 17 Tiergartenstrasse, which runs parallel to Tiergarten Park, where the zoological gardens are found. He was met at the door by Clive, who looked like he had not slept.

"As you can see," he said, looking at the lines of children that seemed to go on endlessly, "we're overwhelmed. We can process a few hundred a day but there are thousands of children and a lot of them are alone."

Basil saw that most of the children carried suitcases, containing everything they possessed. Most of them were dirty and just stood in line quietly because they could not think of what else to do.

"And what happens to them from here?" he asked.

"Once we have processed them and given them identity cards, we put them on trains and send them to Holland where they are put on boats to Harwich."

"And after that?" asked Basil.

"We send our lists to England where volunteers start looking for foster homes for the children," said Clive. Clive pointed to a thin, dirty child sitting in a chair, next to a score of other children. "That little boy," he continued, "came to us from Czechoslovakia. One night in March he was woken up by German soldiers marching into the town square in Ostrava. It was the night that Hitler invaded, and, two weeks later, his mother and older sisters put him on a train to Berlin. They must have heard that we were arranging for children to leave Germany. He slept in the parks for three weeks until someone found him and brought him here."

"Is there anything I can do to help?" asked Basil. He looked at the boy from Ostrava, sitting with the other children, and realised that most of them were younger than his own two children, Howard and Catherine.

"Individually, there is almost nothing anyone can do," said Clive. "Almost every country in Europe is now trying to send their Jewish children to England. When they get there, they are accommodated in camps, private schools or hostels. The government has set up an organisation called 'Care of Children from Germany' to find more long-term accommodation solutions."

"Yes, my wife is one of their coordinators," said Basil.

Clive looked at him for a moment. "Your wife isn't Celia Drewe?"

"Yes," said Basil. "Have you come across her?"

"Come across her?" repeated Clive ardently. "She's often the first person we speak to when we send a group of children to England. You must be immensely proud of her and the work she's doing."

Basil smiled and agreed. He had not appreciated the immensity of the task that Celia faced each day until he saw the lines of children.

"A lot of the children that you see here today will be placed by your wife," continued Clive. "I'm sure that most of the people here would want to pass on their thanks to Mrs. Drewe if they knew you were here."

***

Basil left the passport control office a little before eleven after speaking to Clive about his brother. The line that spread down the Tiergartenstrasse had not become any smaller despite twenty-four staff working continuously at processing the children. Basil walked slowly down the line, which went beside the park and towards the zoological gardens. Many of the children looked hungry, some were crying, and others were hugging siblings or friends. At the end of the line was a little girl, no older than six, standing on her own with a dirty, tear-streaked face. He wanted to stay and help, but he needed to get to Salzburg and then on to Linz. By the entrance of the zoological gardens was a small gift shop. Basil hesitated but went in. He saw a small stuffed toy, fashioned as a gorilla with a button nose and dark brown glass eyes. He thought for a moment, bought it and a bar of chocolate, and went back out and handed it to the girl.

231

"Bitte. Sie heisst Gloria," said Basil. The girl looked at the stuffed toy and then clasped it to her but did not say one word. Basil turned and walked towards the train station. He wondered which of the children he had just seen would be dealt with by his wife. There were so many of them that it seemed a hopeless undertaking, and all he had done was give one child a stuffed toy.

Clive had discovered that the train that Christian was on had stopped in Linz for twenty minutes longer than scheduled. Clive had also said that it could be anything, a German military train going past or a change in the schedule; however, it was a starting point. Before he left the passport control office, Basil arranged for a telegram to be sent to Tomas at the St Gilgen address, saying that he would be arriving in Salzburg in the late evening and giving the name of the hotel he was staying at.

He arrived at eight, after a long day on the train. Tomas was waiting for him and, as the dining room was about to close within the next thirty minutes, they decided to talk over a meal.

"Kit locked up the apartment in Vienna," said Tomas, "and as far as I know got on the train as planned. He intended to come to St Gilgen for a few weeks and then go back to England and then on to America."

"Why America?"

"I don't really know," said Tomas. "I hadn't seen Kit for over a year, and we only ever spoke briefly on the telephone when I called him from Salzburg. A few weeks ago, he had all his belongings sent here. He said he would explain everything to me when he came."

"And so, what happened?" asked Basil.

"When he didn't arrive, I telephoned the apartment in Vienna, but no one answered," replied Tomas, "and then I filed a missing person's report here in Salzburg after a few days."

"And what did the Salzburg police say?"

"They said that if Herr Drewe had not arrived in Salzburg, there was nothing they could do. They closed the case as quickly as possible."

"Is there anything else?" asked Basil. "It doesn't matter how irrelevant you think it is; it may be important."

Tomas sat thinking. There was nothing more he could think of and then he said. "A friend of his, Rachel Kraus, was on the same train with her parents but they wouldn't have been travelling together as she's a Jew."

"Where are they? Can I talk to them?".

"No, they were going on to Marseille and then Palestine."

It was the third day of travelling for Basil and when he arrived at Linz, he was tired. He went directly to his hotel and was again made to submit his passport. Clive had arranged for him to speak to several officials who were charming but could not explain what had happened to his brother. They had contacted all the other stations along the line, and there was no news of Christian at any one of them. By Friday morning he had run out of ideas and places to visit. He decided to walk down to the railway station and speak to the staff there, however, none of the guards said they had seen anything. He returned to his hotel packed up his suitcase once more, arranged a ticket to Vienna and flight back to London, sent Tomas a telegram, hoping he might have news, and ordered a taxi to the train station.

Basil sat looking out of the train window, depressed that his journey had proven fruitless. He had failed to find out anything about his brother and thought that he had let him down. He soon came to the pretty little town of Mauthausen. In the distance, he could see rows of tree-lined lanes with tiny, picturesque houses. Baskets of flowers hung in the porches and in their front gardens were bicycles and toys left by excited children. Behind these houses, and far away out of sight, was the Mauthausen concentration camp where women judged troublesome were dragged under ice-cold showers on winter nights and kept there until they convulsed and died.

Chapter 40

"It was heartbreaking," said Basil, as he sat down in his armchair in his apartment in London. "Lines of children going on for more than a quarter of a mile and everyone doing their very best to get them to safety. Many of them were a lot younger than the twins. I hadn't appreciated the scale of the problem or what you were doing."

"Were they all alone?" asked Celia.

"Some," said Basil. "Clive told me that a few of the children's parents had been killed and others were being detained in work camps. Any Jew old enough to work is being used as forced labour. However, even those who can pay to leave are struggling to get here. I hadn't realised that we were stopping the children's parents from coming to England."

"There's a limit on who we can bring into the country, and we can't check every person that we allow in," said Celia.

Basil started to tap his fingers on the arm of the chair, in the same way that he often did when he struggled to find the answer to a crossword problem. Celia looked at him.

"What are you thinking?" she finally asked.

Basil sat forward in his armchair and looked at Celia. Castle Drogo was almost empty and only his mother lived there, with a few staff and groundsmen. It could house between thirty and fifty children if they employed some nurses and a few more housekeepers and cooks. The children could go to school in Drewsteignton, and a bus could be arranged to pick them up and return them. Basil explained his idea.

"What do you think?"

"Have you asked your mother?" said Celia.

"Not yet, although I'm certain she'll agree. She's always complaining about how quiet it is there." Basil took a breath. "But what about you?" he added. "It's going to mean more work."

"I don't see why," said Celia. "Unless you're expecting me to go there and be the nurse or the housekeeper."

"Of course not," said Basil. "I was thinking that we would take the children temporarily until permanent places to stay can be found. If we simply take thirty children then that would be a drop in the ocean but if we find them permanent homes as well, we could have hundreds of children passing through Castle Drogo. I thought you could help my mother set up a committee to find places in Exeter," continued Basil, "and your mother might want to help as well."

"My mother?" said Celia. "I rarely ever see her."

Basil stopped tapping his fingers.

"It might give her a new purpose since she resigned from the Theosophy Society."

***

Number 19 Mansfield Street, Marylebone, London was a substantial brick building with white Portland stone around the sash windows and door. It was five storeys in height, including the basement rooms that the servants occupied. Celia had never felt it was her home. Her parents had bought the house after the Great War and Celia had never lived there, except for six months when she came back to England from America. She now rarely ever set foot in the house, except on family occasions when it would have appeared strange if she, Basil and the children had not been invited.

"I have to say I was surprised to receive a note from you," said Emily, after Celia was brought into the living room and had sat down.

"I wouldn't have written," said Celia, "except that this is important to both Basil and me, and we think you can help."

"So, you want my help now?" replied her mother. "You have hardly acknowledged me since you came back from India, and now eight years later you come around asking for my help."

"That's not entirely true," said Celia. "You have never approved of me and made that perfectly plain."

"You were having an affair," said Emily, her face flushed. "What was I supposed to do, stand up and applaud you? You ignored me then and you've deliberately ignored me year after year without an apology. Give me one reason why I should help you?"

Celia sat forward. She had dealt with more difficult characters over the last six years than her mother and she believed that what she was doing was too important to let her emotions get the better of her.

"I'll give you ten thousand reasons," said Celia emphatically. "You know what I've been doing for the last ten months with the displaced Jewish children from Europe. It's about them and it's important. But if you want to talk about that affair, then yes, I regret it. However, I don't owe you an apology. I never have owed you an apology. There is only one person to whom I should apologise; however, he doesn't know, and he will never know." Celia took in a deep breath. "So, are you ready to talk to me about helping the refugees or would you prefer to roll up your sleeves and have this out?"

Celia left two hours later, and she was in a determined mood. When each of them had said their piece, her mother had then become surprisingly helpful. She had grasped the problem and realised that this was something where she could use her organisational talents. As Celia was taking a taxi back to Cadogan Square, Emily was talking on the telephone to Lady Frances and a committee for the rehousing of children in Exeter would be formed.

Chapter 41

September 1940

On the 7th of September 1940, a warm, hazy day in London, the game changed. Instead of targeting the Royal Air Force bases, aircraft factories and radar stations, the German bombers began an attack on London, in what became known as the Blitz. Wave after wave of German bombers crossed the coast and instead of splitting up to target air force bases, they continued straight on. The Royal Air Force engaged the German planes at four thirty-five p.m., although overwhelmed nearly ten to one. The bombers reached London at five-fifteen p.m. and started dropping their payload over the docks and the East End. That was the first wave and more bombers arrived over London in the evening. The attacks kept on coming through the night until the sky was lit red. The bombers came the following day, and the day after and the day after that. There was almost no respite for those who lived in London.

"We're not arguing about this," said Basil, as he undid the collar of his uniform. "You and the twins are going to Castle Drogo where you'll be safe."

"And what about you?"

"I have to stay here," said Basil. "I'm a captain in the Judge Advocate General's office and they would shoot me if I deserted."

"And what am I going to do in Devon?" asked Celia testily. Basil went to the drinks cabinet and poured two large gin and tonics, handing one to Celia.

"You're going to do the same as you've done in the past. There is going to be an exodus of children leaving London and you'll need to find them homes to live in while this war continues."

"But I can't do that from Devon," said Celia. "I need to be here coordinating things."

"Nonsense," said Basil. "We're not living in the dark ages; we have telephones at Castle Drogo, and you can work there just as efficiently as you can in London. More important than you and me," Basil took a long gulp of his drink, "we need to think about our children. I can't go and you must be there for them. I can't believe we are even discussing this."

Celia thought about what Basil had said, and while she knew he was right, she enjoyed her life in the city with her friends and everything it offered. She wondered what she would do at Castle Drogo, day after dreary day, and worried she would end up doing nothing more than be a nanny, a teacher or a nurse.

"There was a time," said Basil, "when you said you wanted to live in a castle."

"But we all grow up," said Celia, and as she said it, she wondered how much she had changed in the last ten years. "Anyway," she said, "who is going to tell the twins that they must leave their home and their friends? I think it would be better if it came from you."

"I've already told them," replied Basil, "and although they weren't pleased, they understood why we were making that decision."

"So, you told them without consulting me," said Celia. "You are the limit, Basil!"

Celia put down her glass on the table and went to the bedroom to change. She was meeting some colleagues in the Dorchester Hotel later that evening and would then be going on for a late supper. She was relieved that Basil had said he could not attend and felt irritated with him for making decisions that affected her life, without any discussion. Of course, if he had spoken to her, she would have agreed with him; but that was not the point.

Basil watched as Celia left the room and thought to himself, 'I didn't tell you because you weren't here. You're rarely here.'

***

Basil stood before the War Office building. The imposing Edwardian Baroque exterior was hidden by sandbags and boarding, to stop the windows from shattering. The War Office was open both day and night. On the roof were spotters and those who worked in the building would only go down to the shelters and the sub-basement when the bombers came close. When they fled to the basement, as the sirens sounded, the slamming of iron doors could be heard down at the bottom of the lift shafts. Basil showed his pass at the door. Even though the guards knew him by name, he was still required each day to prove his identity before he was allowed to enter.

Basil made his way to an office at the back of the building where the Judge Advocate General's department was located. He had been assigned the job of looking at the detention and internment of refugees. The government's position was that they should inter anyone if there was the slightest doubt about their allegiance. Publicly the government stated that they hoped all German refugees were loyal to Britain. However, privately Maxwell Fyfe said to Basil that there could be no certainty about this, and the government would be applying a zero-tolerance policy. Refugees had to prove that they were innocent, and Basil had to implement this policy despite disagreeing with it. As Basil sat at his desk on the 20th of September 1940, he was passed a note saying that Maxwell Fyfe had been badly injured in an air attack the night before and was at St Thomas' Hospital.

***

"Malingering?" said Basil, as he looked at the battered and bandaged Maxwell Fyfe with his leg in a cast. Maxwell Fyfe opened his eyes and tried to smile. "Just lie still," Basil continued. "I thought I would see how you are." He pulled up a chair and sat down. "I've brought you a copy of Marcus Aurelius's *Meditations* and some grapes. A friend of mine at university used to go on and on about this book and, as you claim to like history, I thought I would bring you a copy." Basil placed the book on a little table by the side of the bed. He then put the bag of grapes next to it. "Sorry, I ate a few," he added. "They made me wait for an hour before I could see you and it was either reread Marcus Aurelius for the fourth time or eat grapes. The grapes won."

Maxwell Fyfe nodded his head.

"The doctors said you'll make a full recovery in time," continued Basil. "Did you know I was here when I shattered my leg?" He didn't wait for an answer, nor did he expect one as Maxwell Fyfe had closed his eyes. "I was in the children's ward of course, which is on the other side of the hospital. The nurses were much prettier then." Basil picked up the bag of grapes took one, chewed and swallowed it. "They are quite delicious, although I never think to buy myself fruit. I'm surprised I don't have scurvy."

Maxwell Fyfe opened his eyes again and leant towards Basil.

"Could you send a message to Sylvia?" he whispered.

"Of course," said Basil.

"Tell her not to come," said Maxwell Fyfe, who started coughing, "to stay in Liverpool with the girls."

"I'll tell her that," said Basil who placed the bag of grapes on the side of the bed next to Maxwell Fyfe. "I'll leave these there," he added, "and I'll see you tomorrow. Try not to eat them all. Is there anything I can get from your apartment or anything that you need from the shops?" However, Maxwell Fyfe did not answer and was again fast asleep.

***

"And how are things with you?" asked Basil, as he held the receiver to his ear. He had poured himself a large gin and tonic and looked at it.

"Fine," said Celia curtly. "I was sorry to hear about David."

"Oh, he will be up and about in no time," said Basil. "He's as tough as old boots, but he did take a knock. The doctors said he would be drowsy for a few days. When I came back from the hospital, I called Sylvia. It was a job to convince her not to come down, however, I promised I would see Maxwell Fyfe every day and report back to her."

"And are things as bad as the papers suggest in London?"

"Probably worse," said Basil. "Everyone in the apartments has put bedrolls down in the basement. I've slept there two or three times in the last week. The young couple who moved in a few months ago seem to be on tenterhooks and the elderly couple who live above us are pretending

240

that it's just a jolly holiday at the seaside."

"What on earth do you mean?" asked Celia.

"They suggested that we sing 'It's A Long Way To Tipperary' and 'Daisy, Daisy'. All I wanted to do was complete the crossword and get some sleep."

"Aren't you scared?" asked Celia. "I would be terrified."

"When you're down there it's not too bad. The worst time is when you're on the bus going to work, and the sirens start. You jump off and run for shelter and even if my leg starts hurting, I can't stop and then it will ache for the rest of the day."

"Aren't you using the herbs that Majda recommended?"

"Sometimes, but I can't massage my leg the way you do it. How are things going with the waifs and strays that are being sent down to you?"

"They're very different from the Jewish refugees. The Jewish children were so happy to have a home that was safe and quiet and miles away from the troubles of the world. The London children just complain that there's nothing to do. We had one group of children who complained so much we had to send them to a place in Exeter. And it's not just the children."

"Who else?" asked Basil.

"Some of the parents who come to visit their children have also complained. One mother said that it took her nearly a whole day to get here, as she had to take three different buses after she got to Exeter and that by the time she got here, she had to go. I felt so bad for her that I told her to stay for a few hours and arranged for Poley to drive her back to Exeter."

"Do you have enough petrol rations for that?" asked Basil.

"We'll manage," said Celia. "I also heard from Robert. He's got some leave coming up and thought he would come and see us, then drop in on you on his way back. And there's also one other thing. The roof is leaking again."

"Christ!" said Basil. "Will the bills for that place never stop?"

"Your father asked for a castle in the middle of a windswept moor with battlements," said Celia. "And as he used to say: 'What is paradise for one is purgatory for another.'"

***

Robert was a good inch taller than Basil and had beautiful, green piercing eyes – according to his fiancée. His black hair was combed back and glistened with Brylcreem. Eton had changed him, bringing him confidence, and now the war had changed him again. In the time that Basil had known him, he had gone from a little boy who hung to the skirts of his mother to an independent and assured man. He knew his capabilities and his limitations, but then, thought Basil, when you sit in the cockpit of a Spitfire, looking through the crosshairs, you must have a certain amount of confidence but not so much as to be complacent.

"It's good to see you, my boy," said Basil.

"And you, Basil," said Robert. "I've just come up from seeing Mother."

"Any special reason for the visit? I'm not complaining but it is a bit out of the blue." He got up, opened the drinks cabinet, and took out a bottle of gin. "G and T?" he asked.

"Yes, to both questions," said Robert. He followed Basil who held two glasses and wandered along the hall to the kitchen.

"I'm listening," said Basil, as walked towards the freezer.

"I'm going to get married," said Robert.

Basil stopped and looked at his stepson and then turned, opened the freezer door and put two lumps of ice into each glass he was holding.

"Congratulations. I assume to Wendy." He put the glasses on the kitchen table.

"Who else would it be?" said Robert.

"Well, let me shake your hand," said Basil but then he looked again at his stepson. "Damn it, come here – I want to give you a hug."

They went back into the living room with their drinks and sat down.

"Your mother was my first love," said Basil. "I think I fell in love with her in a garden in Thursley when I was sixteen. She was eighteen and the most beautiful person I had ever seen and three years later she went to America, and I never saw her again until she returned."

Basil took a sip of his drink.

"And you never met my father?" asked Robert.

"I once told your mother that she could talk to me about him whenever she was ready, but she never wanted to, except to say that he died in the war."

"She's never spoken much about him to me either," said Robert. "Although I do know his name was Adrian."

Basil put down his glass and turned away from Robert. He looked out the window for a moment and then pulled the blackout curtains shut. In his heart, he had known. There were mannerisms that Robert had which reminded Basil of his brother – the way he stood and smoked a cigarette. There was also the resemblance to his brother so when Robert had said his brother's name it hadn't surprised him. However, Basil knew it wasn't for him to say anything; this was something Celia had to do in her own time.

Basil looked around the room, at a loss as to what to say next, and then saw a copy of Plato's *Symposium*, which he had left on the table to take to Maxwell Fyfe. "Have you read that?" he asked, pointing to the book. Robert shook his head. "Plato said that humans were originally created with four arms, four legs and a head with two faces. Fearing their power, Zeus split them into two separate parts, condemning them to spend their lives in search of their other half. Anyway, that's how I've always felt about your mother. She makes me the perfect whole." He took a sip from his drink. "I think, however, that your mother often looks back at the past, thinking that her perfect other half was killed in the last war."

***

As Robert drove back to RAF Biggin Hill, he thought about what Basil had said to him. He knew that Basil was devoted to his mother, but it was a very English devotion. Basil did not wear his heart on his sleeve – he was just not that type of man. His love was deeper and heartfelt, although someone who did not know him might think it was indifference. His mother was different. At moments, he saw the passion she had and an unstoppable determination to possess whatever she wanted. However, he believed that what Basil had said was true and that her true love lay in the past, with a soldier who died on a battlefield on the Western Front. Robert was unsure which of their stories was the saddest. He felt a spot of rain as he drove his sports car and then the heavens opened.

***

It had been a quiet morning at the War Office as, once again, the East End of London had taken the brunt of the bombing during the night. Basil sat at his desk, with a file marked 'SS *Arandora Star*' in front of him. The *Arandora Star* was a passenger ship that had been sunk in the Atlantic in July three months prior, as it sailed for Canada, overloaded with internees. Half the people on board had died – seven hundred Italians, four hundred and thirty-eight Germans, being either Nazi sympathisers or Jewish refugees, and seamen and soldiers. Basil methodically went down the manifest until he came to the name Abram Rosenthal, which he underlined. He made a note and then opened another file marked 'Rosenthal A.' and placed the note within it.

The story of Abram Rosenthal was not uncommon, and Basil had read similar stories in his case files. Abram's parents had come to England from Germany, and he had been born and grew up in Britain. He had returned to Linz in 1930 on business, where he fell in love, married a local girl and set up a home there. During *Kristallnacht*, he and his wife had been arrested and friends took in their daughter, later sending her to Berlin to join the *Kindertransport*. In 1939 Abram managed to get released from his camp, using money that had been sent by relatives in Britain. A few months later he arrived in England and started looking for his wife and daughter, however, he was immediately arrested and put on a boat to an internment camp in Canada. Abram had died when the *Arandora Star* was torpedoed, and his relatives were now seeking compensation, because, as a British citizen, the arrest had been wrongful.

Basil looked at the application for compensation made by the Rosenthal family in which they claimed monies for 'illegal transportation'. Even though Abram was of alien descent, his registration at birth in England meant that he should not have been deported. Basil checked that all the documents were in order and stamped the claim 'approved'. Basil noted down one outstanding issue – to whom to pay the compensation. There was evidence that Abram's wife had died in Germany, but Abram also had a daughter, Greta. If she was still alive, she would be entitled to the compensation. He therefore dictated a letter to 'Care of Children from

Germany' asking them to ascertain whether the missing child was in Britain and, if so, to establish her location.

Basil would never know that a little eight-year-old girl called Greta Rosenthal was sleeping in a bed in a house in Exeter, clutching a stuffed toy gorilla called Gloria.

Chapter 42

May 1941

Celia put down the newspaper. The bombings of London were decreasing, and those people who had been evacuated were talking about going back home. The German Luftwaffe had changed its tactics in the last six months and begun to focus on other cities like Coventry, Birmingham and Liverpool and now they were targeting shipping, to starve Britain into surrender.

On Dartmoor, behind the solid granite walls of Castle Drogo, it was hard to imagine the barrage balloons high in the sky, sleeping in the Underground, or discussing the Blitz as if it were the weather. London seemed an eternity away and Celia also wondered whether it was time to pack her things and take the children home. She looked at her watch; Basil was coming down later in the morning and she needed to drive to Exeter to fetch him.

"When was the last time you were here?" said Celia, as Basil put his briefcase in the back of the car.

"Nearly three months ago," he answered. "I thought you would have brought along the twins."

"I wanted to talk about something and thought we ought to have a quiet word." Celia got into the driver's seat and Basil looked at her.

"Do you want me to drive?" he asked.

"No," replied Celia. "Hop in."

Basil opened the passenger side door and got in. "Hop in," he said. "That sounds American."

"There are some Canadians barracked at Okehampton," said Celia. "We've been going into town and chatting with them and a few of them have come up to the castle on their days off."

"That must be pleasant for them," said Basil, and he looked over at his wife as she pulled away from the station. "What was it that you wanted to discuss?"

"Whether the twins and I should come home."

Celia took a packet of cigarettes from her cardigan, put one in her mouth and lit it, holding the steering wheel steady with her knee.

"American cigarettes," said Basil, as he looked at the packet on her lap.

"Yes," replied Celia. "The Canadians have everything here from stockings to chocolate. You don't mind me smoking, do you?" Basil decided that the last thing he wanted to do was argue with Celia, given that he had not seen her in months, and said that he didn't mind. "So, what do you think about us coming back? How bad are things in London?"

"Actually," said Basil, "things aren't that bad at all. Surprisingly the bombing has had the effect of making everyone pull together and it was not nearly as dangerous as everyone feared at the start."

"So, you think we should come home?" said Celia.

"No," said Basil, "and if I tell you why you have to promise never to say a word to anyone." Celia looked over at him and nodded. "First, the Germans have stopped for now, but they could restart bombing London tomorrow; and second…" Basil paused. "Celia, what I am going to tell you must never be repeated."

"I won't say a word."

"I would be shot for telling you this. The Germans are manufacturing missiles that can be fired across the channel. No one knows when they will start firing them, but our intelligence is that they may be ready soon – we just don't know. Unlike the bombs which are being dropped mainly on military targets, these missiles can land anywhere."

"I was hoping…" Celia began.

"I was hoping as well," Basil interrupted, "but it's not safe for either you or the twins in London. Staying here is the only way to keep them protected and give them some stability, although I know it will be hard for you."

⁕

It was as if she had seen a ghost when Lady Frances saw her youngest son. In the few months that had passed, he had noticeably become thinner and his hair greyer – even his moustache was tinged with grey. He looked older than his age, and he was only in his early forties. She watched as he limped up the stairs to the dining room – and as he saw her, he hid whatever pain he was feeling behind a smile.

"You're looking well," she said, trying her best to maintain her reserve.

Basil knew she was lying. "You too," he responded.

"Your leg seems to be causing you some discomfort," Lady Frances said.

"I'm struggling to get the herbs I need for the poultice," he said, by way of explanation. "And I had forgotten how arduous the journey here was." He sat down on a chair and his face visibly relaxed. "I'm now going to take a long bath and ask Celia to massage my leg."

VI

Part Six

Chapter 43

25 December 1943

Basil had telephoned and said that he would try his best and come down for Christmas Day but that if he couldn't, the children should still have a special day, as they should not be cheated out of the one day they looked forward to for the whole of the year. However, the war did not stop in London or around the world and those who fought, or drove ambulances, or put out fires, or patrolled the streets had to continue working like any other day. Those who still had shops put up tinsel and streamers, and holly sprigs adorned the barbed wire. The children wanted to celebrate their heroes. The boys asked for model aeroplanes – Spitfires, Hurricanes and Wellington bombers. The pilots were their new idols – "Johnnie" Johnson, "Cherry" Vale and "Ginger" Lacey. All of them had nicknames – as did "Deadeye" Drewe, who was credited with shooting down twelve enemy aircraft.

It was another year that the church bells were not rung on Christmas Day. No church bells were allowed to be rung, as this would mean the invader had come. On Christmas Eve, everyone prayed for a storm, as on these nights the German bombers stayed at home. No one felt sorry for themselves; everyone understood that they were fighting for liberty and that if England failed, the world would be a darker place. One did not think about defeat, as the consequences of that were so terrible. Quietly, and in their own way, the people prayed to the Prince of Peace.

"We'll wait for your father," said Celia, "before we open the presents."

"Are you sure he's coming?" said Catherine, buttering some toast.

"He'll come," said Celia, "or at least he'll move heaven and earth to try. He promised he would do his best, and you know your father is not one to break his word."

"I miss him," said Catherine.

"Me too," said Howard.

"We all miss him," said Lady Frances, as she signalled to one of the butlers that she wanted more tea. She looked towards Celia. "I'm also sorry that your parents could not come."

"Mother is looking after Father," said Celia, "and he refuses to leave their home in London. When I spoke to him on the telephone yesterday, he said to me in a rather fatalistic way: 'You get it – or not! Wherever you are.'"

After breakfast, the family went around the estate to wish each of the workers a merry Christmas. It was a tradition that had started at Wadhurst Hall and had been carried on after the Drewes moved to Castle Drogo. The twins carried bags of small presents – baskets of fruit, biscuits, preserves and chutneys. Little packages of nuts had been prepared for the children. As lunchtime approached, Lady Frances had spoken to every estate worker and then suggested to Celia and the children that they walk down to the gates of the estate and look out for Basil.

"I'm not sure I want to give the children false hope," said Celia.

"He'll come," said Lady Frances, as she watched the twins run off ahead. "Can I speak frankly?"

"Of course," replied Celia, who pulled her coat around her as the wind blew across the moor.

"Why don't you divorce him?"

"What on earth makes you say that?" responded Celia, who stopped and looked at her mother-in-law. Lady Frances also halted. Her coat was unbuttoned but she appeared not to feel the cold.

"I don't think you've ever loved him. I didn't think it when you first came here with him, and I don't think it today."

"It's delicate," said Celia.

"It always is," said Lady Frances.

Celia took out a packet of cigarettes and lit one. She took a puff and slowly blew out the smoke.

"And then there's the children."

"Yes, the children," said Lady Frances. "It's a shame you didn't think about them when you spent that afternoon in the Okehampton Hotel with that Canadian officer."

"Who told you that?" demanded Celia.

"You were seen by someone, if you must know. Who it was is not important. I pretended that I knew you would be there and said that you had gone to arrange the Christmas dance for the servicemen. However, let's not pretend to each other this was an isolated occasion."

"And what do you propose to do about it?" asked Celia, taking another puff of her cigarette before dropping it and crushing the remains into the cinder path.

"I hope I don't have to do anything," said Lady Frances, "because you are going to tell Basil. And let's be clear, I will tell him if you don't. I am not going to have people point at him and laugh behind his back. He deserves better than that."

Lady Frances turned and walked towards the twins who were standing at the gates of the estate looking out across the moor. Celia stood motionless. Lady Frances was nothing if not honest. She knew that if she did not tell Basil then Lady Frances would. She felt a lump in her throat and tears pricked her eyes, as the cold wind beat around her. She wondered what Basil would say and hoped that he would take the news in that cold, reserved manner that he had, and not make a fuss.

***

"What are you reading now?" asked Celia, who swallowed a last mouthful of tea and placed the cup in the sink.

"It's nothing," said Basil, as he closed his book.

"Are you ready to go?" she asked sharply.

"I just need to put my shoes on." He got up and went into the hall.

Celia's father, Edwin Landseer Lutyens, had died on the 1st of January 1944, after battling cancer for three years. He was cremated fourteen days later at Golders Green Crematorium. His ashes were taken from the crematorium and buried in the crypt of St Paul's Cathedral, beneath a memorial tablet designed by his friend and fellow architect William Curtis Green. As the cortège arrived at the cathedral, pigeons swooped down, looking for any crumbs they could eat.

There had been a frosty silence at the crematorium; Celia said nothing but stared ahead with red eyes. Her mother had cried for a few moments, the first time Celia had seen it. Her brother and his wife stood beside her mother, and her sisters huddled in a group with their husbands and children – each of whom wore a dark suit and black tie or black dress. The children held their tongues. Only the babies cried, unaware of the necessity for silence.

Basil stood silently, hardly listening to the service or the long eulogies extolling the achievements of his father-in-law. He was forty-five years old and had nothing to show for his life. He was a moderately successful barrister and a captain in the Judge Advocate General's office, however, if he died tomorrow, there would be no plaque in St Paul's Cathedral and, when his children died, he would be forgotten. He would be erased from everyone's memory like a raindrop in an ocean. He looked down at his polished black shoes. Compared to his father or Lutyens he was not a success. "Must do better," he said to himself. They were the words his father had so often chastised him with when he was a small child.

He looked at his wife standing next to him. They had never been further apart in all their lives. She had admitted to having an affair with a Canadian officer. She did not even fear that he might walk out and leave her. She calmly said that she would remain at Castle Drogo until the war was over, as it was best for the children because they were settled at their school. They could then decide what to do – whether "to make a go of it" – her words, not his. She said that when he visited the children, it was probably best if they had separate rooms. He looked downwards again at his shoes and a tear fell onto the polished leather.

The service lasted less than two hours, and then it was expected that the family wait at the cathedral door and thank those who had attended. Basil stood behind Celia listening to platitudes given solemnly and sometimes sincerely. Emily put on a brave face. It was strange, thought Basil, that she and her husband had spent so much of their lives apart but in the end, in the last few years, they were always together. Lutyens had even said that he loved her more now than the day they married. The human condition, thought Basil, was unfathomable.

***

In June of 1945, Celia finally said that she wanted to come back to London and make a go of it for the children's sake. Basil agreed but with a sense of trepidation. It was easier said than done to forgive and forget, as even a cripple has some vanity. He wanted to be with his children. He wanted his marriage to work, but a lack of trust ate at his heart. For the first few weeks, he and Celia skated around each other, even though they made a pretence to the children that things were back to normal. Celia moved back into the bedroom and shared the marital bed. However, after a month, the war dropped another bomb.

"I'm going to have to go abroad soon," said Basil.

Celia looked at him as she sat in bed reading a Raymond Chandler book, *The Lady in the Lake.*

"Why?" she asked, placing a bookmark on her page. She knew it would be at least another day before she found out whether Philip Marlowe had caught the killer.

"Because they're holding a trial of the Nazi High Command and it will be in Nuremberg," answered Basil.

"I thought that they would have just lined up the High Command and shot them."

"Churchill wanted to do that, but the Americans are insisting on a full trial in front of a specially convened court. Yesterday, Maxwell Fyfe ordered me to attend."

"Was it his idea or yours?" asked Celia.

"Does it matter?" said Basil. "This will be the most important legal case of the century."

"And what about us?"

"Frankly," said Basil, "we are treading on eggshells, and perhaps some time apart will do us good."

"We were apart for over four years," said Celia, "and it didn't do us any good."

Basil bit his lip. He wasn't the one who had had an affair. She was in no position to demand anything of him, and he turned and left the room without another word.

Celia watched as he walked out. She hated his icy indifference and had no way to fight against it. She would have preferred if he had lost his temper when she had told him about the affair, but he just listened to her and said, "I suppose I shouldn't be surprised." He just stoically acknowledged the situation, as if he had been given bad news from a doctor. If the boot were on the other foot she would have packed her bags, slapped him across the face and divorced him. However, he just accepted it like a beaten dog and when she had said she wanted to come back to London with the children he had said, "I want that too." Celia knew precisely what he would be doing now, pouring himself a gin and tonic and then doing *The Times* crossword, and she wondered whether she had made him like that.

Chapter 44

August 1945

A cloud of dust hung over Nuremberg and swirled in the light breeze. The city had been bombed by both the Americans and British, and nearly all of it had been destroyed. It had been taken by the Americans and Russians in April 1945 and the old medieval city, once the seat of the German kings, lay in ruins. In the aftermath of the destruction, the inhabitants of Nuremberg started to clear away the debris and dust that engulfed the city. A decision was made to rebuild the city in the image of what it was before, a sun among the moon and stars, as Albrecht Dürer had described it. Basil arrived in Nuremberg at the end of August 1945. He had been promoted to the rank of major and his first action was to visit the camp at Dachau, which the US Army was using as a prison camp for war criminals and members of the SS. The chilling slogan, *Arbeit macht frei,* was still there on the metal gates as one entered the camp.

When Basil drove out of Dachau, he felt as if he had left a small part of his humanity there. He had known what had happened in the concentration camps before he went, but standing in one, being shown the mass graves, the gas chambers, the furnaces, the bullet-riddled walls and the photographs of those who died, was something quite different. He had seen and defended murderers, but nothing had prepared him for what he saw. He was ashen-faced and angry when he left. Thirty-two thousand Jews had died there and when the camp was relieved there were ten thousand people who could not be closer to death. How could anyone have allowed it to happen? He felt that the world should be dragged to the gates of Dachau to see the horror of it. He was determined that the same thing should never be allowed to happen again and that those who turned a blind eye to what was happening were just as bad as those who actively perpetrated the crimes.

Court Room 600 of the Palace of Justice in Nuremberg had been designated as the room for the trial of the Nazi High Command. The Palace of Justice had been one of the few buildings left unscathed by the Allied bombing and had a large prison complex. Basil was taken to a room on the top floor, where the British delegation had established themselves. Behind an oak desk sat Maxwell Fyfe. Basil hadn't seen him for nearly six months and noticed that he had put on weight, become a little more pear-shaped, and that the top of his large square head was becoming noticeably bald.

"Drewe, I was expecting you a few days ago," said Maxwell Fyfe. "I'll introduce you to everyone shortly. There's over one hundred and fifty of us here, including secretaries, and we're working every hour, but you'll be used to that. Also, I should tell you that presently the phones are out, so it's impossible to call home."

"Sorry for the delay," said Basil, "but I went to Dachau."

"It's not a place you forget," said Maxwell Fyfe.

"No one should ever forget that place," Basil replied.

Maxwell Fyfe looked at Basil, who stood with his hands behind his back. He noticed that Basil was looking older and a little greyer.

"We have pretty much agreed to divide the work up between ourselves with the Americans taking the lead. The Russians will be dealing with the atrocities to the Slavs, and the French – well who knows? I am going to lead the cross-examination of Goering, Keitel and Hess; I'll want some help from you on that."

Even with the windows closed, the noise of the traffic outside the courthouse could still be heard and soldiers were still driving through the city cheering incessantly.

"Usually about this time, we have a meeting to discuss what information we have unearthed. We then have weekly meetings with our counterparts on the Soviet, French, and American teams to ensure that all relevant evidence is exchanged." Maxwell Fyfe stood up. "But be a little careful and don't take anything they say as fact."

They walked down a dusty hallway to a small auditorium where inside was Sir Hartley Shawcross, Britain's chief prosecutor. Sir Hartley was tall and slender and rather better-looking than it pays any man to be unless he is a film star. He looked down from the stage at forty other lawyers, whom Basil joined, and Maxwell Fyfe stood next to Sir Hartley.

"I see some new faces," Sir Hartley began, looking down at the legal team. "I will not pretend that what we must do is easy, and there are still thousands of documents to sift through in the coming weeks and months. Many of these documents will need to be translated; many have been partially destroyed or may be of little or no use. However, we are all here for a common purpose, which is that the truth should be established about the crimes that the defendants have committed, so that their mark may never be erased."

Basil listened as Sir Harley spoke about the work that Maxwell Fyfe had done for the preparation of the trial and Maxwell Fyfe spoke equally favourably about how Sir Hartley was progressing the case. Basil noted the kindness of Maxwell Fyfe's compliments, and he knew that the dour Scotsman thought highly of Sir Hartley, as he was never normally so forthcoming with his praise.

***

There was little to do in Nuremberg at the end of the day. However, Basil was surprised that in the heart of a city which had been substantially flattened, the Allies were able to get better food than he had been used to for the last five years in London. The French had eggs, ham and a seemingly endless supply of wine. The Russians had vodka, sometimes awful, sometimes exceptionally good; and, on one occasion, Basil was treated to caviar. The Americans managed to get chocolate, fresh meat and cigarettes. However, there was precious little that the British had, except cans of bully beef, tinned peas, Spam, baked beans, dehydrated milk and oatmeal.

For some reason that went beyond Basil's comprehension, Maxwell Fyfe seemed to enjoy the food. However, in his first week in Nuremberg, Basil ate very little except Spam and then he started receiving some food packs from Celia with a few bottles of whisky. As soon as news got out that Basil could bring whisky to dinner, his star was in the ascendant.

Maxwell Fyfe had a dry sense of humour, common for a Scot, and an ability to remember even the most obscure pieces of information. His views were more conservative than when he was younger, but then that was no surprise as he had been the Attorney General in Churchill's last cabinet. He was not a natural advocate but was clinically methodical and could drive a witness backwards step by step until they stood on the edge of an abyss and could do nothing but admit the truth. Basil's style of advocacy was different as he had a second sense about people. He instinctively knew when people were lying or when they sought to avoid a subject that they did not want to address. Basil was also a little more flamboyant in his advocacy, his style having been learnt at the criminal bar. Both men enjoyed a drink and each other's company and spent many evenings together talking and therefore it was not long before the subject of Celia and Basil's marriage was brought up.

"And how are things between you two?" said Maxwell Fyfe. "You hinted some time ago that all wasn't well."

"Something of an understatement," said Basil. "Things are, to be honest, a fucking mess." Basil finished his glass of wine. "We're going to need another bottle if we're going to discuss this."

Maxwell Fyfe drained his glass and called for the waiter to bring another bottle of red.

"I suppose we were apart for nearly four years. Celia was at Castle Drogo, and I was in London although I would come down whenever I was able to – but that wasn't often. Things were drifting along, and I suppose I let that happen. It wasn't perfect, but in wartime, you make do. I know she hated being there with nothing to do but I just thought it was best for everyone. Then, last Christmas, she told me that she had been having an affair with a colonel in the Canadian army." Maxwell Fyfe poured them both a glass. "Apparently it had not been going on for long – about three months from what I could gather." Basil stopped speaking and looked at Maxwell Fyfe before adding, "I hadn't any idea and it's rather knocked me for six and all I could say was that I wasn't surprised."

"And how had things been before that?"

"What do you mean?" said Basil.

"Had there been any previous indiscretions?"

"Not on my part," said Basil indignantly. "And as for her, I would say not, although we were apart for quite a long time when she went to India after the children were born. When she returned, she was different."

"In what way?" asked Maxwell Fyfe.

"She said that she needed to do something; that she needed a purpose in her life and that she wanted to work with underprivileged children. She then worked at Dr Barnardo's, and I could tell she was content or at least less unhappy. However, then she gave all of that up to work on the *Kindertransport* programme, which took up all her time. She worked night and day as if she needed to prove something to herself."

"I remember," said Maxwell Fyfe, "you told me that you two rarely saw each other because she was working so much. If I had to guess, I would say that you have both been so obsessed with your respective jobs that you hardly noticed your marriage was drifting apart and then – when she went to Castle Drogo and had nothing to do – she probably recognised that as well. You can't be surprised that she has had an affair. To be honest I'm surprised that you haven't had one as well. You may not be able to forget what has happened, but you have got to be able to forgive her – otherwise, there is no point continuing with your marriage. So, my advice is to speak or write to her as often as you can and most importantly, forgive her." Maxwell Fyfe looked at his friend. "Now, I've said my piece, so let's get roaring drunk!"

***

On the 21st of November 1945, in the Palace of Justice at Nuremberg, Germany, Justice Robert H. Jackson, Chief of Counsel for the United States, made his opening statement to the International Military Tribunal. The day before they had read the indictment. Basil sat next to Maxwell Fyfe as

Robert H. Jackson explained the case against the Nazi High Command. The opening went on for hours and when Basil left the courtroom, he vividly remembered the following, which was how the law had been corrupted and used against the Jewish people:

"The most serious of the actions against Jews were outside of any law, but the law itself was employed to some extent. There were the infamous Nuremberg decrees of September 15, 1935. The Jews were segregated into ghettos and put into forced labour; they were expelled from their professions; their property was expropriated; all cultural life, the press, the theatre, and schools were prohibited them.

"The persecution policy against the Jews commenced with nonviolent measures, such as disfranchisement and discriminations against their religion, and the placing of impediments in the way of success in economic life. It moved rapidly to organised mass violence against them, physical isolation in ghettos, deportation, forced labour, mass starvation, and extermination..."

Chapter 45

14 December 1945

Basil sat in his room in a building opposite the Nuremberg court. He drummed his fingers on the table, slowly and rhythmically, and wondered how he should start the letter to Celia. Their telephone conversations had been cordial and cool, mainly talking about the twins and Robert. However, at the start of the week, the phones stopped working again and Basil sat in front of a piece of paper not knowing what to write.

Dear Celia,

The Opening Statements went well. Yesterday, the Americans dealt with the concentration camps. The absolute horror of what the Nazis did still astounds me, and I still wake up in the night thinking about it. No one who saw those pictures will ever forget them or forgive what was done. It is difficult to understand what drove them to create these camps and then use them as a weapon in the battle against the Jews, against the Christian church, against labour, against those who wanted peace, against opposition or non-conformity of any kind. It was a systematic use of terror where anyone who opposed the Nazis could be confined without trial, often without charges, generally with no indication of the length of their detention. It is something that must never be allowed to happen again.

Basil looked at the letter on the writing table, then picked it up and screwed it into a ball. "Damn it," he said to himself; he thought that the letter read more like a dissertation than a letter to the woman he once loved. "Once loved," Basil said the words out loud, "still loved," he added. He was not sure which one was correct or whether they were both correct or both wrong. Words seemed such an insufficient medium for what he was feeling, and words were his forte. He began again.

Dear Celia,

It's cold here and the wind chills me to the bone. I miss you and our children and the warmth you give me. I don't think I have been so unhappy and lonely, and I realise now that I took you for granted for many years, especially during the war. I know that you must have told me a hundred times how you were feeling but I wasn't listening and did not understand. I must accept that I was partly to blame for what happened and hope that you can forgive me, as I am trying to forgive you.

Basil looked at the last six words. He wondered whether he should change them to "I have forgiven you." He brought his pen close to the paper intending to make the alteration and then stopped. It wouldn't be true, he thought to himself; he hadn't yet forgiven her, and he knew that it would be a long journey. He carried on writing.

I received a telegram yesterday from Tomas Skeres. He said that there was some news about Christian but did not say what it was. I wanted to speak to you about going to Vienna, but the telephones are not working again. I tried to imagine what you would say to me. Should I come home or spend part of the three weeks' break travelling to Vienna to meet Tomas? In my head I heard you say: "Get to Vienna as quickly as you can and then come home." It is what I have always loved about you – that decisiveness, that sense of purpose.

I do so want to be with you and start our lives again and, more than anything, I want you to forgive me.

All my love to you and the children.

Basil

Basil folded the letter, placed it in an envelope, addressed it and went to find the quartermaster to ensure that it would be on the afternoon plane to

London. He pulled up the collar on his army coat, straightened his cap, and then ordered a jeep to take him to the railway station, where the twelve forty-five train would take him to Vienna via Linz.

***

Vienna had been divided by the Allies into five areas, with the old centre being designated an international area. It was governed on a rotational basis by the American, British, French, and Soviet troops. If one did not have the correct papers, one could be stopped in the street and designated for labour service by the Soviets, so Basil always kept his papers on him while he was there and walked with his head downwards. He had the address written on a piece of paper, Tuchlauben 1, Flat 4, and walked purposefully along the pavement until he got there. On the ground floor of the building was a shop, which had been boarded up. At the corner of the building was a column with a statue of a young lady. He remembered the place from the last time he had been there fourteen years earlier. However, Vienna looked so different, a ghost of its past.

Basil rang the buzzer for flat 4. He waited a few seconds and pressed the buzzer again. There was silence. He looked at his watch – it was nearly eight in the evening. There appeared to be nothing open in the dark streets around him and then the door was pushed ajar, and Basil stood in front of a thin, tall man with wispy grey hair in his early fifties. There was a sallowness in his face and dark rings around his eyes that unceasingly looked around. He wore a blue pinstripe double-breasted suit, which was a little too big for him, and a stained white shirt and tie. The years had not been kind to Tomas Skeres.

"Come in," said Tomas. Basil extended his hand. "Quickly," said Tomas, "we can do the pleasantries when we are out of the cold."

Flat 4 was a large apartment, almost twice the size of Basil's four-bedroom flat in Cadogan Square. All the rooms had at one time been ornately decorated with cornices, panelling and chandeliers. The living room had a view towards the quire of the *am Hof* church. However, it was almost devoid of furniture, except for a baby grand piano that dominated the main room. There were shadows where pictures once hung on the walls.

"Your brother loved sitting here," said Tomas, as they walked into the living room. "He would open the windows in summer and listen as the world went by."

"I remember," said Basil. "Where's all the furniture gone?"

"He had it taken to the villa in St Gilgen, except for the piano which he could not remove quickly. Anything else that was of any value the Nazis took, and what else was here has been used for firewood."

"And what about his things in St Gilgen?"

"Most of them are safe," said Tomas. "We packed everything up and hid them. The Germans found a few things, but his art is safe."

"I've never been to the house in St Gilgen."

"It is quite a beautiful villa," said Tomas, "I will miss living there. However, it belongs to you, as does this apartment." Tomas walked to the large window and looked out on the dark square below. "Looking at it now, it is hard to believe that in the early nineteen thirties, Wien was one of the most marvellous cities in the world."

Tomas led Basil into the kitchen and made coffee. They sat at the kitchen table, each cradling a cup in their hands.

"You hinted that there was some news about Christian," Basil said.

Tomas put his fingers to the bridge of his nose and rubbed it.

"I think I told you that Rachel Kraus and her parents were travelling to Marseille and then going on to Palestine."

"You did," said Basil.

"I tried to contact them again after the war ended, I heard nothing and a week ago I received a letter from a friend of the family saying that they had passed away. However, he said that Rachel had never gone to Palestine and that she had been arrested and removed from the train at Linz. They also said that they thought she was alive."

"Alive?" repeated Basil.

"I believe so," said Tomas. "According to the letter, she was taken from the train at Linz and sent to Mauthausen. Her release was paid for by some relatives in England and in August 1939 she tried to make her way to Britain."

"Why Britain?" asked Basil.

"Because she had relatives there who could sponsor her and the borders to Palestine had then been closed by the English."

"So, she might be in England," said Basil.

"She may be."

"And what about Christian?" asked Basil. "Did the letter mention anything about him?"

"Nothing. I don't know whether he was detained at Linz or carried on to Salzburg. I was only told that Rachel was taken to Mauthausen but was released."

"If she got to Britain, she would then have been deported," said Basil, "and I should have her details in my files somewhere." They continued to sip at their coffees. When Basil had finished his cup, he washed it up in the sink and then looked at Tomas. "There's something I want to ask you. I meant to ask Christian when I saw him last, but I didn't raise it."

"What is it?" asked Tomas?"

"It's about Robert, my stepson. Did Christian ever talk to you about who Robert's father was?"

"Why do you ask?"

"I know that Celia and Christian were close friends, and I thought she might have told him."

"As far as I know, she didn't tell him – Kit didn't know for certain," said Tomas.

"But he had some idea. Was it my brother Adrian?" asked Basil.

"Christian didn't want to speculate, but I can tell you that Kit thought that Celia was pregnant when she went to America."

Chapter 46

London was pockmarked. Where buildings should have stood there were piles of rubble, and whole areas that had been flattened by bombs had been cordoned off by the police. These became the new playgrounds for young boys. Basil wondered how long it would take to rebuild the city that had sustained such devastating damage – ten years, twenty, longer? He didn't want to guess but he was sure that the restoration work to the city would be completed, even if it bankrupted the country. Cadogan Square had survived much of the bombing and those who lived in the area and had been unscathed, ruefully smiled when they thought of John Betjeman's plea: 'Lord, put beneath Thy special care One-eighty-nine Cadogan Square.'

Basil arrived to a cold home four days after leaving Nuremberg. He had taken a train from Vienna to Munich and then waited a day for a flight to London. He was tired, as he was unused to sleeping on trains or airport seats. His leg hurt worse than it had done for many years, and he looked forward to sitting in a hot bath. He opened the door to the apartment and placed his kit bag by the door. He noticed that the living room light was on and went in. Celia sat under a blanket with a little Belling fire near her, reading a book.

"I thought I would wait up," she said, "after I received your telegram." She got up and kissed him, and noticed he was sweating. "Are you well?"

"Just a cold, I hope," he said. "All I want to do is have a bath and put on some clean clothes."

"I'll boil some water on the stove," said Celia. "Unfortunately, the boiler decided to stop working yesterday."

When Basil had bathed, and put on pyjamas and a warm towelling robe, he sat under the blanket with Celia with a mug of coffee in his hands. Celia asked about the trial and then about Vienna.

"Tomas told me that just before the war started Rachel had been able to buy her release from Mauthausen. Everything after that is supposition but she may have made her way to England as she had relatives here and then would have been interned and deported."

Basil took a sip of coffee and screwed up his face.

"I'm sorry, I could only get Camp coffee," Celia said.

"Is that what it is?" replied Basil.

"It's a mixture of coffee essence, chicory and sugar," explained Celia. "That's what I was told by the man in the grocer's and it's all the rage now."

"Is it?" said Basil, taking another sip. "The next thing I need to do is check my files because if she was on one of the ships that took internees to Australia and Canada then there will be a record of her on the ship's manifest. It should be possible to find out where she was taken and then we can track her from there."

"And what about Christian?"

"I've no idea," said Basil, "but I feel certain that if we find Rachel, we will be one step closer to finding out what happened to him." Basil put down his cup on the coffee table. "I'll go into the War Office tomorrow and see what I can find. I have two weeks off before I go back to Nuremberg."

"Why don't you take a few days off first?"

"I need to do this," said Basil. "I feel that every day a little more hope slips away."

"Is there any hope? It's been nearly seven years." Celia paused for a second before continuing. "Do you believe there's any possibility that he might still be alive?"

Celia didn't get an answer, as Basil had fallen asleep on the sofa. She looked at him. The war had made him old and tired. He had once been attractive but now that youth had passed, and any memories of desire had become like dull, unwatered roots. Her job had been the wellspring of her existence for so long, covering the emptiness of her life with hours of fulfilling work. She had been honoured with baubles and plaudits; friends and colleagues were effusive in their admiration for her. It was, however, nothing more than a blanket of snow covering a painful loneliness in her life. Basil was trying to make a new start for them, and she admired him for that, but her true happiness lay buried and was nothing but a remembrance of death. She sipped at her tea, now tepid, like her life. When she had finished, she whispered in Basil's ear to come to bed, and he followed her, completely unaware of the world about him.

***

Basil woke late the next morning. He ached everywhere and was sweating profusely. Celia was still asleep, and he put on his robe and walked into the kitchen, where Catherine was eating a bowl of porridge at a table and Howard was listening to the radio and writing on a pad. The twins were both in their pyjamas, with additional layers of clothes on to ward off the cold. Howard sat intently listening to the radio, from which he could just barely hear some song, and would on occasion scribble something down.

"Dad," said Catherine looking up from her bowl, "when did you get home? More importantly, do you know how to make the central heating work? Mum tried but failed and we are all likely to freeze. Isn't the point of central heating that you can just turn a switch and that you don't need a man?"

"It's not as cold as Vienna," said Basil, who was grateful for the robe he was wearing.

Catherine examined her father intently and said, "You don't look well at all. Haven't you been feeding yourself?"

Basil regarded his daughter with her emerald-green eyes under an unruly pile of auburn hair. It made him think of the first time he had seen Celia. Catherine finished off her porridge and then washed the bowl and put it on the draining board.

"Except for the first week there, when I ate nothing but Spam," said Basil, "I have been eating quite well, compared to most people."

"But you look like you've walked out of Auschwitz," said Catherine.

"That's not funny at all," said Basil tersely. "There's nothing funny about

270

those camps. Never joke about them – never."

"Sorry," said Catherine, who lowered her eyes. "I didn't mean..." She didn't finish the sentence.

"Can I get you anything, Dad?" said Howard. "Toast, porridge... I think Mother got bacon and some eggs with the ration cards. There's not nearly as much food here as we had at Castle Drogo."

"What's that you're listening to?" asked Basil, as he put his head next to the radio.

"'White Christmas'. It's a song by Bing Crosby."

Basil listened for a minute and then asked, "What are you writing?"

"It's a cipher. It's a game I play with my friends where we write messages to each other based on the number one single of the Billboard charts in America." Basil raised his eyebrows.

"It's simple," said Howard. "The first line of the song is 'I'm dreaming of a white Christmas' so, I equals 1, m equals 2, d equals 3 and..."

"R equals 4," said Basil.

"No one can break the code unless they know the key, and as the key changes every few weeks it is almost impossible."

"Only a boy would be interested in that," said Catherine.

"I think it's rather smooth," said Basil. "That is the right expression, isn't it?"

"Dad," answered Catherine, "if you have to ask, you're too old to be saying it."

***

The sandbags and boarding around the War Office had been removed. Basil looked up at the Edwardian Baroque building as he arrived, almost hidden in the brown fog of winter dawn. He had taken a taxi to Horseguards Avenue, where hundreds of people were chatting to each other, as if the world had reverted to a kind of normality. Basil entered the building, in his major's uniform, and was saluted at the door and asked to produce his pass. As he walked to the back of the building, where the Judge Advocate General's offices were, people looked over at him and he heard the word 'Nuremberg' said again and again. He tried to be nonchalant, but he still did not feel well. He wanted to look through the documents pertaining to Rachel Kraus and then go home to bed.

"The first file I want to see relates to the SS *Arandora Star*," said Basil to his secretary.

"That's the ship that was torpedoed," replied the secretary.

"I'm looking for someone called Kraus on the manifest."

The secretary duly brought a box of documents relating to the sunken ship. An hour later Basil had gone through the contents of the box finding no mention of Rachel. He was feeling worse as the morning wore on and could hardly focus. He requested more documents of the other ships that took the internees.

"That was also a dead end," said Basil to his secretary, as lunchtime approached.

"Is there anything I can do to help?" the secretary asked.

"A decent cup of coffee, please?"

Basil was halfway through the next box marked '*HMS Ettrick*' when his secretary returned with a cup. He took a sip. It was slightly better than Camp coffee, but he doubted that what he was drinking was derived from a coffee bean.

"Is there anything else I can help you with, Major Drewe?"

"Just some peace and quiet," said Basil, as he continued looking through the documents. He saw the name 'O. Kraus' on the manifest and decided to see if there had been a mistake. He checked against the internees' names, which had been listed on the internment camp records, but it confirmed the name as being 'Otto Kraus'.

By the late afternoon, he had three more boxes to review – '*MS Sobieski*', '*SS Duchess of York*', and '*HMT Dunera*.' He knew he would have to come in the following day to complete the task. His secretary returned asking whether she could get him anything else and he dejectedly shook his head.

Basil opened the lid to the box marked '*HMT Dunera*.' He had dealt with a problem on that ship when it had taken two thousand people to Australia, in what Winston Churchill subsequently called 'a deplorable and regrettable mistake'. The treatment of the internees by the army had been appalling.

The internees had been kept below decks during the voyage and had only been allowed ten minutes on deck during the day to exercise. The guards kept their guns trained on them as they exercised and used their rifle butts to hit the internees who were slow in going back below deck. One guard smashed a beer bottle on the deck and the internees had to walk on the shards of glass when they went below. When the ship arrived in Sydney the medical officer who inspected the ship was so appalled by the condition of the internees that he made an official complaint and the matter landed on Basil's desk. Basil had been equally appalled and took the file to Maxwell Fyfe and recommended that the army personnel face a court martial.

"If we cannot treat those who are the most vulnerable with compassion and respect," Basil had said to Maxwell Fyfe, "then we are no better than the people we are fighting against. It's bad enough that we are transporting these refugees to Canada and Australia, but then to treat them so deplorably makes me ashamed of the uniform I'm wearing." Maxwell Fyfe agreed and gave the order for a court martial to proceed.

Basil read to the end of the file. By this time, he knew that Rachel Kraus was not on the ship's manifest. Basil's eyes were tired when he placed the lid on the box. He had found no trace of Rachel in any of the documents and looked at his secretary.

"I can't find her name anywhere in these documents," he said with exasperation.

"You won't find her in those files," the secretary answered.

"Why ever not?" asked Basil.

"None of the women were sent to the Dominion countries. They were all sent to the Isle of Man."

"Why didn't you tell me earlier?" asked Basil, frustrated by a wasted day.

"You didn't tell me that the person you were looking for was a woman," came the slightly irritated reply.

***

Basil woke up with a groan. It felt like flu, but it probably wasn't. His temperature was ninety-nine degrees, according to the thermometer, and his nose was running. He had wasted a whole day chasing shadows. He hoped that he would feel better later and would then go into the War Office. Celia came in with a warm mug of Earl Grey and a bowl of porridge with honey.

"Eat it," she said in a tone that demanded obedience.

"I'm not really that hungry," Basil responded but knew that objecting would prove fruitless. Celia put down the mug and bowl on the bedside table and was about to leave. "Stay with me, and talk. I never know what you're thinking."

"I'm thinking that unless I get to the shops, we'll have nothing for dinner tonight."

"That's not important," he said. "However, I need to know what I can do to make our marriage work."

"You can't do anything," said Celia, "because you're not the problem."

"I know I promised that I would never ask, but I need to know why you're not happy. Why you've never been happy with this life and why we have to dance around each other and pretend there is nothing wrong when neither of us is happy living with indifference."

"It's not something I can talk about now," said Celia, who turned back towards the door. "When you are better, we'll speak about it. I promise."

Basil slept fitfully until the afternoon and then got up. The twins had been sent out to play with friends so as not to disturb their father and Celia had gone to the shops to buy what was needed for dinner. Basil noticed that the radiators were warm and that sometime in the morning the plumber had resolved the problem with the boiler. He washed, shaved and got dressed and then stood looking out of the sash windows across the gardens. He wondered what would happen in a few years' time when the twins went to university, when Celia and he didn't have them to hide behind and pretend that their lives were happy.

The ringing of the doorbell startled him. Basil's secretary, Anne, appeared at the door.

"What do you know about the Isle of Man internees?" she asked.

Basil looked at her and said, "Assume nothing. I've never had to deal with them and so have never thought about them."

"Well, the women who came from both Germany and Italy were interned at Rushen Camp. It was a camp made up of two villages, Port Erin and Port St Mary, and we just put barbed wire around both villages. The government requisitioned all spare bedrooms, and the internees were housed by families who continued to live there."

"I see," said Basil, but had little idea what she was getting at.

"Anyway, the camp closed three months ago in September 1945, although we commenced releasing people in 1943, after an outcry from the press and several members of Parliament."

"I do remember something about it, now you mention it," said Basil.

"I checked last night after you left and found that Rachel Kraus was interned there and was released in May 1944."

Basil sat forward in his chair. "So, we know Rachel was alive in May 1944."

"That's where the good news ends," continued Anne. "She left Port Erin for London but after that, there's no record of her. She could be anywhere – she might even have returned to Vienna."

Basil ran his hands through his hair. Another dead end he thought.

"I'll keep on looking," said Anne.

She was still there when Celia came home, and Basil introduced her as his secretary who had been assigned to him while he was back in London.

"Actually," said Anne, "I asked for the assignment."

"Why ever would you do that?" asked Celia, sitting down on the sofa.

"Because of what Major Drewe is doing," said Anne. "Everybody in our department is incredibly proud of his role in the trial and, of course, Major Maxwell Fyfe. All of us would give anything to be there to see those Nazis convicted in a court of law. It proves that what we fought for was right and that our sacrifices meant something. I lost my fiancé in the war; he was an engineer in the RAF and was killed when they bombed Biggin Hill."

Anne paused and smiled for the briefest of seconds as she remembered him. "He was killed trying to get our fighter pilots scrambled. For me, what Major Drewe is doing is just as important as what my fiancé or the pilots who won the Battle of Britain did. I know that if he were alive today, he would want to shake Major Drewe's hand and would be bragging about having done so in the pub afterwards."

Chapter 47

Tolling reminiscent bells marked Christmas. All along Sloane Street, Christmas trees were sold. At Sloane Square station they handed out a flower with every tree to remember the seventy-nine people who had died when the Tube station was bombed. At Cadogan Square, they held a carol service and put out candles. Seventy thousand people of all classes wrote to Parliament, expressing their willingness to give up food to help Europe and Miss Vera Brittain urged Parliament to help. It was a testament to an indomitable spirit. As Britain attempted to help those less fortunate in Europe, the toy-starved children of London received gifts from America. Normality was gradually returning to a bombed and battered world and the Adelphi Theatre, in London's West End, put on the pantomime *Cinderella*, with the brilliant Bud Flanagan back as Buttons.

A strong wind had blown down from the north on Christmas Eve, and when the curtains of their apartment in Cadogan Square were drawn back on Christmas Day the windows were covered in dust. Celia made a pot of tea for everyone, as Basil still refused to drink Camp coffee. She put on the grill and toasted crumpets and placed pots of jam and honey from Castle Drogo on the breakfast table. It would be a luxurious Christmas meal at lunchtime – all of which had been given to them by Lady Frances – a goose, parsnips, carrots, potatoes, sausages and bacon. There was also a game terrine, Christmas pudding, eggs, and rich, silky redcurrant jelly. From a cupboard in the hallway, Celia took out a mountain of presents, from her mother, her sisters and her brother. She put them around the Christmas tree, each one with a label and a Christmas wish.

Bleary-eyed, the twins came through to the living room. Basil, unshaven and with his hair sticking up, wandered through. Celia noticed that the twins, who would be sixteen in the following year, no longer ran headlong for the pile of presents. Everyone wished each other a merry Christmas and then sat drinking tea and nibbling crumpets, almost like strangers, waiting for something to happen. It was Basil who broke the silence, asking who was going to get him a present to open, and Howard went over to the Christmas tree, sat down cross-legged and started searching through the pile of presents. Not to be outdone, Catherine joined him as he searched for a present for Basil.

"You've obviously been a bad boy," said Howard, grinning at his father, "I'm not sure that Santa has brought you a present." Basil laughed and Howard took out a small package wrapped in red paper and stretched out and handed it to his father. "It's a tie," he said.

"Don't tell him," said Catherine, hitting her brother on the arm.

"What about me?" said Celia.

Catherine rummaged through the pile of presents. "Oh, you've definitely been a bad girl," she said.

However, unlike Basil, Celia did not laugh.

***

They lay in bed. Celia looked up at the ceiling and Basil lay on his side staring at his wife. In the blackness of the room, Celia could see nothing and Basil could just make out the silhouette of his wife's face. Their breathing was slow and regular, both breathing simultaneously like twins in the womb, and then, suddenly, Celia would take a deeper breath as if something shocked her or disturbed her thoughts and afterwards, her breathing would return to that regular, slow pace in time with Basil's.

"A penny for them," said Basil.

"I was thinking about Catherine," said Celia.

"What about her?" asked Basil.

"I don't know..." Celia paused and took a longer, deeper breath. "I sometimes think she doesn't like me. Am I being stupid?"

"Catherine's always been more headstrong than Howard and has a streak

278

of stubbornness in her which she clearly doesn't get from me."

"Are you teasing me?" asked Celia.

"A little," said Basil.

"Do you think I'm stubborn?"

"Stubbornness or determination – it amounts to the same thing some-times. And yes, you are the most determined person I know. When you want to do something, you do it. You inherited that trait from your mother, and Catherine has inherited it from you."

"But it's not just the stubbornness that she has. I sometimes feel that she disapproves of me."

"Why don't you talk to her about it?" suggested Basil.

"Because I'm not quite sure I want to hear the answer," said Celia. "I was wondering whether you knew what it was about."

Basil sat up in bed. "I don't think it is for me to say," he replied.

"Then you do know," said Celia who turned towards Basil. "You asked for honesty from me, but it cuts both ways."

"All right," said Basil, "if you want this conversation." He closed his eyes and composed himself. "You know my mother told you that someone had seen you with that Canadian officer in the Okehampton hotel – well, it was Catherine."

"But your mother told Catherine I was helping with the Christmas dance for the servicemen," Celia said after a moment's pause.

"Yes, but Catherine didn't tell my mother that when she saw you go into the hotel, she waited outside in the cold for two hours, and saw you kissing him when you left. It's why she's so surly with you."

"And how do you know this?" asked Celia.

"Because she told me, just before I went away to Nuremberg. She didn't want me to go."

"And what did you say?"

"I said that I knew about it and discussed it and that I trusted you as you had promised that it was a mistake and would never happen again."

"But I didn't say that to you," said Celia.

"I know. It was the first time I've lied to Catherine, but it was the only thing I could think of saying that might help her forgive you."

Celia could not stop herself from crying and through the tears, she said, "I'll make that promise now."

Chapter 48

January 1946

Celia read the figures with a sense of incredulity. In Europe, sixty-five million people had been displaced and, in addition, there were ten million Germans who had fled from Poland, Czechoslovakia and Romania when the Red Army had advanced. Many of the displaced persons had been prisoners of war, or forced labourers, or the inmates of the concentration camps. These people were looked after at displaced persons centres. On arrival, they would be sprayed with DDT to prevent the outbreak of diseases like typhus. People of all ages and nationalities lived together in these camps and basic necessities were scarce. Life was hard and brutal. Clothes were washed in local canals and rivers. Slowly, by the truckload, these displaced people were returned home, however, some did not want to go back to their countries from where they had come, and some died.

The United Nations Relief and Rehabilitation Administration, UNRRA, had been set up to provide health and welfare to these displaced persons. As Harry Truman had said, it was not only crucial to win the battle but also to "win peace in the world". Celia had thought about helping with this relief work, but the scale was too large, and all her experience related to helping children find foster homes. Also, in the five years she spent in Devon, she had lost contact with a lot of people, and the organisations that she had worked with had disbanded and others had taken their place. She felt adrift, without sail or oar or controlling hand.

"What is it, Mother?" asked Catherine.

"I have to find something to do," said Celia.

"You could make me a cup of tea," suggested Catherine, but the sarcastic comment did not receive a response.

"Where's your brother?"

"Writing one of his silly codes," said Catherine.

"All right," said Celia, "shall we do something together? Tea at the Ritz, perhaps, or a manicure. A mother-daughter afternoon."

It was not the first time that Celia had suggested that she and Catherine do something together, but it was the first time in quite a while. They agreed on the Ritz and Celia telephoned and booked a table, and they dressed up for the occasion.

The grey of London was forgotten within the hotel's gold-tinted Palm Court. White marble floors shone beneath gilded ceilings and ornate birdcage chandeliers. Tables covered in the whitest of linens with richly padded chairs of golden material were placed around the room. It was exquisitely beautiful.

If the building was beautiful, tea was sublime. It commenced with smoked salmon sandwiches and a lemony butter that cut through the oiliness of the smoked fish. There were cucumber and cream cheese sandwiches, where the flavours were accentuated with dill and mint. Chicken with onion relish was served on malted bread and then, once the sandwiches were cleared away, the cakes, scones and pastries appeared on a layered cake stand. Brimming with clotted cream and strawberry preserve, they were the lightest scones that Catherine had ever tasted.

"Are we rich enough to do this every day?" asked Catherine, as she wiped a smudge of brilliant red preserve from the side of her mouth with a white linen napkin.

"I suppose so," said Celia, "but it does get very boring if you do it too often."

"Is that why you and Dad both work?"

"We work for very different reasons," said Celia. She stopped speaking as the waiter came over with a bottle of champagne and poured each of them a glass. "Your father works because he believes it's a calling and I work because I need to."

Catherine picked up the fluted glass and then looked at her mother.

"Go ahead," said Celia. "But just a sip."

"So, what did you mean when you said that Dad works because he believes it's a calling?"

"He explained it to me once that being a barrister and defending those who needed protection was a public service. He said that it was incidental that he made his living from that work because the primary purpose was helping people."

"What did you say?" asked Catherine.

"I said that if barristers weren't paid, they would all stop working and the few who continued could be counted on the fingers of one hand. Your father shrugged and said that he would be one of them."

"And why do you need to work?"

"That's more complicated. I only told your father the reason why a few days ago and I'm not sure you would want to know."

"You can't stop there," said Catherine.

"Your father said I should tell you. Of course, if you need to speak to Howard about it or Robert you must, but I wasn't planning on telling Howard for a year or two until he's older. Girls grow up so much quicker than boys."

"And what about Robert? Have you told him?"

"Robert was there. It happened on his fifth birthday. It's a day I'll never forget."

Celia told the story as she remembered it. Not every fact was accurate, and the years had changed her perception of some things. She could not remember the name of the middle brother – only Deke and Joshua. She remembered the knife that Deke had as being larger than it was, and she remembered the fear that she had for Robert as he was held on the ground by Joshua Hamilton. She remembered trying to hit the boys with the whip and Deke laughing as she was pulled from the wagon. She also remembered how cold and calm she felt when she levelled the gun at the boy and fired, but she did not say that to her daughter.

"And the nightmares that followed carried on for years. I went to India to get away from things and I started working in a children's clinic there with a wonderful doctor. She told me that in time things would get better if I did something positive that dealt with the consequences of my act."

"And what was that?" asked Catherine.

"Working with the poorest children in the most desperate need. If someone had helped that boy, then what happened might never have occurred."

"I can't believe how brave you were," said Catherine. "I've always thought that the reason you've not wanted to look after us and go to work is because you didn't love us."

"Not at all – never think that. You, Howard, and Robert are the most important people in my life."

"And what about Dad?" asked Catherine.

"Yes, of course. He's important too," replied Celia, however, from Catherine's look, Celia knew that she had not sounded convincing.

***

Basil stumbled into Maxwell Fyfe's office and sat down without even being asked.

"My head hurts," said Basil.

"Mine too, but we were only drinking beer," said Maxwell Fyfe.

"Were we?" Basil poured himself a glass of water and drank it. "I blame the Russians."

"Did you enjoy the party?" asked Maxwell Fyfe.

"It was a singular success," said Basil. "A band, a singer, a juggler, speeches, a game of netball and even a singsong around the piano. We certainly got to know the other legal teams especially the Soviet prosecutor, General Rudenko, and his team."

"Oh God," said Maxwell Fyfe. "I remember now. He's rather larger than life. *Da*... we'll hang every one of them, Comrade David. *Da*, do you like Russian women, Comrade David?... *Da*, you look like a man with appetites, Comrade David." Maxwell Fyfe looked across the table at Basil who had buried his head in his hands.

"You know they were spiking our drinks with vodka," groaned Basil.

"That may explain why I feel so wretched," said Maxwell Fyfe. "I'll ask for coffee?"

"Please," said Basil. "All we had at home was Camp coffee."

"I can't stand that stuff either," said Maxwell Fyfe. He looked at his watch. "We've got an hour before the court session starts. Fortunately, Harry Phillimore is dealing with the morning session today and tomorrow. Was he there last night?"

"He left early," said Basil. "I think he suspected what the Russians were up to and decided to get an early night."

"And how were things at home?" asked Maxwell Fyfe, after telephoning for two cups of coffee.

"I think Celia and I made some progress," said Basil. "She told me about something that had happened to her in America. It wasn't pleasant and I rather wish she had told me years ago so I could have been there for her."

"They do complain that we never listen to them, but then tell us nothing important. Sylvia can be the same, but I'm pleased that you are at least talking about it now," said Maxwell Fyfe.

The two men continued to talk about things that Celia might be interested in, and Maxwell Fyfe promised to speak to Sylvia to see whether she had any ideas. An hour passed and the cups of coffee got cold, then Sir Hartley knocked on the door and said to them, "Hurry up please, it's time."

Chapter 49

March 1946

"That was a disaster," said Basil.

"It wasn't that bad," said Maxwell Fyfe.

"It was an unmitigated mess and may go down in history as one of the worst pieces of cross-examination. Jackson just read from preprepared questions and didn't listen to Goering's answers, and then failed to follow any of them up. You will need to control Goering tomorrow when you cross-examine him."

"The Fat Boy is as slippery as they come," said Maxwell Fyfe, "but at least Jackson brought into evidence all the documents we need. That was the most important thing as it will be the documents that hang him. However, I'll give myself enough time. Did you notice how after every question, Goering questioned the translation or kept on saying he did not understand the question?"

"I did," said Basil. "He just wanted more time to think about his answer. You do know he speaks fluent English and didn't need a translator? My advice, for what it's worth, is to focus on what you can prove – for example, the execution of the fifty British flyers from Stalag Luft III. What you can show is that as head of the Luftwaffe, Goering oversaw the prisoner-of-war camps from which they escaped, and he implemented a policy that escaped prisoners caught by the police would be taken to Mauthausen and shot."

Mauthausen – Basil remembered sitting on a train in 1939 as it went past the little town of Mauthausen, with its white-painted houses and flower boxes. He remembered it was also the camp that Rachel Kraus had been taken to before buying her freedom and coming to England. His efforts to track Rachel down had proved fruitless, and he resigned himself to the fact that he would never find out what happened to his brother Christian.

"You were miles away," said Maxwell Fyfe.

"Sorry," said Basil. "I was thinking about my brother. Let's get back to your cross-examination."

"I had planned that the second part of my cross-examination would deal with the genocide of the Jews. Goering is saying that he knew nothing about the policy to exterminate the Jews."

"You're not going to get him to break down on the stand," said Basil.

"I know," said Maxwell Fyfe, "but what I must do is show him the figures – the four million dead in Auschwitz, the ten million dead across Germany – and ask whether he knew anything about it."

"He will deny it," said Basil.

"But no one will believe him, and he can't deny he knew about the forced labour," said Maxwell Fyfe.

"No, he can't," said Basil, "nor can he deny that he wasn't aware of the directives given to exterminate thirty million Slavs and Russians. However, Rudenko's dealing with that."

***

"What do you plan to do for Easter?" said Maxwell Fyfe, after the cross-examination of Goering had finished and they had returned to his office.

"I'll go home," said Basil.

"Why don't you take Celia away – maybe just for a week? De Menthon has invited the British prosecution team to Paris over Easter."

"The French prosecutor invited all of us to Paris?" repeated Basil incredulously.

"You remember," said Maxwell Fyfe, "that in his opening statement he said that France was looking for the cooperation of all peoples to establish a progressive international society?"

"Yes."

"It seems it wasn't just bluster. The French want to talk about it and Attlee has asked whether Sir Hartley and I would spend some time with them. I'm bringing Sylvia and you could also come with Celia."

***

The taxi pulled up in the Rue Coquillière and Celia got out. A silent crowd was milling around by the entrance of the restaurant waiting and hoping for a last-minute cancellation. People were subdued and the *joie de vivre* seemed to have been sucked from the city. A yellow canopy spread out from the restaurant covering diners on the pavement, who were prepared to sit outside. In the square, the noise from Les Halles, the meat market, rang out, and all around the square waxed paper was blown from the market.

Basil took Celia's hand and led her into the restaurant where he told the maître d' that he had a reservation for two at eight. The maître d' looked down the list dispassionately and then turned to Basil and said in English, "I am sorry, sir, but we have no reservation in the name of Monsieur Drewe."

"It may be under the name de Menthon," suggested Basil. The maître d' did not need to look at the list again.

"Of course, sir. We have a table in the private dining area if that is agreeable, and a bottle of Krug waiting for you."

They walked through the restaurant past rows of brown leather chairs and tables covered in cream linen. On the few empty tables, which had been reserved for later, the napkins were folded like circular tents and silver cutlery was regimentally spaced. The restaurant was filled with a cacophony, and those who had managed to get a table talked loudly so that they could be heard. Glass chandeliers adorned the panelled ceiling giving off a warm yellow light, and from every direction waiters dashed from one table to another either carrying full plates of meat or empty ones back to the kitchen.

In the private dining room, the leather chairs were red and the table linen white. Celia noticed how quiet it was in comparison to the main dining room.

"Would you mind," she said, "if we ate in the main dining room? It seemed livelier." The waiter sighed as if he had been given an impossible task to perform, turned, sighed again as he passed Celia and walked back the way that he had come with all the surliness that only a French waiter can possess.

288

They were given a table near the kitchen.

"Au Pied de Cochon," said Celia, as she looked at the front of the menu where the name of the restaurant was embossed, "the pig's trotter. Not a wholly appetising name."

"We're in the heart of the French meat market area," said Basil. "You can have anything you want from fillet steak to I suppose, well, pig's trotters."

Basil ran his eyes down the menu. They stopped for a second at the range of different oysters and then he considered the crevettes, but he read no further when he saw the steak tartare of Normandy beef. He imagined the rich, red seasoned meat with a raw egg yolk sitting in the middle, perhaps with a dash of tabasco to give it the slightest hint of fieriness. He told Celia his choice of starter.

"And for the main course?" asked Celia.

"I'll ask the waiter for a recommendation," said Basil. The waiter duly arrived as if a sixth sense had alerted him to the fact that he was needed. He seemed indifferent to Celia, explaining to Basil the menu, as he knew that at the end of the evening, it would be Basil who would pay the bill and determine the tip. When Celia ordered the French onion soup, he nodded slightly, as if finding the choice acceptable, however, he did not hide his frown when she ordered the sole meunière. Basil ordered the steak tartare and then asked the waiter for his recommendation.

"The *Tentation de Saint Antoine*," said the waiter, "is our speciality. Saint Antoine is the patron saint of charcutiers." Basil thought for a moment about simply agreeing with the recommendation but having no idea what the 'The *Tentation de Saint Antoine*' might involve, he sought further clarification.

"The *Tentation to Saint Antoine* is a dish of pig's trotters, tails, snouts and ears," said the waiter.

"All served together?" asked Basil.

"Yes, sir."

"No thank you," said Basil. "I have had enough Spam to last me a lifetime."

"Is Spam an English delicacy, sir?"

"You could say that," answered Basil. "I think I'll have the same as my wife."

The waiter left shaking his head, wondering why anyone would come to a restaurant in a meat market only to order fish. The English, he muttered to himself, with their awful coffee and salad cream and their opinion that they are superior to everyone in the world – *c'est ridicule*.

"You know that I said Maxwell Fyfe and Sylvia are here," began Basil. "Well, they would like dinner with us tomorrow evening."

"Any reason?" asked Celia.

"The United Nations are going to ask him to assist in the drafting of a Declaration of Human Rights, which enshrines the principles that were set out in the Nuremberg trial. It will involve going to New York and he thought he would broach the subject with Sylvia when we were there."

"So, he has no idea how she will respond?"

"None at all," said Basil. "He just thinks it may be safer if he tells her when there are people around."

"And what do you want to do after this?"

"I thought about going back to the law and reviving my practice. Maxwell Fyfe indicated that my application for King's Counsel would be nodded through, and I could spend more time with you."

"I think I would like that as well," said Celia.

"Maxwell Fyfe also wants to talk to you about a new children's aid organisation that's being created to provide relief for the children whose lives have been devastated by this war. He thinks that you would be the perfect person to help with it – it's called UNICEF."

***

Celia lay awake in bed in their small hotel room in Paris. She could not remember the last time she had been away with Basil to another country, and she had to admit she was enjoying herself. They had been living separate lives for so long and she wondered whether she could be happy with Basil in the future. She had burnt a lot of bridges, and some of them were still smouldering but Basil seemed capable of forgiving her, and she wondered if the boot were on the other foot whether she would be that charitable. However, he did not evoke in her the same passions that Adrian and Devjeet had done or even the charming Canadian Colonel Landry. She knew that when she married Basil, she hoped he would change, like a chameleon sheds its skin, and become more like his brother. But he hadn't. He was different in so many ways; reserved, stoic and composed, not gallant and dashing.

She thought about her life with Basil, who lay next to her sound asleep. Had she been happy when they first met? They had gone out to theatres, restaurants and polo matches and he seemed to have a key to every door. They were seen in clubs and every fashionable house party – they even had an open invitation to Cliveden and Chartwell. She had enjoyed herself; she had enjoyed the attention. Basil had been a rising star at the time, but it all came to an abrupt halt when the twins were born. And then things just fell apart. They had no sleep. They bickered constantly. As she lay in bed looking up at the ceiling, she wondered how they survived those few years; how they had survived after her infatuation with Devjeet. She hated to think of it as an affair, that seemed so sordid, but she knew exactly what it was.

She could not say that Basil had been a bad husband, as he made every effort with the children. He would take them to museums, or a park, and he arranged flying lessons for Robert when he turned sixteen. He accompanied Howard to cricket matches and was always there for everything that Catherine wanted to do. She remembered that someone had once described Basil as a man of honesty and integrity and knew that was true. Would Adrian or Devjeet still have been with her after twenty years? No, she thought, they were far too interested in themselves.

Basil started snoring. She nudged him, hoping he would roll over. Soon the snoring ceased. She looked at him, with his gaunt face that looked so tired. They would have to muddle through, she thought. She knew now that she had chosen her horse, and it was no longer possible to change in mid-race. She wondered how he maintained that deep and unfaltering belief that he loved her. It was not just an infatuation but a real love that grows over time because you believe that the person you are with was created for you. As she thought about what it meant to truly love someone, her eyelids became heavy.

When she fell asleep, she knew that if her marriage was going to succeed, she would now have to learn to make compromises and accept Basil for who he was.

Chapter 50

26 July 1946

The Closing Submission of Mr Justice Robert Jackson, United States Chief of Counsel to prosecute Nazi war criminals:

"Nor were the war crimes and the crimes against humanity unplanned, isolated, or spontaneous offenses. Aside from our undeniable evidence of their plotting, it is sufficient to ask whether six million people could be separated from the population of several nations on the basis of their blood and birth, could be destroyed and their bodies disposed of, except that the operation fitted into the general scheme of government. Could the enslavement of five millions of labourers, their impressment into service, their transportation to Germany, their allocation to work where they would be most useful, their maintenance, if slow starvation can be called maintenance, and their guarding have been accomplished if it did not fit into the common plan? Could hundreds of concentration camps located throughout Germany, built to accommodate hundreds of thousands of victims, and each requiring labour and materials for construction, manpower to operate and supervise, and close gearing into the economy, could such efforts have been expended under German autocracy if they had not suited the plan? Has the Teutonic passion for organisation suddenly become famous for its toleration of nonconforming activity?"

Basil listened to the submissions. He wondered whether Maxwell Fyfe could have done a better job after his brilliant cross-examination of Goering, which left Goering's defence in tatters. However, while Maxwell Fyfe was meticulous and intellectually brilliant, he wasn't the right man for the main closing submission. More pizzazz was needed, as the Americans called it.

Basil looked at the Nazi High Command as they sat in the dock of the courtroom on the one hundredth and eighty-seventh day of the trial, guarded by seven American soldiers, meticulously dressed and standing to attention. Basil could tell that the High Command were resigned to their fate – death by hanging. The twenty-one Nazi leaders did not seem to pay regard to what was being said, most of them did not even put on headphones to hear the translation of the closing submissions. They had claimed that they had no knowledge of the war crimes and that the events for which they were accused were just the excesses of the Gestapo. Jackson slowly destroyed the defences of each one of them in turn. "Mass extermination," said Jackson, again and again and again. "Twelve million murders. Two-thirds of the Jews in Europe exterminated, more than six million of them on the killers' own figures," continued Jackson. Basil looked at Goering who was grinning and thought that the world would not miss him one iota.

When the closing submissions had finished and the courtroom had emptied, Basil and Maxwell Fyfe left the court building. The noise of demolition and rebuilding could be heard around them. The dark brick building of the court, with its triangular roofs of red slate, was wrapped up in a sheet of dust. Basil turned and looked back at the building, realising that this marked the end of a part of his life. In a year, or a score of years, or a hundred years, people would still talk about Nuremberg and what had taken place. The names of the prosecutors would be recalled with honour, and he would be a footnote, a part of that legal team who had brought the most evil dictatorship in the world to an end. The river behind the court building flowed brown and dirty; the nymphs had departed and the city of the sun among the moon and stars had lost its magic.

They climbed the steps to their rooms and Maxwell Fyfe opened his door. They sat at a table on which there was a chessboard, and, in the quietness of the early evening, Maxwell Fyfe poured two glasses of whisky.

"It will soon be over," said Basil, taking the glass from Maxwell Fyfe, "and we can go home and await the decision."

"Over?" said Maxwell Fyfe. "I think there is enough work here to keep me busy for a lifetime."

"What are your plans?" asked Basil.

"I'll go back to my constituency for a bit," said Maxwell Fyfe, "and then New York to prepare a declaration of Human Rights for the United Nations and, after that, a European convention on human rights. What happened in Germany and what's happening in Russia must never be allowed to happen in any other European country. I want to draft something which is a beacon to those who live in totalitarian darkness that will give them hope of a return to freedom." Maxwell Fyfe took a sip of whisky. "And what about you and Celia?"

"She's taken the job with UNICEF," said Basil. "And we've agreed to talk to each other more and try and do more things together."

"If you both go back to focusing on your careers," said Maxwell Fyfe, "then you'll just end up repeating the same mistakes – or at least that is what Sylvia thinks. If she were here, she would tell you to make sure you take an interest in what Celia does, but you must also find interests together."

Chapter 51

26 April 1949

"The title of King's Counsel has for centuries been a mark of quality that sets a small group of barristers apart. They are the very best from our four shores and the rank signifies the highest regard for legal ability, for diligence, for professionalism and integrity."

Basil listened, after being sworn in as a King's Counsel, to the Lord Chancellor's speech. Next to him, Aubrey St John Stephens looked around him, more interested in Westminster Hall, where the ceremony took place, than the words of congratulation that the Lord Chancellor was bestowing. Although they were colleagues in the same set of chambers, they had nothing in common. St John Stephens believed in the rod whereas Basil preferred the carrot. St John Stephens thought that a defendant should be directly examined, whereas Basil believed in the right of silence. Where St John Stephens boomed out in a courtroom, like an empty kettle, Basil was polite, articulate and firm, and he wondered what strings St John Stephens had to pull to be made a King's Counsel, as, in his opinion, he was at best mediocre.

"Within these walls," the Lord Chancellor continued, "there have been many famous trials, including that of King Charles I, William Wallace, and Thomas More, and it was in this hall that Guy Fawkes was convicted and sentenced to be hanged, drawn and quartered."

The long horsehair wig that Basil was wearing was beginning to irritate him and he felt slightly ridiculous wearing a silk gown, frilled shirt and steel-buckled shoes. The suspenders that held up his socks itched like mad, and he wondered how long the Lord Chancellor would drone on for, as he had a reputation for being able to talk the hind legs off a donkey.

"A word now for your wives and family," said the Lord Chancellor, "who will be proud of your achievements; but more than that, they are equally responsible for your success. They will have suffered through the long hours, late nights, and cancelled weekend trips."

Basil looked out across the hall and could see Celia sitting in the middle aisle, wearing a red pillbox hat with a birdcage veil. She always stood out in a crowd, and he thought back to that ball in Inner Temple Hall where they had met after her return from America. She had flown back from New York just for this ceremony and would be returning to America at the start of the following week. As soon as she had confirmed that she was coming, Basil had telephoned the twins and suggested that they join them for the weekend, Howard from Oxford and Catherine from the Medical College of St Bartholomew's Hospital. Catherine had been reticent, but Basil convinced her saying that he would be disappointed if she did not make the effort.

They began to troop out of the Hall as soon as the Lord Chancellor concluded his speech, and Basil noticed beside him Helena Normanton and Rose Heilbron, the first two women ever to be appointed as King's Counsel. Heilbron, who practised on the Northern Circuit, had been appointed at the age of thirty-four, even younger than Maxwell Fyfe. She had the reputation of being a ferocious advocate and was painstaking in her preparation. As they walked out Heilbron turned to Basil and introduced herself.

"I understand," she said, "that you're a friend of Sir David Maxwell Fyfe, who I know from the Northern Circuit. He asked me to pass on his regards and his congratulations."

"How is he?" asked Basil.

"Surprisingly well," said Heilbron, "given that he rarely stops working."

"Please also send him my best wishes."

"He also said that you were the best criminal advocate he had the privilege of working with, although you used to struggle knowing the difference between the West London Magistrates' Court and the Wimbledon Magistrates' Court. I hope I come up against you in the future."

Basil stifled a laugh as he walked through Westminster Hall and all he could think of saying was, "Really, he remembered that?"

***

They dined that evening at home, with a dinner made by their cook. It was nothing special, just a traditional shepherd's pie with carrots and peas, but Celia said she enjoyed it more than any of the meals she had eaten in her hotel in New York over the last month. The glamour of living in a hotel room had worn away after a few days. She wore the same clothes day in, day out. The menu in the hotel restaurant never changed and if she sat in the bar in the evening there would inevitably be someone there who would try and make a pass at her. She therefore got into the habit of reading a book when eating and would usually go to bed early, unless she was invited out somewhere by colleagues from UNICEF.

"Mostly I read Agatha Christie, although I was given a copy of *The Ides of March*, which is about the assassination of Julius Caesar. I thought it may be something you would enjoy, so I brought my copy back with me."

"Did you enjoy it?" asked Basil.

"In a way," replied Celia. "It wasn't written like a stuffy history book but more like a book on philosophy where Julius Caesar asks himself questions about the meaning of life."

Basil thought for a moment. He wasn't sure that a fabricated story of introspection by one of the great Roman leaders would be his cup of tea, however, he would give it a go. "And what about work?" he asked.

"Work is the last thing I want to talk about," said Celia. "I want to kick off my shoes and not think about UNICEF or its funding for another week. Let's talk about you. I must say I was so proud of you today. You've now achieved everything you ever wanted to. You're now a King's Counsel; what next, a judge?"

"No, not a judge!" said Basil. "It would put a knot in my stomach every time I had to imprison someone, wondering if they were guilty or not. Also, I could never sentence someone to death, as there's no going back when you hang someone. No, I am happy where I am now, as a barrister giving each of my clients the best possible defence they could have."

"Well, congratulations to you," said Celia and raised her glass of wine.

"Thank you," said Basil. "Do you know I received one of the greatest compliments I've ever had today? The young female King's Counsel, Rose Heilbron, spoke to me for a few minutes – she knows Maxwell Fyfe. Anyway, when we finished chatting, she said, I hope I come up against you in the future, and I thought, how perfect."

"I'm not sure I understand," said Celia.

"She perceived me as being a worthy opponent, which for me is real recognition."

Celia smiled. "So, that's what you want to do. Go on being a barrister until one day you die with your wig on in court."

"No," said Basil. "The world is changing, and I think I would like to stop when I am at the very top of my game and walk away."

"And do what?"

"Spend more time with you and the family. Do you know, I saw Robert last week and he took me up in his glider. It was the first time I had flown with him and, to be honest, it scared the hell out of me, but please don't tell him that. I was squashed in like a sardine and thought I was going to be sick more than once."

"How is he and the family?"

"He's in good form and Wendy's fine. Her mother was staying over, which gave Robert an excuse to go out with me. Paul and Grace are little angels, though I had forgotten how loudly babies can bawl."

"You had forgotten – don't you remember what Howard and Catherine were like?"

"I suppose I do," said Basil. "They're coming over to spend the weekend with us."

"You've arranged it. That's sweet of you and it will be nice to see them… both of them."

"Hopefully you and Catherine can spend a weekend without fighting."

"I'll do my best," said Celia. "But she does know how to get under my skin."

"I'll speak to her," said Basil, then he opened his mouth and yawned. "Bed?"

VII

Part Seven

Chapter 52

June 1955

Basil skipped up the eleven stone stairs two at a time and at the top, he stopped abruptly, winced, and rubbed his left leg. What had possessed him to dash up the stairs like an errant schoolboy he could not possibly conceive, and now he felt that sharp, age-old cramping of the muscles. He moved forward gingerly past Garden Court Chambers and saw another seven stone steps in front of him. He took a deep breath. One at a time he said to himself, slow and steady wins the race. Temple Gardens to his right was in full bloom with red and white roses and he felt that the world was back on an even keel. He looked at his watch. He was late but he didn't care.

He gingerly walked up the remaining steps and into Fountain Court, with Middle Temple Hall on his right. The Hall, which had been slightly damaged on its eastern side during the Blitz, had now been repaired. It was a stunning example of an Elizabethan building that had survived the Great Fire of London and had been almost unscathed by the last war. The entrance door to the Hall was newer, built in 1831and above it was a stone sculpted lamb, the crest of the Middle Temple, and, above that, a leaded window. As Basil walked past, he noticed the similarities between this and the entrance of Castle Drogo. He turned into Middle Temple Lane, with his chambers just a few steps away.

Two Hare Court was a red brick building with sills of York stone and sash windows, typical of Victorian architects. Basil's rooms were on the first floor, with a small bay window which looked back down along Middle

Temple Lane. On the ground floor was the clerks' room where the senior clerk, Claude Palfrey, worked; the grey-haired septuagenarian had been there as long as anyone could remember. He ran the set of chambers with military precision. The other clerk was young Arthur Wright, who, at the age of forty-five, was no longer considered young by anyone except Claude Palfrey. Both said "Good morning, sir" as Basil leaned into their room.

"Anything for me, Palfrey?" Basil had expected a short and negative answer, as he was preparing for a trial in two weeks.

"Yes, sir," said Palfrey. "There's a request for an opinion from leading counsel. I've put it on your desk."

Basil let out an audible sigh. "Can't you get someone else, Palfrey? You know I'll be all ends up this week."

Palfrey got up slowly from his chair, straightened his jacket and walked to the door where Basil still stood.

"I'm afraid that won't be possible, sir. It's from the Colonial Office and it's covered by the Official Secrets Act."

"What on earth do they want me to do?" asked Basil.

"I'm afraid you will have to read the brief to find that our, sir," said Palfrey. "I was not permitted to look at it. All I was told was that I would have to clear your diary for the next six weeks."

"Six weeks? Impossible, I have the Ruth Connolly murder trial in two weeks."

"I've passed that case on to Mr St John Stephens," said Palfrey.

"Oh, that's just bloody perfect," said Basil, not even trying to hide his sarcasm.

"You will also be having a meeting with the Colonial Secretary this afternoon."

"With Alan Lennox-Boyd?" said Basil. Arthur looked up from his desk at the mention of the name.

"Yes, sir," said Palfrey.

"And when does the Colonial Secretary get here?" asked Basil.

"Mr Lennox-Boyd doesn't come to you, sir. You go to him. I assume the details will be in your brief."

"Call down, sir, when you need a cab and I'll arrange one for you," said Arthur.

Basil left and started climbing the single flight of stairs to his room. Damn this leg, he thought, it still ached.

***

Basil removed the pink ribbon from the brief and opened the papers. His instructions notified him that he was bound by the Official Secrets Act. The Colonial Office wanted a legal opinion about whether there was sufficient evidence to justify a public inquiry, based on allegations of torture and inhumane treatment of the Mau Mau detainees in Kenya. Basil groaned. It was typical government delaying tactics – instead of holding an inquiry they would just kick the can down the road and ask whether there was enough evidence to justify one. Basil read some of the correspondence attached to his instructions, that had been sent to two Labour MPs, Barbara Castle and Fenner Brockway. It was mostly unsigned and without dates or specific allegations. Basil folded his instructions and retied them with the pink ribbon, picked up the telephone and rang down to the clerks' room.

"Palfrey," he said, "if I remember correctly, wasn't St John Stephens instructed by the government on Jomo Kenyatta's appeal against sentence as the leader of the Mau Mau uprising?"

"Yes, sir."

"So why on earth didn't they instruct him for this?"

"I don't know, sir. The secretary to the Colonial Secretary told me that you had been specifically requested."

***

"Your cab is here, sir," said Arthur, standing by the door of Basil's room. Basil stopped writing and looked up. "And I have your tickets to the Dvořák concert tonight at the Festival Hall." Arthur took out an envelope from his inside pocket and handed it to Basil. "Mrs Wright told me this morning that unfortunately they have changed the conductor."

"Do you and Mrs Wright like Dvořák?" asked Basil.

"Mrs Wright and I," said Arthur, "prefer something less highbrow. Something with a good tune, like *Singin' in the Rain* or *Guys and Dolls*."

Basil smiled and for a moment thought of his brother Christian, who had also liked something with a good tune. He had been missing for sixteen years and had long since been presumed dead. His brow furrowed as he again wondered what had happened to his brother. It was the not knowing that bothered him, like an unsolved clue from a crossword.

He picked up his briefcase and made his way down the stairs. The black cab was across the road; its engine thudded loudly, and a trail of black smoke came out of its exhaust. Basil got in and said, "The Colonial Office." The black cab moved slowly down Middle Temple Lane and came to a stop at Embankment. The taxi driver waited for the traffic to pass for a minute before pulling out and turning right. He blew his horn intermittently to warn other drivers that he had no intention of giving way and accelerated towards Westminster.

"It gets worse every year, sir," the cabbie commented. "If we cut up Horse Guards Avenue, we'll be there in a second, sir."

Basil pulled down the window to let some air in.

"Feel free to smoke," said the cabbie.

"I don't," said Basil. However, the driver pulled out a pack of Players and lit one, taking both hands off the wheel as he did so. The cab went quickly up Horse Guards Avenue, turned onto Whitehall, and as the smoke filled the cab, Basil asked him to stop.

Basil got out and stood for a moment looking at the Cenotaph. He rarely came to this part of town, except on the Sunday immediately following Armistice Day when Celia and he would go together. Basil began walking towards the door of the Colonial Office just around the corner on King Charles Street but stopped and then looked back at the Cenotaph. He remembered something that Lutyens had once said, that the Cenotaph had been originally designed to commemorate the victory over Germany. However, when it had been built people immediately started laying wreaths around it to remember the dead and the missing. Instead of a monument to victory, it became a place to remember the dead.

Basil looked at his watch. He was still a few minutes early and his thoughts drifted to his dead brother Adrian. With every passing year, he thought, his eldest brother was being slowly forgotten. He could hardly remember the things that they had done together and then, once again, he thought about Christian. He had now lost everyone in his family – his father, his mother, who had died the previous year, and his two brothers. All that remained was a cold, austere castle.

***

The Right Honourable Alan Lennox-Boyd was charming and when Basil later recounted to Celia the meeting with the Colonial Secretary, it was this fact, above any other, that stuck in his memory. The Foreign Office building, where the Colonial Secretary was based, was a warren of corridors and rooms, many ornately decorated so that foreign dignitaries could be entertained. Basil, however, was taken to a basement area where the rooms were plain and functional. Lennox-Boyd stood up when Basil entered and shook his hand. There was no one at the meeting apart from Basil, Lennox-Boyd and his secretary because, as Lennox-Boyd explained, the sensitive nature of the advice that the Colonial Office was seeking meant that numbers had to be kept to a minimum.

"I have a meeting in an hour with cabinet," said Lennox-Boyd, who then set out the requirements for the advice. Basil had realised that if he did not take control of the meeting, he would not ask the questions to which he wanted answers. However, Lennox-Boyd was a master of talking and kept going without pause, explaining that Basil had been extended the courtesy of a room within the building for the next few weeks and a driver and that this could be extended if necessary. He handed Basil a small file containing some more letters from detainees and told him that every evening he should put in a request for any documents that the Colonial Office had and, if possible, these would be supplied the next day.

"And with that, he shook my hand and went," said Basil.

"But you have not told me what the case is about," said Celia.

"Well, the letters I received made some allegations of brutality, the same kind of thing that you would have read about in the newspapers. There were about twenty letters and most of them are undated and unsigned. There are only two with signatures but no dates. That's all I can tell you."

"But what did Lennox-Boyd say?"

"He is a master of saying nothing, especially on anything important. He spent ages telling me about the uprising and how some elements within the Kikuyu tribe were seeking independence from Britain, who the British referred to as the Mau Mau."

"So, the long and the short of it is that you were called in to see the Colonial Secretary and left no wiser than when you went in."

"Well, I wouldn't exactly say that. Lennox-Boyd did say the British intervened because the Kenyan government failed to take control of the situation and then every Mau Mau suspect was rounded up and put in detention camps. He said that there is now a growing uneasiness about the time taken over screening those who were detained and uncertainty as to their future."

"And why does the Colonial Office want an advice from you?"

"They want to know if there is sufficient evidence for them to order an inquiry. There are about fifty detention camps," said Basil. "But try as a might, I could not get a straight answer from Lennox-Boyd about exactly what was happening in any of them. Every time I thought I was getting him in a corner he would pick up the pot of tea, smile and say: 'Shall I play mother?' and then proceed to fill up our cups or pass around a plate of biscuits and suggest, with a knowing look, that I take a bourbon. It was quite disarming."

"But you don't like bourbons," said Celia.

"I know," replied Basil.

"And how many did you have?"

"Four," said Basil.

Celia shook her head. She wondered how someone so brilliant and analytical in their career could be derailed with just a little charm, and then she smiled as she realised that that was exactly what their daughter had been doing for the last twenty years. She glanced at her watch – she had to get a move on – and then looked at Basil in his dinner suit and, with his dark hair with streaks of grey, thought he looked quite distinguished. She mentioned it as she walked past to the bathroom, and he blushed.

"Will you ring down to the concierge and ask them to arrange a taxi in half an hour?" she suggested as she stood at the bathroom door.

"No need, the Colonial Office has given me a car for the next few weeks to chauffeur me around."

***

Celia was impressed with the Bentley that had been put at Basil's disposal. The inside smelt of freshly cleaned leather. The driver tipped his cap as they got in and Basil instructed him to go to the Royal Festival Hall. They turned out of Cadogan Square and down towards Sloane Square. The car went along the embankment, back towards the city and then crossed the river at Lambeth Bridge. They were there in a fraction under twenty minutes, and Celia hardly had time to straighten her dress.

"You may have chosen the wrong profession, Basil."

"I am not sure I have the charm for politics," replied Basil. "How was your day?"

"Everything moves so slowly. We had some of the UNICEF committee over from America who I had to lunch with."

"Are they finally setting up a branch in London?"

"That's going to happen soon," said Celia. "We talked about the work we're doing in Europe and the established projects in Asia, Latin America, and North Africa. There's a lot of focus on Africa now."

"And that includes Kenya?" asked Basil.

"Yes," said Celia, "why do you ask?"

"It's just that I might have to go to Kenya, and I thought that we could make a holiday of it, go on a safari. Then, when I'm working, you might be able to get some first-hand experience about what UNICEF is doing on the ground. What do you think?"

"And when did you come up with that idea?"

"I just thought of it. There's nothing certain yet. Lennox-Boyd said that a lot of the information is out in Kenya, and I thought that it may be easier for Mohammed to go to the mountain than the mountain to come to Mohammed."

The Bentley pulled up outside the Royal Festival Hall.

"I'll be waiting outside at the end of the concert, sir," said the chauffeur.

"Thank you, Rodgers," said Basil.

However, before he could get out of the car, Rodgers was opening the door for Celia. People in the queue for last-minute returns turned to look at her and, for the first time in a long time, Celia felt like she was twenty-one again.

Chapter 53

UNICEF began its work in Kenya in 1954. However, instead of simply providing aid to sick and undernourished children, it commenced a programme of training midwives and sanitary inspectors to raise the standards of hygiene across the country. It established training schools, where local women could learn about hygiene and nourishment, and then mobile units went to the villages to pass on their knowledge.

"Our aim is to try and establish a women's group movement," said Celia. "However, there's a fear that what we're trying to do is apply a Western solution to an African problem and there are concerns that our policy will fail. That's why UNICEF has agreed that I can go out there and work on the ground; so, I can report back to them about the problems we're facing."

Basil rubbed his eyes. "I spent all day in the Colonial Office going through thirty boxes of documents called the Swynnerton Plan."

"On the redistribution of land," said Celia.

"How do you know that?" said Basil. "I had never heard of it until this morning."

"Because it's about trying to make the land that the Kikuyu have more productive and therefore reduce the starvation that is affecting them, especially the children. However, what has it got to do with your case?"

Basil rubbed his eyes again. "Nothing really, except it allows me to understand the cause for the Mau Mau uprising. The Swynnerton Plan deals with one cause – and probably the most important one. Fifty years ago, when the land was redistributed, there was not a problem with hunger. Ironically," he continued, "it's because of modern medicines and sanitation that there is now a much higher life expectancy and population. Fifty years ago, there were about a million and a half people in Kenya and now there are six million. The population has grown threefold, but they are still producing the same amount of food."

"It's why all the governmental bodies are encouraging the use of modern farming methods and why UNICEF is supporting them," said Celia.

"But everything is owned in small parcels of land and modern farming methods only work if you combine the land. From what I could gather, the Swynnerton Plan is seeking to bring the land under the control of a Central Province with mass land consolidation taking place. However, there will be some winners and a lot of losers and, from what I can see, the winners will be those who are supporting the government, and the losers will be those who don't." Basil loosened his tie. "On balance, the Kikuyu will end up being better off economically but there are a lot of people who oppose the change." Celia came over and sat next to him on the couch. "From the perspective of some of the Kikuyu," said Basil, "this is a case of stealing from the poor and giving to the rich."

"But there will be paid jobs working on the land and the amount of food grown will substantially increase, which means no one should starve," said Celia. "Isn't the answer for the government to give the Kikuyu back some of the rich pastureland that was given to the white settlers?"

"It's the settlers who control the government," said Basil, "and they would never countenance that. Most of them bought the land generations ago. For them, it's ancient history."

"It's not though is it," said Celia, taking off her glasses and putting them into a case. "Britain has become rich because of the empire. Your father made his fortune from importing tea and coffee from around the world and a lot of that comes from Kenya."

"My father always paid a fair price for what he bought," said Basil.

"That may be true," replied Celia. "But he paid it to the estate owners and not to the people whose land had been taken away from them."

***

Basil sat in his room in the basement of the Colonial Office, wondering what he should request next. The conversation with Celia the night before still played on his mind. He had thought of his father as the successful owner of retail stores across England. He had never thought about what was sold in those stores and how that impacted the people where the goods were produced. In India, thought Basil, where the plantations provided so much tea, the people who worked on the estates were much better off. They had jobs, incomes, homes, and security. However, there was something about Kenya that disturbed him. Here the most fertile lands had been taken away from the Kikuyu. It was true that the British had brought medicines, schools and even the church to Kenya. It was true that many Kikuyu were living and enjoying a Western lifestyle. The British had stopped the internecine wars between the natives and made illegal the slave trade that was rampant across East Africa; but, still, something did not feel right.

The door of the room opened, and Lennox-Boyd wandered in.

"I hope I am not disturbing, old chap," he said, "but I thought I would see how you were getting on."

"A secretary would be a help," said Basil.

"Ah, that's always a problem. Finding a secretary who is cleared to deal with Official Secrets is not as easy as it sounds. Even if you proposed someone, she would certainly not meet the clearance requirements."

"And I suppose a background check was done on me," said Basil.

"Of course, old chap. But as a major in the Judge Advocate General's office in the war, you had the requisite clearance level. It's nothing personal; although I should say you weren't my first choice for this task, but the Lord Chancellor intervened."

"Maxwell Fyfe asked that I be instructed?"

"Yes, the Lord Chancellor thought you would be the right man for this review and said so in cabinet. It seems that he holds you in high regard. Anyway, getting to the more important issue, can I arrange for some tea and bourbons to be brought down to you?"

***

The following days involved box after box of documents being brought to

Basil's room. He was very much left alone, only seeing a receptionist when he entered and left, and an assistant who brought tea and biscuits twice during the day. On his fourth day, a slew of boxes arrived. In total, they contained over a hundred police reports, each with photographic bundles depicting the Mau Mau savagery. Reading the brutal details, and looking at the photographs, Basil thought with a sinking feeling that this all felt horribly familiar – he had seen atrocities like this a decade ago in a camp called Dachau.

***

Celia did not disturb Basil and left him with his thoughts. She knew better than to ask. Something had happened – it may have been something he had been told or seen, and she knew he needed time to digest it before he could speak about it. Over the years she had seen him like this on a few occasions. When his father had died, when Christian had gone missing, after she had told him of her affair, and during the Nuremberg trials. There seemed to be a weight that dragged him down. It was a form of melancholy that he needed to work through. She knew he would shake it off but that it might take time – a few hours or, more likely, a few days.

"Can you get me another G and T?" he asked.

"That's your sixth, Basil," she responded, hoping reason might prevail.

"It's been a long day," he answered, a slight tremor in his voice that he could not disguise.

"I'm here if you want to talk about it," said Celia.

"Not yet," said Basil, "soon maybe." He picked up his glass and finished off his drink. He watched as Celia took his glass to the kitchen. "I think I had forgotten how depraved human beings could be," he shouted after her.

"The things that the Mau Mau have done," answered Celia, guessing at what might have affected him.

"Do you remember me telling you that when some of the camps in Germany were liberated, the soldiers who arrived first executed the German guards?"

"Of course. Is that what's happening in the Mau Mau detention camps?"

"I don't know," said Basil. "However, if it is I wouldn't blame the soldiers

314

one bit." Basil tapped his fingers as Celia returned with his gin and tonic. "Have you got a cigarette?" he asked.

"You don't smoke," said Celia.

"Please, just give me a cigarette," he said, that tremor in his voice appearing again. "I just want to think."

Celia got up and looked at him. She went to her handbag and took out a packet and gave him one and then said she was going to bed. For fifteen minutes she heard him banging around in the living room. She couldn't remember seeing him this drunk and then it went quiet, and she thought he had fallen asleep. It was then that she heard him sobbing.

Celia tried to sleep but the fan by her bed whirred, blowing warm air around the humid room. Basil had stopped crying an hour earlier, and she had gone to see how he was. He was asleep on the couch, an untouched gin and tonic next to the ashtray where the cigarette had burnt down to nothing, leaving a two-inch piece of unbroken ash. She put a light blanket over him and decided not to wake him.

She thought that, for almost a decade, their lives had proceeded smoothly. He had come back from Nuremberg willing to forgive her and had helped her find a role as an ambassador within UNICEF. For ten years they had done things together. He made every effort to take an interest in her work and, after the children left home, they started to go out regularly to the theatre, the opera and classical concerts. On weekends they would sometimes go to Castle Drogo. He bought them both bicycles so that they could go out together and he seemed at his happiest when he stumbled across a country pub, and they sat having a meal before a roaring fire.

He still loved the law and the thrill of standing in front of a criminal court and defending the indefensible. He still loved cricket – and she still had no understanding why. He still loved ancient history but, most of all, he loved his children and grandchildren. Whenever she was away with her work, he would always have one, if not both twins over. He would take them to the newest musicals in the West End or premieres at the cinema. He would have days out with Robert, Wendy and the grandchildren, taking them to the London Zoo, where a favourite for the grandchildren was Guy the Gorilla. They had reached a point when both of them seemed at ease with the world. This new case he had been given therefore troubled Celia, and she worried that it might throw their boat back onto stormy waters.

Chapter 54

July 1955

"I have some news," said Celia. "UNICEF has arranged for me to join a mobile unit on my trip to Kenya. I will be working with a group of American nurses, as I practised nursing in America."

"Why not a group of British nurses?" asked Basil.

"There are none," said Celia. "None of the Kikuyu would be treated by a British nurse, we're seen as the enemy." Celia picked up a slice of toast, put a thin coating of marmalade on one end and nibbled at it. "I am going to be working around the Nairobi area and the Rift Valley. I was told that there were detention camps near there – at Nairobi and the Mbkasi camp, but we don't go into those as they have their own doctors." Basil put down his cup.

"What name did you say? The detention camp, what did you call it?" he asked.

"Mbkasi. Why?" said Celia.

"It's just not a name that I've come across on the official list of camps I was given."

***

"I just thought I would see how things were going," said Lennox-Boyd from the door of Basil's room in the Colonial Office.

"They're coming along," Basil answered.

"And I understand that your request for documents yesterday only had one item."

"You do like to keep your finger on the pulse," said Basil. "I'm just waiting for the documents to arrive; usually, they're here for me when I arrive. However, credit where credit is due, the civil service files everything meticulously."

"Ah," said Lennox-Boyd. "Well, I am afraid we have looked and there is nothing specifically referred to as the Mbkasi detention camp."

"Nothing?"

"Nothing. We can't find any documents specifically matching your request, no Mbkasi detention camp officially exists."

"And unofficially?" asked Basil.

"Unofficially," said Lennox-Boyd, with the faintest hint of a smile, "no Mbkasi detention camp officially exists."

Basil looked at his watch. Nearly ten-thirty. He closed the file he had been reading and put away his notebook.

"Tea will be coming in a few minutes… and bourbon biscuits. Do you care to join me, Mr Lennox-Boyd?"

"I'm afraid I can't, old chap. I have a pile of work this morning and to be honest…" Lennox-Boyd leant in a little as if he were about to whisper an official secret. "I can't abide bourbons."

Lennox-Boyd closed the door as he left. Basil looked at the four walls of the basement room that had been designated to him and sighed. The sun was shining outside, and, for a change, there had been a purple patch of weather. The only adornment on the wall of his room was a print of Queen Elizabeth by Pietro Annigoni. Basil stared at it for a moment and then got up to take a closer look. In the bottom left-hand corner was a small figure fishing for salmon. The original was being exhibited at the Royal Academy and Basil, for a moment, thought that he might take the day off and wander into Piccadilly and see it. Without documents, he could do very little. He opened his briefcase and took out the list he had made of the names of the detention camps. What was he missing, he thought to himself, and why was the list incomplete? He counted the names of the camps on the list; there were fifty-two names. He had been provided with all the official records that the Foreign Office claimed to have and, except for a few cases, where the guards had allegedly been heavy-handed, he could not see any instances of systematic maltreatment.

Something was missing, he was sure of it. He had seen the photographs of the brutality carried out by the Mau Mau to both Africans, who supported the British government, and Europeans. He knew that some of the guards would seek retribution. Basil took out his notebook and started tapping his fingers on the table. Half an hour passed, and Basil had still not written one thing on the list of documents. He looked down at the clean page. Why had Maxwell Fyfe suggested his name, he thought to himself, and he thought about the cross-examination of Goering at Nuremberg by Robert Jackson. It had been awful. Robert Jackson had not listened at all to Goering's answers, but simply placed document after document in front of him for him to acknowledge. The court had been told in exacting detail the complaints made about the concentration camps. The British advocates had submitted hundreds of documents from maltreated prisoners to the authorities as well as complaints from inspectors. Basil had joked later that if the American plan was to bring the Nazi High Command to its knees through boredom, then the strategy of Robert Jackson was working admirably.

Basil got up. He opened the little basement window to let in some air. He could hear the noise of the traffic as it passed down Whitehall, with taxi cabs continually honking their horns to obtain any small advantage. He looked at his watch. It was eleven-fifteen. If he left now, he could surprise Celia and they could lunch at Peter Jones, the fashionable new department store in Chelsea, as Celia seemed to like the place. Basil went back to the table and looked down at his notebook. He hadn't thought much about the Nuremberg trial for nearly a decade. A whole morning at Nuremberg had, in Basil's opinion, been wasted. Maxwell Fyfe had later told him that Goering would be hung because of the documents. One needed to show that the authorities were aware of what was happening and so each letter had to be exhibited.

Basil closed his briefcase and was about to leave when he looked down at the empty document request list. He remembered that at Nuremberg the letters that were exhibited weren't written to the camp commanders, they were written to the local mayor and the authorities. The camp commanders had destroyed the letters on receipt. Basil thought for a moment. He had asked to be provided with official correspondence from the camps. What he needed were letters to the colonial governors, magistrates and the district authorities. He started scribbling on the list the names of each camp and a request for any document sent from there to a magistrate, district authority, police or government body. He then requested internal documents from inspectors, local hospitals and undertakers who had dealt with a detainee from one of the camps. He did not know what would come back, but he was now more certain that he needed to be in Kenya.

At one forty-five, as he was about to leave the Foreign Office building, he handed in fourteen sheets of paper containing requests for documents.

***

"I don't see you for weeks on end," said Basil, "and then you appear two days in a row."

"Well, I heard you had asked for quite a few documents yesterday, and I wanted to make sure that you were hard at work," said Lennox-Boyd. Basil put back the lid on one of the boxes.

"I am still trying to make sense of all of this. Most of the documents I requested must be in Kenya and so are the witnesses. I'm therefore planning to go there in two weeks."

"I know," said Lennox-Boyd, who had a copy of Basil's request to visit some of the camps. "I shall, of course, approve the trip and also we shall send Rodgers with you."

"Rodgers?"

"Your driver," said Lennox-Boyd. "He's quite a capable man if you find the time to chat with him."

"And do you often chat with him?"

"Oh yes," said Lennox-Boyd. "As I said the other day, you were not my choice. I would have preferred St John Stephens. You can rely on him to do the right thing."

"I can assure you," said Basil, biting back a feeling of annoyance, "I will also be doing 'the right thing' as you call it."

"Old chap," said Lennox-Boyd, in a dismissive tone, "what's 'the right thing' for you is unlikely to be 'the right thing' for us. St John Stephens would have appreciated the distinction, which is why I wanted him."

***

Three days later, Basil had meticulously recorded the contents of each box and had identified the documents that he might need to refer to in his advice. It was on the third day that he opened a box marked 'Miscellaneous'. It had details of the Kisumu prison, one of the detainment camps for the Mau Mau. As he read some of the documents, he realised that it was also referred to as Kisuma or Kesumett, depending on the language spoken. While the European settlers had corrupted the names, the people who lived there still referred to the places by their old tribal names. He suddenly realised that if Lennox-Boyd was only giving him things that matched his spelling, he might be missing three-quarters of all relevant documents.

Basil wrote down the word 'Mbkasi'. He looked down the list of detention camps to see if one had a similar spelling. Mbeu and Mkobe camps came closest. He decided to say the word out loud: "Am be kasi, Em be kasi, Um be kasi. Am ba kasi, Am be kasi, Am bu kasi, Em ba kasi." He stopped and repeated the word, "Embakasi". He had heard the name before.

Basil got up from his chair, opened the door, walked down the corridor to a flight of stairs, and went up them as quickly as he could. At the reception desk, he asked whether the Colonial Secretary was in his office and told the receptionist he was on his way to see him. Basil went up another flight of stairs and along another corridor, until he got to Lennox-Boyd's offices. Lennox-Boyd's secretary objected, saying the Colonial Secretary was busy, but Basil knocked on the door and opened it.

"Sorry to disturb you, old chap," said Basil, "but what's the name of the airport we are building in Nairobi?"

"I beg your pardon," said Lennox-Boyd, "I don't think you have an appointment."

"I'll be gone in a second," said Basil. "I was just hoping you could remind me of the name of the new airport we're constructing near Nairobi."

"It's Embakasi airport," said Lennox-Boyd.

"Em… ba… kasi," repeated Basil slowly. "Thank you. Oh, and just one other question." Basil did not wait for Lennox-Boyd to object. "Is there a new detention camp there?"

"No, not precisely," said Lennox-Boyd, who closed the file he was looking at and raised his eyes. Lennox-Boyd put the tips of his fingers together, and slowly and deliberately started to speak. "There is a prison camp for convicted criminals. You should appreciate that those working there have been convicted to hard labour. No person on remand or held under the Emergency Regulations is required to do any manual labour there, unless it is voluntary, and they are then paid the current rate of wages. This was made clear to Parliament in response to a question I received."

"But the prisoners working there are Mau Mau?"

"I believe so," said Lennox-Boyd.

"Then I'll only have one request for tomorrow."

"You're wasting your time if you start looking there," said Lennox-Boyd, "but then, I suppose, it's your time to waste."

Chapter 55

"I met Tom Askwith today," said Basil. "Have you heard of him?" He sat back in his armchair and put his gin and tonic on the side table.

"Asquith, like the prime minister?" asked Celia.

"Same pronunciation," said Basil, "different spelling."

"No," said Celia. "Who is he?"

"He runs the Department of Community Development and Rehabilitation in Kenya. He's the man responsible for setting up the rehabilitation programmes for the Mau Mau. An interesting person in that he spent his first years there as a district officer and was in the British Olympic team twice as a rower."

Celia sat opposite Basil on the sofa. She turned down the wireless as the music to *The Archers* faded and the radio presenter started talking about the following programme. Basil knew too well not to start any conversation that might interfere with her enjoyment of the lives of the people of Ambridge.

"He probably understands more about the Mau Mau problem than anyone I have yet met," continued Basil. "He didn't appear to have one of those 'us and them' attitudes but understood the struggles that the Kikuyu were having when the crisis erupted. He's been trying to explain these problems to Whitehall for the last few years."

"So, did you ask him about whether there had been any violence against the Mau Mau detainees, or can't you tell me that?" asked Celia.

"He was quite reticent about it at the start. He told me that almost every settler in Kenya will have known someone who had been killed by the

Mau Mau and that the murder of his friend Arundell Gray Leakey had sickened him." Basil paused for a moment before continuing. "They made Leakey watch as they murdered his wife and then they marched him to the base of Mount Kenya, where the Kikuyu believe their god Ngai lived, disembowelled him and burned him alive."

"That's awful," said Celia, horrified by what she had heard. "It's absolutely barbaric."

"He said that any violence was likely to have been carried out by the screening teams and in the camps where the hardened Mau Mau are detained because they wanted to exact some revenge."

"The screening teams?" asked Celia. "What are they?"

"When the Kikuyu are arrested, they are screened to determine whether they support the Mau Mau. If they are classified as being 'white' they are released. If they are classified as 'grey' they are sent to a detention camp. If they are classified as being 'black' they are sent to prisons. The 'blacks' will have committed some crime. The 'greys' are those who have shown sympathies for the Mau Mau and have taken an oath and the government wants to rehabilitate them. Askwith told me that as far as he knows, no ill-treatment has ever occurred at any of the detention camps he supervises. However, he wouldn't be specific about the holding camps at Manyani or Mackinnon Road, where there are allegations of mistreatment."

"Did he say anything else?"

"Nothing much. He said that part of his duties had been to inspect the detention camps and to supervise operations and that he did so with the First African Minister. He also said that if he had been aware of any mistreatment, he would have dealt with it." Basil paused. "There was one other thing he did say when I told him I was going to Kenya to see things for myself. He said, 'Speak to Peter Muigai Kenyatta.'"

"Why do I know that name?" said Celia.

"He's the son of Jomo Kenyatta, the head of the Kenya Africa Union, who we've imprisoned as one of the leaders of the Mau Mau uprising."

Chapter 56

The sun came through the window of their flat at Cadogan Square and dust motes danced around the living room. Outside the noise of children playing could be heard, coming up from the gardens. Celia put down the telephone and turned to Basil as he sat in his old, favourite chair.

"I thought we should get away for the weekend."

Basil leaned across to the sideboard and turned down the radio. After two days, the Test match between England and South Africa was finely poised.

"Where do you want to go?" he asked.

"To the castle," said Celia. "I've spoken to the children, and they say they would be happy to meet us there and make a family weekend of it. Even Catherine sounded enthusiastic and said she wanted to bring a friend. It's been a long time since we were all there as a family. The last time was," Celia paused for a moment, "at your mother's funeral. I would like to see everyone before we go to Kenya."

Basil sighed. "It's not that I don't want to go away," he finally said. "It's just that I'm not sure that I want to go there. It holds too many memories."

"Not all of them are bad," said Celia.

"Not all of them are good," responded Basil. "It feels like a mausoleum. I would sell it tomorrow if anyone would buy it. I am one of the major shareholders in the twenty-seventh largest company in England and I feel like a pauper. The cost of the upkeep of the castle is staggering and now the whole roof needs replacing. It was only completed twenty-five years ago! If your father was alive, I would be suing him for so much money you would be able to hear the pips squeak."

"It keeps the past alive," said Celia. "Every time I am there, I remember your parents and your brothers. Anyway, what would you do with all that money?"

"Buy an Aston Martin DB3 for starters," said Basil, under his breath. He knew that Celia had rather a negative attitude towards sportscars driven by older men. Over the radio, Basil could just hear that another English wicket had fallen. He thought about turning the radio up for a moment but had learnt from bitter experience that cutting Celia off mid-conversation was not something one did lightly.

"And we could ask Rodgers to drive us," continued Celia. "He might like a weekend in the country."

"I doubt it," replied Basil, who desperately tried to listen to who had been dismissed. He thought it was Tony Lock but wasn't one hundred per cent certain. He just caught the word 'lbw'. At least Compton will be in next, he thought to himself.

"Why did you say that?" asked Celia. "That Rodgers might not want to come?"

"Oh that, well he might have plans with his own family," answered Basil.

"But he's not married, Basil. Don't you ever speak to him?"

"Well, not often," said Basil.

"Well, he's not married. After the war, he got divorced and he's been single for the last few years."

"And how exactly did you find all of that out?" asked Basil, as he looked intently at Celia.

"There's no secret, dear. When you are buried away in that little room of yours in the Colonial Office, Rodgers will drive me around town and help with carrying any shopping I might need. And, of course, we chat over lunch."

"You've lunched with him?" said Basil, who had now lost interest in the Test match, even though the great Denis Compton was heading to the crease.

"A few times," said Celia.

"And now you're suggesting that we bring Rodgers with us for a weekend away, just after telling me that you lunch regularly with him?"

"Basil, you are the limit. He is young enough to be my son," said Celia, thinking about it for a moment. "Actually, he's a few months younger than Robert." Celia suddenly realised that this conversation may be heading in a direction she had not intended. Basil was not prone to jealousy, but Celia knew it was better to avoid some subjects where her conduct had not been exemplary. "You're not jealous, are you?"

Basil paused. He also had been married long enough to know when Celia was bowling him a googly. If he admitted to being jealous, she would say he was being melodramatic. If he denied being jealous, he would be condemned for taking her for granted. He needed to pad this away from the wicket.

"Of course I'm jealous," he said slowly. "You're still the most beautiful woman I know." It was like a little dance they did on the odd occasion, thought Basil, where one of them would inadvertently make a comment and the other would try and withdraw without appearing to acknowledge that an uncomfortable situation had arisen. Let sleeping dogs lie, his father had often said as he was growing up. Basil had now mastered the art of avoidance and wondered whose benefit it was for.

Celia leaned down and kissed him on the forehead.

"Nice recovery," she said and turned up the volume of the cricket commentary.

***

"And between meadows, soft and full of patience, one path, a pale strip, appeared."

"That's beautiful, Basil. What's it from?"

"A book of poetry I found in Christian's belongings after the war. As we turned into the driveway it came to mind."

"Have you heard from Tomas recently?" asked Celia.

"Nothing for a long time."

The cinder on the driveway crunched as the Bentley moved slowly up the path and stopped before the front door of the castle. The large wooden door opened, and two small children ran out.

"Nana… Grandpops," the two children shouted in unison. Celia got out of the car.

"My little darlings," she shouted back and gathered the two of them into her arms. "You've both grown like weeds." The two children giggled, and Celia kissed them on their cheeks. "And where's Mummy and Daddy?" asked Celia.

"Mummy's unpacking and Daddy's sleeping," said the youngest child, Paul.

"We arrived hours ago," said Grace.

"Well, not hours ago," contradicted Paul.

"It was hours," Grace insisted.

Basil had by this time got out of the car and was carrying a suitcase.

"And don't I get a hug?" he asked and immediately found two small children clinging to his legs.

"Who's that?" asked Paul, as Rodgers walked past him carrying the other suitcases into the castle.

"That's Rodgers," said Basil. "He drove us and he's looking after Nana and me when we go to Kenya. Now go and wake your father and tell him we are here." And as quick as the two children had appeared, they were gone.

"It's lovely to see them," said Celia to Basil. "But I still can't get used to them calling me Nana. It makes me feel old."

"You're not old," said Basil. Celia smiled; however, deep in her bones, she was beginning to feel her age.

Robert was woken by two young children who dived onto him as he slept. He woke with a start and when he heard their giggles he shouted "monsters" at them, and then laughed.

"Nana and Grandpops have arrived," said Grace.

"Come on," said Robert, "let's go and find them. And then we can go exploring the castle. There's a room I want to show you where you can learn about Grandpop's brother Adrian, who died in the war. He was a very special person."

***

"You will join us for dinner tonight," said Celia to Rodgers.

"I was thinking about getting something at the pub," said Rodgers.

"That won't do," said Celia. "If you're going to be chaperoning Basil and me for the next month in Kenya, it's best if we get to know you a little better. Also," she continued, "it would be nice to call you by your Christian name while we are here. Would that be all right with you? It's Iain, isn't it?"

"And we'll have an informal meal," said Basil. "Cold cuts in the kitchen. I'm sure the cook was dreading having to cook for all of us, as well as all the staff."

"That's settled then," said Celia. "We'll see you at seven this evening for dinner. You'll then get to meet our other two children Howard and Catherine."

Rodgers said that he would get himself settled in one of the empty staff rooms in the North Tower.

"Where did you find him?" asked Wendy, after Rodgers had left. "He's a bit broody."

"He was given to us with a car," said Basil. "A perk of being instructed by the Colonial Secretary."

"And you said he was going with you to Kenya," said Robert.

"Yes," said Basil. "He'll be our chauffeur out there."

"More of a bodyguard than a chauffeur, I'd guess," said Robert. Celia looked at her eldest son.

"What on earth made you say that, Robert?"

"The tattoo on his arm, I noticed it when you introduced us. *Per Mare, Per Terram*. It's the motto of the Marine Commandos."

"Well then," said Celia, "I certainly will feel more comfortable having him with us when we go to Kenya."

"Yes," said Basil. However, something made him feel a little uneasy. Why would the Colonial Secretary appoint a commando as his chauffeur? He doubted that it was for his benefit.

Chapter 57

Except for a few rooms, such as the bedrooms and the nursery, Castle Drogo had not changed one iota since the death of Lady Frances. The rooms still looked precisely the same as the day on which she died. In the dining room, the portraits of Sir Julius Drewe and his long-dead ancestors continued to look down upon the table. The library still had the blue velvet chairs placed along the bookcase, and Lady Frances's boudoir still had the photographs that she treasured more than anything. That morning Catherine and Howard had left the castle and walked down to the Teign Gorge and then up past Piddledown Common, where Dartmoor ponies abounded. They arrived back a little before lunch and Howard went off to find Robert and Catherine went into the library.

"How are you, Mother?" asked Catherine, as she saw Celia reading at the table.

Celia looked up from her book. "I'm fine," she said. "Why do you ask? Don't I look well?"

"You are looking happier than I've seen you for years. You're not having an affair, are you?" Catherine had wanted to make it sound like a joke, however, as she was saying it, she had thought about adding the word *again* at the end of the sentence. Celia slowly closed her book and put it down on the coffee table.

"If that was supposed to be a joke," said Celia, "then it wasn't very funny. And no, I'm not having an affair." Celia could feel herself becoming more annoyed as she spoke. "Who exactly would I be having an affair with?"

"Well, there is that moody dish you brought down with you, Iain, your

330

chauffeur. There are more than a few women I know who would be tempted by someone like him. Do you know who he reminds me of?" Catherine again paused. She knew she should just shut up, but she couldn't help herself.

"Marlon Brando?" said Celia, with more than a hint of sarcasm in her voice.

"No, that Canadian army colonel that you were so chummy with during the war."

"I don't know who you mean," said Celia, who picked up her book and opened it.

"You must remember him," said Catherine. "Granny didn't like him one bit. You and he were always gadding around in his jeep. Don't you see the similarity? I have to say they're two peas from the same pod."

"Well then you need a new pair of glasses," said Celia. "He's nothing like Colonel Landry."

"Oh, you *do* remember him," said Catherine, who smiled as if she had won a small victory.

Celia bit her tongue. She could not understand why her daughter seemed to delight in making these little jibes and then watching Celia's embarrassment. Celia had hoped that she would have become more forgiving as she got older, but every time Basil looked tired the barbed comments started again.

"Actually," said Celia, "I was smiling because I'm feeling useful."

"Useful?" Catherine asked.

"Yes, useful. When I go to Kenya I will be working with a mobile unit out in the field. It's a new initiative and I'll be finding out how the money that we've raised through UNICEF is spent. We can make a major difference to the starving children there."

She looked at her daughter, who everyone said was the spitting image of her when she was younger.

"And," Celia added, "your father and I have been going out on the town enjoying ourselves. He took me to a Dvořák concert last month at the Festival Hall."

"So, why is Dad looking so tired?" said Catherine.

"It's because of this case that he's doing," said Celia. "You should speak to him."

"Do look after him," said Catherine emphatically.

"Of course I will," said Celia. "Always."

When Catherine had gone, Celia thought about carrying on reading her book. She looked out from the library across the moorland. It was her library now – hers and Basil's. She had once said that she wanted to live at Castle Drogo and now it belonged to her she felt like a stranger on the few occasions she visited. Sir Julius and Lady Frances still resided there in every piece of furniture that they had chosen, in every fitting and fixture and every painting. After Sir Julius's death, Lady Frances lived there for over twenty years not changing a single thing. Basil was right, thought Celia, it was a mausoleum and not a place to be lived in.

She thought about Lady Frances, who had known everybody's names who worked on the estate. Each day Lady Frances had walked the circumference of the estate, stopping to ask after every person she met. Celia hardly knew the names of ten of the staff. For a few years after the beginning of the war, she and Lady Frances got on as they both helped with the refugees and orphans that were brought to the castle. Then Celia had met Captain Landry and things had changed, and a coldness descended on their relationship. When Celia went back to London, she felt she had spent the last two years there under sufferance. Lady Frances, who would speak to everyone on the estate, rarely said more than a few words to Celia from the moment she found out about the affair.

Chapter 58

"What are your plans when you get to Kenya?" asked Lennox-Boyd.

"I thought you knew my schedule," said Basil looking up from his desk as he closed a file marked Embakasi Airport. "I will be talking to the authorities at three of the prisons as well as inmates and guards. I will then be working in Nairobi at the government's offices inspecting any relevant documents."

"And your terms of reference," said Lennox-Boyd, "you are clear on the scope of your mandate?"

"Of course," said Basil. He had learnt the precise terms of reference by rote. "Whether the Government of the United Kingdom or the Government of the United Kingdom through the British army or the Colonial Administration or members of the security forces acting under their instruction, established or operated a system through which members of the Kikuyu tribe were subject to torture or inhumane treatment."

Lennox-Boyd sat down opposite Basil.

"While you are there," said Lennox-Boyd, "you may hear stories about acts of torture or inhumane treatment. I was told that a Complaints Coordinating Committee was set up by the Chief Secretary in Kenya." He handed Basil a carbon copy of a document dated the 20th of February 1954, which had the word 'Priority' written on the top. "However, the information I've been given leads me to believe that these acts are not being carried out by the British army and are not sanctioned by the British government in Kenya. As you have said, the Colonial Office wishes to know whether the government of the United Kingdom has operated a system of inhumane treatment or given instructions for others under their control to operate a system of inhumane treatment." Lennox-Boyd stopped speaking and looked around the room. "Is there any tea?" he asked.

"It's Saturday," Basil answered and looked at Lennox-Boyd, who seemed exhausted. "Can I get you a glass of water?" he asked. Lennox-Boyd shook his head.

"Some of the guards have been prosecuted and we are investigating other offences. However, this government believes that these are isolated events and have taken place without the acquiescence of the government."

"Is there anything else?" asked Basil, who looked at his watch. He needed to pack up his papers and head back to Cadogan Square, collect Celia and then go to the airport.

"Just one thing," said Lennox-Boyd. He paused. "The British officer who is overseeing the camps you will be visiting is someone you used to know."

"I don't think I know anyone in the army in Kenya," said Basil.

"Brigadier Jonathan Bruton," said Lennox-Boyd. "I believe you were at university with him."

"Bruton," said Basil. "I haven't seen him for nearly thirty years."

VIII

Part Eight

Chapter 59

August 1955

Located in the Northern Frontier Province, Shaba National Reserve is a rugged area of stone kopjes, thorn bush and acacia trees, which is little visited by Europeans. It is an arid semi-desert area, which is set against the backdrop of the sacred mountain Ololokwe. The reserve has a diverse mixture of game – from elephants to zebras, ostriches to black rhinos. However, Basil and Celia were hoping to see one of the big cats, a lion, cheetah, or leopard. As they drove along the red earth roads, dik-diks ran across their path – those beautiful tiny antelopes with incredibly dark black eyes surrounded by a white ring of fur. Many of them were reddish-brown in colour, and the males had small horns. When Celia first saw a dik-dik, a smile spread across her face as she thought that if one of these exquisite creatures could walk on its rear hooves it might transform into Mr Tumnus.

At night the sky can turn almost orange in colour and the trees are silhouetted. There is a warmth that emanates from the evening light, like the glowing embers of a piece of wood. The Samburu tribe have lived there almost since the world was created. They are nomadic herdsmen, who keep mainly cattle and live near the waters of the great Ewaso Nyiro river, which draws the wildlife to its banks and creates an oasis of green in the otherwise arid landscape.

"Don't most Europeans live in the White Highlands?" asked Celia.

"Yes," said Basil, who continued to look for animals as the Land Rover bounced along.

"But why is it called the White Highlands?" she asked.

"It's because those lands were passed to the Crown and all native rights in the land, whether individual or communal, disappeared." Basil looked at Celia. "Put simply," he said, "those lands were taken from the Kikuyu and now only white people can own them, and that's because the White Highlands are the most fertile lands in Kenya."

"The place we are going to, Mrs Drewe," shouted Iain Rodgers from the front of the Land Rover, "only has a few Europeans. We'll be very much alone out there."

Dust from the road, as red as a ripe coffee berry, pillowed up behind the Land Rover as it made its way northwards along the dirt track. Basil sat next to Celia and felt troubled. The holiday had not started propitiously but he thought that bad luck was just an obstacle to overcome. He therefore took every opportunity to look for big game through his binoculars and, if he saw something interesting, he would pass the glasses to Celia. Celia also looked out of the window of the vehicle but without a thought or a care.

"We'll be camping tonight at the reserve," shouted Rodgers.

"And what can we expect to see?" asked Celia. Rodgers spoke briefly with the driver – an African of about thirty years called Nuru.

"Hopefully where we are going this evening, we'll see reticulated giraffes and zebra. Also, there should be elephants and if we're very lucky we might spot a black rhino and some big game."

The sun was starting to go down on the horizon and the heat of the day was waning. The shadows began to lengthen and became a deep purple as Celia and Basil looked out across the scrubland. There was a smell of smoke and dung in the air, even though they were miles away from the nearest village and they heard the occasional shriek of an unseen bird.

"At this time, memsahib, you might see elephants," shouted Nuru over the noise of the engine, "at the rivers and drinking holes." Basil tried again to look through his binoculars into the distance hoping to get a glimpse of elephants. "The bush, it comes alive at night and the jackals and hyenas come out."

"Were there problems with the Mau Mau here?" asked Celia.

"No Mau Mau here, memsahib!" shouted Nuru. "There's more problems with man-eating lions than the Mau Mau."

They made their camp at the Shaba National Reserve, near a patch of acacia trees. Basil's spirits again began to sink when he saw where they were staying. The holiday was not going to plan. After promising Celia a vacation at Treetops, he found that it had been burnt down by the Mau Mau and not yet rebuilt. Their guide and driver, Nuru, said that he would arrange everything and so they set off for Shaba, with the hope of seeing giraffes and big game. Basil had not expected that he would be camping outdoors, as if he were a boy scout. He felt the camp bed and rather suspected that his back would ache the next morning. However, Celia seemed unperturbed, and she sat by the campfire watching Nuru as he prepared dinner and sang happily to himself.

"It's quite desolate here," Celia said, as Nuru stirred the pot of stew over the campfire.

"The earth is quiet here," said Nuru, who lifted a spoon from the pot and tasted the meal.

"I am not sure I could ever live somewhere like this with so few trees and no flowers," said Celia, who was thinking of the green fields of England.

"When it rains," said Nuru, "the grasses and the flowers will spring to life. Usually, the rains come between March and May. It is a time which we call *masika*. The thornbushes burst into bud with their yellow and pink blossoms. You would laugh to see all the colours. Seeds that have been lying under the dry dust for years just come alive and the grasses grow. Even if we don't have rains for years on end the seeds, underneath the dry earth, are still alive, still waiting for the rain."

Nuru started spooning up the stew into metal dishes and then handed them to Celia, Basil and Rodgers. It was rich, with a deep warmth of chilli and pepper and was spicier than Celia had expected. Despite her initial apprehension, she finished her dish. Basil had a second bowl and when he finished it and handed the bowl back, said *"Ashe oleng."*

"You're a Maasai," Nuru said laughing.

"What did you say?" asked Celia.

"It was just 'thank you'," said Basil. "I thought I would learn a few words."

***

Two things surprised Basil the next morning. First, his back did not ache one iota and second, about thirty giraffes were eating acacia seeds in the trees around the camp. He climbed out of his tent wide-eyed and then felt a mild sense of trepidation when he realised how many animals he was seeing. Basil walked slowly towards them, trying not to scare them into running. One of the elegant beasts slowly lowered its head, looked at Basil and gave a low, long-drawn snort. Basil froze. He suddenly felt Nuru's hand on his shoulder and inched backwards until he found he was standing next to Rodgers and Celia. Once he was at a suitable distance, the giraffe went back to grazing.

"How long have they been here?" whispered Basil.

"Ten minutes," replied Rodgers, in an equally quiet voice.

In khaki shorts, without a shirt and with a pith helmet firmly placed upon his head, Basil was photographed by Celia with thirty giraffes standing behind him. After a few minutes, Nuru and Basil inched closer to the herd, but an old bull stamped its foot on the ground and any semblance of courage that Basil had a second earlier dissipated as he realised that this large titan could kill him with a few stamps of its hoof. He had, of course, seen giraffes at the zoo. However, there was something different when there was no cage, when there were so many and when you were standing on a plain in Kenya with the sun coming up on the horizon.

Nuru took them to the pool, which was about fifty yards from the camp and explained that after the giraffes had eaten, they would drink. Downwind and near the pool there was an area where there was a shrub bush, and after searching it for snakes, they settled down and waited for the giraffes to come. The first giraffe that came over splayed its forelegs as wide as possible and bent its neck down to drink. Another came and a third and then they sensed something, stood up, looked around and galloped away.

Nuru slowly cocked his rifle and Rodgers followed suit. Nuru pointed to the left of the pool and both Basil and Celia strained their eyes to search the scrub for any other animal.

"See, bwana," whispered Nuru pointing into the scrub. It was then that the face of a lioness appeared with three cubs in tow. They came to the water, drank and then moved away; perhaps sensing or hearing the click of the box brownie in Celia's hands.

Even though Basil subsequently saw rhinos, herds of elephants and a myriad of antelope, it was this experience of waking with giraffes and seeing a lioness with her brood that Basil remembered most from his safari. In the months to come, he would tell this story to anyone who was prepared to listen to him at his club and to many who did not care to know. On family occasions, armed with a carousel of slides, he would show their adventures in Kenya. Basil would often tell his grandchildren that Celia had failed to photograph the most important moments when he wandered so close to these animals that he could almost stroke them.

Chapter 60

After Shaba, they made their way to the highlands, where the air is cooler. Here the tree plantations cover over half the land and the lower areas have rich emerald pastures where cattle feed. Their safari then carried them to the Maasai Mara Nature Reserve, on the eastern side of the country, where the Great Migration was happening. Hundreds of thousands of wildebeests, zebras, and gazelles were leaving the dry plains of the Serengeti in Tanganyika in search of water and pasture in Kenya's Maasai Mara and would cross the crocodile-infested Mara River to get there.

They stayed in a game lodge in the Maasai Mara. Out in the forests, fifteen miles from their lodge, was a covered platform used to watch animals. It had been built in a large acacia tree and Nuru had used it on many occasions. It overlooked a large watering hole fifty yards in circumference, where during the day the animals came to drink. Nuru shot a small antelope and dragged it to the far end of the watering hole and then they waited quietly. Away in a directionless distance Celia and Basil could hear the low growling of a lion, but it did not come near the kill on the first day. Rodgers sat with his back against the trunk of the tree, his rifle resting on top of his crossed legs. He was his usual taciturn self, and, despite Celia's best efforts, he said very little.

"Aren't you enjoying the safari?" she asked that evening as they got back to the lodge.

"It's not my thing," said Rodgers, with a shrug of his shoulders.

"Whatever is the problem?" asked Celia.

"I prefer not to kill animals."

"But we're only photographing them," said Celia.

"Tell that to the antelope we tried to feed to the lions."

"I'm surprised you're squeamish about the death of an animal after a life in the forces," said Basil, who had been listening to the conversation.

"I'm not squeamish about death," said Rodgers, "but in the army you fight for your country, you have a purpose."

"We could debate that all night," said Basil. However, instead of waiting for an answer, he said goodnight to Rodgers and Nuru and smiled at Celia.

"I'll see you in a minute," she said, sipping at a cup of tea.

Basil went to his room and on the veranda lay in a hammock looking up at the night sky. He felt content as he looked up. The Kenyan sky was clear, and the stars throbbed as if they were a part of some living organism beating with a pulse. Canopus, the brightest star of the Southern Hemisphere and part of the constellation of Carina, shines clearest there. For centuries the Maasai have used it as a reference point for navigation when fishing at night. The Maasai say that the stars burn with such an intensity there because they live in God's country and that they are therefore permitted to see the universe in all its brilliance.

They saw a lion on the second day as it came to the watering hole, thirty yards from the viewing platform. The lion, sensing no danger, lay down with its paws just touching the water and drank from the hole, as a thousand lions had done before. Celia took Basil's hand as they watched the large cat first drink and then sleep. Suddenly, Celia sat up, focused the camera on Basil and took a picture of him unshaven, in his shorts, shirt and boots.

"My own Tarzan," she whispered. Basil laughed and the lion, sleeping by the water, raised its head and bolted back into an almost impenetrable area of bush. Nuru sat up.

"He won't come back now," said Nuru. "I'll pack the Land Rover and we go."

Nuru started collecting their things and took them back to the vehicle.

"I think I'll just go down to the watering hole," said Celia. "Having sat here all morning my legs are aching."

"Do you want me to come with you?" asked Basil.

"I'll be fine. Rest your leg, it's a good walk back to the Land Rover."

Basil watched as Celia climbed down the ladder from the platform and wandered over to the pool. A forest of trees and shrubs spread out in front of her.

"Nuru told me that they call this area the 'Forest of the Lost Child,'" said Basil to Rodgers. "There is a Maasai legend that a young girl who was looking after some calves, fell asleep and some of the calves wandered off into the forest. When the girl woke, she was frightened that she would be scolded by her father and so went into the forest to find them. The calves eventually found their way home but, despite every inch of the forest being searched, the girl was never discovered."

"Well then," said Rodgers, "we ought to keep an eye on your wife. We don't want to lose her. Can you see her?"

Basil looked down from the platform but couldn't see her and then she came into view at the far end of the watering hole.

"There she is," said Basil. They watched as she continued to walk around, and at moments they would just lose sight of her.

"Where's Memsahib?" asked Nuru, as he got to the top of the ladder to take the final things. Rodgers pointed to her. "I'll go and get her," Nuru said, "and you cover her. One of the boys who came with us said that the lion hasn't yet left the area."

"I'll go with you," said Basil to Nuru. He then looked at Rodgers. "Do you have a pistol?" Rodgers handed him his sidearm and asked whether he knew how to use it.

"I was a major in the army," said Basil coldly. He took the gun and quickly followed Nuru. He had done basic training, but it had been over a decade since he had held or fired a gun. The Judge Advocate General's office dealt with paperwork, not weaponry.

"Stay quiet," said Nuru, "we don't want to panic the animal if it's here. It's fed so it will only attack if it thinks you're a threat." As they got closer to Celia, Nuru told Basil to go on alone. "I'll cover you from here."

Basil put his finger to his lips as he approached Celia and whispered in her ear that they needed to go back slowly. He pointed to Nuru who had his rifle embedded in his shoulder and had it aimed at the bushes near them and then he looked towards the viewing platform, where Rodgers stood with his rifle aimed in their general direction.

"The lion may still be around," he whispered, and as he said the words, he could see Celia visibly tremble. "Hold my hand and quietly follow me."

They walked a few yards around the watering hole, and then Basil saw one of the bushes in front of him rustle. He lifted his right arm and pointed the revolver towards it. He glanced over and saw that Nuru had also trained his rifle at the area. Basil suddenly realised that he was holding his breath and tried to recall his training. Breathe as regularly as you can, he thought to himself. He did not know how long he stood without moving; however, when everything seemed quiet, he took a few more steps. Something in the bushes moved. His throat was dry, and he wanted to pull the trigger. However, he knew he had to wait until he saw the lion charging.

"Shoot," whispered Celia.

"Stay behind me," murmured Basil. "I promise you'll be safe."

Celia relaxed. She knew that if Basil promised something, he would do it. No other person she had ever met would move heaven and earth like Basil to keep his word. She squeezed his left hand and noticed that she was no longer shaking. For a moment she thought about whispering in his ear that she loved him, but then thought better of disturbing his concentration.

Suddenly, the bushes parted. Basil swallowed and aimed his pistol. He was sweating and was about to fire when he saw that what had broken cover was a dik-dik. He lowered his gun.

"Oh God, I nearly killed it."

Nuru ran over and a few minutes later Rodgers joined them. Both asked Celia how she was and then Rodgers looked at Basil.

"You've got some nerve," he said, taking his revolver back and patting Basil on the side of the arm. "I don't know if I would have been that cool if I thought I was about to be charged by a lion."

"But it was only a dik-dik," said Basil.

"But you didn't know that."

"We should head back, bwana," Nuru said to Basil. "And let's do something less exciting this afternoon – like watching elephants."

A week later it was with a feeling of dejection that Basil and Celia arrived in the city of Nairobi and said goodbye to Nuru. They had adored their two weeks on safari, perhaps more than any other time they had been together. They had found themselves laughing together; enjoying foods that they would not have touched in London and watching the animals. Celia would often bury her head into Basil's chest and smile as they looked at a watering hole where elephants were bathing. Basil would close his eyes and would feel that he could stay there forever, just listening to his wife talking about everything and nothing.

And so it proved, that love, like rain, cannot choose the grass on which it falls.

***

Nairobi was not an unpleasant city with its wide boulevards, palm trees and modern concrete buildings, and was known as the Green City in the Sun. Cars and buses filled the roads, spewing black soot. There was a large mosque and even a mock-Tudor building, which had been built by a homesick businessman. They were staying at the Hilton Hotel, which was modern and a little ostentatious. Despite the heat, it was expected that men would wear a jacket and tie in the city. Sometimes this took the form of a suit, especially where the man worked in a profession, but more usually it was a safari suit. Celia noticed immediately the smell of body odour, as everyone perspired in the humid heat.

Basil put on a tie and slipped on a jacket of martini-green linen that he had bought specially for the trip from Celia's favourite tailor on Jermyn Street. He had questioned the colour when he bought it but was told that if Edward VIII had one, it should be more than acceptable to any minor dignitary from Africa. It received approving praise from Celia, and he left for the Attorney General's office, saying that he would see her later.

The Attorney General's office was in an area called The Judiciary on the intersection between Taifa Road and City Hall Way. It was in a colonial-style building where the Supreme Court sat and opposite the Kenya National Archives. Basil was met by the Attorney General who walked him through the building, explaining the complex legal system that was used to deal with local matters as well as issues of Muslim law. He pointed out the offices of the chief justice, Sir Kenneth O'Connor, who had presided over some of the Mau Mau trials.

Basil was given a room to work from, a secretary called Njambi and an assistant, Daniel Leech. The Attorney General explained that they would arrange for him to meet with any officer that he requested to meet and provide him with any documents he wanted to inspect. The Attorney General then left, saying that Daniel would take care of his every need and that he would drop in later just to check on things. Later that morning, after Basil explained how he wanted to record all the documents that he inspected, he asked Daniel to get him copies of the complaints of irregular conduct from the Chief Secretary's Complaints Coordinating Committee.

"There isn't a committee with that name," said Daniel.

"There is," said Basil, who reached into his briefcase and pulled out the carbon copy document given to him by Lennox-Boyd. "Give this to the Attorney General," continued Basil, "and respectfully request the documents be here by tomorrow morning."

"You want me to go now?" asked Daniel.

"If you wouldn't mind."

***

Njambi was in her mid-twenties and had received a Christian education. She was tall with demerara-brown eyes, pronounced cheekbones and a straight nose, which suggested European blood in her ancestry. She used hair lotion and hot combs to straighten her hair and wore it in a style reminiscent of the American singer Lena Horne, whom she idolised. She listened to American jazz records when her parents went out and to highlife from Ghana when they were home.

"Explain to me," said Basil as he looked at her, "how did we arrive at this situation?"

"The state of emergency?" said Njambi.

"Yes, what do you think caused it?"

"It's complicated," she answered and then went to one of the boxes and opened it. She rummaged through it for a few seconds and then took out a photograph and handed it to him. Basil looked at the photograph. It was a picture of Chief Waruhiu, one of the Kikuyu chiefs who had for years supported the British against the Mau Mau. He was sitting in the backseat of his spotless Hudson sedan wearing a beige, wide-brimmed hat and a blue linen jacket with a bullet through the forehead.

"Despite having instantly killed the chief," said Njambi, "the assassin shot him three times in the chest. He left the driver and the other passengers unharmed and then the assassin and his accomplices fled, shooting the front right-hand tyre. A few hours later the police arrived and photographed the scene." Njambi looked at Basil. "I can tell you he was not the great citizen of Kenya that the newspapers painted him, and this was not the first time someone had tried to kill him."

"And as a result," said Basil, "the governor-general, Sir Evelyn Baring, introduced a state of emergency, saying he was facing a planned revolutionary movement."

"But there was no evidence that it was a Mau Mau attack," said Njambi, emphatically. "Chief Waruhiu had a lot of enemies and if it was a Mau Mau execution then why didn't the assassin kill the other people who were in the car? It doesn't make sense. The chief's assistant couldn't get out of the car and cowered in the footwell, but the assassin just left him. The driver and the other person in the front of the vehicle ran for cover but only after the first shot had been fired."

"And you don't think it was a Mau Mau killing?" said Basil.

"Some things don't make sense to me. None of the witnesses could describe the assassin or any of the other people there and none of them remembered the number plate of the car. The detective who was appointed to find the killers managed to track them down within days and although each confessed, it was after they had been beaten. The police denied it and said that the killer tried to escape by jumping out of a moving vehicle whilst in shackles and guarded by two officers and the other confessed after he had been beaten unconscious." Njambi took a deep breath. "And then there was the concocted story of a conspiracy where it was alleged that six people had met at Jomo Kenyatta's house in October 1952 to plan the murder. The evidence was so weak and so inconclusive that all six men were acquitted; although, when they walked out of court, they were arrested again and have been in jail since then without charge for being suspected as part of the Mau Mau."

"And how do you know all of this?" asked Basil.

"I was the secretary to the Attorney General at that time, and he was appointed as the prosecutor in that case. Despite overwhelming doubt about their involvement in the murder, two men were convicted and hanged for the crimes."

"You mentioned Jomo Kenyatta. Do you know where his son is, Peter Muigai Kenyatta?"

"He lives in their family home at Gatundu," said Njambi.

Basil reached inside his jacket and took out a piece of paper.

"I'm going to want to speak to him. Could you arrange for this message to be sent to him?" Basil looked at Njambi. "And do it quietly," he added.

Chapter 61

Peter Muigai Kenyatta had a fat, round face, a broad smile and a gap between his two front teeth. He looked younger than thirty-five and when he spoke, even about the most serious of subjects, he gave the impression that he might suddenly burst into laughter. He lived with his mother, Grace Wahu, in a bungalow in Gatundu about thirty miles from Nairobi. It was stone-built with rough wooden doors and a corrugated iron roof. When Basil first saw it, he wondered whether he had been taken to the correct address. It did not look like the home of a political leader, as it was so plain and small. Rodgers had been loath to drive Basil there, but, as Basil had threatened to take a taxi if he did not, he reluctantly agreed. Rodgers waited in the car as Basil walked to the door.

"Thank you for agreeing to see me," said Basil as Peter Muigai Kenyatta opened the door.

"I was surprised to receive your message," said Peter. "You said that you wanted to speak about the detention camps." He led Basil through to the living room where there was a settee, an armchair and a small round dinner table. They sat at the table and Basil took out his pad.

"To understand the problems in Kenya," said Peter, "one must understand the reason why my father was arrested. The British claimed he was part of the Mau Mau, but no one believed that, especially those who knew my father. He wanted to unite the Kikuyu and demand our rights. But he has never advocated violence. The government saw that my father could lead thirty or forty thousand people, and this scared them. When they arrested him, they had already decided his guilt and the trial was just a sham."

"That's not how British justice works," said Basil.

"British justice works just the way the British want it to work. If that involves bribing people to arrive at the decision they want, then that is British justice," said Peter.

"That's a serious allegation to make," said Basil.

"There are a lot of serious allegations regarding the trial of my father," said Peter. "The government's chief witness, Rawson Macharia, is now telling people that he was bribed to make up the story that he went to my father's house, stripped naked and gave a Mau Mau oath while drinking blood."

"I am not here," said Basil "to judge the rights and wrongs of your father's trial or reopen that case. I'm here to find out what happens in the detention camps and Tom Askwith suggested I speak with you."

"Mr Askwith, he's one of the better ones," said Peter. "However, he closes his eyes to what he doesn't want to see."

"What do you mean by that?"

"The camps that are run by Mr Askwith's group aren't the ones with problems, but Mr Askwith does not want to look at the other camps because they're not his problem. He wants to believe that he is part of an enlightened and peaceful empire and, whenever there is something unpleasant to see, he closes his eyes."

"And what," said Basil, "is Mr Askwith refusing to look at?"

"He's refusing to see that the camps that he runs just make up a small number of the total camps in Kenya." Peter talked quickly about the camps, telling Basil that they had been set up to separate the sheep from the hyenas, as he called them. "And there's a process where those who are accused of trying to destroy the British Empire are sent to one set of camps, and those who have not done much at all, except to take an oath, are sent to Mr Askwith's camps. Every Kikuyu is being arrested and nearly every Kikuyu, irrespective of whether they're a man or woman, girl or boy, is then screened."

"Yes, I am aware of that," said Basil. "I understand that it's a process used to determine whether you are a part of the Mau Mau or not?"

Peter explained that on nearly every white settler's farm, there were screening teams. All the Kikuyu who worked on the farms would be questioned. Sometimes this might involve being beaten until you confess and sometimes someone would point you out from a line of people.

"The British," said Peter, "are letting the white settlers screen their workers by any methods. No one seems to care what they do or how they get their information." Peter then went on to confirm that if someone was suspected of taking a Mau Mau oath and could be a threat to British rule, they would be sent to camps like Manyani or Mackinnon, with all the Kikuyu who had been rounded up in Nairobi. The most passionate supporters of the Mau Mau would, however, be sent to Hola camp. Those who were not considered to be a threat but had allegiances to the Mau Mau would be sent to work camps under Tom Askwith's control. If they repented they would be recommended for release and returned to their districts of origin.

"And in the work camps," said Basil, "the Kikuyu were generally treated well?"

Peter let out a sigh. His normal enthusiasm seemed deflated for a moment as he recalled passing through these camps. He then stood up and went to another room and came back with a large envelope stuffed full of letters.

"Read these," he said as he handed Basil the envelope, "they are just some of the stories which we have collected. It was not just beatings that occurred in the camps but rapes and castration. Also, at the work camps you had to start work at sun-up, and you went on to sunset. It was backbreaking and most of the people in the camps had done nothing wrong, except having been forced to take an oath."

"Tell me about the Manyani and Mackinnon camps," said Basil. "You were at one of these, weren't you?"

"You were stripped when you arrived at these places. They made you swim through a cattle dip full of insecticide like you were an animal. The guards stood at the sides and pushed our heads down under the insecticide with sticks. Once you managed to get out you were made to wear yellow shorts and a wristband with your detention number on it."

Peter looked around, afraid that he might be overheard. Despite everyone knowing the treatment that was meted out in the camps, he was embarrassed to say out loud the things that had been done to him.

"They would then search you," he continued. "They would look inside your mouth and make you drop your shorts." Basil looked up from his pad for a moment and nodded slightly, acknowledging how difficult it was for Peter to explain.

"Before arriving at Manyani we had all been searched at least four times. However, here it was to shame you. You were bent over in the courtyard in front of every other prisoner and had a guard open your anus. That's when we met Wagithundia."

"I've not come across that name before," said Basil, making a note of it.

"He was a guard from Tanganyika, a corporal. Wagithundia wasn't his real name, but we all called him that. It's a Kikuyu word meaning 'he appears'. He was this big man and he had something wrong with his skin. He was the ugliest man I have ever seen, and he used to appear out of nowhere and would start beating you for no reason."

"Just beating?" asked Basil.

"Sometimes worse. I remember once, when a friend of mine was squatting over a bucket because he had dysentery, Wagithundia suddenly appeared and grabbed him by the shoulders and jammed him in the bucket. On another occasion when they brought Chief Petersen and some of his supporters to Manyani, they stripped them. I saw them beat them with clubs and mattock handles first. I thought they were going to kill them all." Peter took a breath and then shook his head. "The African guards then got buckets of water and put the chief's head in the water and then lifted his legs so that he couldn't get his head out. Wagithundia then got dirt and stuffed it in the chief's anus and rammed it in with a stick. After he finished doing that to the chief he started on the other prisoners."

"So why didn't the officers stop it?" asked Basil.

"The officers are as bad. The officer in charge of the camp was called Wells and his mother had been killed by the Mau Mau. Whenever anyone raised a grievance, he would say 'Bloody Mau Mau, you all deserve to die.'"

"So, you're telling me that this officer just let the maltreatment happen?"

"He encouraged it. He would get Wagithundia to shackle the prisoners and then make them jump around the compound in their shackles whilst the guards beat us." Peter stopped and again looked around the room. "If they thought you had taken part in any of the Mau Mau attacks, they might even castrate you."

"And what happened to you?" asked Basil.

"Some of what I have just said," replied Peter. "On one occasion I had to run around the yard with a bucket on my head which was filled with excrement. They called it bucket fatigues and they made me do that for hours. If I stopped or spilt any of the excrement, they'd beat me. Finally, when my legs gave way, and I couldn't run any further, I sat there asking them to kill me and put me out of my misery."

"And what happened after that?" asked Basil.

"They went and got Wells, who was with another officer from Nairobi. I thought, that's it and I'd be shot then and there. And then Wells said to me 'Any last words?' and I decided to confess, even though I hadn't taken any oaths. I just told them what they wanted to hear; that I hated the Mau Mau, and I would do whatever they wanted." Basil stopped writing and looked at Peter as he continued his story. "The other officer, the one from Nairobi, was laughing at all of this and told Wells to make me get up, put the bucket of excrement back on my head and run for another five minutes so he could watch. He then made two guards run behind me shouting *memento mori*."

Chapter 62

Basil felt a sense of trepidation as he arranged his first meeting with Jonathan Bruton. He still thought of him as a friend, remembering that year at Oxford when they would be out drinking most nights, where they would go to weekend parties or where he would spend afternoons lying on Port Meadow watching the polo matches and reading the meditations of Marcus Aurelius.

Basil had decided that his first meeting with Bruton had to be a formal one. It would give the wrong impression to meet him socially. However, he did not want to be overbearing and drag Bruton to his office in The Judiciary and therefore suggested it take place at Bruton's barracks in Nairobi. Bruton greeted Basil cordially and asked after the health of Celia and his children. Basil gave a similar greeting.

"Do you mind if we get straight down to business?" said Basil.

"Of course not, Drewe," replied Bruton. "We have plenty of time to catch up out of office hours."

"I would like that," said Basil. "By the way, it's good to see you." Basil paused for a moment and opened his notepad. "How does the Kenyan government plan to defeat the Mau Mau?"

"I can't speak for the Kenyan government," said Bruton, dispassionately, "but my orders are to starve them into submission. That's the key both politically and militarily. We have put barbed wire around their villages and made the forests no-go areas, where people will be shot on sight." He lit a cigarette and settled back into the leather chair behind his desk. "We will also be putting special farm guards around farms so they can't steal food. When the Mau Mau leave the safety of the forests to scavenge for food, that's when we can capture them."

"Is it really that simple?" asked Basil.

"That's the short explanation," said Bruton. "There is a longer one if you need to hear it."

"I would be grateful for a few more details," said Basil. Bruton opened his desk drawer and removed a file marked Director of Operations' Committee on Food Denial Measures. He handed the file to Basil saying that everything he needed to know was there and asking him to return it at the end of the day.

"You know, Drewe," said Bruton, "some people here were a little sceptical about having you come and ask a lot of damn fool questions, but I've rather stuck my neck out and vouched that you're a decent chap. Now, getting back to your question; there are lots of measures we are taking. In my opinion, the most effective is restricting the food allowed in the reserves." He drew on his cigarette. "The problem for a long time has been that during the night the Kikuyu would go into the forest with any extra food they had and feed the Mau Mau. By restricting their food and placing curfews on when they can leave their villages, we are putting a stop to that."

"So won't the Mau Mau just go into the fields and steal crops?"

"Not that easy. We are using the Kikuyu to construct ditches around the forest areas and food stores. Sheep and goats must be brought in from grazing every night and fenced inside the villages."

"So, you're using the Kikuyu as labour?" Basil stopped writing and looked up at Bruton.

"Of course," said Bruton. "Who else is going to do this?"

"And you are paying them for their work?" asked Basil.

"Not my decision," said Bruton. "But, if they want to be fed, they will do the work."

Basil thought Bruton had changed. There was a steeliness that encircled him which had not been there when they were at Oxford. Although Bruton was being genial, he guessed that if he asked the wrong type of question that geniality would disappear.

"Can I ask you how many Kikuyu or other natives have been arrested?" asked Basil.

"The numbers aren't my thing," said Bruton in response. Basil swallowed and took a sip of water from a glass on the table.

"Perhaps I can help you there," Basil responded slowly. He opened his bag and took out a list. "This is a brief to the commander-in-chief of detainees," continued Basil. "You are the commander-in-chief?" Bruton stared at Basil. "And this was sent to you three weeks ago and it says that there are forty-eight thousand, four hundred detainees in work camps and holding and reception camps."

"If you knew that answer," said Bruton, "why did you ask me the question?"

Basil ignored Bruton and took out another piece of paper. He knew that his old friend was not enjoying the reunion but proceeded regardless.

"This," said Basil, holding up a piece of paper, "was taken from a parliamentary question from February last year and shows that up to February 1954, there were one hundred and sixty-five thousand, four hundred and sixty-two Kikuyu arrested and that one hundred and thirty-six thousand, one hundred and seventeen were screened."

Bruton looked at the list. "Yes, I see that."

"My question is, how long are these people held for in the holding and reception camps?"

"It's usually just a matter of days," said Bruton, "or weeks. It rather depends on the resources available."

"Would it surprise you to hear that some people were held for months and in appalling conditions?" Bruton looked at Basil. Basil could see Bruton's eyes narrowing and knew that he was about to cross a line.

"My second question relates to the release of detainees from these work camps. Now that the Mau Mau uprising is coming to the last stages, how many detainees do you plan to release in a month?"

"We are planning to release one thousand, one hundred per month," said Bruton.

"And how many people are still being arrested each month?"

"About seven hundred, more or less."

"So that's four hundred a month or about five thousand a year that are being released. And," continued Basil, "there are about thirty-five thousand detainees. According to my calculations, that means it will take you about seven years to release all the detainees at the current rate."

"Again," said Bruton, "that's a matter of policy. If I am ordered to open the gates of every detainment camp, I will do so tomorrow."

"And my third question is, how many of those that were in holding camps in February 1954 are still there?"

"I couldn't possibly say," Bruton responded.

"But you're the commander-in-chief of the detainees. You must know."

"I'm afraid you will now have to excuse me," said Bruton. "I have a pressing matter to attend to." Bruton stood up waiting for Basil to follow suit, so he could show him out of his office. However, Basil didn't move but put his pen down on the open page of his pad.

"Please sit, Brigadier Bruton." Basil spoke slowly, assessing how Bruton would be likely to respond. "It would be far better that we completed this meeting genially, as otherwise I will have to subpoena your attendance at the Attorney General's office. You are aware I have a mandate from the Colonial Secretary to carry out this investigation and that mandate will be completed by me to the letter."

Bruton was unused to having his authority questioned. However, he also knew the harm that would be done to his career if it became public knowledge that his assistance could only be obtained by court order.

"The choice is yours," said Basil as Bruton took his seat. "I understand that at the start of last year, one hundred and fifty Kikuyu had been executed for Mau Mau offences and ninety-two had died in prison of natural causes."

"I'll take your word for that," said Bruton.

"Would you define malaria as a natural cause?"

"I would," said Bruton.

"Even if a detainment camp is constructed in an area where there is a swamp that is known to have malaria."

"That would be unfortunate," said Bruton.

"I think we can call that a little more than unfortunate," said Basil. "Especially where the detainees aren't even given malaria tablets. However, let's not labour the point. I understand that there have been several civilian deaths caused by officers of the army and that you have decided to deal with these matters by court-martial rather than a trial before the criminal courts."

"I believe that's correct," said Bruton. "It happened during military operations."

"And in the case of the civilian Elijah Njeru Gideon, the two officers who were charged with his murder were fined in total one hundred and fifty pounds and bound over for a year."

"Let's be quite clear," said Bruton, "the decision to try them by court-martial was taken by the Attorney General of Kenya and these officers were then tried by a competent court. That's all I can say on the matter, I was not involved in the decision."

"And what happens when soldiers or police officers overstep the mark?"

"They are dealt with," said Bruton. "Yes, there have been one or two 'bad hats' but let's be clear, for every single European who is killed there are forty African loyalists who are killed. Every black police officer, guard and soldier knows a friend or relative who has been killed by the Mau Mau and it's impossible to stop retributions. We don't support it, but we also can't stop it."

"And what do you say to what's happening at Embakasi, Manyani, Lamu and Mackinnon Road detention camps? Everyone seems to accept that these are the worst camps for atrocities to inmates."

"They are convicted Mau Mau terrorists," said Bruton.

"But you do know that the law doesn't permit torture? You can't simply castrate detainees."

"I am not aware of anything like that. If you provide me with evidence of such things occurring," said Bruton, "then I shall personally deal with them. However, you seem to have forgotten what we are fighting against. You do know about the Ruck family? Roger Ruck was just a farmer and his wife was a doctor, who ran a dispensary to help local Kikuyu. The Mau

Mau hacked them to death and left them on the veranda." Basil could hear the anger in Bruton's voice. "I knew them; they were personal friends of my wife and myself. We often saw them socially. Margaret had seen Esme Ruck the week before when Esme told her she was pregnant. Did you know that the Mau Mau ripped the foetus from her belly? The Mau Mau then went through the house looting and destroying it before they came to the bedroom door of the Rucks' six-year-old son, Michael. They broke it down and found the terrified child hiding. They butchered him, Drewe. They butchered him by hacking him into pieces. I have got dozens of files like this if you care to look. So, yes, there have been a few cases where guards have overstepped the mark, but no one here blames them."

"I've read those files," said Basil, swallowing as he spoke. "All of them. And I've examined every photograph. However, I am not here to judge the Mau Mau. I am here to ascertain whether the government of the United Kingdom has operated a system of inhumane treatment. That is my brief, and the evidence seems to suggest that the problem is rather greater than one or two bad hats, as you call them." Basil stood up, reached into his bag and took out the file that had been given to him by Peter Muigai Kenyatta.

"I had a copy made," said Basil. "Just in case it gets lost."

Chapter 63

The morning had started with a two-hour drive towards Mount Kenya. They passed the old Ritho homestead, near the Aberdare Forest. The burnt, blackened skeletons of round, wooden huts stood accusingly, as they drove towards the newly constructed Ritho village, which had been built further away from the forest. Celia listened as a UNICEF doctor explained to her that two types of villages had been constructed: temporary and permanent. The permanent housing, explained the doctor, would remain after the Mau Mau emergency ended. The temporary housing, said the doctor, was subdivided into punitive villages and protective villages. When Celia had asked what was meant by a punitive village, the doctor told her that the government thought that those villagers who lived there had assisted the Mau Mau.

"And what are the conditions like in these camps?" asked Celia.

"They ain't good. The temporary villages are worse than the permanent villages. The punitive villages are just plain awful, and you wouldn't want to hang out there too long. Infections are rife and most of the children are undernourished."

"And what's Ritho like?" asked Celia.

"It's a punitive village. There's an entrance, a drawbridge and a moat lined with razor-sharp wooden spikes. After curfew, no one is allowed in or out."

"It sounds, well, like a prison camp," said Celia.

"That's what the Kikuyu say, and there are rumours," continued the doctor, "of rapes and beatings by the guards. You get to hear stories that some of the guards are taking revenge for what the Mau Mau have done to their families and friends."

From a distance, the Ritho village looked bucolic. Each of the huts was round and separated from the next in regular and orderly lines. The huts were of a post and pole type of construction, with thatched roofs. Women sat around small campfires and the men herded cattle. However, the closer they got to the village the more Celia noticed. There was a fence that enclosed the village and the only way in or out was via the drawbridge. A guard post was at one corner, where armed soldiers were watching the villagers. As the Land Rover pulled up, she could smell that the sanitation was appalling. The river, from which the Kikuyu had to get water, was over a mile away.

"Just one other thing," said the doctor. "We were told that you worked in New York for six years. If you speak, and I don't recommend that you say much, try and sound less British and more like an American."

"What do you mean?" asked Celia.

"Like you don't have a plum in your mouth," answered the doctor.

Celia got out of the vehicle and what she saw made her heart sink. She watched as the Kikuyu women, children and old men came to the drawbridge and stared at them. They all seemed miserable, underfed and dirty. They were different to the Maasai, who wore colourful clothes which they wrapped around their waists and over their shoulder. The Kikuyu women often only wore cloths around their waists, although they adorned themselves with beaded necklaces and earrings. The cloths were a dirty ochre in colour and many of the women shaved their heads. The nurses were starting to set up their mobile units from the backs of the vehicles and Celia asked if she could help.

The children that were brought to the mobile unit looked equally as undernourished as the adults. They were emaciated and Celia could see their protruding ribs. Many of them wore nothing but a piece of cloth with a hole for their heads to go through. She wanted to pick them up and hug them. However, even though they lived in desperately poor conditions, some of the children seemed to be excited by the presence of the mobile unit while others cowered away.

"We give 'em sweets," said a young American nurse, "after they've had their injections. It's the only reason they don't all run away."

Celia noticed how many of the women who brought their children to be inoculated seemed distant. Their eyes were dark as if the life had been beaten out of them. This wasn't life, thought Celia, it was a struggle for survival, and she felt ashamed that her countrymen had done this to them. The women that looked at Celia showed either complete apathy or hostility and Celia felt uncomfortable every minute she was there. On that first day, Celia regretted her decision to come. What UNICEF was trying to do was like putting a sticking plaster on a festering wound. Inoculations would stop outbreaks of diseases, but what these people needed was food and water, and it was the one thing that the government was depriving them of in their war against the Mau Mau.

In other circumstances, some of the women who lived in the village may have been described as beautiful. However, the weight of a constant struggle for those essentials left everyone looking older than their years. Beaten down by back-breaking work and starvation, all that was left within them was a feeling of anger. The Kikuyu had first been stripped of their ancestral lands and moved to reserves. However, in the war against the Mau Mau, they had been moved into villages which they could not leave, encircled by fences, towers, and trenches. The land was also not suitable for their needs, often away from the rivers in plains without a tree or a shrub, bare and brown.

Celia was the oldest person in the UNICEF group by almost twenty years, and the age difference placed a barrier between her and the other nurses. She was amazed how the nurses seemed immune to the hardship of these people, constantly laughing and talking, and she fondly remembered her time as a nurse in the war and then in America. They were a group of people who had come to Kenya because they thought that they could help and, for the people they treated, they gave them some hope. She gravitated to the eldest of the American nurses, who was pleased to chat with Celia, especially about her time in New York. During that first morning, Celia inoculated over a dozen children and handed out malaria tablets to anyone who would take them. She also gave away two boxes of sweets and, if the women had any misgivings about Celia, this did not extend to the children.

They stopped at lunchtime and Celia felt just a few heavy drops of rain. A minute later the heavens opened. It was an unexpected downpour for August, as there is often little rain. The raindrops cascaded down like a waterfall and within minutes their camp was flooded. The Kikuyu women and children had already run back to their huts when there was only a smell of dampness in the air. The nurses packed up quickly and they headed back to Nairobi.

When she arrived at the hotel all she wanted to do was take a long hot bath. Basil drew the bath and then let her soak undisturbed for an hour.

"How long do we have before we have to go out?" she asked as she stood in the doorway of the bathroom, smelling of lavender soap and wearing a white robe with the name Hilton stitched into the front.

"A couple of hours at least," said Basil, as he looked at his watch. "The reception starts at seven, but we can arrive a little later."

"Remind me later to tell you about the awful village I visited today," said Celia. "Something needs to be done about those places, but just now all I want to do is close my eyes." She went into the bedroom and, before her head had even warmed the pillow, she fell asleep.

***

The Muthaiga Country Club in Nairobi had its stucco walls painted a flamingo pink and had, through the last forty years, hushed up more than one scandal. As one approached the entrance to the club, the staff stood, impeccably dressed in tasselled tarbooshes, cummerbunds of silk the colour of a bishop's robe, and white jackets. The head waiter was dressed in a gold-braided bolero jacket.

The reception had been organised by the Advocate General to introduce Basil to Nairobi. Sir Evelyn Baring, the governor, accepted an invitation and therefore any discussion that this should not be a white-tie event was instantly quashed. When he had heard that a Queen's Counsel was coming to review the Mau Mau detainment camps, Sir Evelyn had remarked "Let's see the whites of his eyes."

Basil and Celia arrived at seven-fifteen and were whisked into the main reception room where Celia was introduced to the Attorney General, Eric Griffiths-Jones, and his assistant Daniel Leech. After the introductions were done, the Attorney General made his excuses and asked his assistant to show Basil and Celia around the club and remind them of the rules.

"So," explained Daniel, "the reception rooms are to our right and the bar is straight ahead but I'm afraid that it's gentlemen only," he said, looking at Celia. "We are rather a traditional group. However, if you need anything just ask one of the 'boys' and they'll bring you whatever you like." They walked slowly through the reception room, with Daniel stopping every few steps to introduce Basil and Celia to someone whom he thought was vaguely important.

"And, of course, you know Brigadier Bruton," Daniel said, as he saw an officer in formal mess dress in the corner.

"We were reacquainted this morning," replied Basil. They wandered over. If Bruton was annoyed with Basil, he did not show it and said how well Celia was looking.

"And it's a social occasion," said Bruton to Basil. "So, there's no talking business."

"Are you based here in Nairobi," asked Celia, "or in Mombasa?"

"Mainly here," said Bruton. "They have me working behind a desk most of the time."

"And what is there to do socially here?"

"Tennis, if you like the game, and of course swimming."

"And do you play tennis?" asked Celia.

"Badly," replied Bruton. "My wife plays occasionally. I play a little polo, but I'm getting too old for it now."

"And where is your wife?" asked Celia.

"Somewhere," said Bruton. "I'll introduce you when I see her." Bruton looked around the crowded room until he saw her. "There she is," and waved at her.

Even though nearly forty years had passed, Celia would have known

Margaret Ellis anywhere. Margaret walked towards them nonchalantly, a glass of champagne in one hand and a cigarette in the other. She stopped for a second to say hello to someone and, as she turned back towards them, Basil noticed she was spilling her drink.

"Celia," said Margaret, "I heard you were coming."

"Margaret," replied Celia. "You haven't changed a bit."

"Do you know each other?" asked Basil.

"We were acquainted when we were young," replied Celia.

"We've also met before," said Margaret to Basil. She stared at him as if he were not there. "At one of Jane Facey's lunches in remembrance of your brother." She swayed slightly and smiled just a little too broadly. Margaret then turned to Bruton and said, "It was all long before we got engaged." Margaret waved over one of the waiters with a tray of drinks and reached for another glass of champagne.

"Haven't you had enough?" whispered Bruton.

"It's been a long afternoon and what else is there to do in this godforsaken place but drink?" said Margaret, taking a good sip from the new glass of champagne.

"You'll excuse us," said Bruton to Basil and Celia, and took Margaret's arm. However, Margaret shook him away.

"I hear that you're stirring up trouble," she said to Basil. "Jonathan says that you're pointing the finger at the very people who are keeping us safe."

"It's the truth I'm looking for," said Basil.

"Is it?" Margaret added. "Really?" She laughed again. "I think you're here betraying the people who have made your family rich. The tea and coffee farmers, who are being dragged from their farms and butchered."

Basil was about to respond but Margaret kept on talking.

"They're decent people who have given everything to this country. What you're doing is a betrayal – something your wife knows a lot about."

"I beg your pardon," said Basil and stared at Bruton, hoping he would take control. However, Margaret had not finished and turned to Celia.

"I hope you don't mind me saying, but I wasn't surprised when I heard you had married him." She laughed, with no hint of amusement. She took hold of her husband's arm, to steady herself from falling over and then laughed again.

"Shut up," whispered Bruton. Margaret ignored him.

"You always wanted to live in that castle, and it seems that it didn't matter which brother it was with."

Basil looked at Celia.

"It was a schoolgirl infatuation," said Celia. "This is not the place, Margaret."

"It was a lot more than that," said Margaret.

"Leave it, Margaret," implored Celia, who started to blush.

"You even wrote to him after he was married," continued Margaret, pointing towards Celia with her hand still holding the glass of champagne. "Didn't you have any shame?"

"Shut up, Margaret," said Bruton, who started to drag her towards the exit.

"How do you know about that?" said Celia.

"His wife," said Margaret, pulling her arm from Bruton's. She looked at Celia. "Jane, my friend, she was sent that letter you wrote after Adrian was killed."

Bruton again took a grip of Margaret's arm again and squeezed it.

"And your son was born just nine months later," Margaret said.

"You're saying nothing that I don't know," said Basil. "And you're drunk." Basil looked at Bruton. "Get her out," he said quietly but firmly, "she's making a spectacle of herself."

"Jonathan told me that you always wanted to emulate your brother. I'm just surprised that it extended to picking up his leftovers."

There was a moment when Basil felt his blood surge. If it had been a man speaking to him, he would have hit him. People around them had stopped talking and were looking in their direction. Basil continued to stare at Bruton.

"Get her out, now!"

Basil and Celia watched as Bruton pulled his wife towards the exit.

"I think I preferred standing between you and a lion," said Basil quietly, "than you and that woman. Now, take a deep breath. There was nothing she said that I didn't know."

"You knew?"

"I suspected Adrian was Robert's father," said Basil. "And Robert knows as well."

"Why didn't either of you say anything?" asked Celia.

"It was always your secret, and the time didn't feel right just to raise it after so many years."

Once Bruton had left, the people who had been staring went back to their own conversations and soon the incident had been forgotten like the wake of a small boat in the ocean.

After they had moved to a quiet corner, Basil asked Celia if she would like to talk about her relationship with Adrian.

"If you tell me something about him first," said Celia, "then I will tell you something I should have told you thirty years ago."

Basil thought for a moment.

"It was Bruton who made me promise to think about Adrian with only affection and not with sadness. I had been grieving for nearly a year and then one day Bruton stopped me and made me make that promise and I've tried very hard to keep it. Every year when we go to the Cenotaph I stand there and think about one thing that Christian, Adrian and I did together."

"And what was the last thing you thought about?" asked Celia.

"When Adrian was at Cambridge, he rowed in the boat race against Oxford. We drove up to Mortlake to see the race and stood at the finishing line in tails and wearing top hats. It was a wonderful day out. Mother was as proud as can be, and father was pretending he didn't care but you could tell he did. The finish was extremely close right up until they crossed the line and Oxford won by a whisker. Despite having lost, Adrian wasn't dejected but just said that they would have their revenge the next year." Basil then talked about how they had gone to dinner at the Petersham Hotel on Richmond Hill and how the next morning Christian took a tin of watercolours and painted the Petersham meadows, in the same spot where Turner had painted them one hundred years before.

"Adrian," said Celia, "was the person I dreamed of when I was a girl." She looked at her husband in his mid-fifties. "He was just like Errol Flynn, gallant, handsome and carefree, and he made my heart race every time he looked at me. I suppose that I measured our marriage against that feeling and that was unfair of me. I also think that because you were his brother, I always wanted you to become more like him, but you have so many other qualities and for years I took you for granted. I am so sorry for that and then you stood in front of a lion for me."

"It was a dik-dik."

"But you didn't know that. What I'm trying to say, Basil, is that you have many of the characteristics that your brother had and others that he didn't, and I didn't see them because I was looking in the wrong direction."

Daniel Leech found them huddled away and informed Celia that the head of UNICEF in Kenya had arrived. Basil let her go and wandered around the club. The reception room was filling up with smoke as people stood in small groups chatting, and he wandered outside into the mild August evening to get a breath of air. As he stood in the doorway of the club, a large black Rolls-Royce pulled up. Wearing the full panoply of the governor general, Sir Evelyn Baring got out of the car with his wife, Mary, a petite and demure woman dressed in a silk gown with white gloves. Caught in the doorway, with nowhere to manoeuvre, Basil decided to bow as the Governor General went past, however, instead of going straight on, Sir Evelyn stopped and extended his hand and Basil introduced himself.

"Just the person that I wanted to speak to," said Sir Evelyn; "and you're here waiting for me at the door."

"What would you like to discuss, Sir Evelyn?" asked Basil.

"What you're going to write in this legal opinion to the Colonial Secretary," said Sir Evelyn. "It's got everyone on tenterhooks here." Sir Evelyn looked at Basil. "However, that will have to wait until later, the Advocate General is inside, and it's bad form to keep him standing there for too long."

Basil walked behind Sir Evelyn as they went through to the main reception room. He wondered what he would say when he told him that he could not talk about the legal opinion, even to him, as it was covered by the Official Secrets Act.

Chapter 64

Jonathan Bruton arrived at the Hilton Hotel in his Land Rover at precisely six-thirty in the morning. Whereas he would usually have had a driver take him, Bruton had insisted that he take Basil around the camps. As always, his uniform was washed, pressed and immaculate.

"Jump in," he shouted, as he saw Basil in his suit standing in the entrance lobby. As Basil got into the vehicle, Bruton thought that green linen was probably the worst choice of clothes for a trip up country. "Camouflage," said Bruton, as Basil settled himself in the vehicle.

"What do you mean?" asked Basil.

"The green suit, Drewe. Are you hoping that if we're attacked in the forest, the Mau Mau won't spot you?"

"Of course," said Basil, "avoiding a fight is a mark of honour."

"Marcus Aurelius?" asked Bruton.

"The bible," answered Basil.

Bruton pulled away from the hotel and into City Hall Way before turning onto the main road out of the city.

"Well, that got a little fiery last night. I was aware that Margaret knew Celia, but I had no idea that they disliked each other."

"I didn't even know that Celia knew Margaret," responded Basil.

"According to Margaret, there was an incident…"

"I don't need to know," said Basil, interrupting Bruton. "It's a matter between them and nothing to do with me."

As they went into the country and headed for Ngenya Camp in the Kiambu District, Bruton seemed to relax. The roads were unmade, and a trail of reddish-brown dust rose behind them. It was a verdant forest area that was interspersed with tall grasses and bamboo. It was unlike the arid Northern Territories or the savannah of the Maasai Mara, with its many short, bushy trees dotted around the landscape. Basil was also pleased to be out of the city with its pollution and acrid smells and into the countryside.

"You know, Drewe, you're making your life far harder than it needs to be. They're not a bad lot here when you get to know them."

"Doesn't it depend on which side of the fence you're standing?" replied Basil.

"I'm a soldier," said Bruton. "I don't have the luxury of being able to choose which side of the fence I stand on. I simply carry out the orders that are given to me."

"That's far too easy an excuse," said Basil. "Every prisoner of war that is captured is subject to the Geneva Convention and that requires that they are humanely treated and protected against violence and insults, and that reprisals against them are prohibited."

"That would be all well and good," said Bruton, "if we were at war, but we're not. The Mau Mau are not an army, and their men do not have a rank and number. They are nothing more than butchers and terrorists and are tried and convicted to death or hard labour." Bruton put his foot down on the accelerator. "And don't suggest that we're bound by the European Convention on Human Rights, because you know we're not."

"I wasn't going to," said Basil, quelling Bruton's rising hostility. "Did you read those letters I gave you?" he asked.

"I read them," said Bruton, "but most of them seem completely unsubstantiated."

"Individually that may be right," said Basil, "but together they form a compelling case against the authorities," said Basil, as he peered into the distance, "and not all of them are uncorroborated."

"So, a few officers in detention camps have gone too far," said Bruton. "When I find out who they are, I'll deal with them."

"You think," said Basil, turning to look at Bruton, "that pushing a broken bottle into a woman's vagina and causing her a miscarriage is just 'going too far'. Do you think that crushing a man's testes by squeezing them with pliers is just 'going too far' or beating a man until he dies? Bruton, these things are beyond the pale!"

"As I said, Drewe, give me proof and I'll make sure any infractions are punished."

"You know what is going on here, Bruton and you're turning a blind eye to it."

"You're wrong!" said Bruton. "I will punish any infraction of our military code."

"And how would you deal with someone who made a prisoner run around carrying a bucket of excrement on his head until he collapsed?"

"There was no permanent injury to the Kenyatta boy and having him denounce the Mau Mau cause has shortened this uprising and saved countless lives."

"Is that how you justify it, Bruton? You do the things that no one else is prepared to do so that we can all sleep safely in our beds?"

"Yes," said Bruton. "You may not agree with it, but if your friends or family had been attacked by the Mau Mau, you would be thanking me now."

They arrived at Ngenya Camp. On the gate, someone had put up a sign which read 'Labour and Freedom'. The hairs on Basil's neck went up as he read it. He had seen almost the same words when he walked into Dachau.

***

Every village that Celia attended had been constructed in the same way and was surrounded by a fence or barbed wire and gun towers. The young American nurse described it as 'villagisation'. Basil had not mentioned it, as he seemed only interested in the cases of torture within the detainment camps. The American nurse explained that for the last two years, the Kenyan government and the army had been relocating the Kikuyu and that last year it had become a widespread policy. Celia was told that over half of the Kikuyu, Embu and Meru tribes had been relocated to these concentrated villages, which they had to build. All the construction work had been done quickly and when the Kikuyu had moved in, the usual health and sanitation measures had not been completed.

"Charity and goodness seem to have been forgotten," said the nurse. "The Kikuyu can't feed themselves and the British seem determined that they should not have an extra loaf of bread, which might be given to the Mau Mau."

"I know," said Celia, "although, how do you deal with people when they're prepared to carry out the atrocities that the Mau Mau have done?"

"No one is saying that the Mau Mau are right and yes, I know people in Nairobi whose friends and relatives have been killed. However, doing this is not right either. Two wrongs do not make a right."

Celia agreed. From a week of visiting these villages, she knew that most of the Kikuyu saw their detainment as a punishment and, for many who did not support the Mau Mau, they were being punished for the crimes of others.

***

"He was a complete shit, and all I did was waste a day," said Basil as he paced around their hotel room.

Celia lay in a bath full of bubbles. "It's unlike you to swear," she remarked.

"It was perfectly orchestrated," continued Basil. "Here was an exemplary example of a camp where the habitation and sanitation were perfectly acceptable, and the detainees were given things to do. I was even introduced to one detainee who was doing a course in journalism remotely."

"What did you expect?" asked Celia. "That a brigadier of the British army would take you to a camp where the conditions were horrific?"

"He had already rubbed my nose in it by quoting the law at me," added Basil.

"I can imagine you found that galling."

"Especially as he was right on each point," added Basil. "He'd had a good briefing from the Attorney General. At the end of the tour of the camp, he told me that all the camps under his command are run in the same way and that this should feature in my report. I said to him that I hadn't seen all the camps under his command, and he replied that that wasn't his fault and could be remedied if I stayed longer."

"Well, you did say that Jonathan was nobody's fool."

"What makes it worse is that while everyone talks about there being a war against the Mau Mau, that phrase is a complete misnomer. There is no war in the legal sense of the word because the Mau Mau are not an army but a collection of gangsters and terrorists who are fighting for a cause. It seems to me that if there is a legal case by those who have been tortured then it is one in the civil courts."

"You sound disappointed," said Celia.

"I'm just feeling frustrated. Bruton is taking me to Embakasi camp tomorrow. However, he's already explained that this is a prison camp and therefore it does not fall under the jurisdiction of the British government but the Kenyan authorities. There are some six thousand prisoners there and since they have been convicted of offences, they are subject to hard labour. I won't see anything there except prisoners carrying out hard labour and if there have been any infractions no one will say a word. It's going to be a waste of time. We wrote the Nuremberg Charter so that we could prosecute a country that committed crimes against humanity, and now here it is, happening again."

"So, if crimes against humanity have been carried out in Kenya, why isn't the United Kingdom liable under the Nuremberg Charter?"

"Because it only applies to war criminals from the European Axis. It simply can't be used for anything else. That's why Maxwell Fyfe worked on the UN Declaration of Human Rights and the European Convention on Human Rights but, as Jonathan emphasised to me, it can't be used because Kenya is not a signatory to it."

"You seem to be between a rock and a hard place," said Celia. "I certainly don't envy you. What are you going to do now?"

"I'll write my advice based on the law and if I can't find anything that shows an established system then I shall state that. What about your day?"

"It was soul-destroying," Celia said. "The conditions in the villages where the Kikuyu have been relocated are truly appalling. I don't know where to start – everybody, even the children, were starving and were being held prisoner. I felt embarrassed to be English, and I never thought I would say that about my country. We must do something about this, Basil. I'll write to UNICEF, but it needs the government to change its policy."

"I'll do what I can to help you," said Basil, "but it's difficult."

***

A few days later Basil and Rodgers drove towards the detainment camp at Manyani. Basil was relieved that he was not going with Bruton, who had gone there the day before to ensure that Basil's visit went smoothly. He had little doubt that they would be putting on a show for him when he arrived and that there would be a dozen or more detainees ready to tell him how well the camp was run and how well treated they were. He was struggling with drafting the advice and only had one more day before he returned to London. He was grateful, therefore, to be able to sit quietly for a few hours, gather his thoughts and think about what he would present. He drummed his fingers on the dashboard as the vehicle sped along.

"What is 'wilful blindness'?" Basil said as they headed towards Mlolongo.

"I'm afraid I don't know," said Rodgers, "you're the lawyer."

"Sorry," said Basil, "I was talking to myself. Wilful blindness is when everyone knows that something is happening, but nobody wants to be told about it because they then must do something."

Rodgers started slowing the car down and Basil looked at him.

"There's a herd of zebra to our right," said Rodgers. "Do you want me to stop so you can photograph them?"

"No," said Basil. "We don't have time, it's another four hours to Manyani isn't it?"

"Four, maybe five," said Rodgers.

"The thing about wilful blindness," Basil continued, again more to himself than to Rodgers, "is if we can prove it, then the cases of torture, which everyone knows occurs, will amount to a breach of the UN Universal Declaration of Human Rights and Britain's a signatory to the Declaration, although Kenya isn't."

Basil stared ahead at the long road in front of him, ignoring both the countryside and the herd of zebra.

"As the paramount colonial power, it could be argued that Britain owes a duty of care in law to those people who have been tortured." There was another silence as Basil thought through the argument. "However, this all happens to Kenyans in Kenya, and Kenya is not a signatory. And my terms of reference restrict me to look only at whether there is a system established through which the Kikuyu peoples were subject to torture or inhumane treatment."

It made Rodgers start when for no reason and completely out of the blue, Basil shouted, "Celia, you angel!"

Basil sat quite smugly for a few seconds before Rodgers asked, "Aren't you going to explain?"

"I've been looking at the wrong thing," said Basil. "I've been fixated on all the cases where torture occurred, and I missed the bigger picture."

"Which is?" said Rodgers.

"Although there have been dozens of cases of torture where guards have been prosecuted, I can't find any evidence of an 'established system'. In nearly every case, the torture has been due to retaliation because of what the Mau Mau have done."

"So, what is this established system?" asked Rodgers.

"It's what's happening in the villages," said Basil. "At Nuremberg, the allies relied on the following as inhumane treatment – the segregation of Jews into camps, their forced labour, having jobs taken away, and the expropriation of property. This was how the Americans opened the trial. I remember sitting listening to the opening next to a friend of mine, David Maxwell Fyfe."

"Then why are we still going to Manyani?" asked Rodgers. "The villages are in the opposite direction."

They pulled over, ignoring the herd of zebra, took out a map and placed it on the bonnet of the Land Rover. They both studied the map, with Rodgers pointing out where the Kikuyu villages were. A zebra looked at them, its white ears standing up and its tail swishing as it stood in the grass, not fifty yards away. A small, thin mane of beautiful black hair, which ran from its head to its shoulders, waved in the light breeze. The stripes on its face were closer together than the stripes on its body and its black eyes watched the two white men who appeared, for no purpose, to have simply stopped their journey.

"They did the same thing in Malaysia," said Rodgers.

"Were you there as well? For a chauffeur you are remarkably well travelled," Basil remarked, without taking his eyes off the map.

"It was just one of my many jobs for the Colonial Office," said Rodgers, who ignored the sarcasm.

"And the term for what you're doing now is a 'babysitter' I believe?"

"As I said, I have a varied role."

"That sounds a little more ominous."

"Let's just say that after all this is over and you go back to your normal life, you wouldn't want to bump into me again."

Basil stopped looking at the map and turned towards Rodgers.

"What are we going to do?" he asked. "We agree that going on to Manyani would be pointless and that the villages of Kiambu, Nyeri, Murang'a and Embu are too far away. What's left?

"Are you asking me?" said Rodgers.

"Yes," said Basil.

"I would suggest that we sit here for an hour or so and watch the zebras. You can take some photographs and we have some bottles of beer in the back of the Land Rover. We can then drive back to Nairobi and, if I were you, I would take your angelic wife out for lunch and let her go shopping. Also, when we don't show up in Manyani, your friend Bruton will be frantically running around wondering what you're up to."

Basil smiled to himself, and they fetched a rug from the back of the Land Rover and sat watching the zebras.

"What did you find out about the people who wrote those letters?" asked Basil when they were comfortable, and both had a beer in their hands.

"It was difficult," said Rodgers. "No one talks here, especially to Europeans. However, I went to the hospital where the woman who had the miscarriage was treated and saw her records. It confirmed her injuries but nothing about how they occurred." Basil took a swig from the bottle of beer.

"What did you mean when you said I wouldn't want to bump into you again?"

"Do you want me to spell it out?" said Rodgers.

"I think I do," said Basil. "Robert, my son, hinted at it but I would prefer to hear it from the horse's mouth."

"My work involves cleaning up messes. I'm here because if there had been problems with the Mau Mau, I hope I would have been able to deal with them."

"You kill people?"

"Your words, not mine," said Rodgers. "If the government feels that it may be embarrassed by a situation that it cannot resolve, it might send me to clear up that mess. Of course, my instructions come in a roundabout way. People like Lennox-Boyd don't dirty their hands."

Basil raised his bottle and clinked it on the side of Rodgers's bottle.

"Here's to never seeing you again," said Basil.

"And here's to never seeing you," responded Rodgers.

IX

Part Nine

Chapter 65

1 December 1955

Certain people cannot be judged by their looks. It does not matter whether they are rich or poor or from a village or city. They may be as tall as giants but walk unnoticed and have no claim to the world's stage. Their beauty lies in what goes on inside their hearts and minds and often they will have an unassuming and quiet modesty that appears to many as shyness. Some people are born this way, and others are moulded by events that changed their lives. These people will often shun the company of others when childhood exuberance has faded. These people see the world for what it is, and they see that when the music changes, they must learn to dance a different rhythm.

"If a country cannot look in a mirror," said Basil, "and see itself for what it is, then that is a poor state of affairs."

"And if it can't?" said Celia.

"Then someone has to say something." He reached out his hand and took hers. "You know, I'm terribly proud of you. I would not have been able to complete my advice if you had not asked the UNICEF nurses to send you photographs of each of the villages they visited." Celia looked at her husband, as Basil continued, "And how many letters have you written to UNICEF and your MP? Twenty? Thirty? And now they are raising the matter of the Kenyan villages in Parliament. I know you're frustrated that everything is moving so slowly, but things are changing because of what you saw and what you are doing."

They walked towards Castle Drogo. The octagonal tower of the entrance hall dominated their view. Basil stared at the granite stonework, at the windows and then, looking further downwards, at the rampant lion over the principal door – the Drewe heraldic emblem, with its one paw outstretched and the mouth gaping. Basil admired the exquisite detailing carved by the stonemason, Herbert Pallister. Below it was the inscription *Drogo Nomen Et Virtus Arma Dedit* – 'Drogo is the name and valour gave it arms'. He smiled to himself and felt that his father would have been proud of him if he had read his advice to the Colonial Secretary.

"So, when did you submit your advice?" asked Celia.

"Last night," said Basil.

"And what did it say?"

"You know I can't tell you that," said Basil. "But I do expect that it might also have some repercussions. And now I'm planning to take some time off."

"And what then? Back to your practice?"

"I don't know," said Basil. "I thought I might retire. The world is changing and all the certainties that I grew up with are being questioned. It's not a bad thing but I'm getting too old to change and it's time for a younger generation to mould their future."

They walked into the castle and heard their two grandchildren calling them to come through to the dining room.

***

Later that evening, after Basil had again shown them the carousel of slides from their trip to Kenya, Robert sat with his mother as she read a book. He didn't know what had changed but knew that something had. A wall that had once separated his parents seemed to have toppled down. Basil and Celia were animated when they spoke to each other, and it reminded Robert of when he and his wife first met. They talked about their trip with a familiarity, and each would finish the other's sentence. But most of all Robert noticed that when his mother looked at Basil her eyes shone, and he had not seen that since he was a boy when they went to India.

"Are you going to stare at me all night?" asked Celia, as she placed her book on the table. "If you have something to ask me, just come out with it."

"It was nothing," said Robert. "It just seems to me that you and Basil enjoyed your trip."

"We did," said Celia. "More than anything I have done in a long, long time."

"I'm so pleased," said Robert. "There was one other thing I wanted to ask you." He paused. He had wanted to have this conversation with his mother all his life but did not know how to begin; and, not knowing how to begin, he asked something completely different. "Do you know what Basil wants for Christmas? I thought I would buy him a tie as usual."

Celia looked at her son, with his strong jaw, straight nose and beautiful green eyes. He was just as handsome as his father, perhaps more so. However, she loved his independence and the way that he was his own man. He had learnt that from Basil.

"Don't buy him a tie," said Celia. "Strictly between us, I think that he will retire next year."

"And what are you getting him?"

"Tickets for all of us to New York, to see a Broadway premiere next March – it's called *My Fair Lady*. I telephoned Sylvia Maxwell Fyfe and she's getting us in as her brother Rex is starring in it."

"I didn't think that a musical was your cup of tea," said Robert.

"Basil seems to like them – something with a good tune he says." Celia suddenly felt tears welling up and reached for her handkerchief.

"Are you all right, Mother?"

"Yes, I'm just being silly," said Celia. "I just thought about Basil's brother Christian. He used to say the same thing." Celia once again looked at her son. She knew that he still hadn't asked the question that he wanted to ask, so decided to put him out of his misery.

"Do you want me to tell you about your father, Adrian?"

***

A week before Christmas, Celia and Basil drove into Exeter. She cursed quietly as she crashed the gears and told Basil that he needed to buy a new car. Basil hardly heard her as he watched the world speeding by. They parked near the cathedral and, after putting on hats, gloves and scarves, walked into the shopping area. It was another freezing December morning. Celia reached out her hand and took Basil's.

"You seem distracted," she said, as they walked along the main shopping thoroughfare.

"I had a call this morning from the Colonial Secretary."

"What about?"

"It seems my advice was given to the Attorney General in Kenya. The Right Honourable Alan Lennox-Boyd wanted to know if I was just stirring a hornet's nest or whether there was any substance to the matters I raised. It appears that the Attorney General decided to cover his position and came out saying that he was equally concerned. Lennox-Boyd is now deciding what he does next."

"What did he say to you?"

"He wanted to know if I was prepared to withdraw my advice."

"To which I assume you said, no," said Celia.

"Or be less forthright in some of my criticisms and I again said, no. Lennox-Boyd then made some veiled threat about my career, and we rather left it at that."

"So, what do you do next?" asked Celia.

"We get the grandchildren their Christmas presents and then a spot of lunch," said Basil. "Do you have any idea what they want?"

"Paul wants a train set and Grace wants something called a Tiny Tears doll."

The toy shop was on two floors. It held what Basil could only describe as piles of cheap plastic junk on the ground floor. There were puppets and marionettes and an array of girls' dolls with accessories to match. The shop assistant, a young lady in her early twenties, said that if the child liked words, then Scrabble was a new game that could be enjoyed by the whole family. However, it was on the first floor of the shop that Basil fell in love with the Hornby railway models and completely overspent on a present for his grandson Paul.

"You know," said Celia, "you can't have favourites."

"There's no point," said Basil, "having a small track that just goes round

386

in a circle. If my grandson is going to have a train set, then it should be a proper train set."

As they paid, the shop assistant asked whether they wanted the presents wrapped and tagged and they watched her as she carefully cut paper and wrapped the presents.

"You must have a very big house," she said, as she wrapped the third train set box.

"We live at Castle Drogo," said Celia.

"I know Castle Drogo," replied the assistant excitedly, who looked carefully at Celia. "And I also remember you. When I was a child, I was evacuated there for a few weeks after coming from Germany. You won't remember me because you must have had hundreds of children coming through, but I always used to carry around a stuffed toy, which made me feel safe." Celia and the assistant swapped addresses and Celia promised to come and see her again the next time she was in Exeter.

"It's strange," said Celia to Basil, as they left the shop, "how coincidences like that happen?"

"I suppose it is," answered Basil. "Do you remember her?"

"I'm afraid not." She looked at the name on the piece of paper – Greta Rosenthal. "But I would love to find out how her life has been over the years."

Chapter 66

7 January 1956

London was grey and drab and a heavy fog had fallen. The buildings had lost all definition in the murkiness of the smog. The roads were gridlocked, horns blaring, drivers shouting, and there were the inevitable delays on the trains and Underground. Basil arrived in chambers twenty minutes later than usual. He unbuttoned his coat, took off his scarf and placed his bowler hat on the peg of the door. He was coughing as he stood in the kitchen making himself a pot of tea and despite Arthur Wright offering to make it for him, he refused.

"We were all sorry to hear about your decision to retire, Mr Drewe. You'll be missed," said Arthur.

"I'll miss being here," replied Basil.

"Have you got any plans for your retirement?"

"Some travelling," said Basil. "I would like to go back to Africa; however, Celia wants to take me to India to a place called Meghalaya."

"And have you thought about returning to Kenya?" asked Arthur.

"No," said Basil. "I think that things out there are getting more difficult. If the settlers and the authorities continue to treat the native peoples like third-class citizens, then our time in Kenya is at an end."

"And will they be better off when the British leave?"

"Some will be, some won't. One half of the country hates the other because it embraces Western values, and that half hates the other because it sees them as backward and barbaric. The Kenyans are doing horrific things to each other. There is a lot of animosity, and there is no medicine except time that can cure that kind of hatred."

"I've always thought that Britain was a force for good in the world."

"I believe that it has been," said Basil. "But a lie will spoil a thousand truths, and we have been lying about what is happening there."

"And have you heard anything further from the Colonial Secretary about your advice?"

"I'm afraid, Arthur, that I seem to have rocked the boat and I don't think we'll be seeing any more work from the Colonial Office. When I last spoke to Lennox-Boyd he was more than a little frosty with me."

"There was one other thing," said Arthur, as he reached inside his pocket. "I have the tickets for you and Mrs Drewe to the ballet this evening at the Royal Opera House."

***

There dwelt in Golders Green in London a thin woman of forty-five, of forceful disposition and married to a diamond merchant, Mr Goldmann, who worked in Hatton Garden. She lived in a detached house and in the summer, she would display in window boxes a variety of pansies, violas, and petunias. She had black hair, which would have gone grey if she had not dyed it regularly. Her cheekbones were high, and her brown eyes often flashed ferociously. On the rare occasions when she could be cajoled into doing so, she could stand on her toes like a ballerina, and she would proudly tell people that she once danced at the Vienna State Academy of Music and Dramatic Art.

It would not be untrue to say that the 1950s had been a good decade for those who traded in diamonds. Mr Goldmann's Christmas present to his wife had been a car, a Ford Consul, in two-tone green and white with white-walled tyres. She had wanted a car for some years to allow her to take her children to school and to the clubs which they attended. She had got a driving licence some years earlier but rarely had she been allowed to drive her husband's car. It was therefore with some trepidation that she got into her car on the evening of the 7th of January 1956 and headed towards Hatton Garden to pick up her husband. As she drove past Regent's Park, the fog seemed to get thicker and with her headlamps on full beam, she continued through Marylebone, Soho and into Convent Garden, missing her turn along Holborn.

***

Celia had met Basil at chambers, and they walked along the Strand, on to Catherine Street and then Bow Street, where the Royal Opera House is situated. Celia joked that it might be the last time they did anything cultural for a while if they were moving down to Castle Drogo. Basil suggested that they get a television set.

"Isn't that Iain Rodgers over there?" said Celia suddenly and pointed towards the steps of the Opera House.

"Where?" asked Basil. He stared across the road but couldn't see him in the murkiness of the fog.

"Over by the doorway," Celia said, and Basil looked again. "I'm sure it's him."

"Just wait here for me."

"Don't be silly, Basil. Let's cross together and say hello."

"Celia, please, do as I say. Just wait!" However, Celia started crossing a few steps behind and Basil turned to look at her. "God, you'll be the death of me!"

He did not see the car as it came around the corner and when he did see it, with its full beams on, he had no time to move. Celia closed her eyes and screamed as she heard the thud. When she opened them, Basil was lying on the road; the car had stopped, and the driver was looking down at him. A throng of people rushed forward from the Opera House, and Celia pushed her way through the crowd.

"Call an ambulance," she shouted as she got to Basil's body.

Basil lay on his front, and blood seeped from a gash in his forehead. A man had placed a coat under his head.

"Call an ambulance," she shouted again. She put her fingers on Basil's neck, trying to find a pulse. She couldn't feel one.

"Basil," she cried.

"Get something to cover him," someone said. Celia stood up.

"They've telephoned for an ambulance."

Celia could not tell who was speaking and looked around, ashen-faced.

"Do you know him, miss?" a police officer who'd arrived on the scene asked.

"That's the driver."

"He was just standing in the middle of the road."

None of it made sense to Celia, and then she felt a hand on her shoulder, and she looked up to see a policeman in uniform.

"I said, do you know him, miss?" the police officer repeated.

"He's my husband," replied Celia, her voice cracking.

"Stay here, miss, there's an ambulance on its way."

In the dark and muffled evening, Celia suddenly heard a bell. At first, it appeared far away, but over the next minute or two it got louder as it came closer. The crowds parted like a biblical sea and within a few minutes, two men were examining Basil.

"Just stay here, miss, they know what they're doing," said the officer. Celia watched as they strapped Basil onto the stretcher and moved him into the ambulance. The policeman went over to speak to the ambulance crew quickly before returning to Celia.

"Is he alive?" she asked.

The policeman nodded. "The ambulance crew said he could just about speak."

"What did he say?" said Celia.

"Your husband asked whether he had been hit by a ball from Freddie Trueman."

Chapter 67

April 1956

The charge sheet against Rachel Goldmann alleged dangerous driving. For some reason that Basil could not fathom, Claude Palfrey insisted that chambers would prosecute the case; saying that it was a matter of chambers' pride.

The brief was given to St John Stephens who complained bitterly that he would be giving up a whole day to do something that would earn him nothing. Basil complained that he would prefer to prosecute the case himself than have St John Stephens do it, to which Palfrey looked at him sternly and said, "A man who represents himself has a fool for a client."

Monday morning at the Bow Street Magistrates was usually a dark affair. There would be a 'rat-tat-tat' before the court usher entered and uttered the words, "Court rise." The three magistrates would take their seats on the bench, and the presiding magistrate would ask the usher to call the first case. On a Monday morning, it was usual for the first few hours to be taken up by those who had been bound over for the weekend. This would inevitably be a rag-tag bunch who had been charged with drunk and disorderly or breaking and entering. The more serious cases were usually listed during the latter part of the week. It was therefore with some surprise that the three magistrates looked out into the well of the court and saw in front of them Aubrey St John Stephens QC in all his finery.

"Your worships," said St John Stephens, "I appear for the Crown in this matter and my learned friend Mr Carman appears for the defendant, Mrs Rachel Goldmann. It is the Crown that brings this case, and it is the Crown that must prove it."

St John Stephens looked up at the bench and hoped that they would believe that he would not be there unless this woman was guilty. "The facts of the case are quite simple; my client was on his way to attend the opera…"

"Objection," said Carman, who stood up. St John Stephens glared at him.

"Your objection, Mr Carman?" the presiding magistrate asked.

"Mr Drewe is not my learned friend's client. My learned friend represents the Crown."

St John Stephens forced a smile, acknowledged his error and continued.

If Basil had been allowed in the courtroom before giving evidence, he would have thoroughly enjoyed St John Stephens's humiliation before this young barrister who was still doing his pupillage and objected to the many procedural errors that St John Stephens made.

"If my learned friend has no objection," said St John Stephens, exasperated, "I would like to call my first witness, Mr Basil Drewe QC."

Basil confirmed his name and his address at Castle Drogo, Drewsteignton, Devon. As St John Stephens started his examination-in-chief, however, the objections for leading the witness and hearsay came thick and fast from George Carman until the presiding magistrate suggested that if this case were to be finished today, Basil should be allowed to give evidence in his own words and "without the assistance of leading counsel". Basil finished his evidence and waited in the box ready to be cross-examined. He suddenly felt quite nervous at the prospect.

"You said," Carman began, "that you started crossing the road without your wife."

"Yes," said Basil.

"And that you stopped in the road to make sure she was following you?"

"No," said Basil. "I told her not to follow me."

"And could you explain to their worships why you did that?"

"Because I wanted to speak to Mr Rodgers on my own. Iain Rodgers was the person she thought she had seen on the opposite side of the road."

"So, Mr Drewe, you were standing in the middle of the road looking at your wife and having a conversation with her. Would that be a fair summation of your evidence?"

"Nor precisely," said Basil. "The only thing I said to my wife was 'wait there' or something to that effect."

"You don't remember what you said?" asked Carman.

"Not precisely," said Basil.

"And you weren't on a pelican crossing, were you?"

"No."

"Even though there was one just twenty-five yards further down the road."

"If you say so."

"Oh, I do say so, Mr Drewe. Let me put it to you, Mr Drewe, that your wife saw someone, and you walked out in the road without looking and stopped in the middle of the road to carry on talking to your wife."

"The car came out of nowhere."

"It didn't come out of nowhere, Mr Drewe. It turned into Bow Street twenty yards further up the road and proceeded into Bow Street slowly. There is no suggestion that my client was speeding. The only reason you were in an accident was because you were standing where you should not have been."

The case was finished by eleven o'clock. George Carman made a no-case submission at the close of the prosecution evidence and the magistrates dismissed all charges. Basil looked across to Rachel and mouthed the word "sorry", but she was busy talking to her barrister who came over to Basil and said that his client wanted to speak to him.

"It was when you said Castle Drogo," said Rachel. "Christian had mentioned the name once to me, but I couldn't remember it." Rachel sipped her tea from a stained white porcelain mug in the canteen at the Bow Street Magistrates. "I brought him over to England in 1931 for his father's funeral and then I stayed in London with relatives. I think that was the only time he mentioned the name Castle Drogo."

"You're the dancer," said Basil.

"Ballerina," Rachel corrected him.

"And you were with Christian when he tried to leave Germany in 1939."

394

"Yes," said Rachel. "He was going to Salzburg, and my family and I were going to Marseilles."

"So, please tell me, what happened?"

"I had gone to check on him when the guard arrived. He checked our tickets and because I was in first-class, he told me to get back to third-class. The guard was shouting that I couldn't be there, and Christian was trying to calm things down saying that I had come to check on him. I went back to third-class and thought nothing of it but when we got to Linz, we were both taken off the train. I told my parents that they should go on without me and that I would follow on the next train."

Rachel looked at Basil with tears in her eyes. "Please, go on," said Basil.

"I had expected that we would be reprimanded and then allowed to get on the next train. I thought we would just need to apologise and then everything would be all right. However, as soon as the train stopped, we were arrested by a German Gestapo officer and taken to the Gestapo headquarters. Christian seemed resigned to what was happening and said almost nothing. I was crying. Another Gestapo officer was waiting for us there."

"Do you remember his name?" asked Basil, who was trying to take in every word Rachel said.

"No," replied Rachel. "He just said, as we came in, 'Welcome, Herr Drewe,' and then we were taken into a room, both of us. The officer started provoking Christian and was calling me a dirty Jewess. He was shouting all sorts of vile things; it was horrible. I just thought, 'Keep quiet, for the Lord's sake keep quiet', and Christian did until the officer turned to the soldiers and told them to take me to Mauthausen."

Rachel sipped at her tea again. Basil knew not to interrupt her. He could tell she might break out into sobs at any moment.

"I think Christian knew," continued Rachel, "that if I was taken to Mauthausen I might never come out, so he demanded to speak to the commanding officer. The German Gestapo officer laughed at him and told him he was in no position to demand anything and that he was speaking to the head of the Gestapo in Linz. I think the officer then repeated his command to take me to Mauthausen. Christian could have stood there silently, and I am sure that if he had done that he would be here today, but he stood his ground and said that he wasn't going to allow them to persecute women and children."

"That sounds like Christian," said Basil.

"Then suddenly," said Rachel, "the officer took out his baton and hit Christian around the head. He went down and stayed there for a few moments and then slowly got back up, rearranged his glasses, and said nothing. The officer moved closer to Christian and was about to hit him again when he lashed out and hit the officer with a punch to the side of the face. The officer lost all control and knocked him down again and I ran over to help. I shouted at Christian to apologise and shut up and when I started crying hysterically, they dragged me away from him and out of the building."

"Is there anything else you can tell me?" asked Basil. "Did you hear where they took him?"

"Nothing," said Rachel. "That's the last time I saw him. I hoped that when they had beaten him unconscious, they might let him go." Rachel stopped, unsure whether she should say something more but decided to continue. "Just before I was taken away to Mauthausen I heard a shot. I don't know if they killed Christian or whether it was something completely unrelated."

"And do you think he's dead?" asked Basil.

"I don't know," said Rachel. "All I can tell you is what I saw and heard. I would like to believe that he is happy, wherever he is. There is one other thing." She reached into her pocket and took out a St Christopher. "After he was hit and fell his St Christopher came off. I picked it up but couldn't give it back to him. When they dragged me away, he shouted, 'Keep it safe', or 'It will keep you safe'. I don't know, but I carry it whenever I go out."

She handed the St Christopher to Basil. "By rights it's yours," she said.

Basil looked at it and could feel engraving on the back. He turned it over and stared at the one word etched there, 'Rose'.

Afterword

A Remembrance of Death is a work of fiction, although those who look closely enough may discover a grain or two of truth.

I started compiling ideas for *A Remembrance of Death* about six months before my debut novel, *Of All Faiths & None,* was published. While *Of All Faiths & None* was an anti-war novel that dealt with the effects of the First World War on two families, I wanted *A Remembrance of Death* to be different and intended to write a story about living with loss and the grief that war brings. As the relationship between Basil Drewe and Celia Lutyens developed, the story also found a theme of loving a person who does not return those feelings. Although the story is set against the backdrop of some of the most horrific events of the twentieth century, ultimately it is a story of hope and how love can be found unexpectedly. As Lutyens says in *Of All Faiths & None,* "only Time is capable of understanding how valuable Love is."

The other underlying theme of the book was prejudice and our attitude to those from different cultures. Britain has often been a country of contradictions. The *Kindertransport* programme was something that Britain should be rightfully proud of, as part of the struggle against Nazism. Similarly, Britain raised living standards in many countries it ruled, but not always without cost. However, there have also been many inhumane events such as the 'Dunera Boys' incident or the villagisation programme that the British implemented in Kenya, which features in the novel. The reader is encouraged to look at their country in the cold light of day, not through rose-tinted spectacles, and remember that a lie will spoil a thousand truths.

The writing process for this novel was very unstructured. I had a few ideas and then just wrote, and the story took me wherever it went. Basil Drewe was always intended to be the main protagonist, and I initially had the idea of recounting his story in flashback. Celia Lutyens played almost no part in my original thinking. By October 2022, the working title was *Memento Mori*, and I had written two hundred pages. The novel started to take shape as I continued revising it and I changed the title to *A Remembrance of Death*. Following some initial feedback from friends and family, I carried out another substantial redraft, developing the characters and then submitted the book to Dominic Wakeford, a developmental editor at Reedsy. A further redraft followed where I again focused on developing the characters of Celia and Basil. I have tried to make *A Remembrance of Death* historically accurate where possible. However, it is a novel, and the two main characters are fictional creations.

A Remembrance of Death was written in sections and each section deals with a distinct period and a distinct place.

The Oxford chapters were difficult to write, as I wanted to avoid a comparison with Evelyn Waugh's masterpiece, *Brideshead Revisited*. So, I deliberately chose a darker, sombre Oxford, which was suffering at the end of the First World War. Fortunately, there is a wealth of material about life in Oxford in that period and I discovered that the first Indian DPhil student attended Oxford in 1916 at Balliol. This gave me the idea of bringing in the character of Laxman Chaudhury and allowed me to hint at the underlying racism that permeated this elite society.

The Ojai chapters were written in two parts. Initially, the story of Celia in Ojai was about forgiveness and her return to England, with the aid of Krishnamurti. Krishnamurti lived in Ojai during this period, as recorded in Mary Lutyens's book *Krishnamurti: The Years of Fulfilment*. When my first draft was reviewed, it was suggested that these chapters could be developed further, as the readers had enjoyed the reunion between Celia, who had been the main protagonist in *Of All Faiths & None*, and Krishnamurti, the heralded World Teacher. In Steinbeck's *East of Eden* there is a line about a schoolmistress from a town near Ventura who had been raped. As Ojai is close to Ventura, this gave me an idea for a twist in the story and the

Hamilton boys were created. Their importance became fundamental to Celia's journey.

The England chapters were intended to reacquaint the reader with many characters from *Of All Faiths & None*, including Sir Julius, Lady Frances and Christian Drewe; Lutyens and Lady Emily; Jenny Stanton, Margaret Ellis, and Jane Facey. I also brought in a new character, David Maxwell Fyfe, who would later be with Basil at the Nuremberg trials. David Maxwell Fyfe was a complex man in real life. He was a passionate advocate for human rights but when Lord Chancellor, was fervently against repealing the penal laws against homosexuality.

The India chapters are, perhaps, my favourite section of the novel. I went to Sri Lanka and then Nepal for work and fell in love with the Indian subcontinent. In my research, I was fortunate enough to find an article about the inauguration of New Delhi, which I hope has allowed me to give an accurate flavour of the time. Lady Emily, who was judgemental in *Of All Faiths & None,* is a more complex character here, and Lutyens is again the 'honest' onlooker whose stories always have an element of truth and warning. There is one scene where I was influenced by Somerset Maugham's *The Painted Veil*: "A sudden knock on the door made them stop and hold their breaths." Like Kitty Garstin, Celia is on a journey of discovery although the Indian chapters mark her nadir. The reader may disapprove of Celia, but they should also understand what has brought her to where she is. These chapters also allowed me to bring back Laxman Chaudhury and introduce the reader to his sister, Majda.

The Second World War chapters focus on the fragile relationship of Celia and Basil and the disappearance of Christian Drewe. During this time antisemitism was rife throughout Germany and Austria, and I felt it could not be ignored in the story. Unlike the First World War, this was a war that came into people's homes and listening to radio broadcasts from the time gave me a sense of the desperation and suffering that people went through. It was also a time that my parents spoke about, where families were torn apart, and people lived in constant fear of being bombed.

The Nuremberg chapters serve two purposes. First, they set the scene for what comes later in the Mau Mau uprising. Quotations are taken from transcripts of the trial. The cross-examination of Goering is a summary of what took place, and the buildings are described from video footage and photographs. Events such as the 'party' were taken from letters David Maxwell Fyfe wrote to his wife Sylvia. Second, these scenes mark a change in the relationship between Basil and Celia with both characters recognising their flaws.

The London chapters, where Basil is asked to provide an advice on the Mau Mau uprising, have been substantially edited to ensure that the story was not swamped by legal anecdotes. Basil is now very much his own character, tapping his fingers while he considers a problem and enjoying nothing better than listening to the cricket on the radio while doing *The Times* crossword. Celia is also living a comfortable existence, listening to *The Archers,* attending concerts and reading books.

The Mau Mau chapters were, however, the reason why I wrote this novel. The safari story was again intended to show a change in the relationship between Basil and Celia. I read Joy Adamson's *Born Free* to form a picture of Kenya in the 1950s, remembering the film from the late 1960s. I had an interest in the history of the Mau Mau uprising as my father was an insurance clerk in Kenya during the Emergency Period and on rare occasions spoke about his time there. However, it was not until William Hague made a statement to Parliament on the 6th of June 2013 that I realised that the British time in Kenya was not a golden period in its history. Hague said, "The British Government recognises that Kenyans were subject to torture and other forms of ill-treatment at the hands of the colonial administration." This led me to undertake my own research, which included reading Caroline Elkins's Pulitzer Prize winning book *Britain's Gulag* and Hugh Bennet's *Fighting the Mau Mau.* I also visited the Kew Archives. Documents to which Basil refers in the novel can be found there and were previously classified.

The characters within the novel are a mixture of real and fictional people. Although there was a real person called Basil Drewe, who owned Castle Drogo and was a lawyer of Inner Temple, that is where the similarity with Basil Drewe in the novel finishes. The character of Celia Lutyens is entirely fictional. With the character of Krishnamurti, I have attempted to summarise his philosophical teachings on subjects like forgiveness, enlightenment, and the independence of India in a way that is accessible to modern readers. Similarly, with David Maxwell Fyfe I have tried to make him the respected and brilliant lawyer that he was. Tom Askwith's views on the Mau Mau uprising were summarised from his writings at that time. The dialogue within the novel is, however, purely fictional as is the story.

I would like to thank everyone who has helped with this novel. First and foremost, my wonderful wife Keren for her support and constructive criticisms. Thanks also to Eoin Tweeddale, Louise Witt, Kim Brown, Lee White, Mandy Ribekow-Evans, Barbara Lawrence, and Amanda Tweeddale who all agreed to help and had to suffer through a poorly written initial draft of the book. Once again, the brilliant cover photograph was created by Patrick Dodds who also read and commented on the early drafts of the novel. Thanks to my developmental editor, Dominic Wakeford, who has cleared away the unnecessary verbiage and suggested edits to help the reader understand the characters of the book, and finally to Robin Seavill for his brilliant copy editing of the manuscript, his assistance and insightful comments on all aspects of the book.

If you would like to find out more about the characters and the background to the novel, visit my website at https://www.ofallfaiths.com/ and sign up to my mailing list at https://www.ofallfaiths.com/contact-8 to get free stories, my blog and newsletter.

If you have enjoyed the book, please leave a review on Amazon or Goodreads. Your reviews are invaluable for an author.

Thank you,

Andrew

About the Author

Andrew started his working life as a chef and six years later went to university to read law. He worked as a criminal barrister between 1992 and 1994 and was then employed as a construction solicitor from 1994 to April 2021, when he gave up his legal practice to work full time writing novels and the occasional book on arbitration law.

Andrew started writing *Of All Faiths & None* in 2004 as an anti-war novel. In 2010 he completed a first draft. It was not until he decided to retire in 2021 that he came back to the novel and employed editors and book designers to complete the work. The novel is centred around Castle Drogo, the last castle to be built in England and was published in September 2022. The book won numerous awards. *A Remembrance of Death* is Andrew's second novel and has already been shortlisted for the Yeovil Literary Prize 2024.

You can connect with me on:

🌐 https://www.ofallfaiths.com

Also by Andrew Tweeddale

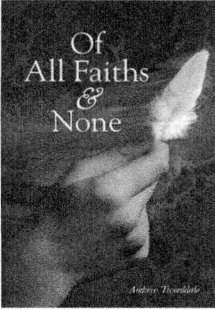

Of All Faiths & None

https://www.amazon.co.uk/All-Faiths-None-Andrew-Tweeddale/dp/1739612205

In the autumn of 1910 Edwin Lutyens, the renowned architect, receives a commission to design a castle on Dartmoor – Castle Drogo. His daughter, Celia, is enamoured with the project dreaming of chivalry and heroism and becomes infatuated with the owner's son Adrian Drewe. The story moves to 1914, and the start of the Great War, where Adrian Drewe and his younger brother Christian enlist in the army for very different reasons. The story jumps from the battlefields of the Somme to London and to Castle Drogo, where the characters are reunited for brief periods. Faith and love are stretched to their limits as each character is affected by the relentless brutality of the war. *Of All Faiths & None* is the story of a lost generation. It is a novel that focuses on the relationships of the characters until those relationships are shattered. It is a coming-of-age tale and a social commentary on the tragedy of a needless war.

Printed in Great Britain
by Amazon

57066839R00228